For the luckiest

Prologue

'Sure you're not coming down with us, Cass?'

My dad was leaning on our fence, facing across the sun-browned field to the sea, and he glanced back over his broad shoulder at me. It was late into the season, early September, so his face was weathered and darkly tanned, his natural paleness only visible in the crevices of the crow's feet around his blue eyes.

He looked disappointed. He was always disappointed when I said no. He could not imagine a world where anyone willingly refused a dive, especially me.

And I gave him some casual, offhand answer, I can't even remember what it was – perhaps I said I was tired. Perhaps I lied and said I was coming down with a summer cold. All I knew was that it was my day off and I didn't want to dive the *Undine* that day. I wanted to lie on the deck of the boat in my tiny green bikini, to sunbathe, to read, but mostly, if I was honest, to fantasise about my kinda-sorta boyfriend Ben.

I didn't realise it, but this was to be my last real memory of my father.

That said, I know I must have spoken to him afterwards – he would have stood behind me in the little wheelhouse of the *Mustang Sally*, 'backseat steering' as my mother would have said, laughing. He never trusted me to find the bobbing hazard buoy, despite having done it a thousand times before.

He would have muttered instructions and observations as the other three suited up, and everybody checked each other's gear, and would have made rubbish little jokes and offered that tiny nervous cough of a chuckle after them, as had been his habit his whole life.

It's funny that he had these anxious tics above the surface of the water. Below it, his unruffled bravery was a matter of legend. Complete strangers had approached me all my life, in dive shops and bars and on social media, to tell me about it, and about how inspirational he was to them.

I remember other things about that day instead. I remember that my sister Sid had on an expensive new drysuit with pink flashes on the sides, and I had to fasten it up for her while she wriggled within like an eel to get comfortable. I could smell the coconut oil she smeared on her long curtain of glorious fair flyaway hair to protect it against the salt, something our mother had taught us to do. Beneath our feet the *Mustang Sally* tossed us gently up and down, tugging against her anchor, and it made us both giggle as we fell against each other.

'Stand still. You'll get your hair caught in the zip,' I said.

'All right, all right, hurry up.' Sid loved to dive, was impatient to get into the water.

'Hold on . . . there. Done. That suit is *way* too small.'

'Cass, it's supposed to be tight . . .'

I took half a step back from Sid as the boat rocked beneath my feet and bumped backwards into Adam, who was holding Sid's diving belt, threaded with her weights.

'Oh, sorry,' I said, righting myself.

He laughed. 'It's no problem.' His hand was momentarily around my arm, steadying me. It felt warm against my skin. 'The sea's lively today, eh?'

Adam had just started work at Blue Horizons a couple of weeks ago – he'd come down from a dive shop on the Scottish borders, murmuring something about 'family reasons' in his low Southern accent. It seemed indelicate to pry any further.

And just like all the new guys, he had made a beeline for Sid before the end of his first week.

I walked back to the bench and slumped down next to Jimmy as Adam decorously hung the weight belt around Sid's waist. He checked the strap while she tested her regulator with a short, huffing breath, distantly oblivious to him.

'Another one bites the dust,' Jimmy muttered under his breath, raising a dark eyebrow at me. He was already in full kit, only his face poking out of his drysuit.

I've known Jimmy for most of my life, or at least ever since we came to Anvil Point as little girls. He and his wife Mandy had just moved up from Bradford a year or so before we arrived. It was they who took care of us when my parents flew all over the world to dive.

He was the nearest thing Sid and I had to an extended family.

'Hmm.' I gave him a tiny smile.

'Everyone ready?' called Dad.

There was a murmur of assent.

'We'll be forty-five minutes, Cass, if that,' said Dad, advancing to the back of the boat.

'Okay.' I shrugged at the ocean all around. I don't think I was even looking at him. 'I'll be here. Have fun.'

I remember that they all jumped off the transom of the boat one by one, each with a thunderous splash – my dad, Sid, Adam, Jimmy – but by then they were covered by their diving masks – they had become faceless, neoprene beings as they splashed down into the royal blue of the Atlantic, only Sid identifiable by her too-tight pink flashes.

They would have gathered, a bobbing quartet, before my dad raised his hand at me. I doubtless waved back as they vanished beneath the surface in a stream of bubbles.

I can't remember that part exactly, but I think, if anything, I was probably pleased to see them go, already fishing my novel and water bottle out of my backpack, my patterned beach towel under my arm. Finally, I would get some peace and quiet.

We had come out to check on the wreck of the *Undine*, which had sunk in mysterious circumstances more than twenty years ago. It lay some hundred feet beneath the *Mustang Sally* and had somehow become our responsibility.

My dad was a famous person in our small but international community, an athlete with a life of firsts – the first to dive to the bottom of the Manniton Hole in the Caribbean, the first to sound out the southern reaches of the Black Belly Cavern System beneath the Appalachians, and the first to explore the wreck of HMS *Chivalry* and take those fantastic images of its silent, coral-studded gundeck, with that great white shark looming out of the darkness of the hold like a pale revenant, its belly shining in the gloom.

He'd had handsome sponsorship deals in his time, most of which had gone into sending me and Sid to private school.

Now he had 'retired', allegedly, to concentrate on running the dive school off the Cornish coast where he was born. But as Sid and I constantly chirruped at him, he was doing the exact same things, just in less exotic places and for much less money.

I rolled out my towel on top of the wheelhouse, checked the time on my phone – 3:14 p.m. They would be gone for three-quarters of an hour, tops – they would just check that the wreck was still safe, that the trail plaques were still readable, and that nobody was stealing from or damaging the wreck in the meantime. It was a box-ticking exercise.

Ruffling the pages of my book to find my place, I felt again that little stab of guilt that I'd not offered to accompany them.

I was leaving – heading out to Australia for my year's secondment at the Institute of Oceanography – and it would be the first time I'd left my dad and Sid since my mum died two years ago. I was conscious I should be spending more time with him.

Sid will still be here when you go, I reminded myself. She's the eldest, anyway. You're not totally abandoning him.

Then why did it feel like I was?

I let out a long sigh, and my brow fell on to my forearms and their slimy residue of sunscreen.

Maybe I shouldn't go.

After all, Ben was here.

Hmm, Ben. I picked up my phone, checking it for texts.

I'd been seeing Ben since late July. He'd told me, as we lay spooned around one another in his room up above the Wreckers, that he'd be thinking about me every day, and the thought of his warm voice, his large and sensitive hands, filled me with a low, sweet yearning that made my belly flutter as it pressed against the towel.

'Maybe you could visit me,' I'd said. 'In Queensland.' I'd tried to sound casual, unforced, as though suggesting that we buy an ice cream on the beach.

His face had frozen for a second.

'Yeah, maybe,' but I'd heard that hesitation, and he knew I had.

I shouldn't have said that, I thought, smiling at him, shrugging it off. I was always pushing him too hard. He kept telling me he wasn't ready for a relationship, for commitment, after what had happened with his last girlfriend, but I just couldn't seem to stop.

I turned over on the towel and shut my eyes against the blazing sun.

After what seemed a long while of trying and failing to read, I glanced at my watch.

It read 4:05 p.m.

I frowned, surprised, and sat up, scanning the horizon.

I wouldn't have described myself as worried, even then, though my dad had always been a stickler for keeping to a dive plan. They were all experienced divers, after all, with air tanks that we'd filled that morning with Nitrox, using our own compressor. Under normal circumstances, any one of them could have made that air last for up to an hour if they had to.

But I felt, despite the glorious sunshine, the glittering ocean, that familiar sense of chill disquiet that came over me whenever I thought about the *Undine*, locked in the rocky embrace of the sea's floor beneath my feet. She was, after all, a mass grave – a rusting steel mausoleum where everyone on board had drowned.

I stood up, stretched, fooling myself that I had meant to get up anyway, that I'd had enough sun, and it wasn't that I wanted to go down to the deck and look for their heads breaking the surface.

After all, I reasoned to myself, pulling on my light shirt

against a wind that suddenly felt faintly cold, they may have just found something interesting down there. I shaded my eyes against the glare, scanned the shifting surface of the water.

Come on, I thought. Come on, come on now.

My hair stirred in the rising wind.

Suddenly, a sign.

It was a popping trail of bubbles, some hundred feet away, too far away from the boat. One black-clad head, then another.

I breathed a sigh of relief. At last. I waved over towards them.

But there was no wave back. Instead, they both raised their arms out of the water, and with a shiver of dread I recognised the diver's distress signal.

I couldn't tell who it was at this distance, but I thought one of them might be Jimmy.

Nor could I turn the boat towards them. Not till I was sure they were all on the surface. I couldn't risk scraping the whirring propellers over their heads.

'What is it?' I screamed at them.

No answer. Just that arm signal, twice more.

And then two more heads bobbed to the surface, and I was in the wheelhouse, turning the *Mustang Sally* around, and she was responding slowly, all too slowly, and as I drew near I could see Sid in her pink flashes, her mask and regulator thrown back, and in her arms my father floated, eyes closed, as still and pale as the dead of the *Undine* ever were, with a thin foam of blood dripping out of his nose and into the dark blue water.

Two Years Later

'It's nearly dark out there – look.'

Livvy had climbed up on the overstuffed gold brocade sofa to peep through the ancient windowpanes. Empty glasses sour with beer and abandoned playing cards were strewn at her bare feet as she pointed her narrow, freckled face through a chink in the heavy curtains.

'Well, yeah,' said Jake, in contemptuous deadpan. 'It will do that. It's fucking night.'

It wasn't even funny, or remotely clever, but somehow the other two still fell about in hysterical laughter.

They had been doing that all day. Part of it was the booze and pills, she knew, but not all.

'Sorry, Liv. But you just keep asking for it,' said Jake, not looking particularly sorry, as he pushed his vaper between his pale lips and leaned his back against the foot of the armchair. A thin stream of steam burbled out of the end of the device.

She hadn't asked for it, not really, she thought to herself, as she sank back on the cushions, but it was pointless to fight about it.

There were only two more days to go until she went home.

Then she could get on with never having to speak to any of them ever again.

When Jake had suggested this, them all coming out to his parents' holiday house in Cornwall, she had been so thrilled to be finally accepted into their circle. There was always a buzz of excitement around Jake – he said and did whatever he wanted, and never cared what other people thought. She had fancied him like mad ever since Freshers' Week, had contrived to be at the same parties and social events as him. That was how she had ended up befriending Hannah, an arch and willowy business admin student who had gone to school with Jake, and who Livvy wasn't sure she really liked.

Nevertheless, when Hannah had rolled up in her little green Mini five days ago, Livvy had jumped in, her bikini line freshly shaved and her scarlet and purple overnight bag slung over her shoulder. She had not looked back.

The first night had been so promising – the house was huge and amazing, with its real fireplace, and its ancient, blocky furnishings and heavy fabrics, its retinue of stopped clocks. It was like something out of a du Maurier novel, she said, and Jake had merely shrugged.

He told her it had belonged to his Cornish grandparents, and they had died too recently for anyone to sell it yet without paying massive taxes on it. He was lying on the gold brocade sofa at the time, staring up at the mock Georgian chandelier. Livvy had admired the way his thick, dark eyelashes fluttered over his hazel eyes like moths' wings, while simultaneously marvelling at the idea of being able to own two houses at once and be in no hurry to sell either one.

He'd seen her watching him and offered her a slow, wicked smile that made her heart pound a frantic bassline.

Everyone had been exhausted after the long drive, and there had been a frenzy of hugging. They had played cards and drank, the others making mean little comments about some friends who had cried off at the last minute, before erupting into peals of cruel laughter. Livvy had stayed mostly silent, smiled too much, stirred restlessly.

The next morning she woke, hung-over and hungry, and decided to shake off her misgivings. She had been longing for this holiday so much, she told herself, that there was bound to be a sense of anti-climax now she was finally here. She was just tired after the long drive, and having to cope with Hannah, who had a talent for issuing occasional barbed compliments that did nothing but make her feel insecure ('Love your make-up! I could *never* get away with that eyeshadow . . . ')

But Livvy hadn't known at the time that this would now be the pattern for their days and nights. Jake didn't want to swim or hike or explore, which meant that the others didn't want to either. Instead they hung around the house, only leaving for meals and big rounds of drinks at the Jolly Wreckers, the pub in the village, lavish outings which burned through Livvy's tiny reservoir of funds at a terrifying rate. They didn't even want to sit on the beautiful pale beaches with her – Hannah had merely drawled that 'the sun is really bad for my skin, but don't let me stop you, Liv.'

Instead, Jake had stayed in and played tunes on his lap-top, nodding along complacently with every beat. Seamus had urged him at one point to keep the noise down, and this made Jake turn the music up, till the heavy old house shook and an incipient headache lurked constantly between Livvy's brows, waiting for its moment to spring forth.

Within twenty-four hours her crush had died stillborn in the cramped, monotonous conditions. Jake wasn't some free-thinking maverick or rebel, merely a petulant child used to getting his own way.

I am such an *idiot*, she had mumbled into the soft feather pillows of her bed, her eyes wet with fury, after he'd spent the evening making fun of her accent – 'Eee Mum, I'm missing Corunn-ay-tion Street' – and she understood that his needling hostility towards her was growing because he realised, on some subconscious level, that she had gone off him.

And since Hannah was her lift, and Hannah was going nowhere – hanging on Jake's every word, squawking out loud laughter at all his shitty jokes – and Livvy was flat broke, she was stranded here until at least Friday.

It was suddenly all more than she could bear.

'I'm just going to stretch my legs,' she said, getting to her feet.

'Get some firewood while you're out there,' called Jake to her departing back. 'Can't all be living in mammoth skins and clubbing sabretooth tigers like you Northerners.'

Again, that peal of asinine laughter as she forced her feet into her pumps.

'Go fuck yourselves,' she murmured as she slammed out of the kitchen door into the garden, disappointed that she'd not had the courage to say it loud enough for them to hear.

By the time she crossed the field to the dark shape of the woodshed she was already texting, the evening dew wetting her feet through her thin cloth shoes:

Mum – pls can u lend me money 2 cm home tmrw am??? 😩 ❤️ Can't afford the train! Promise I'll pay u back from September student loan!!! Lxxx

A beat, then she added:

Missed u loads!!!!!! Lxxx 😔 😊

She stopped, staring into the phone, waiting, all around her the field growing darker. The woodshed was already little more than an oblong lump against the dark smudge of yew hedge. The bars of the metal farm gate shone palely in the last rags of dusk, and the lane beyond was empty.

A cool breeze ruffled through the thin tendrils of hair on the back of her neck, and it smelled of the sea.

She realised she was holding her breath.

More?! You already owe us 400. Are you ok? ❤️ 🙂 X

She was light-headed with relief, giddy, and she had a flash of insight then into how miserable, how distressed she had been.

Yes! I'm fine. Just want to get home. Thank u!!!! 🙏 😊 Lxxx ❤️

There was no reply then, not for the longest time, and Livvy started to grow anxious, fidgeting with her clunky amber necklace, the phone in her hand a little glowing beacon in the dusk, and now the brightest thing for miles around.

She was distracted by a faint whistling.

Someone idling up from the village, along the farm lane – probably a dog walker. She waited for them to pass the farm gate, but strangely they did not appear.

The sound of footsteps ceased.

She frowned into the empty darkness around the gate, with a flicker of trepidation.

How much are we talking? Another 200? x

Livvy's heart soared. She was *leaving*.

YES!!! Tha

'Excuse me? Hello?'

A man was standing against the metal gate. His voice was vaguely muffled, and she could just make out a scarf drawn around his mouth and nose.

Livvy jumped, nearly dropping her phone, and let out a little shriek.

'Sorry! Didn't mean to startle you.' He stood back from the gate, his head turning up and down the farm lane, as though searching for something. He was holding what looked like a map. 'I think I'm lost. I'm looking for Anvil Point?'

'Oh,' said Livvy.

She knew the way to the village. She'd taken it the first day, with her towel stuffed into her canvas tote bag, her jaunty sunglasses perched above her forehead despite the faint grey mist.

'It's that way,' she pointed to the right. 'Back the way you came.'

'It is? Yeah?' He took another few steps backwards, nearly vanishing into the darkness. 'I . . . Oh, thanks.' He glanced at the map. 'But it looks like the road forks – which way do I go?'

She did not remember a fork in the road, but that did not mean that there wasn't one.

She approached the gate, reluctantly, not sure why but there was something about him that didn't sit right with her. Some people were still wearing masks, of course, she thought, regarding the scarf pulled up to just under his nose. But who did that on a deserted country lane?

Still, she didn't want to appear rude.

'If you just follow the main path,' she said, staying a careful few feet away from the gate, 'you should be all right.'

'Oh, okay,' he said. He was peering at the map again, and she realised, with a flutter of horror, what was bothering her.

It was barely light enough to see his eyes.

There's no way he could read a map in this.

She swallowed, hard.

She had to get away.

'Anyway, it's not far, only twenty minutes.' Her voice was high, tense, and he glanced up sharply at her.

'Is that so?'

And there was something else in there now, a visceral familiarity, something warm and gloating.

Run, said a voice inside her head.

Just run.

Livvy abandoned politeness, abandoned dissemblance, and started to pound back across the field, but already she could hear the steel sing as he vaulted up over the gate, and though the house was only five minutes away, with the golden light shining out through the chinks in the heavy curtains, it might as well have been on the other side of the world.

She opened her mouth to scream and a kind of tangled hitching noise came out, little more than a squeak.

And as she did his hand curled fast in her thin dark hair, hurting her – he was so fast, how was he so fast?

'What's your rush?' he breathed into her ear, his voice smiling, almost playful, as his arm locked around her throat and she was pulled backwards across the grass, her heels digging frantically into the earth to stop her progress.

Livvy struggled, clawed at him, tried to kick him, tried to scream, until he punched her so hard in the side of the head that her vision wavered and the few sprinkling stars in the sky above doubled.

She was limp with terror as he dragged her into the covering darkness of the woodshed, and the sky vanished.

He did not speak again.

2

'You all right there, love?'

I blinked myself awake, an act that felt like swimming upwards through a sea of wallpaper paste.

When I had left our house of mourning almost two years ago, my plans had been simple – to complete my year's internship in Australia, then to return to Britain the following summer. Sid had been adamant that I go – she would take care of the business – something she had been primed to do since Dad had acquired it, and she was, despite our loss, surrounded by good friends. Our dive shop, Blue Horizons, would be fine.

Reluctantly, I'd got on the plane.

But despite everything, happiness had stolen up on me from behind, like a kidnapper. I was seduced by Australia, by the blue depths of the Pacific. I became submerged in the work – quite literally, most days. By Christmas, I was barbecuing swordfish on the blazing beach with my housemates while we drank ice-cold lager, and even though every new experience, every new friend, made me conscious of the void that existed where I would be telling Dad about this, somehow it grew less hollow, less bitter, as time drew on.

Sid also seemed to be recovering, slowly but surely. The dive school was thriving, she told me, and sometime in late October, a month after I left, she started seeing Adam. That Christmas, he surprised her by jetting her off to somewhere in the Dominican Republic (she sent a flurry of images to my phone, of them both lounging on beaches and holding on to brightly coloured and plumed cocktails, smiles and heart emojis scattered over all her communiqués like digital glitter).

I couldn't have been happier for her, and I thought Dad would have been happy for her too, though I must confess I was a little surprised.

I wouldn't have thought Adam was her type.

At any rate, I told myself, I would soon be home for the summer, and able to judge for myself what her type was.

But then Covid had happened, the destroyer of lives and all plans. By March the next year the borders were closed. In the meantime, Blue Horizons was forced to shut its doors and all lessons stopped. Even if I'd come home, I would merely have been another mouth to feed.

I'd had no choice but to stay away, and to keep staying away.

The upshot of this was that I had not seen my hometown for the best part of two years, and my exhaustion and homesickness made it feel insubstantial, as though I had turned a corner in a dream and found myself here, rather than travelling ten thousand miles to arrive.

'Yeah, sorry, just tired,' I said, hoping that would be the end of the conversation.

The taxi driver's eyes flickered towards me in his rear-view mirror, like a bright chirpy bird's.

'Oh yeah?'

I think I was out of luck.

My eyes fluttered shut again. I am just resting them, I told myself. I am not falling asleep. Honest.

'Come far, then?' he asked, after a few moments.

I'd been travelling for forty hours at that point, at least twenty-three of them spent crushed into a tiny economy seat on an airplane.

Small talk was the very last thing in the world I wanted just then.

'Yeah, from Queensland.'

'Have fun?'

'I . . . yeah.' I sighed, softened. 'Still, it's nice to be back.' I let my eyes slide closed again.

'So where are you headed to in Anvil Point?'

'Blue Horizons,' I said, happy for once to be offering tangible information that would get me closer to my goal. 'The house, that is, not the dive school.'

'Oh yeah, I know the house, all right. Up on the cliff. To be honest, I thought the dive school was shut.'

'No,' I said, finding the energy through my exhaustion to be surprised. 'It opened again six weeks ago.'

'Yeah? If you say so.' He glanced at me in the mirror. 'Used to be really popular, it did, now, not so much.'

I stirred on the backseat of the cab, unpleasantly surprised.

Sid had been so effusive in her calls, then her emails as her calls petered out ('Always so busy!' she'd write). She never seemed to stop.

In fact, it was this busyness that had finally lured me back across the equator. Blue Horizons was horrendously short-staffed, said Sid. There had been something hesitant, almost wistful in her words, and I realised instantly what was being asked of me.

Jean-Paul, my supervisor at the Institute, had been very understanding.

'We will hold your role for you as long as we can,

Cassandra,' he'd said, his long, thin fingers stroking through his beard. 'We'd love to have you here full-time. And I know your family is important to you. But as for the visa situation . . .'

I knew what he meant. There was no knowing how long it would be before the backlog in visas that Covid had caused in Australia would be sorted. The borders were still closed. If I left the country now, it was not clear when, if ever, I would be able to return.

I was taking a risk with my future and I knew it, but when your family calls, you have to answer.

And I wanted to see Sid.

So here I was.

'Really?' I asked the driver. 'I heard the dive shop was busier than ever.'

'You did?' His eyes met mine in the rear-view mirror again, bright, curious. 'Maybe. I dunno. Apparently some new guy took it over.'

A sense of relief washed over me then. He'd obviously got his wires crossed somehow.

'My sister Sid is the owner,' I said. 'It's run by a woman.'

He widened his eyes at me, as though I was the mistaken one.

'Right.' He blinked again, and the short, unsure way he said it made me think he was humouring me.

Exhausted as I was, I was not expecting that first flush of emotion upon turning up the winding, cracked road to Anvil Point. The village was there below, a small crowd of white-painted houses looping around the grey harbour walls and stretching up the nearby hills in narrow arteries, the sea beyond ivory and dark blue and thrashing against its pale strip of pink sand and pebbles. On the prominence overlooking Anvil Point was the cluster of buildings that was our home.

I realised I was about to start crying, facing the roll call of all who would not be here to welcome me as we cranked our way up the steep and meandering driveway to the house.

'Where shall I set you down, love?'

We were passing the huge glasshouse structure that covered our indoor training pool. Through the windows, all was silent and empty, boxes of kit racked against the far wall.

'The house, thanks,' I said, trying to keep myself under control. The sea air was forcing its way in through the tiny crack in the driver's side window and though cool, it smelled of salt and fresh air. I sucked it in, savouring the taste of home.

The taxi pulled into our gravel driveway, and he got out to unload my luggage, making theatrical little sighs at its weight. I'd been carrying this stuff across the country for the last seven hours so I was perhaps not as sympathetic as I should have been.

'This looks heavy,' he said mournfully, reaching for my dive kit.

'No, it's all right, I'll handle that,' I said quickly, darting forward to swing it out of the boot.

That stuff may be heavy but it's fragile. The last place you want to find out somebody's damaged it is a hundred feet under the surface of the sea.

I paid him, waiting for Sid to emerge from the house to greet me, but there was no sign of her.

I sighed and turned around as the taxi rumbled away,

alone for the first time in hours. Not even the cat was turning up to welcome me, it seemed.

My tiredness had morphed from a kind of confused fug to something sharp, almost too alert. I was getting my second wind, perhaps, or maybe it was just a sense that something was off.

I walked up the wooden steps – they looked weathered, we had to take care of these things living so close to the sea – and now I was here I realised the whole place had a slightly neglected air. The plant pots on either side of the door had housed two lavender bushes, and both now appeared to be dead. There had always been a windchime hanging from the awning over the porch that sang out tiny atonal notes in the sea breeze, a purchase of my mother's, and this had vanished.

I rang the bell, but instead of the sound of the buzzer I was greeted with silence.

Staring through the frosted glass of the door, I could see nobody.

I knocked this time, loudly, and stood back, waiting.

Then, like a pale flame, the distorted figure of someone who could only be Sid was making her way down the stairs. She seemed to be moving slowly, or that could have been a factor of my tiredness. I thought of Sid as someone who was always in flight – rushing to the boat, rushing to the pub, rushing down to the sea from the beach.

This new dilatoriness made me uneasy.

The door swung open.

'Cass!' she cried, and I was suddenly in her arms, after a kind of weird, hesitant pause. I had only a second or so to get over my shock, to smother my surprise at the change in her.

'Oh God,' I gasped. 'It's so good to see you! You look well,' I lied.

'Oh, I don't know about that.' She wouldn't meet my eyes. 'How was your journey?'

'Dreadful,' I stammered, with a little fake laugh. 'But it was always going to be dreadful, so let's not even. How have you been? How's Tallulah? What's been going on?'

Her hair, her beautiful long golden hair was all gone – replaced by a sharp, asymmetrical bob that somehow made her look older. She'd gained about thirty pounds as well, by my guess, and it didn't sit well on her.

More to the point, I also thought she looked tired, with dark smudges under her eyes. Sid had no business looking pale – even in the depths of winter she was constantly outdoors, constantly on the sea.

Something of my feelings, despite my best efforts, must have shown in my face.

'It's the hair, isn't it?' She twirled a couple of strands between her fingers.

I felt sick. 'Sorry,' I said. 'It was a surprise.'

'I know, I know. But it was such a faff to look after, you know? With working so hard it was just getting in the way.'

I stared at her. Her hair had been, to use the hackneyed old phrase, her crowning glory – a shower of pure gold that had made her look like a fairy-tale princess. The boys in town had called her Rapunzel.

'And anyway,' she said, still not meeting my eyes, 'Adam likes it short. Says it shows off my bone structure more.'

'Of course, of course, it looks great, now I'm used to it,' I lied again. It did indeed show her bone structure off more – the slightly crooked nose from where she'd broken it against the stone pool lip as a child, and the broad chin we'd both inherited from Dad, tiny defects the hair had distracted the eye away from and which now lay exposed.

'Anyway, I am *so* glad to see you. I've missed you so much. It must have been a wrench to leave Australia. I know you loved it there.' And she hugged me again, and this time her hug was tight, genuine. 'How did you leave them at the Institute? Bet they were sorry to see you go.'

'They were lovely,' I said, remembering my conversation with Jean-Paul. 'They couldn't have been nicer. They . . .' I had nearly said 'want to offer me a job' but managed to bite this off. I could not possibly talk about leaving again so soon.

In fact, I couldn't have, even if I wanted to. I had given up my visa and the door to Australia had slammed shut behind me. For the foreseeable future, I was here.

'Come in, come in,' she said, taking me by the hand with a shadow of her old impulsive intimacy, and leading me into the kitchen. 'I'll make you a cup of tea.'

'Oh Sid, bugger tea,' I laughed. 'Have you got any wine?'

'Oh,' she said, stopping short so I nearly ran into her.

I squinted at her. 'What's up?'

'It's just that Adam's planned a nice meal for later, so I was saving the wine for then. He'll be back from the dive school at seven.'

I glanced sideways at her. Before I'd left for the journey home, the agreed plan had been to go to the local pub, the Jolly Wreckers, for dinner.

'He wanted to cook, you see.'

'Ah,' I said. 'Okay then. That's great.'

Though, if I'm being honest, my heart sank a little. I'd been hoping to set off for the Wreckers as soon as may be.

I wanted to run into Ben again.

When my dad died, Ben and I had trailed off – with the funeral, the organising, ultimately my leaving – we had mutually agreed to end it.

But eight months later, in the midst of lockdown, I'd been surprised by a new follower on my Instagram account, where I posted occasional images of sharks and other marine life I captured on camera.

This time, I'd posted a picture of myself on the patio in our Townsville house. It was sometime in June, so I was clad in a light sweater and jeans against the mild winter evening, gazing mournfully out to sea. Nine tenths of my diving had been cut so I was mostly doing research from home. I forget what the caption was, something maudlin and moody like *Someday I'll be back out there*, I think – and within moments an image appeared in my DMs of Ben and me, arms around each other's waists, laughing under the fairy lights in the Jolly Wreckers beer garden. His hair had been a fluffy dark halo around his long face.

Remember this?

We'd kept in sporadic contact since.

Maybe, I'd allowed myself to think on the way home, perhaps by now, absence had made his heart grow fonder. We could start again properly, on a new, more equal footing . . .

In short, I was desperate to see him.

Still, this gesture of Adam's, to cook for me, was lovely and I was determined to appreciate it. Adam had been looking after my sister while I was away, after all. It would be good to spend quality time with them both, maybe even get them to come out to the pub with me later.

'Sorry, Cass. There isn't a bottle open,' said Sid, looking anxiously into the fridge. 'I can get you a beer . . .'

'It doesn't matter. Tea will do. I'm parched.'

As Sid moved off towards the kettle, a small grey cloud suddenly leapt up on to the table in front of me, making a series of low yowls.

'Tallulah! How've you been, baby girl?' I reached out to take her in my arms.

She wouldn't let me hold her – from the glint in her golden eyes I was a truant and still in trouble, it seemed – and she turned small twirls on the table, as though unsure where to put herself.

I could have been imagining it, but she seemed thinner to me, her cries a little desperate.

'Shoo! Shoo, you silly cow, get off!' Sid glanced at me. 'Sorry, Cass. Adam goes mad when he sees her up here.'

I almost said out loud, *So? She lives here.*

But I didn't. In fairness, we were forever trying to persuade the cat not to get up on the kitchen surfaces. Instead, I picked her up despite the way she froze in my arms, and kissed her downy head, setting her in my lap.

She quitted it immediately and, with immense offended dignity, trotted out into the hallway and vanished up the stairs.

Sid threw an affectionate glance after her. 'So, the cat's still a bitch.'

'Yeah.'

We talked at the kitchen table for a little while, as she shared the small news of the village and our friends, gossiping about them in a way that she would never have considered doing in her texts and WhatsApp messages.

'Have you seen much of Ben about?' I asked her, trying to sound nonchalant.

'No, not really.' She shook her head. 'We've barely stopped working.'

This had been a constant theme in her calls, emails and texts – she was working so hard, working all the time, we are working 24/7 – and despite my tiredness and trepidation I couldn't help but hold it up against what the taxi driver had told me on the way down.

'So, how's business been?' I asked, deciding on a direct approach.

She went still for a long minute, as was her habit when caught in a lie, and my alarm was back with a vengeance.

'Oh . . . well, you know, with the lockdown and all, and then the new place that opened up at the Lizard last year, it's not been as much as we'd like. To be honest, Adam and Jimmy are handling all the figures now, but it's been harder to fill the classes.'

'I see,' I said.

'And there's been a lot of staff changes as well,' she said, looking down at her cup.

'Yeah? Like who?'

'Oh, Nathan left in the spring, as you know. And Elna –'

I was astounded.

'Elna left? *Elna?*'

Elna was a South African who had been here for seven years and was practically a member of our family – to the point where nobody would have batted an eye if she'd sat down at our dinner table without being invited.

'When? Did she go home?' I asked. She'd sometimes talked about this, but with no real enthusiasm. Perhaps something had happened there and she'd had to return.

'No.' Sid bit her lip. 'I think she went over to Devon in the end.'

'*Devon?* Why?'

Sid looked away. 'I dunno. Didn't suit her here any more.'

I stared at her. 'You never said.'

'Well, you know, I didn't want to worry you.' She looked shifty. 'I know how you get. But people told me it's normal, when, you know, there's a change in management, and with Dad not . . .'

We paused, and the moment itself seemed to tremble, this first time we had acknowledged to each other the hugeness of our loss since I had come home.

'Yeah,' I said softly. 'That makes sense.'

'Yeah,' she said, blowing out gently. 'It's been a transitional period.'

I looked up sharply at her. It didn't sound like a phrase she would use.

'Jimmy's still here, isn't he?' I asked. Shit, if *Jimmy* had left . . .

She grinned, clearly glad of the change in subject. 'Of course! He's still the same.' Her gaze moved away. 'I would have asked him up to dinner, but to be honest . . .' Her voice lowered and her head dipped towards mine, though only I and possibly Tallulah were in the house. 'I don't think he gets on that well with Adam.'

'No?'

'Well, you know Jimmy. Wildly overprotective.' She managed a little shivering false laugh. 'Especially since Dad . . .'

I glanced at her, but she wouldn't meet my eyes.

Jimmy had been Dad's diving buddy that day on the

Mustang Sally, so he was the one who'd been responsible for keeping an eye on him.

All we'd ever learned about his death was that Dad had been distracted away from the guideline somehow, and had swum away from Jimmy. It had been Sid who had found him next, floating unconscious ten feet below the surface, and pulled him up with her.

We think maybe that he'd been entangled or stuck in the wreck, since there proved to be nothing wrong with his equipment – and in his efforts to get free overexerted himself and used up his air that much faster than the others. Once he ran low and since he was alone, he would have faced a stark and terrifying choice – to swim to the surface from great depth too quickly before his air ran out, and risk a fatal case of the bends, or to drown.

It was this ascent that had killed him.

The truth was that enclosed wreck-diving is potentially dangerous, even for the most seasoned professionals, and it could have been anything that triggered his accident. We had learned to come to terms with the idea that we would never really know the details.

'You'll probably see Jimmy tonight in the pub.' Sid raised an eyebrow at me. 'He's not stopped asking about you. You always were his favourite.'

'Stop it,' I said, and yawned hugely, not taking the bait. 'Sid, I literally cannot keep my eyes open. I have to lie down just for a bit if I'm going to be conscious for dinner.' I gave her a rueful smile.

She didn't smile back, looked embarrassed. 'Um, Cass, sorry, your bedroom isn't ready – we didn't have time. Can you go in the guest room until we sort it out?'

'What? Oh, don't worry about the bedding and all

that . . .' I flapped a hand at her. 'I could sleep on a park bench, the way I feel. Can you give me a shout half an hour before?' I stood up.

She didn't move.

'No, I mean Adam made that room into his office. He liked the view – sorry, we were going to change it back – we've been talking about it all week – but it's just been so crazy that . . .'

There were soft red blotches appearing on her throat, as they did whenever she was uncomfortable.

'It's all right,' I said, trying to sound cheerful, though there was no denying that I felt the dull ache of disappointment tightening my throat.

I would have thought that Sid would have been as excited to see me as I was to see her. If our situations had been reversed, getting her room ready would have been part of that pleasure.

I had, after all, blown nearly all of my meagre inheritance from Dad in buying a horrendously overpriced ticket to return here.

'Cass, I'm really sorry.' She knew me, after all. Her voice had gone up an octave, almost trembling, and this, too, was new.

Usually, when Sid was pressured, she found the best form of defence was attack.

'Just go in the guest room tonight and we'll move it all back in the morning, yeah?'

I smiled at her, crushed my feelings down. 'Yeah. Sure thing.'

3

When I woke the sun was setting outside – and I was lost, disoriented – where was I?

I was in the tiny, cramped guest room, my suitcase standing upright at the foot of my bed like a sentry, and through the small window I could see the patch of lighting from the kitchen. There was a radio playing somewhere, and the sound of the sink being filled with rushing water. There were also quiet voices, having hushed conversations.

At my back, Tallulah stirred with a soft sigh. At some point she must have come in and lain down on the bed.

I sat up, my neck stiff, my eyes and throat dry. Within me the ache for more sleep was like a physical pain. I glanced at my phone. It was nearly eight o'clock.

I staggered to my feet, into the bathroom. I felt filthy and travel-stained, so I decided on a quick shower, letting the cool water wake me while I considered all that I had learned so far.

Despite everything, I couldn't shake my disquiet. The change in Sid was too great. Could it really all be explained by grief?

And hard on the heels of this, a sharp memory from my journey.

Apparently some new guy has taken over.

Come on, I told myself. You're just tired and overwrought. You just need to give things a chance.

*

Coming out of the shower I briskly towelled off and put on a T-shirt and leggings. I was raking a comb through my hair in front of the mirror when there was a knock on the door.

'Two secs,' I called out.

On the other side was Adam, looking just like I remembered him, with his square face and large grey eyes.

'Oh, hi . . .'

'Hey Cass!' he said, and to my surprise lunged in and engulfed me in a huge bear hug. I could feel his arms flex around my waist, his breath on my shoulder, my breasts crushed against his chest.

I froze, too astonished to move, as with a final squeeze he let me go.

'Welcome home! Sorry about the mix-up with your room. It's just got such a great view, and with one thing and another we forgot to change it back in time. We'll sort it out tomorrow.' He hitched up a wide smile. 'Hope you're hungry!'

'I . . . sure, sure, I haven't eaten since this morning.'

'Come on down when you're ready. Can I get you a glass of wine?'

Finally, some good news.

'Um, sure, yeah, that would be lovely . . .'

'Red or white?'

'Oh, white, please. I'll be down in two ticks.'

He smiled again, vanished.

I watched him retreat down the hall, swing round the bannister, his feet thumping quickly all the way down the stairs, as though he had inherited Sid's missing energy.

When I tramped downstairs, my wet hair wrapped up in a towel, I saw that the table had already been laid. The barbecue grill had been lit in the back garden, and through the open windows I smelled charcoal and smoke.

As I emerged into the kitchen, Sid looked up from where she was mashing potatoes by the stove, her face flushed with the effort, her pale blue top damp with sweat and steam. It was a little burst of shock to see her without her gorgeous hair again, but I quickly suppressed it.

'How do you feel?' she asked.

'Much better,' I said, drawing out a chair, and I smiled at her, because she seemed strangely anxious. There was a full glass of white sitting on the table, so I presumed this was my place. 'Can I help with anything?'

'Oh no, no, it's all done nearly.' She was back to pummelling the potatoes. 'So you slept okay?'

'Oh yeah. Like a log. I'm going to stay up now. Somebody told me that the way round jet lag is to force yourself into your normal routine.'

Sid nodded. 'Good plan.' Then she gave me a sly little wink. 'And that way you get to head off to the pub and check on Ben before bedtime.'

She grinned, and suddenly I recognised the old Sid, perhaps for the first time since I had arrived.

But something caught at my attention in what she'd said, like a snagged thread.

'Well, you're coming to the pub too, aren't you?'

Her eyes widened, then moved away shiftily.

'Oh, I'd love to, but I'm just exhausted, Cass. Another night, yeah?'

'Sure,' I said brightly, trying to keep the brittle disappointment out of my voice. 'Of course.' I decided to change the subject. 'What's for dinner?'

'Steak,' said Sid.

'Fantastic,' I said. My mouth was watering.

'Hey hey, ladies,' said Adam, carrying in a big plate, its contents covered in a white tea towel. 'Hope you're hungry!'

He came up behind Sid and kissed the crown of her head. 'Mmm, looks great.'

'I've tried to get all the lumps out.' She sounded distressed. 'Think it's . . .'

'It'll be fine.' He put the plate down on the table, glanced over at me. 'So how was Australia?' he asked. 'You know, Sid never actually told me what you were doing over there. Some kind of ocean science, right?'

'Yeah, I was seconded to the Institute of Oceanography for a year. Well, that was the plan.' I shrugged helplessly. 'In the beginning. Just a year. To study sharks.'

'Sharks?' He peered at me in amusement as he picked through the cutlery drawer, raised an eyebrow.

'Yep.'

'What sort of sharks?'

I drifted for a moment, lost in happy memories. 'Well, all kinds really, but the main project was about grey nurse sharks and the effect of shark culling techniques on their population.' I sipped the wine. 'Y'know, sharks don't get great press, and it affects how humans deal with them . . .'

He laughed, hugely, abruptly, as though I had said something patently absurd. 'They have to be *free*,' he sang, opening his arms dramatically. 'To live, to love, to eat people . . .'

I raised an eyebrow at him. 'They *very rarely* eat people.'

'They only have to eat you once, Cass.' He gestured at me with the fistful of steak knives he was holding.

36

'Maybe,' I conceded with a laugh. I glanced over to Sid, to include her, but she was not looking at us, still focused on pounding the potatoes.

'So, I presume you saw lots of sharks,' said Adam.

'Not as many as I would have liked.' I sighed. 'Once the lockdown started I spent a fair amount of time confined to barracks. But I got out a few times, at least in the beginning.'

'Well, it sounds a great life,' he said with a sigh. 'All right for some.'

'Maybe.' I took another sip of the cool Pinot Grigio and pulled the towel off my head, letting my hair free to dry in the warm air. 'Are you sure I can't help with anything?' I asked.

'Absolutely not.'

Sid set down the dish of mashed potato on the table and Adam moved to sit down – not taking the seat opposite me, but instead moving to the head of the table, pulling the chair out, settling into it.

I froze.

He was peering at me, surprised. 'Is something wrong?'

The chair at the head of the table had always been my dad's place. A palimpsest of memories flooded in then – Dad sitting there dishevelled, fresh out of bed, monosyllabic until every drop of his coffee was finished, while the morning sunlight bathed him. Dad sitting there in the low dusk, surrounded by friends, a glass of wine at his elbow, telling some tale of his adventures in the depths of the sea. Dad sitting there, his face lit up in wonderment and delight, as I told him about being accepted for my internship, my impending trip to Australia . . .

To now see someone else scrape that chair across the

floor, sit in it, lean back against that wall, was suddenly more than I could bear.

Pull yourself together, I told myself firmly. He's not doing it deliberately.

Stop making this weird.

Or at least any weirder.

I hitched up an apologetic smile. 'No, no, I'm fine. Sorry, I'm a bit spacy. My head doesn't know what time zone I'm in.' I rubbed my eyes, wondered if I was kidding anybody. 'I keep tuning out. I'll be better with something to eat.'

'Well, that's a hint if ever I heard one,' Adam replied archly, glancing over at Sid, who was sliding into the chair next to him. He drew off the tea towel from the plate he'd brought in.

Beneath it lay a mass of burnt meat in a pool of its own blood.

Sid actually clapped her hands together in delight. 'Oh, it looks fabulous!'

I wanted to throw her a quiet look of *really?*, but managed to stop myself.

I didn't know what was the matter with me. I seemed to have been possessed by some evil spirit. It was a dinner and someone had cooked it for me. I should be grateful they'd made the effort. I felt a heat on the crown of my head, and glanced up to see Adam's ardent grey eyes, almost devouring me. I too was expected to offer praise, I saw, and I supposed it was the least I could do.

'Yeah, it looks great,' I said. 'I'm starving.'

He lingered on me for another millisecond, as though he'd heard the false note in my voice, before dropping a piece of steak on to my plate. There was nothing for it but to buckle in and make the best of it.

'Thanks,' I said.

Sid looked anxious.

I did not know what to say or do for the best, but I resolved to roll on through as though nothing untoward was happening. I picked up the spoon from the potatoes, dropped a dollop on to my plate.

Conversation continued throughout dinner, though I noticed it seemed to be led by Adam. For all her stated enthusiasm, Sid poked through the food with her fork and drank. In fact, she seemed to drink a lot – a glass and a half to every one of mine.

Adam however, kept better pace with me.

'It'll be good to have you in the dive shop – they talk about you all the time,' he said, then sighed. 'They've missed you.'

'I . . .'

Suddenly my eyes were welling up.

I knew very well who they missed.

'I . . . sorry. Sorry.' I put my fork down, dabbed at my eyes with my hands. 'I just . . . it's a bit overwhelming to be back after . . . Anyway,' I said. 'It's nice to be home. And I won't be going anywhere for some time now.'

Sid's hand snaked across the table, closed around my own, squeezed. 'I'll bring up the dessert,' she said, getting up and heading down the steps to the cellar fridge, and Adam merely nodded, watched her go.

'You know, it's a nightmare at the shop at the moment,' he said. I glanced over at him. 'We can't seem to find the right people. So it'll be just you and Erik tomorrow for the Advanced Wreck. I've got a class in Newquay.'

'Really?' I hadn't seen it on the shop's online calendar, but then I hadn't looked since before I got the plane.

'But Erik is a good guy,' Adam continued. 'And of course, you should know the *Undine* like the back of your hand.'

I smiled – a thin, ambivalent expression, as Sid returned, carrying a tub of the local ice cream.

My dad had known the *Undine* like the back of his hand too, but it hadn't stopped him from making an uncontrolled ascent from depth that had ended up giving him the bends, and ultimately killing him.

My shoulders and neck ached with tension as I climbed the stairs after dinner.

I tried to think what could be causing it – the kit I'd been carrying across the world, the stress of travel, my frayed and wobbling circadian rhythm?

Back in the guest room, I downed the last two of my Australian Panadol, washing them down with the warm dregs of my water bottle. I threw on a pink dress, thought it looked a little desperate, took it off again, put on a yellow silky top, took it off, put the dress on again.

A little light make-up, a slick of coral lipstick later, and I peered into the tiny mirror. My hair, though dark unlike Sid's, was bronzed by the sun and my freckles were in evidence, and I thought that even though I was tired I looked pretty good.

'Hang on,' said Sid as I tripped lightly down the stairs towards the door. She'd appeared out of the living room, quietly, startling me. How like a ghost she was in her own house. 'How are you getting there?'

'I'm walking,' I said. 'It's only the village.'

Her expression was unreadable. 'I wouldn't do that.'

'What? Well, I have to. I can't drive. And you can't drive.'

She sighed. 'I know. I just think maybe you should get a taxi . . .'

'A taxi?' I let out a sharp laugh. 'Don't be silly. It's fifteen minutes on foot, if that . . .'

Her face didn't change. 'Some girl went missing from Bryn Tawr, and they haven't found her yet.'

I froze. 'What do you mean, missing?'

Sid shrugged. 'I mean missing. Someone grabbed her when she went out for firewood.'

'From Bryn Tawr?' I thought about that for a second. 'Off Linden Lane?'

'Yeah.' Her lips thinned as she grimaced.

'Who was it? Anyone we know?'

She shook her head. 'Some tourist,' she murmured. 'Livvy Something, she's called. She's been missing for nearly two weeks.' She lowered her voice. 'The police have been everywhere, blocking off Linden Lane, asking in the pub . . . You'll see the posters for her in the shops on the way in.'

I widened my eyes at her.

'Just be careful,' said Sid, leaning in to kiss my cheek. 'That's all I'm saying.'

4

This conversation with Sid left me glancing anxiously over my shoulder as I trudged down the private footpath over the steep headland to meet the main road.

It wasn't far, but a challenging walk in bad weather, or when you were coming home from either of the village's pubs the worse for wear and in high-heels. I have lost count of the number of grazed knees, ripped tights and twisted ankles Sid and I collected over the years.

The road was well-lit once I reached it, and lined with stray houses that gathered closer together the nearer you got to the high stone walls of the harbour. Soft yellow lights glowed within homes and shops as evening fell, and I was relieved to see them as I drew close. I already felt happier once I was within the village proper – its post office, its chemist, the newsagent whose floorage was largely taken up with piles of touristy tat.

I wasn't used to feeling unsafe here – it was an alien, disorienting sensation.

All was shut for the night, except for the little Co-op.

Sure enough, in the window was an A3-sized poster with the word MISSING over the top. Below it a girl stared out, offering the camera a shy smile. She had pale eyes and heavy brows. The picture looked like it had been taken for a driving licence or an ID of some kind.

Poor thing, I thought, I hope she turns up, and I ducked into the shop to say hello.

June was sitting at the counter, her dark corkscrewed hair tied back from her face. She looked just the same.

'Cassandra!' She lit up. June, though she looked little over thirty-five, was the village matriarch and the source of all true news. 'Your sister said you were coming home. You do look well! How was it?'

'Very nice,' I said, grinning.

'Is Australia like they say? Barbecues and surfing?' Her eyes glowed with pleasure. 'I've always wanted to go, you know.'

'It was at first,' I said. 'Then the pandemic happened and . . .'

'I bet you didn't want to leave,' she said cheerfully, ignoring this last. 'You've not missed much here, let me tell you.'

I laughed. 'I doubt that.'

'Where you off to?' she asked, but there was something shrewd in her voice, as though she guessed what I was about. It is a talent, but nothing gets past June.

'I just had dinner with Adam and Sid up at the house. Adam did a barbecue. And then I was going to nip into the Wreckers . . .'

'Oh yeah,' she said, breaking into a huge smile. 'Adam's lovely, isn't he? Really takes care of your sister. You know . . .' she trailed off, as though aware she was heading into fraught territory, 'considering how she's been.'

'Yeah?' I studied her serene, open face. What did that mean, *considering how she's been*?

I had the unpleasant crawling sensation then that I was well behind the times.

'Oh yeah,' said June. 'He's so good to her.'

And as much as it hurt to realise it, she would be more likely to know than I.

*

43

The Jolly Wreckers was full to the brim, and after what I'd become used to in Australia, it gave me a frisson of shock to see it.

But I shouldn't have been surprised, not really. Anvil Point has always been the same. We're miles from the nearest village, nestled in our own little cusp of the coast, mostly concerned with fishing and farming, and with only the yearly influx of middle-class tourists with sharp accents and spotless Range Rovers to break up our quiet lives.

There were other things to worry about here apart from social distancing – such as catch quotas and coastal erosion. As Tony, Ben's father, had been fond of saying, Coronavirus could tear off a number and take a seat.

Speaking of Ben, there he was, in skinny jeans and mask and a Jolly Wreckers T-shirt with CREW printed in big letters on the back. He was murmuring to a pretty girl behind the bar, counting something off on his fingers. The girl was clad in an identical shirt to him, her loose topknot slipping sideways in the summer heat, her make-up shiny.

There was a dreamy tilt to her chin while she looked up at him that gave me pause.

He spotted me first.

'Cass!' he shouted, springing away from her, and I caught her simmering glance at me before I was suddenly enfolded in his arms, squeezed tightly, before he put his hands on my shoulders and pushed me back, studying me.

'What?' I asked, laughing. 'What is it?'

'I can't get over how tanned you are!'

'I know, I know. It was blazing all the time. There was no way round it . . .'

'You look *fantastic*,' he said with feeling, and a certain element of surprise.

I blushed under his appraising gaze. 'Uh, thanks . . .'

'C'mon, what are you drinking?'

'Um . . . got a JD and Coke?'

He grinned behind his mask. 'Yeah. I've got a JD and Coke.' He steered me through the crowd, 'Follow me.'

The evening whirled around me. I chatted to old school-friends, their parents, to fishermen and farmers, as though I'd never been away, catching up on all the small news, answering the same questions again and again. *How was Australia? Must be miserable to be back, right?* And occasionally, almost murmured, as though in concern or embarrassment, *How is Sid?*

'She's fine,' I responded loyally.

Every so often Ben appeared at my side, almost posses-sively, before departing in a flurry of elbows whenever a queue started at the bar.

Eventually, on the dot of 10:50 and with a theatrical flourish, Ben tapped the ship's bell behind the bar with a steel rod, and his voice rang out – 'Last orders, please!'

He looked straight over at me and winked.

Afterwards we drifted out into the beer garden alone, to the picnic benches strewn with party lights and winding vines and flowers. Ben sat back into the one in the far cor-ner, his mask pulled down. With his dark eyes and impish dimples, the decorations floating around his corona of dark curly hair, he looked like a garlanded Greek god.

I slid over the sun-warmed wood of the bench in front of him, which brushed against the bare skin of my thighs under the little pink dress.

'So how does it feel to be home?' he asked, cocking his head at me.

I shrugged. 'Good. A bit dreamlike, to be honest, but that might just be the jet lag.'

He smiled at me, that lopsided, generous smile, and for the faintest of moments, it felt a little artificial.

But then it was gone, and there was only us, and the murmur of conversations all around us, and behind that, the nearby splash and whisper of the sea as it butted up against the harbour walls.

'What have you been up to?' I asked.

He shrugged and his gaze swept his surroundings. 'This. And the craft brewery.' He nodded towards the dray shed at the back of the pub. 'Not much room but at least it's free.'

He'd set up a tiny business brewing beer in this shed with his mate Jack, and they were currently selling it as 'Shipwreck Sauce' to the tourists that passed through the pub. His Instagram was full of images of him and Jack, a blow-in hipster with a beard like a spade who'd gone to school with Ben, handling barrels and carrying crates with appropriately moody masculine vigour.

'How's it all going?'

'Good,' he said, with a slightly disengaged air that made me wonder how true this was. 'Okay.'

I took away that it was a sore point.

I smiled flirtatiously at him. 'I'd like to try it some time, but I have to warn you, I'm not a beer person.'

He snorted. 'Maybe you will be, after this.'

'Maybe.'

'It's great that you're back. Now you'll get the chance.'

'I missed you,' I said, deciding to take a risk.

Again that smile, but I had the sense he wasn't really looking at me. Instead, he looked away over my shoulder, waved at someone I presumed was coming out of the pub.

'I missed you too,' he said, turning back, letting his fingers close over my hand.

'Hey.' I regarded him for a long moment. 'What do you think of Adam?'

'Adam?' His smile dropped, a frown crossing his tanned brow. 'Why are you asking about him?'

'Why not?' I gave him a small shrug, trying to stay light, stay flirty, letting the chunky bracelet on my wrist clatter playfully as I did so. 'You know. He's with Sid. I'm curious. What sort of guy is he? I didn't really spend that much time with him, you know, before I had to leave . . .'

'Oh, he's great!' Ben's smile hitched up, and I wondered for a moment whether he had been worried I was going to ask him something difficult. 'He's a really cool guy. He's in here all the time. He's really been helping us out with the beach barbecues . . .'

'Cooking? For the Wreckers?' It was all I could do to keep my face from betraying me.

'What? No!' Ben leaned in, those kissable lips drawing closer. 'Just between us, he's a terrible cook. Absolutely hopeless. But when we were having the first barbecue, you know, during the break in the middle of last year, he was dead helpful. Really pushed the events, you know, to his customers, even though he couldn't book dives for them. Set us up with good suppliers. Constantly hyping up Shipwreck Sauce to everybody. Such a nice guy. Funny, you know?' Ben sighed, sipped his beer. 'It's great that he's stayed so positive, with everything that's gone on.'

47

I nodded. 'Yeah. I suppose the pandemic hit everyone hard, and then that girl going missing . . .'

He waved this away. 'No.' He reconsidered for a moment. 'Well *yeah*, all that too. But it's not just that.' He shrugged. 'You know, with your sister and everything . . .'

My smile slipped. 'What do you mean?'

'Well, it's got to be difficult for him,' said Ben, his eyes growing compassionate and soulful. 'Your sister, you know, with all the problems she has, she's got to be hard work. We don't see her down here much any more, and when we do, she's not . . . she's not the same. Not like the old Sid. I mean, it's probably not that surprising, considering what happened with her dad.'

I blinked at him.

'*Your* dad, I mean.' He looked embarrassed, as though aware he had strayed into difficult territory. I knew of old that Ben did not like difficult territory. 'I know Adam works hard, doing stuff to look after her, to make sure she's okay. She's in safe hands.' He squeezed my fingers. 'You don't have to worry about her, that's all I'm trying to say.'

I felt a kind of chill come over me then, something that the warm wood and his molten eyes could not allay. What did that mean, *all the problems she has*? I knew that Sid looked defeated and her shorn hair and sallow skin warned me that she was not consistently happy all the time, but she was hardly a basket case.

'What kind of problems?'

He stirred on the bench, suddenly uncomfortable. 'Oh, I dunno. I hardly see her. You should ask Adam.'

I will, I thought.

It came to me in a flash that many people seemed to

think that Sid had 'problems' and yet nobody seemed to be able to verify what these problems actually were, because they never saw her.

Was it true? But how would I know either way?

It *could* be true.

I'd been gone so long.

Sid could be in real trouble, and I'd just never picked it up.

The night seemed cold now. I suddenly realised that I wanted to go home, regardless of my previous plans, of the way his bare leg had now drifted towards my own under the table, was rubbing against my ankle.

I wanted to set eyes on Sid.

I put on my own bright smile.

'You know, Ben, it's good to be back. But I'm exhausted. I'm too jet-lagged to think straight.' I took my hand out of his, reached for my bag. 'I'm going to head back to the house.' I stood up, pretending not to see his surprise, his disappointment. I leaned in and kissed his warm cheek, and felt a stab of regret for the evening I was giving up that hit me somewhere between my heart and my loins. 'We'll catch up later, yeah?'

5

'Hello, stranger.'

I had just come out of the beer garden gate, hitching my bag over my shoulder, and I turned on my heel, startled to hear the familiar voice.

'Jimmy?'

He was lingering on his own by the stone front of the pub on a gnarled wooden bench, his legs crossed at the ankles, the blue glow of his vaper a firefly in the warm darkness, lighting up his aquiline nose and dark eyebrows.

'The wanderer returns!' he smiled, and I realised he'd been waiting for me.

'Oh my God, Jimmy!' I exclaimed, as he rose to his feet.

I was suddenly smothered in a huge bear hug, and then lifted up as he'd used to do when I was a little girl. I laughed out loud.

The tiny wrinkles in the creases next to his eyes were a little deeper, and there were a few more sparks of grey in his dark brown hair. But his happiness in seeing me was unfeigned. That had not changed.

'Look at you! Brown as a berry!' he said, putting me down. 'You look like a million dollars. Adam said you were coming back today. How are you doing?'

'I'm fine,' I said, grinning at him. 'They tell me you lot can't do without me.'

'They are absolutely right,' he said. 'I hear you're taking a class out at the shop tomorrow.'

'I am,' I declared. 'You're short-handed, apparently.'

'And where are you off to now?'

'Home.'

'Not on your own, I hope.' His smile slipped into something more serious. 'It's not as safe as it used to be around here.' A pause, as he considered me in the glow of the harbour lights. 'Come on, girl, I'll walk you up there.'

'You don't have to . . .'

'No, I really do.' His face was serious, and I saw resistance was futile.

'Then be my guest.'

Cheerfully I fell into step next to him, and we ambled back up Fore Street, and in the background I could hear the low sounds of chatter from the pub behind us, and below all, the omnipresent whisper of the sea.

'I would have thought Sid would have come down,' I said to him after a little while. 'People seemed to think she's not been much in evidence. Though it would make sense if she's been so busy with the shop . . .'

'She doesn't often come, no.' I sensed rather than saw his shrug. There was something cool in it, as though he didn't quite approve. 'I think she's just fallen out of the habit of it, more than anything.'

I fell silent, thinking.

'It was hard, losing Dad . . .'

He sighed. 'Yeah. And the business reduced to just selling kit for eighteen months didn't help. It's been tough.'

A few more moments of companionable silence passed, as I looked sideways at him.

'How long has Adam been living in the house?' I asked. 'Do you know?'

He shook his head. 'I don't. Not exactly. But he was

spending a lot of time up there pretty much the minute you were gone.'

'That's . . . I mean, Sid would have needed somebody.'

'Yeah.' His footsteps seemed to fall out of rhythm with mine for a moment. 'Absolutely.'

It was too dark to see the ocean itself now, so the ships in the English Channel seemed to float in mid-air, tiny islands of light spaced in a semi-regular line, making their way to all four corners of the world.

'Glad to be home?' he asked after a long moment.

'Yeah,' I said. 'Yeah, I think so.'

Before long we had reached the little footpath that led steeply up across the clifftops towards the house. I could see it standing high on the bluff in the distance, a few faint stars flickering above it.

All the house lights were switched off, including the porch light. Had Sid and Adam gone to bed? I was tempted to text Sid, glanced sideways at Jimmy as he opened the kissing gate to let me through. It could wait.

'So,' I said, as we tramped up the narrow path, long grass whispering as it brushed against my dress, his jeans. 'Who's the new barmaid?'

'Bella.' He shrugged. 'Moved up here a couple of months ago. She's on her gap year, but instead of sodding off to Thailand or India like they do, she's doing this.'

'Yeah. They normally get someone in for the summer at the Wreckers, don't they?'

'Yep. Why are you asking about her?'

I didn't know why. I was remembering her limpid gaze upon Ben, her sour look as he'd sprung away from her towards me.

'No reason. Think she might be sweet on Ben.'

His profile against the moonlight was taut, the lips curling in a snarl. 'Never liked that boy. Too much like his father.'

I glanced at him, surprised at this sudden burst of feeling, but he said no more, crunching up the last few yards of the hill to our house in silence.

Miles out to sea, I could hear a plangent slow bell tolling – the Manacles cardinal buoy, at a guess. You could hear it all the way up here if the conditions were right – a faint, silvery noise warning of the terrible danger beneath the calm seas.

I would be heading that way tomorrow, back out to the slumbering hull of the *Undine* for the first time since Dad had died.

I had been trying not to think too hard about it.

There were three Xanax in my bag and I'd better take one the minute I got in if I wanted to be awake and lively for the Advanced Wreck class we were teaching tomorrow. I would need my wits about me.

We had reached the driveway. I should probably offer Jimmy a cup of tea, a drink, but I was dead tired, I realised, swaying on my feet after the climb up to the house. This was it for me.

'Thanks for seeing me back. Can I ring you a taxi, Jimmy?'

'Don't be daft.' He waved this off, already heading away down the drive, back inland. 'Night, Cass.'

I watched him vanish into the dusk as the Manacle bell tolled faintly in the background, before I turned to let myself into the house.

'Caaaaassss!' yelled Georgia, as though I had been discovered alive in the middle of an Andean plane crash after six months, instead of appearing over Facetime just thirty-six hours after she'd dropped me off at the airport. She turned away from the phone, yelling to the lads on the balcony with their mismatched mugs of coffee – 'Hey, it's Cass!' and I waved back at their shouted yells of *'Hellloooo, Cass!'*

Georgia looked fresh and pretty, her dark hair pinned back in a strict pattern of bright red barrettes, her mouth glossy with lip balm. She must be diving today. 'You're there at last! How was the flight? How are you? How's your sister?'

'Good,' I laughed, wondering where to start with this laundry list of questions, considering that honest answers were probably surplus to requirements. 'I'm okay. Just got in this afternoon.' I glanced at the time on my phone, at the bright stars shining in through the guest bedroom window. A moment of dislocation fell over me then, like a fainting spell. I didn't know how I felt. 'That was . . . wow, it seems forever ago . . .'

Right now, it was just past 8 a.m. in the sun-drenched duplex in Bushland Beach where we had all lived in unlikely opulence, due to Kyle knowing someone who knew someone who had been seconded to Jakarta and needed 'responsible' people to look after his house for a peppercorn rent.

Soon, they'd all be piling into Georgia's Jeep and heading off to the Institute to start work, but for now Kyle and Dan were having their first cup of coffee while looking out across the bay from our patio, Magnetic Island a mirage in the background of my phone screen.

It was winter in Townsville now, but the weather would be warm, fine, like a summer's day here in Anvil Point.

I missed it suddenly, with a gnawing ache.

'Well, you'll be back before too long, I hope,' said Georgia. 'Have you told them about the job offer yet?'

'Not yet.'

'No?' A flash of surprise in her dark eyes.

'I just got here.'

'Ah well. There's plenty of time, I guess.' Her brow furrowed. 'As long as you're okay.'

'Yeah, I'm fine, just tired. It's late here . . . just got back from the pub.'

'The pub, yeah? Did you see Ben then?' She drawled out the word 'Ben' with theatrical pleasure.

'Might have done,' I replied archly, and she let out a staccato burst of laughter.

'Good on you. Was he just as you remembered him?'

'Pretty much.'

'And Sid, how is she?'

I paused, for just a fraction too long.

Georgia comes across as this daft, bubbly ditz as a rule, and so it is easy to forget that she has four degrees and is in fact as sharp as a scalpel. She tilted her head at me, a questioning look in her eyes.

Sid and Adam had appeared to have gone to bed when I arrived back at the house, throwing my keys in to the little bowl in the hallway and calling out their names. It was not unreasonable – they both had busy days tomorrow and it was a Sunday night – but as much as I'd wanted to check in with Sid, I'd also felt strangely relieved to find myself alone, and I didn't understand why.

I had so much I wanted to discuss with Georgia, things I couldn't even have raised with Jimmy, but as I opened my mouth, the dense silence of the house seemed to rush in around me. I didn't know who might still be awake, might overhear me.

Instead, I just smiled. 'She's fine. Busy, apparently.'

A beat.

'Are you sure you're okay?'

To my amazement, I was welling up with tears.

There was a moment of silence.

'Yeah, I'm okay,' I said, and managed a smile for her which must have been more convincing than the others, as she returned it. 'It's just jet lag. I'm probably making a big deal out of nothing. And you know, with my dad gone, it all takes getting used to. Coming back to the old house . . . I don't know, Georgia, I'm just knackered. I'll ring you later, when you've got time to chat.'

Her gaze was soft. 'Ring me anytime you like, mate. And get some rest.'

6

The next morning the sun was full and brilliant. Even the sea could not flap away the muggy, hazy heat of the day.

I'd had a quick cup of coffee and slice of toast in the kitchen with Sid, who'd sat there in a tatty red tartan dressing gown that I'd not seen before.

I gazed at her curiously.

'Aren't you going in with me?'

'Um, no, not today.' She waved a dismissive hand at me, didn't meet my eyes. 'I've got some things to do here. I need to clean out the training pool before the next class.'

'Oh.' I looked around. 'Where's Adam? He must have left early.'

'Yeah,' she nodded. 'He headed out half an hour ago.'

I'd wanted to talk to her about my night at the Wreckers, but she didn't ask and now there wasn't time. I'd overslept with the pill I'd taken so the subject would have to wait.

As I emerged into the daylight, our swanky, nearly-new Audi Q7, emblazoned with the Blue Horizons logo, was gone from the driveway, but our old van was there.

I lowered my kit carefully into the back and jumped in.

Turning the key I looked down the drive – I'd forgotten how high and steep it was, and it was nerve-racking steering the clunky Ford Transit around the hairpin bends to the main road, bounded by its iron rails, the sea flashing blue and white beyond them.

You'll get used to this again soon enough, I told myself, as I pulled on to Fore Street. Everything will be like you never went away.

Somehow I wasn't convincing myself.

The dive shop is perched by the fishing harbour, next door to the old lifeboat station, as though sheltering in its shadow.

I pushed open the glass door festooned with its array of stickers – *Scuba Magazine's Top Ten Dive Shops 2017!* and supplier logos – expecting a welcoming coolness, but if anything, it was hotter and closer in here than outdoors right now.

There were no customers, and no sign of the class yet. At the reception desk, a tall, broad-shouldered man with an angular face was leaning over a keyboard, frowning into a screen. He was typing something in carefully with two thick fingers, pausing every so often to squint at his handiwork.

Despite the bell, I don't think he'd heard me come in.

'Hi,' I said, 'I'm . . .'

One of those fingers was held aloft suddenly, silencing me.

'Wait,' he rumbled at me. I detected a trace of accent, something Scandinavian perhaps.

He leaned closer to the monitor, hitting one key with a loud clack.

'I must do this now or I will . . .' *Clack.* 'Forget.'

Then a final *click*, and he drew back from the computer and faced me, but with a distracted, argumentative air, as though he expected, at any moment, that the machine would start answering him back.

'Hello,' he said gravely. 'Can I help you?'

'Hi,' I began again. 'I'm Cass. I'm here to lead the Advanced Wreck class?'

He frowned at me.

'The eleven o'clock class?'

Yes, I thought and nearly said – eleven o'clock, the hour between ten and twelve – before cutting this off. I was still tired, I realised, and it was making me irritable and difficult to be around. I needed to put a lid on that, and immediately. Apart from being personally obnoxious, I couldn't have the clients see it.

'You are Grace's replacement?' The man peered at me.

'I . . . I don't know if I'm a replacement. Who's Grace?'

'Irish diver. It doesn't matter. She quit last week.' He narrowed his eyes at me. 'You planning on staying?'

'Um, well, I hope so.' I shrugged. 'I'm one of the owners.'

For the first time since my arrival I had the sense that I was marginally more engaging than whatever was happening with the computer.

'Hmm,' he said. 'The little sister.' He peered down at me. 'And the shark expert.'

Patronising as the first part sounded, it was all broadly true.

'Yes.'

A beat of silence.

'Hmm,' he growled again. His expression was impassive, unreadable. 'Interesting.'

I waited for a second or two for this pronouncement to be elaborated upon, but nothing further was forthcoming. Instead, he stood up, and I had a sudden sense of how enormous he was – at least six foot four, and built, as Jimmy would have said, 'like a brick shithouse'.

'You know where everything is, yes?'

'I . . .' I glanced around this new, dilapidated version of my parents' business. 'I think so.'

He nodded. 'Good. We meet the class in thirty minutes.'

He escorted me to the back of the shop regardless, and pushed open the door into the reception rooms for customers. These looked unchanged, at least – plain walls, whiteboards, safety posters, trolleys for coffee and tea and soft drinks and little bottles of water.

'How many people are coming?' I asked him.

'Six,' he said.

'And you're diving with me?'

'What do you mean?'

I felt a little stir of alarm.

'We're going to need more than one instructor to six clients. You're coming down too, aren't you?'

'No,' he said. 'You are alone. Underwater, at least.' He pondered this for a moment. 'I will be porting gear. Someone has to stay on the boat anyway in case of emergency.'

'But . . .' I didn't understand. Adam had said someone called Erik would be diving with me. I'd assumed that meant that somebody *else* would be watching the boat. We normally had, as a minimum, a ratio of one instructor to four divers underwater. That ratio would be higher in a risky advanced class like this one. 'It's not safe!'

'They do it this way all the time,' he said. A shrug.

'Hang on, maybe I can get Sid to come out. She's back at the house. She could . . .'

His dark blue eyes settled on me, confused at first, and then with a tinge of pity.

'Cressida never comes in here. She has nothing to

do with the business here, has not for months.' His expression was compassionate yet strangely defiant, as though he was expecting this information to be poorly received.

'I . . .' This was a revelation. It was certainly not what Sid had been telling me. *Always so busy!* I had given up expecting her to answer any kind of texts during the day – was lucky to get her to answer me at night too, now I thought about it.

And I had not questioned it, as previously Sid had been my father's right-hand woman. She had handled the organisation and admin. There had always been a tacit understanding that when the time came, she would be the one to inherit the headship of the shop.

What was going on?

And it wasn't just Sid that had me worried. One thing you are never normally short of in a dive shop is volunteers. Helping others in training dives is the way to become a dive instructor, and lots of people want to become dive instructors. It beats TEFL and waitressing as an international gap-year job by anyone's standards.

All my life the shop had been filled with a moveable feast of tanned, gregarious and mostly young people who lived in bikini tops and swimming trunks, eager to dive every day of the week, often without pay.

Where had they all gone?

I opened my mouth, turned to my companion.

But somehow, he seemed to sense my question.

'Coronavirus. Not so many people travel abroad now. And the English ones . . . there is a new place near Coverack. Many go there.' A beat. 'There are more opportunities.'

I glanced at him.

'But not for you?'

'No.'

'Right . . .' I didn't know what to say, so I offered a little nervous laugh. 'Looks like it's just us then. Let's start again. I'm Cass and I'm guessing that you're . . .'

'Erik.' He gravely took my hand in his own warm, coarse one and with old-fashioned courtesy shook it, and the unusual gesture stunned me into surrender. Who shook hands nowadays? 'Erik Magnusson.'

The bell at the front desk dinged, a faint, tinny sound. It was too late to change course now, I realised, glancing up at Erik.

I was the only instructor. I would have to be enough.

Class was up.

The class itself consisted of two couples, one pair middle aged and the other young, who seemed to live within five miles of each other in Surrey and were all perhaps from one family, and a single florid bald man from Leicester with Navy tattoos and a wedding ring, who was friendly enough but quiet.

The sixth was a blond twenty-something American called Russell, who immediately started to talk to me about my father.

'Such an awesome diver, man.' He shook his head. 'Such an inspiration.'

'Thanks – we miss him a lot,' I said, making myself smile gratefully. Smiling is what I normally do during these classes, at least while we're above water – I give them a short lecture on the history of the area, the history of the wreck, and do a presentation on the plants and animals they can expect to see on the reefs that the wreck has created, before I move on to the technical skills they will have to master to pass the course.

I had been a little disturbed to find that the PowerPoint presentation we normally run, while the clients drink their coffee, hadn't been opened on the laptop since March 2020. There must be a newer one somewhere. When I got the chance, I would have to ask Erik about it.

But it wasn't an emergency, as very little had changed, I suspected. Most of the people who come are already experienced anyway, hoping to rack up their wreck dives with a view to advancing to pro diving. The lion's share of them know what they're doing long before they arrive.

This group was no different – I'd looked through their logbooks and licences, and they'd dived all over the world, but never with us before, except for the red-faced bald man, Keith Hart, who'd come a couple of years ago. I wondered if he remembered how vibrant and busy the place had been then, and this was what was making him quiet.

I felt ashamed, diminished, at this thought, as though he'd found me begging on the street.

'So, this is the *Undine*,' I said, leaning over the laptop while our logo appeared on the big TV monitor. 'This is where we'll be going this morning.'

I hit *Next* on the presentation.

It showed a grainy digital photo of a medium-sized cargo ship, resting in port. On her prow was painted the single word *UNDINE* with *PORTSMOUTH* underneath.

'Believe it or not, she's actually Russian – she was built

in Murmansk in 1989, commissioned by Clartel International Shipping.' I reached down, took a sip of my Diet Coke.

The next slide was a technical drawing of the *Undine* in 3D that we'd commissioned a local artist to do.

At the back of the room Erik stood against the door, his brawny arms folded against his tight T-shirt. He was paying close attention, it seemed, which surprised me. He must have seen this information dozens of times.

A tiny whisper of suspicion opened up within me. *Hadn't he?*

'So, the *Undine* and her two sister ships were all similarly built, about 260 feet long and 55 feet wide, and had a complement of twelve crew. On the night she sank in May 1998 there were ten people aboard – two of them had gone AWOL in her previous port, so there's some speculation that under-manning was a contributory factor in her sinking . . .'

'What happened to them?' asked Eleanor, the younger woman, her face shiny with sweat. The air conditioning wasn't working in here. Something else that needed fixing, it seemed. 'The crew who vanished? Why did they leave?'

I shrugged. 'We don't know. They just never turned up for work again after getting off the ship in Falmouth.'

'I heard that one of the engineers had a dream,' said the older woman, Ruth. She was a tiny sprite of a woman with white hair. 'He wouldn't get on the ship, and he persuaded his best friend not to as well.'

She glanced around the others, as though to impress this supernatural circumstance upon them all.

Keith gazed at her with an expression like pity.

'They probably had a feeling that there were problems with the ship,' murmured Erik from the back. 'If they were engineers, they would not have to dream something like that to know it.'

'I suppose,' said Ruth, with a shrug that clearly said she liked her version of the story better.

Everybody likes their own version of the story better, I have learned. The *Undine* is wreathed in sorcerous romance, and we have never been in the business of puncturing these fantasies.

My parents found that they proved highly profitable over the years.

'So, she had four decks,' I continue, 'of which about three survive and two are diveable. The superstructure at the stern, which holds the bridge, is in the process of rusting through the main hull and has already collapsed inside. Needless to say, we'll not be going anywhere near that end of the ship, as it's very dangerous.' I offered them a forbidding glare. 'Just to make sure you know that.'

Silence followed. At the back, Erik wore a shadowy expression that might have been a smile.

'Of the three decks that survive,' I held up my light pointer to the next slide, a picture of the *Undine* underwater, pinched between great rocks as if by fingers, her middle bent on either side, 'this is the top deck. You can see two cargo hatches, both rusted shut. That's quite a nice dive, obviously with no penetration elements.' I ran the light pointer over to the back of the ship, where the superstructure and radio mast were visible, pointing upwards though clearly collapsing, like a drunk at a party who's starting to ask wearily when the Uber is coming. 'As

I say, we're staying well away from the stern of the ship, you can see the state it's in.'

They nodded.

'The next slide is . . . ah, there we go.'

There were tiny intakes of breath.

'This is the hull breach in the front of the *Undine*, in the prow, where the lettering was in the first picture.'

The hole gaped before us, as big as the doors in the Houses of Parliament, while mackerel swam before it in a great shoal. Within, a shadowy floor sloped backwards into darkness.

'So, this is the second deck of the wreck itself. The hole was punched in it by the Manacles as it sank. This is where the fixed line is. It's the only diveable penetration part of the wreck and the one you'll be visiting today.'

I folded my arms, regarded them all.

'You'll be marked on your buoyancy and ability to dive without stirring up silt and damaging the wreck, on your light handling, on your mapping and your ability to lay and follow lines. The main line in the *Undine* goes as far as the crew lounge, so from there you'll have to lay a line as far as the upper cargo hold. It's about forty feet in a fairly straight line.'

Keith grunted. 'That seems a lot.'

'Yeah, but this part of the wreck is nice and wide, so you shouldn't have any problems.' I turned to them all. 'But if you *do* suddenly feel claustrophobic or anxious, don't be embarrassed. It happens to some very seasoned divers sometimes. Very little sunlight can get in there and the *Undine* deck is at 94 to 101 feet, so you will be liable to some nitrogen narcosis and may get woozy even with

Nitrox mix in your tank – do not be embarrassed. Let me know and we'll get you out.'

They were nodding, the men almost dismissively.

Nobody foresees that happening to them until it does, after all.

'As for the rest of the ship,' I said, 'the bottom deck, or the Forbidden Hold, you couldn't get into even if you wanted to. When the superstructure first started crushing the steel below it, it sealed that deck off from the open sea. Nobody has been in there for about fifteen years.'

'What's in there?' asked Ted, Ruth's husband.

'Nothing of note,' I said. 'Most of the cargo, which I think was tools, was salvaged after the sinking. The middle deck was full of farm machinery bound for North Africa, and a lot of that was too dangerous to move and so left in the ship. You'll see it there during the class, though you won't be able to go anywhere near it.'

'How can you be sure this Forbidden Hold is empty?' asked Russell, the American, his eyes alight.

Here we go.

There is a little community online that is convinced that the inaccessible bottom hold of the *Undine* contains all manner of interesting things – rifled antiquities from the old Soviet Union, secret weapons, drug-runners' gold – you name it, we've heard it.

'Everything in there was salvaged shortly after the ship sank,' I said, trying to stay patient. 'Until 2001 you could actually dive the Forbidden Hold. My father has pictures of it . . . had pictures.' I corrected myself, and as I did, I felt this twanging disorientation, as if I had just stopped myself from tumbling off the edge of a very steep cliff. 'I can send them on via email if you're really interested.'

I glimpsed Russell's face, a sceptical crease to his brow being ironed smooth as he caught my eye.

'All right,' I said, rising to my feet. At the back of the room, Erik uncrossed his arms. 'That's the talky part over. Let's go diving.'

7

The back of the van was roomy but untidy and largely windowless – normally we like to take the clients in the relative luxury of the Audi people carrier and the other instructor will bring their gear in the van, but Adam was off for his class with it. I wondered when he had left – normally we would take the class into the dive shop for a presentation before driving them to Newquay, but I had seen no sign that other people had been in the reception rooms before us.

Next time I'd get up earlier than him and nab the Audi first.

But still, we had clients and that was all that mattered, people who paid us a lot of money, and whom we could make happy and who could recommend us to their friends.

I climbed into the van next to Erik.

Time to launch into the introduction. Even after two years, I knew it by heart.

'Hi, everyone,' I said. 'So we're going to drive on over to Porthoustock and take the inflatable out to the wreck site. I know some of you have cave-diving form, but I absolutely have to warn you, that while we've never . . .'

I paused, suddenly breathless.

I had been about to say what we always said, 'While we have never had an accident at the *Undine . . .*' but of course it wasn't true.

I could not escape the feeling I was falling, somehow. I

could see them all staring at me, their faces blank with confusion . . .

Then Erik spoke.

'We've never lost a client while diving the *Undine*,' he ground out. 'And since everyone will follow instructions, that will not change today.'

He offered them a long, level look in the rear-view mirror, as though to imply that even if the disobedient didn't drown, fatal consequences could still potentially be arranged for them.

'Yes, thank you, Erik.' I took a deep breath, tried to calm my breathing, my ratcheting heart. I hitched up my smile. 'We just need to follow instructions. And everything will be fine.'

The sun was full and hot now as Erik pulled the van into the car park, which is little more than a marked-off extension of the beach, dark with gritty sand and pebbles.

Porthoustock is a deep cut in the surrounding headlands that opens up into a narrow cove, reached by a steep, violently zigzagging single-lane road that is shaded by eldritch trees. Houses cling to its edges, with stepped hedges and driveways with Land Rovers and trucks parked in them at perilous angles.

For many years aggregate was mined here, and a disused stone mill made out of black rock dominates the beach on the left, and on the right a tall, jagged hump of broken stone, the remains of an old quarry, blocks out all views on that side.

Standing on the black beach, you can only see straight ahead and out across the sea, as though the landscape has imposed blinkers on you.

It's supposed to be an area of 'Outstanding Natural Beauty' and the clients often ooh and ahh over it, but I find it faintly sinister in all weathers, with its dark, gravelly shore and claustrophobic cliff walls.

The clients piled out of the van, blinking in the flooding sunlight, as Erik silently moved to carry their kit to the beach in big plastic container bins marked with numbers. In the meantime, I pointed out the old lifeboat station to them, painted a defiant white.

'It's so hot,' moaned Eleanor, the younger of the two women, while her husband/boyfriend David checked her weights. I was beginning to realise, somewhat uncharitably, that Eleanor was a bit of a moaner generally. Her coffee was too strong, the van ride was too loud, the boutique hotel room she had stayed in last night had been too small and her journey up from Godalming too long. 'I'm so *hot*.'

'You will be cold soon enough.' Erik stood by the inflatable, staring out to sea. He had not even turned around.

'Yes, yes,' I said quickly, diving into the breach, while ensuring each pair had checked each other's kit. 'Sea temp is only twelve degrees, so it will be a little parky but nice and clear.' As I approved each one they were sent off to the boat, their masks and fins in hand, their scuba tanks jostling heavily against their backs.

Soon all were seated, and with me in front and Erik at the back, we purred forward in the inflatable into the lively slapping water, scented with salt.

Despite my fretful, anxious morning I felt, for a moment, a singular peace. I had grown up here, after all, on and below these brilliant waters, and for the first time I felt I was finally home.

'It's a beautiful day,' said the older woman, Ruth, her short white hair ruffling in the wind. She shut her eyes, turning her face up towards the sun gratefully, and I smiled. A beautiful day. Yes. Fortune had favoured us.

I glanced out. 'That's the Manacles, there,' I said, pointing over the side of the boat, and everyone craned to look.

The ocean was flat, surprisingly calm. But every so often, as the sea shifted and scudded over them, the sharp tooth of some hidden dark brown rock would poke upwards through to the surface, as though the water was barely hiding a bed of nails. Nearer the coast, some of these spires of volcanic rock were as tall as a man. Some merely peeked out from the blue expanse, no larger than a shark's fin. And some made no impact on the water at all, but you could see them, lurking patches of darkness in the deep, mere feet from the surface.

'I can't see much of anything,' said Ted, squinting under his shading hand. 'I expected to see something.'

'That's the point,' observed Erik quietly from the back. 'At high tide, ships can't see them either.'

'Oh,' Ted said, getting it.

'You might think the name Manacles is to do with handcuffs,' I continued, 'but it's actually a Cornish word, *Meyn Eglos*, the Church Rocks.'

Another coincidence. Church Rocks because they were near the old church at St Keverne's, whose tower stood proud from the hill and for many years had been the main sight landmark for shipping here.

But church rocks are also gravestones.

What the *Undine* was actually doing here, in this dangerous patch of rocky reef where over a hundred ships have sunk, is still a mystery. In life she had been unremarkable; a medium-sized cargo ship only ten years old, and she had just left Falmouth after putting down and picking up some passengers before sailing on to Algiers.

At 9 p.m. on 23 May 1998, all was calm and quiet. Though night had fallen the breezes were balmy, and visibility good. On board were ten people – Captain Tom Rawlings and nine crew.

At that time, the *Undine* should have been firmly ploughing along the English Channel with the wind at her back, thirty miles from shore.

And yet she wasn't – she was sailing, full speed ahead, alongside the treacherous walls of the Lizard, and nobody knows why. She was first spotted by a farmer who was walking his dog above the cliffs near St Keverne's. He watched her as she tore over the top of the submerged Voices, which gouged a great furrow along the bottom of her belly. With her speed she was able to get free, to reach the deep water on the other side of the rocks, her entrails haemorrhaging into the cold sea, but she was mortally wounded and falling into the depths with a cacophony of shearing metal and thin, high, desperate screaming from the people on board.

By the time the hastily scrambled Coverack lifeboat reached the site there was nothing but floating lifebuoys and corpses to mark where she had been.

There hadn't even been time to launch an escape. The fittings for both of the *Undine*'s lifeboats were discovered here five years later, resting under the disintegrating wreck, in the exact places they would have been when still attached to the ship.

There were no known survivors.

Because she is so well preserved, there is no doubt as to what happened to the *Undine*, but the bigger question is how. Nobody knows how she managed to be so perilously off-course, and how out of ten people, nobody realised the danger much, much sooner.

There are a number of theories, most of them human error or even mass suicide, as well as more exotic variants, such as Cornish wreckers, hijack, ghost ships, freak waves, sabotage and ancient curses.

But despite all the YouTube documentaries, no solutions.

My parents used to run a Christmas competition online where the person who submitted the best theory would win a £100 voucher to spend in the shop. The winning entries tended to be dramatic rather than convincing.

In short, your guess is as good as mine.

8

Below I

As I roll over backwards off the inflatable and into the water there is, as always, that rush of fingering cold and I gasp, part in shock and part in pleasure, as the water searches out every nook and cranny – my ears, my wrists, and leaks faintly but insistently into the neoprene collar and cuffs of my drysuit. My teeth clamp down on the rubber mouthpiece of my regulator, release it again as I fall for a few feet into the deep blue weightlessness before righting myself, poised in the sea.

It's cold – so much colder than the seas of Australia. I had forgotten how cold the Atlantic is.

I touch the thin yellow line of rope that descends from the buoy all the way down to the *Undine*, tugging experimentally, and it is as taut as a bowstring, full of springy life against my hand. I feel like I could pluck it, like a harp.

The others are at the surface, their fins pumping softly, treading water, and I take a second to assess them, sucking in air, making my regulator gasp like aching lungs, before blowing out a stream of bubbles that brush my hair and face.

It feels like a homecoming.

I kick upwards, join the others on the surface, and as it breaks the light breeze flickers around me, the sun blazing on to the crown of my head.

They seem like a good group. They've already changed their snorkels for their regulators and look ready to go, their swimming relaxed but strong, except for Russell, who is kicking a little too hard to stay up – it speaks of someone with bad *trim*, the ability to control their buoyancy and movement, but it's not terrible, just not very good.

He's the one I need to keep an eye on, I see.

I gesture with the OK signal, which is exactly what it sounds like, thumb and forefinger making a circle, the other three fingers held spread out – are they good to go? – and they all reply with the same.

The inflatable is behind me, and Erik is on board, his brow creased with concentration as he hovers near the diving buoy that will tell passing shipping that there are people underwater here. His dark blue eyes flash at me, then away.

As sun-drenched and lavish as the sea is, as confident as the group looks, as familiar as I am with diving . . . try as I might, I cannot shake a tiny flicker of foreboding, more chill than the water. There should, in good conscience, be another dive leader out here with me.

They are looking towards me, a faint question in their eyes, behind the silicon shields of their diving masks.

I hold out my fist to them, my thumb downturned. *Descend.*

I wait as they check their dive watches, the horizon, their buddies – I am buddied with Eleanor and David – and then we are all sinking slowly beneath the surface, letting the air out of our BCDs which drains away into a thin stream of bubbles, falling feet first into the blue darkness below.

The water envelops us.

The others are falling too, in slow, steady measure, Russell a little too fast for my liking. I gesture at him to slow down, and as I do, a single porbeagle swims by – just a baby, only three feet long but recognisably a shark with bright round eyes and stout little body and toothy mouth that looks either very pleased or very angry, depending on your point of view. It lingers for a moment then vanishes downwards in a flash of silvery grey and white when I point it out to the others.

I smile. I realise, yet again, that when I am in the water I feel truly alive. And this sighting – a common enough fish for this part of the world, admittedly – feels like a good omen.

It's strange but true.

Sharks make me happy.

As we sink the reason for its presence becomes clear – a whirling cloud of mackerel, a living metallic storm blowing above the rusting steel skeleton of the *Undine*, which starts to glint now through vivid blue water and its partial covering of shells and seaweed.

Even through the water, I am aware of a gathering excitement in the other divers, grinning at each other through their masks, perhaps increasing the speed of their descent, just a fraction, hoping I won't notice.

I glance at my dive computer. Thirty feet down.

Full fathom five thy father lies . . .

I blink this thought away, though it has stung me, and threatens to distract. Russell is definitely descending too fast now, nearly four feet lower than the rest of us, and I signal at him to slow down. Behind his eyes there is a flash of banked impatience before he complies.

In a hurry to see the wreck, I guess. Well, that's fine, but he needs to stay close if he's going to pass the course. There are no marks for being a maverick down here.

I am heading for a patch of bare seafloor where we will stop, in the lee of the Voices, one of the most notorious rocks of the Manacles, which juts upwards into a triangular point ending about twenty feet below the ocean's surface.

I point it out, while the ghost sun shines above it, pale rays filtering down through cold water and bright fish and sharp rocks.

They follow my gestures, nod.

It's considered bad form to disturb the seabed and the creatures that live there with our footprints, so we turn slowly on to our bellies, float a few feet above it.

For a few moments, the others are too stunned to do much else. Even for me, who has seen it before, the view makes the hair on the back of my neck stand up, twitching in the chilled water.

The *Undine* lies on her ripped belly. She is trapped on both sides by ragged volcanic rocks and flagged with banners of coral and seaweed and crusted with shells. Her bridge has collapsed down into the hold under its own weight, but in her rocky tomb, sheltered from the currents, the main structure is surprisingly intact, and the interior yawns open near the torn metal beneath her prow: a beckoning darkness welcoming you in.

Ruth is already fumbling for her camera as her husband looks on, her awe and her gloved fingers making this awkward until he reaches up and holds it still for her. Eleanor and David clasp hands. Keith, who I know has seen it before, is nevertheless still spellbound, hardly any bubbles appearing out of his mask. He wants to be careful. You should never hold your breath while scuba diving.

But Russell is darting forward, barely able to contain himself, and I think for a minute I am about to lose him until he grudgingly seems to recall that this is a class and not a pleasure dive and swims to the edge of our circle.

There can be no words, so in a series of compact gestures I tell them — *stay together, stay by me, are you okay?*

They reply that they are.

The reason wreck diving is considered an advanced form of diving is because it is potentially dangerous. The peril is not just because the wreck could fall in on us, though obviously that is a risk. At Blue Horizons, as the legal guardians of the *Undine*, part of our role is to check the wreck constantly to assess how safe it is to enter.

The main danger on an enclosed wreck, however, is that you are no longer in open water.

When divers talk about *open water*, it simply means that there is nothing between you and the surface — no roof, no structures, nothing to navigate — and you can come back up whenever you want.

In practice, of course, you can never just come up to the surface whenever you want, even in open water.

The deeper underwater you are, the more pressure you are under — not just you, but also the air you are breathing into your lungs from the tanks.

And in a fairly shallow dive, your air is just that usually — common or garden fresh air — a bit of oxygen, a bit of carbon dioxide and some other stuff, but air is mostly — about seventy per cent — made up of nitrogen.

Nitrogen, under normal circumstances, doesn't affect

you at all. You don't need it to breathe. It's just kind of *there*, floating around, and you and it are mutually indifferent.

Under pressure, however, such as when you're deep underwater, you and standoffish, socially distant nitrogen start to engage in hitherto unforeseen ways. While you float at the bottom of the sea, it is dispersed into your blood through your lungs under high pressure, and a surprising thing happens when you start to rise to the surface. If you rise too quickly, it can't be breathed out in time. It expands, as gases do when pressure lessens, into tiny bubbles in your blood.

These bubbles can make you sick. Sometimes very, very sick.

It is called decompression sickness, or 'the bends'. And if you get it badly enough, you will need to be put back under pressure, as quickly as possible, usually in a barometric chamber if you are lucky enough to be within emergency ambulance distance of one.

Sometimes you are lucky, and it happens near shore.

Sometimes, you are miles out to sea.

Which is what happened to my dad.

I urge the others to follow me into the dark hole in the *Undine*'s chin, gesturing silently at them to be careful on the torn and rusted shreds of its hull as we follow the yellow line within. A single white ghost crab is tapping along the surface of the hull, vanishing inside as we approach.

As I guide them in, I glance upwards, to where the inflatable sits on the surface of the water, looking impossibly distant, a little black smudge against the sky.

I realise I am consciously trying not to think about my dad's last hours.

Within, all is gloomy darkness, the sediment being disturbed by our movement and the spumes of bubbles we give off, despite everyone's best efforts. Once again, Russell is ahead, floating at the top of a rusting stairwell without stairs, his head poking through the roof of the ship. I feel a twinge of cold displeasure.

I switch on my torch, and the whorls of fish lurking within scatter away into the gloom like so many glittering arrows. The white light reveals a steel room once painted cream and now red and grey with patched rust.

It's the old mess, and on the right you can see the ovens and hobs, crusted now with barnacles and the waving tentacles of anemones. The light plays over them as I move the torch over the cupboards above, their doors rotted away, revealing shelves full of debris.

I shiver faintly against the blue cold.

I urge the little party to switch on their own lights. I watch them keenly – being able to swim and hold the light at the same time is one of the dive skills I'm here to assess. They seem okay with it. I gesture at them to follow me, towards the empty stairwell.

Today the group is going to learn to lay a line down from the *Undine*'s main line, a fluorescent yellow nylon rope that stretches like an artery from the mess to the lounge. A wreck like this is a labyrinth and we negotiate it by tying threads together to create lines that will take us in and out of the maze. I am going to watch as they attach a side-line to the main line and together we are going to pass through the mess to the crew lounge and then through the double doors into the upper cargo bay, with its rusting thicket of farm machinery once bound for Algiers. Once they've all done that to my satisfaction, we'll be ascending again with a five-minute safety stop.

I feel a prickle of unease as I consider once again that I am the only instructor here. If something were to happen . . .

I shake my head, dismissing the thought. Nothing is going to happen. You've taught this course dozens of times. You're just tired. Everything is going to be fine.

We pass by the empty stairwell, and I have to tug Russell back. Another strike against him. Instead, we swim, trying to avoid excessive movement, ahead through a doorway, the steel door having swung open and rusted into position.

Within is the crew lounge, with the old cream paint appearing in patches through divots of shellfish and the lost, gloaming light filtering in through the windows, illuminating nothing. I turn the dive lights upon the broken plastic furniture with its freight of barnacles.

Ruth's hands are moving to her camera, they are all reaching for their cameras, all of them except Russell.

I look around, and a lance of icy fear goes through me. This time he has vanished.

Now I am the one in danger of holding my breath. I force myself to breathe, to calm down, to concentrate on the steady flow of bubbles coming out of my mask. He can only have swum ahead to the upper cargo bay, I tell myself. He is testing me, for any number of reasons. Because he's overconfident. Because he's hyper-enthusiastic. Because he's that kind of spoiled guy that doesn't like to take orders from a woman. By the time we kick through to the deck he will be there.

So, let's go.

I gesture to the others to stay where they are and move off towards the open hole where a pair of double doors used to be, scarred with shipworm around the frame, and emerge into the upper cargo deck.

This is the most dangerous room that students visit on the course, though not the most dangerous room in the *Undine*. It is a wide space, about forty feet across and a hundred feet long, and the back of it is full of rusting farm machinery.

When it was loaded, it was in neat, tied-down rows, but the sinking and the years of currents have scattered it into a steel hedge of metal thorns – the baskets of diggers, the turning blades of ploughs, the bulky rectangles of engine housing – all these have tumbled into one another and fused together into an undifferentiated pile of scrap, with the occasional gleam of the original paint sometimes flickering through as you turn your dive light over it.

All this is lying under a layer of grey dust which has blown in through the open port windows, and spiny lobsters clamber over the rotten girders of the deck, indifferent to my presence, protected in their chitinous armour.

The first thing I notice is that Russell is not here either. In fact, the undisturbed dust suggests he never came in here.

I turn around, surprising the others as I skim past them, heading back to the empty stairhead we passed on the way in. My heart is thudding, and I must control it because the more anxious you get down here, the quicker you use up your air.

I am such a fool. My father would be horrified. He would never in a million years have consented to take six divers on a training dive alone.

And here I am, finding out why.

The stairwell links the mess to the lower bowels of the ship, in particular the engine room.

I float before the void, considering the broken metal stair where the risers used to be.

We don't take people down below the entry deck, and certainly not down here. The whole weight of the *Undine*'s upper decks is constantly pressing down on the lower because, unlike other wrecks, it fell the right way up, and is wedged that way in the rocks. Every year the girders that keep its iron skeleton intact warp and rust . . .

Bubbles rise from the stairwell.

I must go after him.

9

Everything seems to happen in slow motion from here.

I suspect, at first, that I am more irritated than alarmed by Russell's disobedience, more furious at the affront to my authority. He's left the line. It is an automatic fail for a penetration dive course, which is bad enough, but it also means the others can't continue until I bring him back under control, and while they have the air to complete the course, they don't have enough to float around all day.

On reflection – and I will spend a long time reflecting on this day – it wouldn't take much to make me angry. I have underestimated how tired I am – how hopelessly jet-lagged.

I signal again for the others to stay still, then push down after Russell, into the whirling vortex of silt his passage has raised up in the rusting stairwell. My flashlight reflects only its muddy, sparkling particles for a moment or two, so I have to wait for it to calm, to show me the line again, giving his reckless foolishness a head start on me.

Fuckity fuckity fuck, I think to myself, air bubbles grazing my face as I equalise the air in my mask. Look, mate, if you want to pitch up here and waste £400 of your money that's fine, but don't waste everybody else's . . .

I slip down after him into the clearing water, Russell's silty wake functioning as a trail ahead of me. I think I can even make out the disappearing ends of his fins as he swims away below.

What's he doing?

He's searching for the Forbidden Hold, of course. There's a certain kind of guy that always does this. I can see that he's fastened a GoPro to the top of his diving hood, filming his own stupidity.

I sink after him, straightening up near the bottom of the ruined stairwell, craning my flashlight into the darkened passageway ahead, the open doors to the crew cabins fused open on either side.

It is a great place to get lost, I realise with a sick start. But to my surprise I can see him clearly, just a few metres ahead, and at the same time there is this strong cold current coming down the gangway, chilling my hands, the exposed skin outside my mask.

I pause, disturbed. Usually there is no real current down in this part of the ship. It's what keeps things preserved.

Where is it coming from?

Disquieted, I surge forward, grabbing Russell by one of his fins. He moves to kick me free, thinking he's snagged himself on something, but I tug insistently, three times, and he turns, sees me.

There is an instant of shock there, some inkling that something has gone wrong, as though he's been sleepwalking and I've woken him. He holds up his hands, an automatic gesture of surrender, and I wonder for the first time whether it is wilfulness that has made him do this or perhaps something more sinister, like nitrogen narcosis – the Rapture of the Deep.

At any rate, he is pliant now, as I signal for him to follow me back.

The cold current is pretty strong, I realise, my hair streaming out in it as he passes me. It is as though I am caught in a high wind. It seems to be coming out of the deep darkness ahead of us in the direction of the engine room.

I shine my light past Russell and into the distance but can see nothing but the crushed bulkheads and decks, dotted with starfish and lying as they always have.

Peculiar.

I have never felt this before, and change is not a good thing on the *Undine*.

Never mind. I can worry about it later.

I somersault backwards, twisting to face the way we had come, a length of old line below me, something we've left on a previous dive.

We are passing outside one of the abandoned cabins, the steel bulkhead still intact, though the door itself is long gone, popped out and lying on the cabin floor. I fin past it, ignoring it, and glance behind me to see if he is following.

Russell is stock-still in the water, as though he has been turned to stone, his flashlight pointing into the cabin doorway, only tiny bubbles coming from his regulator. Irritation flares up in me, turning to hot anger as he once again abandons the route and swims into the cabin.

Damn it. The others are alone up there . . .

I go to follow him, chasing him with my own flashlight, the current resisting me. This new current is troubling me. I want to be gone, back to the rest of my class and the relative safety of the upper deck. I quickly check my dive computer – I have another half-hour of air. I need to bring him back now if there is any hope of salvaging the dive for the others.

I round the doorway, pointing my light into the cool

darkness, and he is suddenly there, barrelling into me with a terrible strength, knocking me down backwards into the mud, his face round-eyed and blind with panic, his regulator hanging out of his open mouth, struggling to get past me and away.

Through the water I hear his scream.

Such is his strength, his terror, that his kicking feet pummel me forward through the door, knocking my arm-mounted flashlight off and leaving me floating through the cabin in total darkness.

Shit. *Shit.*

I must get to him.

I scrabble at my light with desperate fingers, trying to turn myself upright in the black velvet womb of the cabin. Nothing happens. I must have broken it. I have no way of knowing which way I am facing, which way is out, or even which way is up or down.

Calm, calm, Cassandra. You are feet from the stairwell. This way is up. Feel the bubbles rising against your cheek?

In the dark, something large brushes against me.

I wonder for a horrid instant if it is Russell – it is something heavy and motionless, without volition. I reach out to grab it, but it slips out of my glove, and anyway, it cannot be him. Whatever it is, it is cold and organic, perhaps seaweed or some piece of debris, knocked free by the current.

I whip my back-up light off my belt and switch it on, point it into the darkness in front of my face.

And there she is.

She is mere inches from me, as though she has been trying to kiss me with that lipless mouth. What is left of her dark cloud of hair swirls around her head, drifts against my cheeks like a caress.

Her eyes . . . her *teeth* . . .

For a long, still moment, I am held within her sightless gaze.

I scream, push her away, her bare flesh cold and gelid against my palms, her skin sloughing from her like rags, the flashlight winking out as in my terror I accidentally press it off.

Do not panic, I tell myself, again and again, straining to hear my dad's voice in the words. *Never panic.*

The light flicks back on as I press it.

Air gasps through my regulator in vast, shuddering breaths. She is falling backwards against the cabin doorway now – I must have pushed or kicked her, and her pale arms, the bones showing, trail in front of her through the water, as though she had been reaching for me.

She is between me and the way out.

Do not panic.

I am hyperventilating, and this is a dangerous, dangerous place. I do not have time to wonder about this dead woman, how on earth she ended up here. Russell could be lost and drowning right this very instant. I have left five other divers by the line; anything could have happened to them.

This cloying terror, my horror and disgust – I cannot do this now.

I have to get past her and find Russell.

I train my flashlight completely on her, as though I expect her to spring to sudden, malicious life, to leap forwards, but it is worse somehow – she simply drifts, empty and vacant and hideously changed by death.

I swallow hard, my heart pounding, my bubbles flooding into the tiny cabin.

Do not panic.

And a memory flashes up, of my father, murmuring to my mother about some trip he had been on, the police had called him in . . . I have never seen a dead body underwater before, but my dad had – he had often been called in to recover drowned divers in wrecks and caves.

You can be brave, like Dad, I think to myself. You must be, because you need to move her and if you don't you will run out of air and die here.

You just need to reach out, with one arm, and gently push her out of the way.

It is all I can do to come even a foot closer to her, where she floats like a ghost.

Without looking I reach out, brush her aside with my forearm, as though it is nothing, and I think I have got away with it until she doesn't so much move away as twirl in place, as though showing off an invisible dress.

Desperate, freezing and terrified, I push again, and she moves back, though reluctantly, her glassy limbs trailing behind her.

But I don't care. I am swimming out the door, stirring up great wallows of silt looking for Russell, and for the broken stairwell that will lead me up and out of this nightmare.

IO

I had persuaded myself that I was glad Russell had taken no really serious injury as Erik drove us, stony-faced, to Falmouth Royal and left us to check into A&E.

I think I managed to keep thinking that for at least the first two hours of the four we spent there, while I fetched weak hospital coffee back to our cheap hospital chairs and he angsted about whether he would need to have his head shaved.

'I think they just clip it around the wound if you get stitches,' I offered eventually, as I sipped the coffee. It was amazing to me how something with so little taste could be so unpleasant. 'It happened to my sister once.'

I was texting Sid, since she had not yet picked up the phone, and I was recalling that day – we had been diving the Hole of Ha together off Corfu, with only each other for company while my parents lazed on the boat we'd hired. I had been no more than twelve years old. The weather had been sultry, the Ionian Sea a glittering cobalt blue, the cavern beautiful and secretive. She had swum up behind me to pounce on me underwater, and hadn't realised she'd scraped her scalp until we got back to the boat, and her golden waterfall of hair dripped thin rivulets of scarlet on to the deck. My mum had been horrified, but Sid had only laughed.

She'd always been fearless, and the memory made me smile, despite everything.

In A&E with Russell Bowermann, cut his head. Nothing to worry
about. Dead body found on Undine tho. Call me. x

I had discovered Russell scrabbling out of the stairwell,
in his own storm of whirling silt, his eyes wide. He was
fighting his way towards the exit through the hole in the
Undine's bow, his legs bicycling away, producing much
effort but little progress.

As I calmed him down and guided him and the others
up to the boat their confusion and disappointment were
almost palpable, even underwater. And how could I blame
them – they had paid a lot of money and made their
arrangements months ago.

We would have to offer them all refunds, I realised, as
they slowly rose. So much for my first day back.

Russell. If Russell had not gone off on his own, we
would never have discovered the dead woman in the
cabin. I blinked, and once again I could see her dreadful
face, the waving tendrils of her dark hair.

How long had she been down there?

And how had she got down there?

Who was she?

'Hey,' said Russell.

Two porters wheeled an old woman past us. She was
wrapped in an orange blanket, her white puff of hair
emerging from the top.

Russell glared at her. 'Hey,' he said again. 'We were in
line before her.'

I cast a sideways glance at him, trying to control my
annoyance. 'If they are seeing her first, she must be sicker
than you.'

He sighed heavily, like a petulant child, and threw himself back in his seat.

'What's taking them so long?'

'They're busy,' I said.

'Could you go ask when they're going to see me?' He dabbed at his head again, looked at the bloody paper he was holding to it. 'It keeps bleeding.'

Yeah, it will do, if you keep prodding at it like that, I nearly said, before biting my tongue.

I had to hold it together.

'I mean, could you ask them?' he said again, waving the scarlet tissue in my face. 'We've been here for what . . . two hours . . . ?'

'Two hours and eleven minutes.'

'They might have forgotten about me.'

'They'll come get us when they're ready. They see people in order of how injured they are.'

He snorted.

'Oh yeah, you guys have the NHS here, don't you?' He let out a sarcastic chuckle. 'Total socialist nightmare.'

By half two, as he endlessly asked 'Does it look bad? Does it look really bad?' I was wondering if it might have been better if he'd been brought in unconscious.

By four I was considering how I could induce that unconsciousness myself by hitting him repeatedly with one of the plastic chairs littering the waiting room. I was so tired I could feel my eyes starting to glide shut despite Russell's constant chatter.

But then, whenever I shut my eyes, the woman was there.

Who was she? Impossible to tell her age, with her bloated belly and ragged skin, the glassy opaque walls of her blinded eyes.

She could have been a drunk skinny dipper who'd drowned by accident, perhaps, or fallen off a boat when she went up to the deck, leaving her lover asleep in their yacht . . .

Or maybe something more sinister.

She had looked nothing like the person in the poster in the Co-op window.

She had looked nothing like anything I had ever seen before.

Erik had given me Adam's number, but he wasn't picking up – I guessed he was somewhere under the Atlantic still, though it was getting late and he'd left early for his class – surely there would have been time to glance at his phone?

But most worrying of all, there was still no answer from Sid. Perhaps she was away from her phone – she'd told me she was cleaning the training pool, so she might not have brought the phone in with her. I left another desperate message on her voicemail, before giving up.

I wanted to text Ben, but I told myself that he'd be working right now. If I'm being honest, I don't think I could have coped with my disappointment if he didn't respond.

'I mean, do you think it will leave a scar?' Russell was turning this way and that, trying to angle his head so I could see the thin bloody line in his scalp.

I had to admit, annoying as he was, it was a fair old slice, at least three inches long and deep too.

It all made me very uneasy.

Depending on how vindictive Russell proved to be, considering this was all his fault, I felt things could be shaping up to be a potential lawsuit. Thank God we were insured. And, up till my dad's accident, we'd always been fairly lucky that way.

No, I realised. Luck had nothing to do with it. Dad had run a tight ship.

Much tighter than you and Sid.

Almost against my will, my head was sinking backwards against the wall, my eyes closing as I wondered what Dad would say about this.

I missed him terribly at that moment, with a stabbing ache.

'Are you drunk?' Russell asked suddenly.

I jerked awake. 'What? Of course not.'

'You look like you're about to pass out.' His eyes narrowed at me.

'No. I'm just tired. And it was a very stressful day,' I gritted my teeth. 'And I flew in from Australia the day before yesterday.'

'Yeah? Should you be taking groups out into unsafe environments if you're falling asleep like that?'

My heart skipped a beat.

'I'm falling asleep because we've been here for four and a half hours,' I said, hearing an alarmed trembling in my voice and hating it.

Oh God, I thought. Oh God.

Stop it, just stop it. This happened because he didn't follow instructions. He failed the course. And that's a conversation that Sid can have with him. She booked him.

But still, he had frightened me. This was all we needed – I was too tired to teach, I was unfit . . .

'Look, Russell . . .'

'Cassandra Brownrigg?'

I startled, looked up. Why were they calling me? I glanced quickly at the reception desk, festooned with posters warning me not to assault the staff.

Standing there, their faces patient and dour, were two policemen.

'Hey.'

It was drawing into evening now, but the sun was still high. I hadn't heard Jimmy approach me as I sat on the bench overlooking the harbour, staring out to sea, the wind tugging at my hair.

He'd walked up from the shop. I should have been expecting him, really.

'Hey,' I replied, not turning round.

There was a long pause.

'You all right?' he asked me gently.

'No,' I said, sliding my sunglasses up my forehead. 'I'm not all right.' Every time I closed my eyes, she was wafting before me again, a creature out of nightmare. 'Not really.'

He slid on to the bench next to me, bundled into his leather jacket. I glanced sideways at him. His gaze was fixed on the police boat anchored just off the Manacles. Beyond it, the coastguard boat floated, keeping watch.

'Poor Cassie.' He reached around behind me, squeezed my shoulders. 'You're not bargaining for that on a teaching dive, are you?'

I shrugged. It felt childish, self-indulgent to talk about my feelings after my encounter with the woman in the *Undine*. Something told me that of the two of us, she had the infinitely superior understanding of suffering.

'How long have they been down there?' he asked after a moment, nodding towards the police boat.

I shook my head. 'Not sure. An hour, three quarters maybe.'

'Do they know who she is?' he asked me, glancing out to sea.

I shook my head again.

'Did they ask you to show them exactly where she was?'

'No,' I said. 'No, they didn't.'

The thought of going back down to the *Undine* made my heart pound all over again. I didn't know what we were going to do about that, or even when we would be allowed to dive it once more.

It had been all I could do to draw a sketchy map on a bit of napkin (this would become Exhibit TP/BHAP/1 during the inquest), to explain the layout and condition of the wreck to the stocky, earnest-faced police divers in their black drysuits, and then to be pathetically grateful to be excused from any further duties, slinking down the pier to this bench as they'd gathered their equipment, then offered me a wave as their boat pulled out into the water.

There had been something in their expressions that said they understood my condition far better than I did.

'Hmm,' he said. I leaned into his encircling arm. 'And they've no idea how she got there?'

I shook my head. 'They seem to think she just floated into the wreck from the ocean.'

Silence fell for a long moment.

'Really?' he asked.

'It's possible, I suppose.'

Though for my own part, I wasn't so sure. Something about it felt wrong, scraped against my knowledge of the sea. I was remembering that new current.

Once again, I saw her face, and found I couldn't think about this for a second longer.

'I know it's a shock. Especially if it's been down there a while . . .' A pause. 'Well,' he said. 'You've never seen a dead body before, have you?' He was not looking at me, instead staring out to sea, to the boat.

'No.' This was a lie. I had seen my dad. And my mum, after a fashion, when she'd died about five years ago. After the car accident the funeral directors had had to do a lot of work on her, to the point that she'd resembled a dressmaker's mannequin rather than a human. Sid had been too distressed to even look at her.

But that wasn't what Jimmy meant, and I knew it. He meant a dead body in the wild sea, a lost one, somebody who needed to be recovered.

My father had encountered many such people, I knew. In fact, in the living room back at the house, we had a beautiful sea-green Lalique vase Toni McCormack had gifted my dad after he'd recovered her husband's body from a cenote in Mexico, three years after he had gone missing.

My dad was fearless. This small act of grace – guiding the police to the body – would have been second nature to him.

My sense of disappointment in myself was crushing me.

'You'll be fine,' Jimmy said quietly. 'The first time's the worst, you know?'

'I . . .' I swallowed. My mouth was dry. 'Yeah, I suppose.' I pushed my damp hair out of my face. 'I wonder who she is.' A beat. 'Was.' I looked at him. 'You don't think she's that missing girl, do you? Livvy Simpson?'

'Who knows?' Jimmy shrugged. 'She could be anyone.

Don't forget, we're right on the Channel, it's one of the busiest waterways in the world.'

'I suppose,' I said doubtfully.

'Erik says she was in one of the cabins.' It was a statement that sounded like a question.

'Yeah.'

'How did you end up down there? Erik says a student went rogue . . .'

'Oh,' I said bitterly, 'he went rogue all right. You know, thinking back, I'm pretty sure he joined the class just so he could look for the Forbidden Hold. He'd a GoPro, so he's probably on YouTube or TikTok.' I blinked, realised with a kind of distant surprise that I was nearly in tears. 'I had to go after him. There was only me.'

He sighed. 'Yeah. It's a very different set-up now from when Rob ran things.'

'Different or not, Jimmy, this was an advanced wreck class. There should be at least one other person under the surface with me. Why did they schedule two classes today with not enough people to run them?'

'There was another class today? First I heard of it.' He looked for a moment as though he would say more, but he merely shook his head. 'I don't know, girl. Everything would have been scheduled before Grace left, I guess.'

I was shivering, I realised, and gently Jimmy's jacket was being dropped over my shoulders.

'We should go. You're freezing. There's nothing more you can do here. They'll . . .'

'No,' I said, surprised at how forceful I sounded.

I couldn't leave. I had to see them bring her up. If I didn't, I realised, she would be down there in my imagination forever. I'd never be able to dive the *Undine* again for fear of meeting her once more.

My panic, my terror, my crushing failure to control my students – I felt every particle of it as I watched one tiny black-clad head and then another bob out of the water above the *Undine*.

One of them was speaking now to someone on the boat, presumably through a radio, and a long basket was being lowered to the water by the uniformed officers on board. The divers took it and pressed it beneath the waves, vanishing.

Moments later they reappeared, signalling.

In silence Jimmy and I watched the black body bag being borne up the side of the vessel. The dead woman, contained now within her plastic envelope, seemed curiously flat, as though, like a jellyfish, once removed from the water she could no longer hold any kind of shape.

The basket disappeared over the side of the boat, and Jimmy and I sighed, almost in unison.

'Come on,' he said, touching my back through his jacket. 'Let's go.'

I shook my head, shifted on the bench.

'Not yet. In a minute.' I turned to look at him, smiled reassuringly. 'I just need a minute.'

I didn't notice him leave, I don't think. I glanced sideways at some point and could see him further down near the sea wall, turning his head back towards the boat every so often.

For my own part I just stared out to sea, watching the lights on the police launch as it motored over the surface of the waves, pulling aboard the warning buoys they had dropped earlier, and then finally roaring away at speed after a quick wave and hail to the coastguard launch, which soon followed them.

Within fifteen minutes it was as if nobody had ever been there. The tide had come in, covering the tops of the rocks of the Manacles, which returned to their treacherous slumber beneath the waves, and the sun was low and red.

I breathed in, alone at last for the first time since my ghastly discovery.

It was time to go home. To explain to Sid and Adam exactly what had happened. But somehow, despite the cold breeze, my aching limbs, I could not find it within myself to get up, to move.

It was as though the basilisk gaze of the woman in the *Undine* had turned me to stone.

'Hi, I'm home,' I called, opening the front door, but nobody answered. The television was murmuring in the living room. Perhaps they hadn't heard me over it.

I pushed open the door, poked my head into the room.

The curtains were drawn, despite the deeply reddening sunset, and I suspected they had never been opened today. A mug half-full of tepid tea and a plate of toast crumbs sat on the coffee table. Apart from this, the room looked tidy but smelled stale.

There was no sign of Sid, however.

Never mind. She couldn't be far.

As I toiled up the stairs, almost drunk with exhaustion, Tallulah was sitting outside the closed door to my old bedroom, as though she had something to tell me.

'Hey, gorgeous,' I said, leaning down to run my fingers over the silky dome of her head, which she permitted for a few moments before moving away.

On an impulse, I pushed my bedroom door open while she watched.

At first, I didn't recognise it. My poster of Klimt's *The Kiss* was gone, the framed photos of me and my friends likewise vanished. My desk had been moved sideways, against the big south-facing bay window, and a laptop and a printer sat upon it. My bed had been pushed against the far wall, and some magazines and pieces of paper lay on top of it, held down by a coil of electrical cord.

This was much more than Adam moving his stuff in here temporarily – he had repurposed this room, and the photos from the childhood I had spent in this room, the friends I had, and my very family, had been replaced by a poster for *Once Upon a Time in Hollywood* and some kind of framed certificate from a university I didn't recognise.

He hasn't had time to change it back, remember, I tried to tell myself, but the fact was that he had made this room shamelessly his own.

And the thing was, that wasn't the worst of it.

The worst was that Sid had not tried to stop him.

I knew I had been bruised and battered by today, and it was making me sensitive, but try as I might, I could not shake the irrational feeling that he had somehow *supplanted* me – in my own home, and in my sister's affections.

Tallulah watched me stamp across the hall and let myself into the tiny guest bedroom, her golden eyes thoughtful.

13

'What are you talking about?' asked Sid, her eyes hard and horrified. She had leapt to her feet.

I'd found her sitting in the living room when I came back downstairs, curled up on one end of the couch, her vague welcoming smile dying on her lips as I had merely stared at her, in growing astonishment.

She clearly didn't know.

How could she not know? I'd been texting and leaving voicemails all day long . . .

'I *said*, there was a dead woman on the *Undine*.'

'What? Who?' asked Sid, blanching, gathering her dressing gown collar in her fist at her throat. 'Not one of the students?'

'No, of course not. I don't know who she was! I left you a billion messages about this! Why didn't you answer your phone?'

'I didn't have it.' She dismissed the question with an impatient gesture, as though I was trying to change the subject. 'Where was she? This woman?'

'She was in one of the cabins on the lower deck.' I shut my eyes, perhaps to shield myself against the memory. 'I think she'd been there a while . . .'

'The lower deck?' Sid's face contorted dangerously. 'What were you doing down there with a *class*, you muppet?'

'Obviously I didn't *take* them down there!' I replied, stung. 'A client swam off on his own once we got into the ship.' I wiped at my brow, the skin still tight and crusted with dried salt. 'Russell Bowermann. Swam down the bow stairwell after jamming his GoPro on, not a care in the world.'

She shook her head, her mouth twisted into a humourless half-smile. 'There's always one.' She crossed her arms. 'So, what happened?'

'Well, I went after him. Had to leave the others up in the cargo deck . . .'

Sid was aghast. 'You *left* them there? That place is a death trap!'

I shrugged helplessly. 'What was I supposed to do? I was the only instructor!'

Sid sighed, as though she had plenty she would like to say. I had it in my head to remark that it was easy enough to judge these things when you were a hundred feet above sea level, in your living room on the sofa where you'd clearly spent the day in your dressing gown, but decided that however satisfying that might be, it was not terribly helpful.

Wasn't she meant to have been cleaning the training pool today?

'Anyway, he wandered off into one of the cabins . . .'

I paused, remembering that moment, and found it hard to breathe.

'. . . and there she was.'

Sid was silent. She knew what the sea could do to a person. We both did.

'How do you think she got there?' she asked eventually.

I shook my head. 'I don't know. The police suggested she might have drifted in somehow.'

'Really?' Sid looked sceptical. 'Through the hole in the

bow?' She paused, thinking. 'The cabins are quite deep inside the ship.'

'I don't know what they thought,' I said. 'But something had changed down there. There was this new strong current running through the gangway on the lower deck.'

'A new current?' She craned up at me.

'Yeah. Just the lower deck, though. Upper was the same as always.' I faced her. 'Have *you* noticed a change there?'

'Me? No.' Sid shivered. 'But I haven't been down as far as the lower decks since . . .' Her face crumpled for an instant before smoothing out again, so fast I could almost persuade myself I had imagined it. It wrung my heart to see it. 'I leave that to Jimmy and Adam if I can.' She ran her hand over her mouth, something she did when deep in thought. 'Hmm,' she said ultimately. 'Did the police say anything else?'

'Yeah. They're going to do a more thorough search of the wreck.'

'They are?' She brought her knees up to her chest. 'How long will that take?'

'I don't know. They didn't say.'

'We have a penetration wreck class there in two days . . .'

'Well, I don't think they'll finish searching the *Undine* in two days.' I shrugged. 'Erik's contacting all the clients booked for it. Just in case.'

'Can't you phone the police? Find out how long it will be?'

I frowned. 'Why can't you do it?'

A single blink, as though I had taken her by surprise, then – 'Who was this woman? Was she a diver, do you think? Or a swimmer?'

'I don't know . . .' I was not enjoying having to think

about this. 'Hard to say.' I swallowed, lowered my voice. 'I couldn't tell anything like that about her. She was naked.'

'Oh,' said Sid, in a tight little voice. She regarded me in silence for a long moment, gnawing on her thumbnail.

'Could it have been Livvy Simpson?' she asked.

'The missing girl?' I shook my head. 'I don't know. I couldn't tell.' I bit my lip. 'She was in such a mess. But she had long hair. Dark . . . maybe with streaks. But mostly dark.'

Livvy Simpson had gone missing ten days ago. The woman on the *Undine* . . . I was no expert but I knew that the sea could easily have done this to her in that time, if the conditions were right . . .

Once again I was in that dark cabin with her, while she grinned at me.

'Are you all right?' asked Sid, peering at me. 'You look as if you're about to faint.'

'I'm fine.' I swallowed. 'I guess we'll just have to wait and see what the police say. Anyway, I don't want to talk about her any more.'

We'd ordered in a Chinese takeaway from the shop down in the village and were eating it in the kitchen. I was surprised when Sid proposed it, as I had the impression that Adam had no time for fast food.

She didn't suggest ordering anything for him.

I looked sideways at her. 'Russell Bowermann was asking after the Forbidden Hold in the orientation session, you know.'

'Of course he was.' Sid rolled her eyes, barked out a humourless laugh. 'They always do. What is it they think is in there? The Ark of the Covenant? The Treasure of the Sierra Madre? Shangri-fucking-La?'

I smiled despite myself. 'Content makers gotta make content, I suppose. Bet you any money he's some social media maverick.' I sighed. 'That's all we need. Maybe I should look him up.'

'I wouldn't do him the favour.' Sid sniffed, stabbing at her Kung Po prawns with her fork. 'They get paid by their views, you know.' She shrugged. 'You said he hurt himself?'

'Yeah. Cut himself. Quite bad. About three inches.' I demonstrated on my own head, approximating his injury.

She sighed again, and this time there was something hard in it.

And with the acute sensitivity of a sister, I understood instantly that this was a reproach addressed to me.

'What?' I asked.

'You know, Cass, you're supposed to be able to control a group when you take them in there. Didn't you tell them not to wander off?'

'Of course I told them!' I said, my face flushing. 'It didn't help that I was the only instructor diving with them. Why was nobody else put on with me?'

She rolled her eyes again, only this time in a way that made me want to strangle her. 'Do you even need somebody else for, what, six divers . . . ?'

'Yes!' I snapped. 'Yes, we do! We've been open again for lessons for less than two months and already we've had an accident!'

I took a deep breath, gathered myself, pushing my food away. I wasn't hungry any more. 'Do you think Dad would have taken a class that size down with just one instructor and no assistant?'

Her eyes glinted in sudden anger.

'You know, he probably wouldn't.' She let her fork drop to her plate with a tinny clang. 'But he was *Dad*. He wasn't living with a business that has been shut for nearly eighteen months. He had people *throwing* themselves at him to work for him.' She swept her hand restlessly through her short hair. 'We have to manage life the way it is *now*, Cass. Six students to one instructor may not be what we're used to, true, but it's not like we're breaking any rules.' She hissed out a sigh. 'You could always have said something to us at the time if you were that bothered.'

'When?' I asked, incredulous at the unfairness of this. 'I knew nothing about it until they'd practically all arrived! And I thought that Erik would be coming with me.' I folded my arms tightly. 'What was I supposed to do? Cancel?'

Fraught silence.

'It was supposed to be Grace doing it with you,' said Sid, picking up her cup of tea, then seeming to realise it was undrinkable, with a scum of milk on top. 'She just stormed out. Don't know what that was about.' She shrugged hugely, as if helpless. 'Left us high and dry.'

'Yes, so people keep saying, but that was last week,' I said, trying to resist the urge to shake her. 'I mean, why didn't *you* come?' I gestured around me in a sarcastic sweep. 'It doesn't look like you've had much else on.'

And she froze, like a deer in headlights.

'What?' I asked, less angry now than baffled. 'What is it?'

'I've had a cold,' she said. 'I couldn't go. I won't be right to dive for a week at least.'

I peered at her. She hadn't seemed ill.

But maybe she was, I thought, with a little stab of guilt.

It would explain a lot – her lassitude, her unkemptness, the way she was hiding in here in the middle of the day with the curtains drawn, something I would never have imagined her doing before I left.

'So how did you leave it?' she asked, not meeting my gaze. 'With this Russell guy?'

'I think he's going to be trouble, Sid. He was making noises about "unsafe environments" at one point.'

We raised our eyebrows at one another, a tiny moment of sisterly unity. Nothing about the *Undine* was safe and only an idiot would think of describing her that way. 'You really think he's going to kick off?' she asked.

'Yeah, he might. Because generating scandal is content too, right?' I rubbed my face. 'I hope Adam had better luck on his dive,' I said, letting my tired eyes close.

'What?'

'Adam's dive. He was going to Newquay . . .'

She seemed puzzled, her brows wrinkling. 'That's not till tomorrow.'

I sat bolt upright. 'That's not what he told me. Where is he then?'

'He went to visit his sister.'

'What – he went to visit family?' I stared at her. 'You mean he took our expensive people carrier on a personal trip and left our paying customers to rattle around in the van?'

'I . . .' She had flushed bright red, and there was something so stricken, so guilty, in her face I almost, almost but not quite, was tempted to drop the subject. 'He probably wasn't thinking. Sorry, Cass. She has a lot of emotional problems, it's such a huge worry for him . . .'

'Fucking hell, Sid!'

'Cass, you don't understand, he's under so much pressure . . .' She paused, as though something had struck her. 'You're right. I know you're right. I'll talk to him. I'll remind him that the Audi's for the business, primarily.' Her face cleared, softened. 'Things are going to get better now you're back. I can feel it.'

I wanted to argue with her more, to pursue the entitled selfishness of someone who treated our property like his own.

And something else too – he had definitely told me he was taking a class out today over dinner last night. I had not imagined it.

Sid stood up, and for the first time looked purposeful. 'Come on. I'll make you some fresh coffee.'

'Sid?' I asked, watching her.

'Yes?' She swept her plate off the table into the dishwasher.

'Why didn't you have your phone with you today?'

'What?' she asked, and there was something studied about it, as though she had not heard me when I knew that she had.

'Why wouldn't you have your phone? You've not been anywhere. You had it yesterday . . .'

She was reaching up into the cupboards and then stilled for an instant, a tiny telling pause. 'Adam has it.'

'What?'

'He took it with him.' She sucked in a sharp breath, as though expecting a quarrel. 'I've been wasting a lot of time browsing social media, Cass. It's not a good idea, you know, with the state of the world. When the pandemic was on . . . I was so depressed, you know, and he worries about me. So, he takes it with him, so I'm not tempted to doomscroll.' She tried on a little fake laugh.

I simply stared at her. 'He keeps your *phone*?'

'It's not like that, Cass. I ask him to do those things. I mean, I want to be more disciplined, and he just helps me out, you know?' She hadn't turned around, but her voice ratcheted up, and I could tell I was upsetting her.

I sighed, tried to find a place to start from that wouldn't infuriate her, wouldn't make her shut down.

Be reasonable, Cass.

'How long has this been going on?'

'I . . . I dunno. A little while . . .'

I was too stunned to speak as the implications became clear.

'What happens if there's an emergency? If someone needs you?'

She gave a series of little shakes of her head. 'Don't be silly. Obviously he can unlock it and answer it if he has to. It's not switched off.'

'But he doesn't answer it! He hasn't answered it all day!' I stared at her, disbelieving. 'How are people supposed to contact *you*, Sid?'

She scowled. 'Stop making a big thing of it, Cass. He tells me if someone has been in touch.'

'Well, he hasn't, and . . .' But just at that moment, the implications hit me like a gut punch. I could barely breathe through it.

'*Has he been reading personal texts I send to you?*'

She turned to face me, and I saw she was growing red, pink patches spreading up her throat and into her cheeks.

'I doubt it. Anyway, you don't really send me anything that personal, do you . . . ?'

'Sid, this is so out of order . . .' I ran my hands against my scalp, as though trying to hold my flying thoughts in. 'I can't even . . . have you any idea how controlling and weird that sounds?'

Her eyes narrowed at me.

'He takes your phone so you don't "waste time" looking at it or talking to people . . .' I could be handling this better, I thought, taking in her stricken face, the way her hands balled into tense little fists – but I just couldn't seem to stop myself. '. . . but if Adam really wanted to help you, he'd be helping you get back to work.'

'What does that mean?'

'Helping you to dive again.' And the words came out, despite my best efforts. 'Helping you get over what happened with Dad.'

Her mouth set into a tight line, and I felt a tiny pinch of satisfaction, as I had when we were kids, and I knew I had said something that had drawn blood.

'I'm *fine*.'

'You are not fine. I know you're not fine. *You* must know you're not fine. We were under huge pressure at work today, Sid. A lot of bad things happened. And as far as I can tell, you've spent the whole day sat around in your dressing gown.'

'I've been ill!' Her voice squeaked on the last word, and knowing her as I did, I realised with steely sharpness that it was a lie, she had never been ill, or perhaps had had a sniffle a week ago that she had been wringing the very last drops out of, like she had when we were little girls at school.

'Then why are the guys at the shop telling me that you never go in there?' I folded my arms at her.

She flinched. 'How would they know? They're not there all the time. Which one said that?' Her lips drew back over her teeth. 'Jimmy, by any chance?'

'Does it matter which one said it, if it's true?'

She glanced down, seemed to be thinking, then threw up her hands dismissively.

'Okay. It's true I'm not taking classes out to the *Undine* so much any more.' She raised her head, met my gaze. 'Can you blame me?'

'No, I don't blame you for that. But I may blame you for handing everything over to your boyfriend, who tells people he's the manager now but who we can't get hold of when we find a dead body in the shipwreck!'

'What's your point? Yes, Adam helps me with the admin.' Her voice was high, strangled with anger and something that felt a little like fear. 'Obviously. You *knew* this. I told you . . .'

'Sid, on this showing he couldn't run a piss-up in a brewery.' Even as my next words came to me, I knew it was a bad idea to say them. I just couldn't stop myself: 'The only thing he seems capable of running is *you.*'

Her chin came up, her lips curled into a contemptuous snarl. 'What would you know about that? You've never had a relationship that ran for longer than six months anyway.' She sniffed. 'At least a real one.'

'Well, if this is what a "real" relationship is supposed to be like, you can count me out – what kind of controlling weirdo drives around, in the company car, might I add, with their girlfriend's phone with him all day, just so she won't use it? You know, just to reiterate, there was a fucking *dead woman* out in the *Undine*, and oh, a student nearly drowned and cops, actual policemen, were questioning me about it – where the fuck was he? Where were you?'

I could feel the spittle landing on my chin, hear my ratcheting fury, yet somehow I was incapable of controlling myself.

'Oh, calm down, Cass. Stop being so dramatic. You *always* do this!'

'No, I will not calm down!' I leapt up from the chair, blazing. 'The shop's an absolute mess. I couldn't even move back into my room and you've both known I'm coming for *months*. It cost me every penny I had to buy that plane ticket . . .'

Something caught in her eyes, some moment of hesitation.

'All right,' she said, holding out her hands, palm outwards, a gesture of surrender. 'I agree. That's not right, that shouldn't have happened. And it's one thing for me not to have the phone when there's no classes on and the shop is shut, but – we're back in business now and you must be able to get hold of me. I get it. I do.' She inhaled, seemed to think again. 'I'm sorry. I know it was terrible today and you felt you were beached up on your own. But what good does it do us to fight about it?'

I opened my mouth to speak, because of course I was still angry, but then realised – she's right, for once. A big screaming row was not helping anyone now.

I deflated, sat back down in the wooden kitchen chair.

'All right, fine,' I said, hearing how much I sounded like a sulky teenager. I needed to pull myself together. 'Do you want a glass of wine?'

A little flicker in her eyes then. 'I don't think . . .' She licked her lips, seemed to change course in whatever it was she had been about to say, and I had a sense it might have been about whether Adam would approve or not.

Once this occurred to me, it set off a tiny boiling in my blood. I could feel my face harden, and she must have seen it.

'Yeah,' she said, brightening. 'Sure.'

14

'So, I take it that it didn't go too well with Ben,' she said as she opened the second bottle of wine.

'What makes you say that?'

'You came home last night.'

There had still been no sign of Adam, and it was now dark. Sea mist had drawn down, veiling the stars, the lights of the ships, and our windows opened only on to silky blue darkness, as though we were underwater.

I didn't want to tell her that the reason I'd come back home last night was because I was worried about her. I was angry with her, after all – angry at how judgmental she'd been about my attitude to the dive, angry about her relationship with Adam (Oh my God, he confiscates her phone during the day! How messed up is that?), angry at how she'd lied about the business and her part in it.

Angry that she hadn't been there for me today.

But at the end of it all she was still my sister.

'I don't know.' I swiped at my mouth with the back of my hand. 'I'm just keeping him in suspense.'

And there matters rested for a few minutes, as we sat at the kitchen table, wine in hand, in almost companionable silence. Far out to sea was the low blast of a foghorn.

I looked at her. For the first time in forever, everything seemed to be almost normal between us.

'How long have you not been diving?' I asked, holding the wine glass close to my breast.

'I dunno.' She refilled her empty glass.

Sid drank a lot, I was starting to realise.

'I mean,' I continued, deciding to save this observation for a better moment, 'has it been since the accident?'

'No.' She shook her head, unsteadily, and I realised she was getting a little tipsy. 'It wasn't a straight away thing. It just kind of crept up on me, you know?' She drank, a big gulp. 'It was okay for a month or two – till the end of the season really. I thought everything was fine, I thought . . .' she paused, rubbing at her face, 'that it was what Dad would have wanted, you know? To carry on as normal?'

I nodded. I would have thought that too.

'But when the spring came round again, I . . . I just couldn't face it. Like, not just the *Undine*, but any diving. But it was all right. There were no classes with the pandemic, so I didn't have to if I didn't want to. Adam started to help a lot more with the admin and things, so I didn't have to get so involved.' She shrugged emphatically. 'And I was grateful, you know?' She drained the glass, gazing at me over the rim all the while.

I realised now what was upsetting me so, what kept making me want to fight with her. She had given off the impression for nearly two years that things were under control, that however hard it all was she was loving it, and I had let myself believe that, despite every red flag, because I needed it to be true. I wanted the job at the Institute. I had fallen desperately in love with Australia and wanted to go back there.

Selfishly, I had needed to believe that Sid was happy and prosperous here, and whether I wanted to blame Adam or not, it was very clear that she wasn't.

'But you're back now,' she said, as though reading my

thoughts. 'I mean, I know we need to keep a closer eye on the shop and all, but everything is just so messed up with Covid and, you know, everyone is in the same position . . .'

From the hallway came the sound of a key turning in the lock.

He was whistling as he passed along the hallway, sounding as though he didn't have a care in the world.

It seemed to me that Sid froze, just for a tiny second, before getting to her feet and moving to the dishwasher, starting to pack every single thing lying out into it with a barely restrained energy – teaspoons, her empty glass, the mug I'd been drinking coffee out of previously.

'Hello, ladies,' he sang out, coming into the room. He audibly sniffed the air. 'Been painting the town red, have we?'

Despite my best efforts, my blood began to simmer. Where the hell had he been all day with Sid's phone, in the middle of our emergency?

'Hello, Adam,' I said evenly. 'Yeah. We're having a drink. It was a very challenging day.'

Sid did not reply, instead busying herself with wiping the tops, her face flushed. In a way, this was making me angrier than he was.

I wanted to get up, snatch the cloth out of her hand, tell her to pull herself together.

'Challenging, eh?' He offered a sympathetic smile. 'Why, what happened?'

He was dressed in a blue cotton shirt, long-sleeved, and he smelled faintly of cologne. He'd shaved since I saw him last, and his trousers were ironed. He looked like he'd come home from Casual Friday at the office, followed by after-work drinks at the local wine bar, rather than visiting his sister.

He too carried the faint whiff of beer.

I didn't smile back. Instead I explained my day to him, in short, terse sentences.

He blinked at me, his face paling. 'What?'

'Yeah. A dead woman. And me on my own with six student divers.'

He licked his lips.

'Sorry, Cass, I don't do the rotas,' he said. 'That's Sid and Jimmy's department, isn't it, love?'

Sid glanced up, as though this was news to her, then quickly ducked her head down again. 'Yeah.'

'I know it's not what you were used to. But we just don't have the staff we did before the pandemic.' He cocked his head to one side, his expression conciliatory. 'We have to manage with what we've got. Still, I'm sure it was all a horrible shock. What did the police say?'

In the meantime, he had drifted over to the chair at the head of the table, and with a little pause and twitch, as if to make himself extra comfortable, sat down.

Sid was carefully wringing and rinsing out the blue cloth she'd used to wipe the tops. Everything was now pristine and tidied away, as though she and I had never been sitting here, except for my lone half-full glass of wine.

I had a sense of myself as the outstanding object, another thing that by rights ought to be tidied away too.

Sid's servile reaction just filled me with the urge to resist.

'Why did you tell me you were running a class in Newquay today?' I asked him.

He glanced up at me.

'I never said that,' he answered, frowning. 'I was always going to visit my sister today,' he affected wounded surprise. 'The class is tomorrow.' Something in his face hardened, his eyes growing narrow, cruel. 'I think you misheard me.'

'I don't think I did.'

He leaned back in the chair, his head tilting ever so slightly, almost as if to say, *Ah, are we having trouble out of you?*

'Sid, did I not tell you I was visiting my sister today?'

Sid stilled completely, and I once more had that sense of her as someone I did not know.

'I . . . I can't remember . . .' she stammered. 'But that sounds right, yes . . .'

His silence was pointed, as though waiting, while I felt my cheeks redden in rage and embarrassment for her.

'Fine,' I said, as resistance was clearly pointless. 'Though, while I'm here, could I ask you to please not take the people carrier out on personal business when we've got paying customers that have to rattle about in the back of the van?'

'Of course, if you like,' he said calmly, but there was a flush of red in his cheek, in the fine capillaries in the skin of his ears. It occurred to me in a flash of insight that his will in this house was probably rarely contradicted.

'But, you know,' he said, with an elaborate shrug, as though he was indulging me, those wide grey eyes appealing to me, 'I hardly think it makes much difference, Cass.'

'Yes. Of course,' I said. 'That's why my parents spent fifty thousand pounds on a people carrier with a custom paint job. So it wouldn't make much difference.'

His face set like concrete.

And with that, I had no option but to drain my glass in silence and walk out the door.

As I stalked through the hall, I could hear the tinny clink of Sid putting my empty glass in the dishwasher alongside the others.

15

My mobile phone was ringing in the little guest bedroom.

I sat up groggily, reached for it. It was 5:54 a.m.

What the hell?

Georgia had provided me with a trio of sleeping pills in a little plastic baggie when I left Aus, slipping them into my make-up bag with the prim-faced discretion of an upmarket drug dealer. I'd told her I wouldn't need them, and she'd removed them, only to replace them later when my back was turned during the packing.

This had proved to be yet another occasion where she knew better than me.

I'd popped the second last night and managed to fall asleep almost immediately. I was still drenched in chemical fug as the phone rang on and on and on . . .

I picked it up, held it to my ear as I lay semi-conscious. 'H'llo?'

'Hi, is this Cassandra Brownrigg I'm speaking to?'

It was an English accent, Home Counties.

'Whuh?' I rolled over on my back.

'Sorry, I appreciate it's very early,' the voice went on. 'I just really need to speak to . . .'

I rubbed my eyes, tried to gather myself together. 'I'm Cass Brownrigg,' I mumbled.

'Oh great, that's great!' he said with a little false laugh. 'My name's David Neville. I'm a reporter with the *Daily Mail*.'

I blinked. 'What?'

'I was just hoping to do a piece for our readers on what that must have been like – to discover Livvy Simpson's body . . .'

'Livvy Simpson's . . . ? I'm sorry, h-how did you get this number?'

'Oh, a friend of yours – hope I haven't got them in trouble! I appreciate it's early, but you have to have realised, Cassandra, the enormous public interest in this case . . .'

'I don't know anything about any case,' I said quickly, trying to process all this. 'I was in Australia until a few days ago.'

'Ah, I see, I see. This must be an even bigger shock than I realised, then. You know,' he said, 'it's quite a story, you finding this girl in such a lonely, hostile environment. Everyone said she was in quite a bad way . . .'

She was there again.

I saw her as she had appeared in that terrible moment when I'd switched on my back-up light, leaning forward as if to kiss me, or to whisper secrets in my ear.

'It must have been *so* traumatic . . . I mean, I understand your father passed away after an accident on that wreck . . .'

'It's six o'clock in the morning,' I said, teetering between a thudding tiredness and a keyed-up hypervigilance. 'I don't have any thoughts.'

'I know, but I just wanted to catch you while the body is being identified . . .'

A strong sense came over me then, of this woman stripped and ragged, floating in a little cloud of her own decaying blood, without even a scrap of cloth to cover her face in the privacy of death.

'I'm sorry,' I said. 'I don't think the police would like me talking about this to you.'

'I understand,' he said warmly. 'But I'm more interested in your own impressions. You know, Cassandra, we could make it worth your while to share this with us. Perhaps as much as ten thousand pounds, depending on what you . . .'

I tapped the call off, lay back down, staring at the ceiling.

Pale dawn light was seeping in through the open curtains, colouring everything a milky yellow.

Poor Livvy. It was a good thing she'd been found, I thought, though a sad one. Better for the sake of her family that she'd turned up, in any state, no matter how horrible, rather than to have vanished forever and never be found.

But finding this body was also a thing that would have consequences, I realised. For me. For Blue Horizons.

Immediately, as though it had overheard my thoughts, the phone was ringing again.

'All right, now I want to see you put your equipment on,' I announced to the group, my voice carrying across the chlorinated water, amplified by the glass ceiling and walls. 'Remember to check your buddy as they do theirs!'

I was teaching a Discover Scuba course for complete beginners with Jimmy in the indoor pool.

This morning the eight people that had signed up were more nervous than usual, put off by the small gang of reporters and photographers that had somehow taken all the parking spaces near the pool and who were hovering outside the house.

Sid was in the house, as far as I knew, but had shown no

interest in anything happening at the front door. We hadn't spoken since last night. I hoped she was following up with my disappointed dive class from yesterday.

Somehow, I had a feeling she wasn't.

The knot of reporters had worked out we were in here and were now clustering outside near the pool door, the frosted glass making them look elongated and gauzy.

They were making me nervous too.

What the hell could they want? I wondered, as I talked a skinny eleven-year-old boy through the right way to hoist an air tank on to his back. When murder victims are found by dog walkers, which is what invariably seems to happen, you don't have the press reporting on their lives. They are incidental cast. Why were these journalists after me?

'It's the novelty, I suspect,' Jimmy had remarked laconically as he zipped up his wetsuit. 'You can see their point. It's a good story, you know – the girl everyone's been searching for, and the "cursed" shipwreck,' he made little air quotes with his fingers. 'They can take some pictures of you into the bargain. Everybody loves a good-looking woman.'

I sighed. 'Don't be ridiculous.'

'I'm not being ridiculous,' he said. 'I'm being a realist. But they'll get tired of it eventually. It'll be a nine-day wonder.'

'If you say so.' I had glanced doubtfully at the full car park as I tied up my hair out of my face.

'And if we don't talk to them, they'll get tired more quickly,' continued Jimmy. 'You'll see. If they start to get pushy, we can get the police involved to move them on. *They* won't want us gobbing off to the media, I'm sure.'

This seemed like a plan to me. 'Okay.'

He reached up, and in a gesture I hadn't seen in him since I was a little girl, he rubbed my cheek with his thumb. 'Don't worry about a thing, Cassie. It'll be all right.'

I patted his hand. 'Thanks, Jimmy.'

So for now, I was walking from pair to pair of my students as they stood at the edges of the pool, checking their equipment, tightening straps here and there, tucking in lines. The children chattered excitedly to each other, and it always gives my spirits a lift to watch them. This is the time to get people interested in the sea, which takes up most of our planet and is heartbreakingly vulnerable to human abuse.

It's my little chance to save the world, to let them experience this hidden realm and grow to value it, and I needed to take all the chances I could.

They were all kitted up now and had been so patient and adorable, so it was time to give them what they wanted and let them jump in and breathe underwater.

Jimmy was going to handle the adults at one end, and the children were left to me. They were like a huddle of eager goslings as I led them to the lip of the pool.

'All right, Rashad,' I said to the first one, a boy so excited he was literally jiggling from one small foot to the other, his fins flapping against the deck. 'You're going to hold your mask to your face like this,' I demonstrated, 'stick one foot out like this,' I raised my own leg up high in front of me, 'and step into the water. That way, it's less likely to get into your mask and up your nose.'

He nodded, his snorkel waving back and forth frantically.

'Good. You ready?'

The snorkel waved even harder.

'Excellent.'

I stood back, giving him room, and he raised his leg as I had done . . .

Suddenly the pool door opened, letting a swirl of dry air into the humid glass room. A close-cropped man barged in, wearing a Barbour jacket and with a camera slung around his neck. He was looking around quickly, and then his eyes lighted on me . . .

The interruption was so unexpected, the boy, who had been stepping off the pool side at just that moment, turned to look, falling awkwardly into the water with a cry more of surprise than fear.

I jumped in after him – he was weighted down with nearly 20 kg of dive kit, after all, and if it carried him down headfirst – it didn't bear thinking about.

The water closed over me as I kicked towards him, saw instantly he was all right. He was breathing through his regulator like a natural, wriggling about in the water like a lithe spider, and in very real danger of swimming out of my grip and on to his own adventures in the dive well in the centre.

All of which was great, of course, but you shouldn't run before you can walk.

I gestured up and he followed me, our heads breaking the surface together.

We emerged into a cacophony of shouting.

'. . . this is PRIVATE PROPERTY!' Jimmy's voice boomed – the glass walls seemed to tremble with it. 'We're teaching people here – there are *children*! You could have killed somebody!'

'I'm sorry, mate, I only wanted . . .'

'GET OUT!' Jimmy yelled. His face was scarlet. 'Get out before we call the police!'

The class stood around, in stunned silence, as the man backed out, once again reiterating his insincere apologies. I lifted Rashad out on to the lip of the pool and followed him, throwing our fins up on to the edge. His mother was already hurrying up to us.

'Are you all right, girl?' Jimmy asked, then leaned down to Rashad. 'Are *you* all right, lad?'

'We're both fine,' said the boy with guileless confidence. 'I was really good at diving. Cass worries too much.'

I laughed out loud, while Jimmy tousled his head, his mother reaching us. 'What was that?' she asked. She looked frightened, borderline angry. 'What on earth is going on here?'

'A reporter,' I told her. I needed to calm this down. The other adults were craning over at us, peering out of the glass to the little knot of journalists, and a couple of the children looked anxious.

We just couldn't catch a break, it seemed. Discover Scuba is meant to be *fun*. More to the point, if they enjoy it, the clients will often go ahead and book their open water certification with us, which is where we make the money.

I gritted my teeth.

Whether they liked it or not, these people were going to have a good time.

'It's okay,' I said, raising my voice so they could all hear me. I pushed my wet hair out of my face. 'It's absolutely nothing to worry about. It's about the . . . crime scene we found yesterday at the wreck site. The police have asked us not to talk to the media . . .' I shrugged. 'So you can safely ignore them.'

'They found that missing girl out there,' muttered one of the men to Rashad's mother. 'Yesterday. Or they think so.'

Her eyes went saucer-round. 'Oh.' She looked at me in amazement. 'Really? That was *you*?'

I opened my mouth to say something polite and non-committal when suddenly she was before me again.

Only this time, it was different – previously, I had closed my eyes, and it had just been a tiny flashback, a couple of transparent still images, distressing, but soon gone.

This time, though, my eyes were open. It was simply as though the whole pool, the people, the damp chemical air just faded out, and I was back there, underwater in the cold ocean, dozens of feet from the surface in a black box of absolute darkness, while mechanical breaths sighed in and out of my lungs.

The dark filled me with overwhelming terror, but I knew that if I switched on the back-up light she would be there waiting for me, with her floating hair, her swollen white belly taut and mottled and ready to give birth to nightmares.

Suddenly Jimmy had taken hold of my shoulder, as though pulling me back out.

'Now, now,' he was saying, and he sounded very far away, but thankfully growing nearer, and the people had returned, and the sour smell of chlorine, and the giggles of a little girl dancing at the edge of the pool, eager for her turn to dive. 'You all heard Cass. We can't talk about it at all, to anyone, while it's all ongoing. Come on, everyone, let's get back to diving.'

I nodded, being incapable of anything else, and managed to raise a half-hearted smile.

'You all right?' asked Jimmy into my ear.

'Yeah, yeah. Just had a bit of a wobble, is all,' I murmured.

'Better now?' He lifted one dark brow.

'Yes, I think so.' This wasn't entirely true, but at least the vision was now gone, leaving only the wash of emotions in its wake.

Jimmy at least was satisfied. He nodded, stepped back as I stood up, clapped my hands brightly.

'Okay, everybody,' I shouted, 'back to your places!'

16

It was nearly lunchtime – the clients had all been sent off to the showers, after being shown how to stow the gear away in the numbered plastic crates. I was about to follow them when Jimmy simply said 'Cass.'

I looked round. A man and woman were standing at the open pool door, the man in a rumpled jacket and tie, the woman in a severe grey trouser suit and cream shirt.

Instantly I had the sense that these were not journalists.

'Hi – Miss Brownrigg, is it?' asked the woman. She had large, serious blue eyes, wavy brown hair trapped behind her head in a big tortoiseshell clip.

I nodded.

'We're from the Falmouth Serious Crime Squad. This is DCI Trevelyan and I'm DI Rebecca Small. We were hoping to have a word with you.'

She was striding towards me, not waiting for permission. Her suit was sharp but cheap, and her ears pierced three times, twice on the lobe and once high up on the cuff, though she wore no jewellery there. Something told me that her current outfit was a uniform of sorts, and that she would have looked very different if I'd met her while she was off duty.

'Of course,' I said. I was conscious of being clad only in my red swimsuit, and pulled a nearby towel around my waist. 'What can I do for you?'

'Actually, we had some more questions.'

The other detective, Trevelyan, trailed behind her, looking around at the pool, at Jimmy, anywhere but at me. He had a wide mouth, set into a grim, displeased expression.

'I understand your family are the legal owners of the wreck the body was found in?' he asked.

'Oh no, not owners,' I said. 'We're the *licensees.*'

Their confusion was obvious. 'Licensee . . . ?' DI Small asked.

'Yeah, sorry. We're in an arrangement with Historic England to look after the wreck, and in return we develop it for commercial use.' I tightened the towel around me, as the man seemed to be getting increasingly uncomfortable. 'We keep an eye on the *Undine*, and hand in annual reports on how safe it is to dive. We're caretakers, basically.'

Jimmy nodded next to me.

'In return,' I said, fighting the effort not to shiver now the pool house door was open, 'we can develop dive courses around it, and set up dive trails. It's actually a really important site – we don't have a lot of penetration wrecks in the UK outside of Orkney . . .'

'Right. So, your dive shop has exclusive rights to dive there, then?' he asked.

Jimmy snorted.

'Oh no,' I replied. 'Not at all. Anyone can dive there; it's not policed in any way.'

They exchanged a swift glance.

'I mean,' I continued, 'we stick up signs warning people that areas of the wreck are unsafe, and we can refuse to take people that are unqualified on dives that we ourselves run, but there is absolutely nothing to stop any member of the public pitching up in a drysuit and a scuba tank and going anywhere they like in it.'

'And they do,' chimed in Jimmy. 'Even the silly buggers.'

'Yeah,' I agreed, with a grim smile. 'Especially them.'

'So, just to be clear, anybody can get inside the wreck, if they wanted to?' The woman offered me a keen glance.

Jimmy and I nodded in unison.

'So, would you say you had a lot of divers doing that? Just turning up on their own?' DCI Trevelyan asked Jimmy.

'Oh yeah. Sometimes in summer there could be half a dozen boats there at once. It's a worry,' Jimmy said, throwing a sidelong glance to include me. 'It's amazing there haven't been more accidents in it, to be honest. It's a very dangerous proposition, the *Undine*, because it's lovely clear water but deep – a hundred feet deep. But the clear water tricks folk into thinking they're nearer the surface than they really are, lulls them into a false sense of security, if you like.'

I nodded in agreement.

'Yeah,' I said. 'Dangerous or not, the *Undine*'s location is marked on all the navigation maps and there's nothing to stop anyone rolling up in a boat.'

Suddenly I got it. Why were they asking about divers turning up alone in relation to the missing girl? A girl with no wetsuit, or any business being inside the wreck?

There could only be one reason why they were asking questions about who had access to the *Undine*.

'You think someone *hid* that body down there, don't you?' I asked. 'That they hid Livvy Simpson in the wreck?'

They both seemed to freeze, and I realised in an instant I had it absolutely right. That was exactly what they thought.

'She's still not been identified,' said DI Small, but she threw a look at her partner. 'We're still waiting for DNA.'

I felt sick. Despite all logic, and in the face of all the journalists camped on my doorstep, I realised that there was a tiny part of me that had wanted to believe that this was an accidental death, some tragic drowning.

And all for nothing, for it seemed that the woman in the *Undine* had been murdered.

'Well, what did you think of that?' Jimmy asked after they'd gone.

There had been a couple more questions – had I seen anything else suspicious or unusual? Had anybody been hanging around the wreck recently? But other than what I'd already told them I couldn't help them.

Eventually Jimmy had stepped in, pointing out that I needed to get changed, and they had left, with the ominous promise that they would be in touch again soon.

'I thought the police frogmen told you that girl just floated in?' Jimmy rubbed at his damp scalp with a towel.

We were both rattled.

'Yeah, that was their guess before they went down to the *Undine*,' I was whispering, even though we were alone. 'But Jimmy, you know, it didn't sound right to me even at the time. If she floated in through the upper decks, or the hole in the front, there's no way she would have ended up in one of the cabins. That new current would have kept her out of the stairwell.' I stilled, as the implications became clear. 'It would have pushed her out of the ship, probably.'

And the police divers had probably worked that out after going down there, I realised, and experiencing it for themselves.

Hence the visit just now.

'That's all very well,' said Jimmy. 'But who would put a dead girl in the *Undine*? That's a mad thing to do. People are diving it dawn to dusk. You'd be *seen*.'

It was true. It made no sense.

I was exhausted, I realised, and there was still so much to do.

'Jimmy, I'm going to have a shower and head on down to the shop,' I said. 'I want to have a look through the stock.' I rubbed the towel over my head. 'Are you going to clean out the pool?'

'I was, yeah.'

'Great. If the police come back with any more questions, tell them I'm just down the road.'

'Sure thing, girl.' He squeezed my shoulder on the way out. 'See you tomorrow.'

While I showered, I hoped forlornly that this would be the end of the matter. All I did was find a body. Frankly, as selfish as it sounds, I was eager to be done with this business, to return to normal.

Don't be this way, I told myself sternly. That woman – who probably was Livvy Simpson, though the police had refused to confirm it – had a family, people who loved her, people who were mourning her. Her killer must be caught. I needed to do everything possible to further that agenda.

And I will. I will, I promise.

But there was no denying, I thought, letting the hot water pummel me while I slicked shampoo through my hair, that the mere thought of discussing or even thinking about the dead woman in the wreck filled me with a hysterical dread.

I understood that this feeling, whatever it was, appeared to be getting worse and not better over time. Yesterday I had been shocked but able to discuss it with the police divers with some measure of normalcy.

Today I was trembling as I sat myself down on the changing room bench, rubbing another damp towel over my head before throwing it at the laundry basket, lost in my own dark thoughts.

Come on, Cass. Pull yourself together.

I turned upwards to grab my bra from the hook and in the corner of my eye, I caught a glimpse of something on the other side of the room.

There was another woman in the changing room with me.

She was also naked, her long dark hair streaming in wet rivers over her moist, gleaming back and obscuring her face, one arm raised above her head towards something behind her . . .

I opened my mouth to cry out in surprise, and as I did the woman did too, and in a split second I recognised her as myself – wide eyes with shadows like bruises, the little anklet tattoo of wildflowers, her mouth a perfectly round O of terror.

For a moment I had been a stranger to myself.

Oh my God, you are now *literally* terrified of your own reflection.

How Sid would have laughed! In my head, I was already composing this incident into the anecdote I would have told her over dinner in the old days, before I had gone away.

I missed her wildly in that moment, as though she had died and I was grieving her.

I pulled my knees under my chin, thinking.

There was no denying that I had reservations about Adam, and I was troubled by how obsequious my sister was around him, by their dishonesty with me.

But the fact remained that I had come all the way from Aus at fabulous expense, turned my back on my own dreams and ambitions, to help her out. However fraught I was feeling right now, this was still the plan, and I was going to stick with it.

I would try again with Adam.

I could do that for Sid's sake.

'Get over yourself,' I said aloud to the mirror, while combing my wet hair straight.

17

'Oh,' I said. 'Hi.'

I had been sidling around the door to the shop, head down, trying to avoid any journalists lurking nearby, so when I glanced within and saw Erik standing there regarding me, his muscular arms folded over his chest, a hot blush stole over me from my navel to my hairline.

'They've all gone,' was all he said in response to my greeting. 'I think the police spoke to them.'

'Oh, have they? Oh good,' I replied with a ludicrous fake nonchalance, as though he hadn't caught me sneaking backwards into my own shop. 'That's . . . good. Yes.'

I thought I caught the very slightest hint of a smile, quickly banished, as he turned back to the computer.

'It hasn't stopped them calling, though.' He looked down at the phone on the desk. 'We are sending everything to voicemail now.'

I threw back the hood I had been hiding under and surveyed mine and Sid's tiny empire. It looked every bit as disorganised as it had yesterday, and it smelled faintly of dust and rubber and salami sandwiches.

'I wanted to do some tidying,' I said.

He nodded gravely, not looking up, but offered me a *be my guest* gesture, spreading his hands wide.

'What are you up to?' I asked, seeing he was back on his nemesis, our computer.

'I am processing the refunds for the dive yesterday.'

'Did we persuade any of them to rebook instead?' I asked hopefully.

He merely shook his head at me.

Great, I thought. Just terrific.

I turned back to the shop.

Everywhere was dust and broken and lost tags, and after an hour I noticed that though the high street was as full and busy as it was every day in season, not a single person came into the shop.

'This bothers you,' he said after a while, as I turned away from gazing at the crowded street beyond, sighing.

He was leaning forward on the counter, his chin resting in his hand, watching me.

I didn't reply immediately. I was conscious of how inadequate we all were – me in my under-supervised dive, Sid hiding in the house in her dressing gown – and it made me ashamed. Mum and Dad would never have tolerated any of this.

'Yeah,' I said. 'It . . . it didn't used to be this way.'

He considered me, then nodded.

'Also, I think you do not want to be alone with your thoughts right now.'

I was momentarily too shocked to reply.

He was absolutely right.

I nodded.

He inhaled, his gaze drifting to the ceiling, as if he was lost in unpleasant memories of his own.

'These things – I know a little about them.' His heavy chin dropped to his hand again. 'The important thing is to know when it is getting too much. You can see things sometimes and they . . . they can consume you; do you understand?'

I knew he meant the woman on the *Undine*, and I definitely didn't want to talk about her.

Instead, I nodded again.

He stayed there for a long moment, looking at me, as though unconvinced I *had* understood him, but not inclined to press the issue. Then he sighed, as though defeated, and sank back to his computer. 'Did the police tell you when the *Undine* will reopen to divers?'

I shook my head. 'No.'

'That is unfortunate.'

'I know, believe me.' I folded my arms across my chest tightly. 'We're probably going to have to cancel the next class. And when it does reopen, it's going to need a new survey.'

He stared at me. 'A survey?'

'Yeah. There's a new current in the lower section. Near where we found the . . . you know.' I swallowed. 'Probably worth checking the structure.'

I had nearly said, *I'll have to check the structure*, but at the last minute had changed my mind.

If I could offload that task on someone else, I would. Hopefully Jimmy could sort it out.

'A new current?' He lowered his brows at me, as though he could read my thoughts. 'Interesting,' he said, before turning back to the screen.

When I picked up my bag ten minutes later, suddenly too tired to continue, and voiced my quiet goodbyes, he glanced up briefly with an acknowledging nod. But somehow I felt his eyes against my back all the way up Fore Street.

18

I had come back desperate for a nap, and to turn over what Erik had said in my mind.

I wondered what it was that he had seen, back in his past, that had made him so sensitive to my feelings. I would have to ask Sid and Adam about him, find out if they knew anything about his history.

The house had seemed empty when I opened the door, a couple of bottles of wine by way of peace offering clanking gently in my bag. The living room was empty but this time the curtains were open. I wondered if Sid had gone out.

I stowed the wine in the fridge and headed upstairs, poked my head in my old room. Everything looked exactly as it had yesterday – no attempt had been made to move anything.

I opened the guest bedroom with a disgusted shove of the door. On the bed, Tallulah stirred awake, stretched sensuously and yawned in greeting, and I felt a flicker of comfort in it.

I looked around the room, letting my fingers stroke through her luxurious cloudy fur. I didn't want to stay here tonight, but on the other hand, I didn't want to look like I was avoiding Sid and Adam, even if it was true.

I glanced at my phone. Nothing from Ben.

Well, it was understandable perhaps. I had run out on him the night before last. Maybe it was up to me to make contact.

Hi – what are you up to tonight? xxx

I wondered if the three kisses looked desperate, then realised I had already sent it and there was nothing I could do.

Ah well. In for a penny . . .

I lay down next to the cat, and the next thing I knew I was waking hours later to fourteen missed calls on my muted phone – all numbers I did not know – and the smell of cooking, something tomatoey, maybe pasta sauce.

Once again, I had that strange, disorienting feeling of being totally lost – not even sure which continent I was on.

And a single text from Ben:

Sorry Cass, busy tonight! Maybe catch you later?

I breathed in, biting down on my disappointment at this curt reply, and trying to shake my head free of my dreams. I had been underwater, in the darkness, trying to find that fluorescent yellow line that ran through the centre of the wreck, to escape, aware that every minute my air was running out and the woman in the *Undine* was looking for me.

She had something very urgent to tell me and I absolutely did not want to hear what it was.

I sat up in bed, my head resting uncomfortably against the wall, to listen to my voicemails – a parade of solicitous men and women all of whom wanted to talk to me about the woman in the *Undine*. They'd all seemed to stop calling about four o'clock, which I found odd. After the way I'd been woken this morning, I knew they didn't keep conventional office hours.

I carefully deleted every one, letting my head fall back, and then opened the BBC News website.

LIVVY SIMPSON: BODY IN SHIPWRECK NOT HERS

Police have confirmed a woman's body found within a Cornish shipwreck a hundred feet below sea level is not that of missing woman Olivia Simpson.

Olivia Simpson, 19, from Radcliffe, Manchester was reported missing when she went out to fetch firewood on the evening of 18 June while holidaying with her friends. Her phone was found abandoned in the grass near the farmhouse where they were all staying. She has been the subject of an extensive search.

A woman's body was found yesterday within the wreck of the *Undine*, a popular site frequented by scuba divers, by a dive instructor two miles from shore at Porthoustock and about 60 miles (96 km) from Bodmin. MV *Undine* is a merchant vessel that sank mysteriously in 1998 with the loss of all ten crew and lies at a depth of a hundred feet.

Devon and Cornwall Police said that while the body had initially matched descriptions of Olivia Simpson, DNA testing had ruled out that it belonged to her.

They also added: 'Livvy is a popular, hard-working young woman and a brilliant student, beloved by her family and friends, who was abducted while on holiday. We are appealing to any members of the public that know anything about her disappearance to come forward. Her family and friends are desperately worried about her. If you happened to be in the area of Anvil Point between 8:15 and 9 p.m. on the 18th of June, and saw anything suspicious or out of place, anything at all, please contact us urgently.'

The woman discovered on the *Undine* still remains unidentified and her remains do not match any currently reported missing person. The police have refused to rule out that she died through foul play and could not say how the woman ended up in the wreck.

I leaned back against the bedhead, stunned.
I had not found Livvy Simpson after all, it seemed.
But in that case, who had I found?

As I appeared at the kitchen door, sleepy and reluctant, Adam was sitting at the big oak table in my dad's chair, peering into his iPhone, a mug of coffee at his elbow. He was dressed in a pale-yellow rugby shirt and blue shorts, his feet bare.

'Hello, Cass,' he said, his expression mild.

I was being offered a truce, I realised. All things considered, I was inclined to accept.

'Hi, Adam – had a good day?' I glanced around. There were signs of activity – a spatula in the sink, red as though dipped in blood, a few crumbs of cheese on the counter.

No sign of Sid though. I glanced up at the clock: it was 5:50 p.m.

He yawned, stretched, just like the cat had. I had the sense he'd been sitting there with his phone for some time.

'Not bad. Went to see my sister in Redruth again after the class.' He rubbed his face. He looked tired. 'She's got terrible anxiety so she's not doing so great. Especially with all the publicity at the moment.'

'Publicity?'

'Yes, your body was all over the news today.'

I felt the hint of rebuke – that by discovering the body

of this missing person, I had somehow been instrumental in disturbing the mental health of one of his family members.

I had an irrational desire to justify myself but managed to bite this down.

Be civil, Cass.

'Yeah,' I said, taking a seat. 'Apparently it wasn't the woman everyone's been looking for.'

He shrugged, not looking away from his phone. 'I know. It's a shame, isn't it?'

A shame? That was a peculiar way to look it.

But maybe he was right. If she was dead, discovering that this was her body would at least have meant closure for her family.

I ran my finger over a dent in the wooden surface of the table. 'I guess all of this begs the question, though, who is our woman in the *Undine*?'

'Could be anyone.' Another tiny, single-sided shrug from him. 'Sad but true. Probably someone unlikely to be missed, if she's not been reported as gone yet.'

'I'm sorry to hear your sister was affected,' I said gravely. 'Nothing serious, I hope?'

'Yes, I'm afraid it is serious.' His square face grew wry. 'But since it's not likely to change, there's no point in dwelling on it.'

I nodded wisely. There was no way to ask any more questions about that, and he was clearly not in the mood to volunteer much more.

And maybe, I thought, his sister's illness was at least contributing to his behaviour. If so, I could see how it might make him difficult, how Sid might wish to propitiate him . . .

'How did your course go today?' I asked.

'Fine. Lots of awkward questions.' He bent back to his phone. 'As you might expect.'

'Sounds like mine. Never mind, I can think of a cure for that . . .'

I had pulled open the fridge door. My bottles of white wine were chilling in there, and since I felt I had earned a drink, I pulled out a Sauvignon Blanc, made to tear the plastic covering off the cork.

I turned to find him staring at me, his eyes narrow.

'It's a little early to start drinking, don't you think?' His voice was tight.

'No, I don't think it's too early.' I shrugged, but underneath I was disquieted. I remembered his arch reference to painting the town red last night, how nervous Sid had been.

It was setting off a simmering in my blood, despite all my promises to myself to behave.

'Do you want a glass?' I held up the bottle.

I was expecting him to refuse, but instead he looked away with a reluctant sigh. 'I suppose it wouldn't hurt.'

I fetched a trio of glasses, the third for Sid, and uncorked the wine in silence. What the hell had that been about?

The answer seemed obvious. He doesn't have a problem with drinking at this hour – he has a problem with *you and Sid* drinking, full stop.

Speaking of which . . .

'Where's Sid?' I asked. I had been expecting her to appear at any moment, but it was only just occurring to me that the house was silent.

'In bed,' he said, reaching out for the glass. 'She's not feeling too well.'

I felt a kind of sinking dread. It made sense; I knew that all that attention on the diving school would have been overwhelming for her. When Dad died, she hadn't stirred out of the house for a week.

'Oh, shall I pop up and bring her . . .'

'She's sleeping,' he said instantly.

And the thing was, she could have been sleeping. Especially if she'd been ill.

It was just that, for some reason, I didn't believe him.

'Ah.' I looked around me, and because the situation called for it, took a big glug of the wine.

He was drinking and had turned back to his phone again. The silence was awkward, oppressive, but I was reluctant to break it.

Maybe I could do something useful instead.

'Did you cook already?' I asked, trying to inject a note of enthusiasm into my voice.

'What?' he asked, not raising his head.

'Something smelled nice,' I said. 'I wondered if you'd eaten already. If not I could make . . .'

'Oh, we didn't cook,' he said, not meeting my gaze. 'I ate at Jem's and Sid's been in bed all afternoon. Perhaps you could get a takeaway.'

I blinked at him.

This statement was blatantly, demonstrably false. The scent of simmering tomatoes and herbs had seeped through the whole house, had visited me in my bed. The oven gave off a dying heat I could feel from my seat at the oak table. The dishwasher rumbled away next to the sink.

I didn't want to sit here with him any more, I realised. I wanted to go out, and I didn't care where I went or what it looked like.

'Takeaway sounds like a plan,' I said, straining to keep my voice normal. I swept up the small piece of film wrapping I had taken off the top of the bottle, stood up. The swing-top bin was in the corner of the room, next to the oven, and as I opened it to throw the wrapper away, I glimpsed a wet mess of red sauce and pasta at the bottom, as though a whole baking dish had been tossed into the rubbish.

What the hell?

I let the lid close, hiding the mangled remains. Why would you throw all that away? And lie about it?

Had he fought with Sid? Was that why she was upstairs now?

'The phone was ringing off the hook in the shop earlier, according to Erik,' he said, not looking up from his phone. 'Reporters wanting to talk to you.'

I looked over at him. 'I know, they broke into the Discover Scuba class this afternoon. I thought Jimmy was going to deck one of them.'

'The quickest way to have made them go away would have been to do what they wanted,' he said. 'They were offering excellent money, weren't they?'

I was too surprised to respond for a moment.

'I don't think the police would have liked that . . .'

'The police aren't paying our bills. You know we're haemorrhaging money. You could have probably got ten grand out of them just to tell them what they would have found out in the end anyway.'

I froze.

Ten grand? That was the sum the reporter had mentioned to me this morning.

How had he known that?

Because he'd spoken to them, of course.

'And while these journalists are hanging around we can't even do our jobs properly. Customers can't phone the shop. We might as well have had some cash out of them.' He sniffed. 'And now since the dead body in the ship is not even the right girl, we've missed the opportunity.'

I was horrified – by his coarseness, by his lack of empathy.

'Well, I'm very sorry you feel let down by my failure to sell somebody else's tragedy for money.'

'It's not me that's let down,' he said, and I felt that hint of rebuke again, no longer hidden. 'I mean, obviously it's very sad that this woman drowned, I'm not saying it's not. But you might want to think of consulting with Sid for a change before you turn down cash like that . . .'

Consulting with Sid? I saw, in a flash of insight, that to have consulted with Sid would be to consult with him.

And even if I had been inclined to accept the offer of cash, in what world did Adam think he would have been entitled to any part of it?

Apparently some new guy has taken over.

A flare of hot rage moved through me, and I was done trying to control it.

'There's absolutely nothing to talk about. How is appearing in the media talking about dead bodies in the wreck going to achieve anything but frightening customers away?'

'But . . .'

'We're supposed to be encouraging people to dive here again, not peddling horror stories in the papers.'

'That's all very well, Cass,' he said, trying to sound

reasonable, but his gaze was stony. 'But don't you think you should be checking in with Sid first?'

'Well, if that's a problem, I expect to hear that from Sid, and not you,' I replied, trying to control the tremor in my voice. 'And you know what? Seeing as you've already given yourself a day off this week and are at a loose end, make sure you get your stuff out of my room tonight, please.'

He turned back to his phone, tutting in disgust.

I have no idea if he looked up while I stalked out, but I do know he didn't reply.

19

'Cassie!'

Jimmy was still in his work clothes, a T-shirt and a pair of faded jeans. His bare arms were tanned and sinewy. He wrapped them around me and squeezed me tightly. 'I wasn't expecting you!'

Despite my mood, this raised a tiny smile in me.

Sid has always claimed that I was Jimmy's favourite – and in justice to her, and uncomfortable as it makes me to admit it, I think that's probably true. He seemed pleased to see me, at any rate.

It made a nice change that someone was.

'Hey, Jimmy. Can I come in?'

His keen grey eyes narrowed at me.

'Sure you can . . . what's up, girl? Is something wrong?'

I shrugged. 'I . . . yes.' I could feel the tears pushing against my eyelids, starting to wet my lashes. 'Something's very wrong.'

Without another word, he stood back from the door to let me in.

In many ways, it was Jimmy and his wife Mandy who raised us in Anvil Point while my parents dived all over the world.

Of the two of them, even now, it's Jimmy I remember. Jimmy who had time for us, who was affectionate and hugged and kissed us, who when we weren't diving took us out at the weekends to movies and zoos and to point at the gorier places of interest in National Trust castles, who taught us to fish for sea bass off the pier end.

It was Mandy who silently brought up the rear, bearing plastic Tesco bags that seemed to not just weigh down her sloping shoulders but also, judging from her trudging gait, her very soul. The bags were full of cheese and ham sandwiches with Branston pickle, Walker's roast chicken flavour crisps, little boxes of orange juice and tiny red Cox apples that crunched loudly when you bit into them. Sometimes there would be a couple of bars of Dairy Milk. This menu never varied.

Somewhere there is a big photo album of all these trips, the only remaining evidence of Mandy's dour presence in our lives – up in the loft, I think, where all the photographs of those years live. Now I think about it, it's strange that it's up there, instead of with the other three albums in the big dresser in the living room. Perhaps, in retrospect, my parents were uneasy with how often they abandoned us to pursue their dreams, though at the time I don't remember us being unduly troubled by it.

Or at least that's how *I* felt. I can't speak for Sid. I feel like I can't speak for Sid a lot lately, if I'm honest.

Every so often I think I should bring that album down, reunite it with the others, and yet somehow, I never do.

On their free weekends, they'd travelled all over the country for his diving, and she dutifully accompanied him, even though she was frightened of the water. When I think of Mandy, I think of *duty*.

This is why it was such a shock when Mandy left Jimmy, sometime after my fourteenth birthday, absconding into the night with only her heroically ugly tartan suitcase to her name.

I remember being, in some indefinable way, secretly relieved.

That said, Jimmy must have loved her. He'd never remarried, or, as far as I knew, even dated much. He went chasing after her – was gone for ten days, up in their old stomping grounds in Yorkshire, badgering her to return by all accounts.

But she never did.

Sid and I did not mourn her.

His living room was exactly as I remembered it. The inherited Persian carpet, the old squashy blue leather sofa, the campy lamp in the shape of a leaping salmon giving off its antique yellow light, and the rustic mantelpiece above the wood fire, with pictures of all my family resting on it.

My eye was drawn to one – Sid and I, in matching ruffled pink gingham bikinis, holding up crabs we'd caught off the end of the harbour wall, laughing at the camera with square, gappy teeth and unfeigned joy. Mandy stood behind us, and had even managed to raise a smile.

I remembered that day. Sid could have been no older than seven, I would have been six.

'Yeah,' he said, having spotted my interest. 'You were cute kids.'

I looked away, sat down on the blue leather, letting my bag drop to the floor. I was in no mood at that moment to recall our happier, less complicated youth. 'If you say so.'

He knew me too well, his gaze sharpening. 'What's up?'

I opened my mouth, shut it again.

'That man,' I said. I offered him a tense little shrug.

'What man?' He was taking a seat next to me. 'What's the matter with you, girl?'

'Adam.'

He tilted his head at me. 'What about him?'

'He's ... Jimmy, I just need to know – what's been going on with Sid?'

'Sid?' His brows drew together. 'How do you mean? I know she's been down a lot lately ... though with all that's happened, and the state of the world, you can hardly blame her ...'

'I mean,' I said, frustrated at my own bewilderment, 'all the time I was in Aus she was telling me that she's been so busy, that they're both working so hard, but ... it's just not true, Jimmy. Even in the taxi down, the driver was telling me that "some new guy had taken over".' I swiped at my wet face with my hand, 'And Erik tells me Sid doesn't set foot in the place any more.'

'Now, now, Cass, calm down. *Nobody's* been setting foot in the shop till recently. We've been shut with the pandemic ...'

'But the shop itself should still have been open for sales – even if they couldn't teach! They haven't been able to keep staff, or replace the stock, and ... and ...' I took a deep breath. 'And tonight he had the nerve to tell me off for not talking to those journalists for money. I should have consulted with Sid, apparently. Because of course he's got Sid wrapped round his little finger. You should see the way she jumps around him! Argh!' I growled, my helpless rage boiling over. 'I'm not sure who I'm madder at, her or him! I'm ... I'm worried about her, Jimmy!'

He sighed. 'Cass, I know it's difficult to come back and find this strange man there, but he's been good for her ...'

'Has he?' I nearly shouted, spittle landing on my lip. 'Everybody keeps telling me this – everyone in the pub, *oh, what a shame about poor Sid, isn't Adam so good to her!* But it's not how it looks when you spend any time with them both, Jimmy! He controls what she drinks, who she speaks to . . .'

My voice was raised, and I had the sense of myself sounding like a crazy person.

Jimmy's appraising expression was doing nothing to disabuse me of this notion.

'I know you don't believe me,' I said, throwing my hands up. 'And everybody seems to love this guy, but I don't think he's this saint who is helping her. I think he controls her, so he can strut around and pretend to be a dive shop owner. I . . . I *hate* him!'

For a long moment I sat there, breathing hard, while Jimmy regarded me closely, his hand on his chin.

Eventually he sighed. 'Listen, love, maybe he's not who you would have chosen for her . . .'

'Damn right I wouldn't, Jimmy. You know, he keeps her phone with him during the day . . .'

His eyes narrowed. 'What do you mean, he keeps her phone?'

'Just what I say!' I shrugged hugely. 'Keeps her phone with him. So she doesn't "waste time" doomscrolling. That's why she never replied to any of my texts or calls yesterday.' I snorted.

Jimmy blinked.

'Honestly, the sheer *greed*, Jimmy. He was having a go at me for not taking the money from that reporter. He already knew how much I'd been offered! He'd probably been scouting around for what we could get! Maybe even suggested it to them! As if, in any universe, us talking up finding a dead person in the *Undine* is going to help the business in some way! The *nerve*. And the *stupidity*.' My breath hissed out from between my teeth. 'And he's the *manager*, apparently.'

Jimmy was silent for a long moment.

'Well, she *could* have made him up to manager,' he said, scratching his cheek, as though deep in thought. 'I know he's involved with the banking and accounts. She didn't say she'd promoted him, though.'

'Hmph,' I said. 'This manager thing is just something he tells people, probably.'

He shook his head. 'I dunno. He does seem to have come into some money recently.'

'What?' I asked, a chill passing through me. 'How do you mean?'

Jimmy paused, as though he had said too much, and looked away, embarrassed. 'I mean, I don't know what she's paying him.' He scratched his scalp. 'But he's always flashing his cash. Got new clothes. And I know he's bunging money to that sister of his.'

I went still. 'Really?'

Jimmy appeared oblivious. 'But I don't know. He might have money of his own. He's always been a bit flash. So who knows?'

I didn't reply. My mind was running at a thousand miles an hour.

It had only just occurred to me that Adam must have access to my family business's bank accounts.

20

I woke on Jimmy's blue leather couch, to the sound of seagulls crying through the porthole windows.

For once, I realised, I had woken up at the right time for my time zone – morning sunlight was flooding the living room and I could hear Jimmy pottering in the kitchen, an electric kettle murmuring.

I sat upright, pushing off the green blanket that must have been thrown over me in the night. It smelled vaguely of coffee and the animal scent of Jimmy.

What time was it? I searched for my phone, found it lying underneath my hip. The warm screen read 7:12 and I'd had a text at 2:14 a.m.

It was Sid. It simply read: *where are u?*

A sharp pang of guilt then. A girl had been abducted from this very village, after all, so it was no wonder Sid was worried. I should answer that, however annoyed I was at her, and I did, quickly texting *Stayed at Jimmy's.*

'You're up,' said the man himself, coming in with a mug of coffee.

'Yeah,' I rubbed my bleary face, pondering my phone. 'Sorry for crashing out like that.'

'You're all right.' He gestured dismissively, as though this was of no moment. 'Better you were here than trying to walk home at night. Especially lately. Did you sleep well?'

I smiled at him, grateful. 'Like a log. And without pills,

for the first time since I got here. This couch is comfier than it looks.'

He nodded in approval. 'I've only got toast,' he said, and looked out the window with a scowl, as though to warn the weather to behave itself. 'Want some?'

'No, thanks.' I wasn't hungry. I set down the mug. 'I probably need to get going after this.'

He raised his eyebrows. 'The shop doesn't open until nine.'

'I know,' I said. 'But there are a couple of things I want to tackle there first.'

21

I let myself quietly into the silent shop. I had things to do today.

The first was to look up the class schedule for the week.

This weekend had nothing scheduled, which astonished me. We were in high season. We should have been able to fill every day of every weekend through to October.

I scowled and opened up the achingly slow desktop computer out on reception.

The bank's website opened from the bookmark, and I typed in our details from the password manager on my phone.

Click.

The username or password is not correct.

Dammit.

A few more tries convinced me of the truth – the password had been changed. Perhaps not that strange considering I'd had no cause to access it for the best part of two years, I tried to tell myself, though my heart was already beating faster.

I'd never had the account on my phone – before I'd left, it was my dad, Jimmy and Sid that had handled the banking, but I'd known his password on the work computer for emergencies.

Maybe I could ask the bank to set me up, since I was a

director, but who knew how long that would take? And whether I would be able to keep such access secret from Sid, and more importantly, Adam?

I'd have to risk it. I didn't want to tip my hand to either Sid or Adam right now.

I sighed. So much for quickly checking out the account.

And I had one more thing to do, and I was not going to enjoy it.

Very disappointing
Reviewed by DiveCrazy3848, 21 June 2021

Very sad to see what's happened to this once excellent dive shop. They cancelled on us the night before a Wreck Diving course after me and the wife had travelled five hours to get there with two hours notice. No apologies. No explanation, something about problems with the boat. Luckily we were passed on to AquaCulture in Newquay who were an absolute joy to dive with – thanks Alan for the scalloping tips!

SHOCKINGLY UNPROFESIONAL!!!
Reviewed by BlakeneyLass, 14 June 2021

Worst dive shop in cornwall now, Run by rob brownriggs daughters and they are moneyhungry and dont seem to care he must be turning in his grave,, sent me down with broken depth gauge and manager rude and dismisive when I pointed it out, made out like I was just a moaner. New diver had to make ascent alone when problems with regulator I was shocked – think they are shortstaffed and manager lazy our divemaster grace was the only good thing about the whole trip would give no

stars if I could so if you dont want to drown avoid BLUE
HORIZONS!!!!

Great dive, terrible dive shop . . .
Reviewed by xxSpursForever67xx, 12 June 2021

Had a bad feeling when I showed up at the shop as the
guy 'running' the dive (I use this phrase loosely) couldn't
run a p**s-up in a brewery. Lost our names, lost our
booking, though Grace and the older guy (sorry didn't
catch his name – Timmy or Jimmy I think) were nice and
helpful. The guy in charge couldn't even work his own
new expensive dive computer and Grace had to show
him how. Sarcastic and rude, hardly checked anybody's
equipment but possibly a good thing as he might have
killed them at the rate he was going. An hour late getting
out to the Undine wreck site as boat out of diesel
(couldn't you have fuelled up BEFORE the paying customers arrive?) and not enough instructors to divers so
all felt very haphazard.

But the Undine is a wonderful wreck – a real once in a
lifetime dive. I was with less experienced friends this trip,
so next time might try the penetration dive. But not with
Blue Horizons I'm afraid . . .

I glanced over the photos included in the site. There
were the early ones – the *Mustang Sally*, the new people
carrier, sharks and sea anemones flashing through the
corridors of the *Undine* while divers waved, gave happy
thumbs up signs underwater. My dad posing with various
visitors, which made my chest squeeze tight. *Why aren't you
here, Dad?* Sid and I smiling on the prow of the boat in

mocha brown tans and flimsy bikinis. Then the pictures changed – close-ups of broken equipment, dirty changing rooms. There were a couple of a young woman in a dry-suit with a big toothy smile and dark henna-red hair – this must be Grace, I supposed, who'd quit the week before I arrived.

At the moment we were averaging three stars, and this was over the life of our business, I suspected, when we had never been less than 4.9 when my dad was alive.

I couldn't read any more. I leaned back in my chair and buried my head in my hands.

At this rate, I thought, was there anything left to save? What did I hope to achieve?

The door opened, the bell giving a little chime.

I glanced up.

Sid was standing in the doorway, her expression shifty and also – and this was the thing that broke my heart – vulnerable.

We regarded each other for a long moment.

'Hello, stranger,' I said.

She didn't respond, but came further into the shop, stopping at the desk.

There was something very strange about her affect, as though she had not been in here before. Or perhaps it had been so long that she'd not had a chance to see the change in the place.

'Where were you last night?' she asked. 'We were worried.'

The temptation to tell her to *drop the we* was successfully resisted.

'I don't know why you can't make the effort to get along with Adam,' she said, not looking at me. 'You don't have

164

to be best buddies with him. But he's with me now. We're a couple. And if we're going to save the business . . .'

'Well, I'm glad you're thinking of saving the business. Though maybe it would have been better to think about it before all these reviews started appearing.' I roughly turned the monitor around to face her. 'This is the worst dive shop in Cornwall. Apparently.'

Her face tightened, but she didn't seem inclined to read the screen. I realised, with a little shock, that none of this was a surprise to her.

And that gave me pause.

'Sid,' I said, as gently as I could, 'what is going on?'

She bit her lip, stayed silent.

'Sid?'

'I . . . I just can't do it any more. Any of it. And you may not like him, but Adam h-helps me. He's under so much pressure. I keep *telling* you this, and you keep not hearing me. He's got me to worry about. He's got his sister to worry about. I'm not asking for much, but just a little . . .' She sighed. 'He's taking me away.'

'What?' I had a sudden vision of men in white coats turning up for her.

'He's going to encourage me to dive again. He thinks if we go somewhere nice, somewhere low pressure, I might – I might get back into it.'

It was my turn to be silent. Despite the fact that it left us short-handed again, this was, on the face of it, a great idea.

It was just that I didn't trust him to do a single thing he said.

'Where is he thinking of taking you?' I asked.

'I don't know,' she said. She wouldn't meet my gaze, and I wondered what was up. 'Malta maybe, or Egypt . . .'

I blinked at her.

'Where are you getting the money for that?'

She flushed, angry, and I realised immediately it was the wrong thing to say.

'Adam has money. He inherited some recently. What are you trying to imply?'

'I'm trying to imply that a week diving in high season is expensive.' I was trying to stay calm, finding it hard. For God's sake, Sid *knew* this.

'It's not a week. It's just four days. We'll be back by Tuesday.'

'You're going *tomorrow*? You were just going to leave me here on my own with a day's notice?'

'Why is that a problem?' She crimsoned. 'There's no classes . . .'

'You know, Sid, it's not like I think you don't deserve a holiday. But does it have to be right this minute? I mean, they just found a dead woman in the *Undine* and . . .'

'I should have known you'd be like this!' she hissed, suddenly venomous.

I was bewildered. 'What are you . . . ?'

'You've only been back four days and already it's all about *you*, isn't it? Accusing Adam of taking over. Moaning about the work. Sodding off to Jimmy's for the night without even a message when there's some psycho running around Anvil Point attacking women – we were both *so* worried! You never even texted us back to let us know whether you were alive or dead!'

'I did text you!' I blurted out, stung at the injustice of this.

'You know, Cass, I didn't want to believe it, but Adam says you're just jealous at seeing someone else happy . . .'

A white heat seemed to envelop me, and before I could stop myself I said:

'*Happy?* Is *that* what you are?'

Her eyes blazed. 'I absolutely can't be arsed with you when you're like this.' Her voice was high, hard. 'It makes me *insane.*'

I was about to open my mouth, to protest again, as the words died in my throat. A flash of cunning struck me.

Let her go. Let her go and take him with her.

Use this time to get to the bottom of what's been going on here.

But I was still unbearably hurt by her doubt of me, her disloyalty. So, Adam had told her he thought I was jealous. Adam, who had her phone, had told her I hadn't texted her back . . .

We would see about Adam.

'Enjoy your trip!' I called out bitterly behind her, as she stormed out the door.

I got back to the house late, reluctant to return any sooner.

After a day spent in the shop, fighting with the bank about access, I'd driven out to Falmouth in the van, had a quiet dinner by myself out by the docks, watching the cruise ships sail in and out as the sun set, had a chat with Georgia.

Finally, I remembered something I'd been meaning to do.

I took out my phone, opened YouTube and searched for Russell Bowermann.

As suspected, he did indeed have a YouTube channel. I watched a couple of his videos – the first where he dived Hauley Pond in Kentucky, absurdly describing it as a 'highly dangerous cave dive that had claimed many lives!!!'

(the cave itself barely qualified as a cavern, and the deaths had been more due to inexperience and alcohol rather than technical diving). This and a few more like it showcased his bad trim and taking of stupid risks, but I saw nothing about the *Undine*.

Or at least not yet.

Dusk had deepened into night, and the air had grown chilly. I pocketed my phone and stood up.

To my relief, the whole house was dark as I drove the van back up, but still, as I hopped down out of the cab, searching for my keys, the silence gave me a chill.

Who knew who was lurking in the darkness?

After all, if this Livvy Simpson hadn't been able to be safe here, in our quiet village in her holiday home, who was to say that I would be?

I stood for a long moment, listening, but heard only the faraway tolling of the Manacle buoy.

I quietly let myself in, not keen to see either Adam or Sid. Two suitcases were already resting at the bottom of the stairs.

Once I crept up them, I saw to my surprise that my old room had finally been cleared out. It was sad-looking and none too clean, but Adam's things were gone, including the bedding off the bed. None of my things had been returned, giving it a shiftless, uninhabited air, but still.

It was a step in the right direction.

It was too late to move across – I would do it tomorrow once they were gone. I quietly let myself into the guest bedroom.

Once I was there, lying flat on my back staring at the ceiling, of course I couldn't sleep.

There was a soft scratching at my door. Someone had not forgotten me. When I creaked it open, there was Tallulah in her cloud of grey fur, and she shouldered her way in and up on to the bed with the air of someone on important business.

'Hey, Ladycat,' I said, sitting down next to her and scratching her between her tufted ears while she meowed softly at me. 'I missed you,' and she looked away contemptuously, because that's what she usually did.

I lay down on the bed, curled around her, and she stretched out under my hands as I ran them along her flanks.

'Someone needs feeding up,' I said.

'A-rouw.'

Yeah, Tallulah. Me too.

I rolled on to my back, while Tallulah kneaded the top of the duvet with her paws, her face a picture of concentration.

Everything just felt wrong. Like Sid's early night had last night. Like this sudden whirlwind trip abroad. Ben hadn't texted me since last night. His last message – *Maybe talk to you later!* – had set me off worse than explicit rejection would have.

Surely he knew how horrible it had all been. Surely even as a friend you would offer a tiny crumb of support.

It was all just . . .

The only thing that was the same was Jimmy. That was something.

I didn't think I felt tired, but somehow, without trying, I was fast asleep on the bed, sinking into unquiet dreams about the *Undine*.

22

'Well, shit.'

Shannon was breathing hard.

She'd been looking for a romantic Gothic getaway, it was true, but she was already getting far more than she'd bargained for. Still ten miles from St Ives and she was stranded alone in Olly's massive, unwieldy car on a narrow, high-hedged country road. And in near total darkness too.

The only illumination was the inanely blinking hazard lights on either side of the car windows, revealing and then concealing an uneven green verge and a stretch of potholed asphalt. Not a single glint of moonlight penetrated the leafy overhanging branches.

'LOW AIR PRESSURE IN RIGHT FRONT TYRE,' said the car's user screen, with a little picture of the offending tyre accompanying it, as though worried she couldn't read, or tell left from right.

She didn't know what she'd hit, probably a pothole, but she'd felt the bump and the bang, as the car exploded into a litany of electronic warnings and the wheel juddered beneath her hands.

She had steered it, heart racing, into the side of the narrow road, narrowly avoiding burying it in the leafy yew hedge.

In addition to the screen message there was a gentle but insistent repeating chime, and she couldn't for the life of her work out how to turn the sodding thing off.

'Yes, yes, I know,' she hissed at it, unsnapping her seat belt and turning off the ignition.

This seemed to do the trick.

She sat back in the huge seat and sighed. Olly's car was so expensive and high-tech it was effectively impenetrable to her.

She should have come in her own little Mini, and not let him talk her into this, she thought with a sigh.

Now what?

She had changed a tyre once before, assuming there was even a spare, but it was years ago, just before starting uni, and she'd been with good-natured friends and in broad daylight. Furthermore, she hadn't still been in her work suit, now damp with chilled sweat after her near-death experience, and the cute pair of black Bottega Veneta mules that clicked seductively as she roamed the marble corridors of Braybeck & Kemp, but which she suspected would have a hard time coping with the soggy grass of the verge and its edge of spilled soil.

This was so stupid.

'There's nothing to worry about. The car practically drives itself,' Olly had boasted.

Wish it would do that now, she thought. For fuck's sake.

This whole break was supposed to be a treat, something she'd been looking forward to for months after grinding, fifteen-hour workdays and thankless weekends spent in front of the laptop. She was making all this money, Olly said. It was time to start spending some.

And yet everything today had been oddly ill-starred, full of unpleasant portents. She'd come into work at dawn even though she was supposed to be on holiday, because of course there were things to finish off before she left, because nothing ever stopped at Braybeck & Kemp, no matter how hard you might wish it. She'd arrived to find an email from her top portfolio client, cross because she'd contacted him too late the previous evening. She'd emailed her boss, Helena, about it, who'd been unexpectedly sharp with her.

The day had passed in an ominous fug of anxiety.

She should have changed back into something more suitable for her rugged Cornish week away when she'd returned to the flat, but the new flatmate had been having a screaming row with some guy on the phone and Shannon had simply picked up her pre-packed case and fled into what she called Olly's 'Chelsea Tractor', then spent ten minutes trying to work out how to start it – there was no visible keyhole for the ignition – while trying not to punch the dashboard.

Well, there was no need to punch anything now, she told herself sternly. She needed to phone the AA, though when they asked where she was, what the hell was she supposed to tell them? She'd been following the satnav through winding country roads for hours in the dark.

She wanted to curl up on the front seat in weariness and misery. She'd been driving for six hours already, most of the way in bad traffic. She was exhausted.

Don't be stupid. Pull yourself together. Phone them. They'll find you eventually. They've got this thing where they prioritise single women stranded on their own, don't they?

When she lifted the phone off the passenger seat, though, there was a single bar of signal, not enough to call anybody.

She realised, with a little pang, that what she really wanted to do was phone Olly.

That too was off the table.

'Shit.'

She threw the phone on to the passenger seat in disgust. Looked like she was walking to somewhere with a landline – there was a farmhouse a few miles back, with lights . . .

At the very least, she could get her trainers out of the suitcase. Comfy shoes would make everything better.

As the door swung open and she half-stepped, half-jumped down into the sinking grass of the verge, she was struck by the silence. She could hear nothing – not wind, not birdsong, not even the roar of the A-road she'd left behind a mere twenty minutes ago.

Instead, there was only the very slightest rustle of leaves, as though they were whispering to each other, and the sweetish, earthy smell of rotting mulch.

She could see fifty feet in front and thirty feet behind the car in its head and taillights, and after that, absolutely nothing. Not even the sky was visible. The darkness was velvet and absolute, almost solid.

The thought of walking anywhere in it filled her with horror.

'Right,' she said to herself, to break the silence, and immediately her voice felt too loud to her, like the crack of a rifle. Instead, she fell into a watchful quiet, stumbling around the car to the blood-red lights at the back, pressing and manipulating the stupid key until suddenly, like a vampire's coffin yawning wide, the boot opened in slow motion.

'Ahah!' she said, feeling a tiny, ridiculous burst of pride. *Behold me! I am mistress of technology!*

Her trainers were at the very bottom of her suitcase, of course, and she didn't have time or patience to repack or even zip it shut. As she leaned on the tailgate and threw one mule into the mess behind her it seemed to her that things were getting lighter – perhaps she was growing used to the dark – or even better, someone was coming.

A vehicle was drawing near, and suddenly it was upon her – some kind of van – she had broken down on a bend, and any inattentive driver would plough right into her.

This one, however, did not – instead roaring past her before she could even attempt to flag him down.

'Wait!' she yelled, waving her arms after him, her remaining shoe tumbling off her foot as she ran into the road, hearing her voice shrill with panic. 'Wait!'

Miraculously, the van stopped. It waited for a fraction, just long enough for her to wonder whether this was a good idea, when suddenly a man's head in a fisherman's cap poked out of the driver's window.

'Sorry, love, didn't see you there! Are you all right?'

'Um, yes – I mean, no – the tyre's burst – and I've got no phone signal, and . . .'

'Oh, right!' The van's white reversing lights glowed alive and he was rolling very slowly back to her. 'You're in a dangerous spot here, love. Let me have a look.'

He pulled up on the verge right in front of her and jumped down. He hurried towards her, his face hidden in the shadow of the van, and she felt, in that instant, a sudden urge to run, to flee into that bible-blackness and take her chances there, but just as suddenly it was gone – wiped away perhaps by his business-like smile, the way he seemed to be more interested in the problem of the car than in her, in the way that men often are.

'Where you off to?' he asked, swiping the hat from his head while he surveyed the car.

'St Ives. My boyfriend's rented us a cottage for the week. He's flying in but asked me to bring the car up.'

'Very nice,' he said, peering at it, then into the boot. 'Are these yours . . . ?'

'Yeah, sorry,' she flushed, quickly snatching up her lacy underwear and stuffing it into the case before standing back, keeping her distance. 'I was just getting my trainers out now, and . . .'

He simply chuckled.

'I . . .' He was gingerly lifting the case out of the way. 'I don't see a spare in here, love. The nut for it would be here.'

The colour drained from her face. 'What? There must be a spare.'

'Not necessarily.' He did not seem concerned. 'Sometimes these premium cars have run-flat tires.'

'Run-flat . . . ?'

'Yeah. They're a new thing. They're reinforced. So, you can keep driving on them for a while, get to a garage.' He had removed something from the back of the car, about the size of a laptop but thin. 'If it's that, you're laughing.' He turned to her. 'Here, take this.'

He had given her a little free-standing hazard sign, the kind you place on the road, in light reflective paint.

'They can still blow out though,' he was saying. 'And the roads round here, they're not the best.' He glanced up and down the road, then back at her, winked. 'Our road tax in action, eh? Let me have a look, you might be all right – which one is it?'

A little sigh of relief went through her, a slight unhitching. She might be able to just drive out of this.

'Oh, the front right tyre.'

'All right. You go put this in the road, about twenty feet up, so no one runs into the back of us, yeah?'

'Oh, sure, yeah . . .'

Twenty feet. That would be just on the bend, still in the reach of the taillights.

She bent down, arranged it carefully near the verge, where car headlights would pick it up.

'Will that do?' she asked, turning around, and saw to her surprise that he was nowhere near the car, in fact he was walking right up to her, fast, too fast, and suddenly there was a stunning blow to the side of her head and everything went black and grey and she was sliding downwards, down to the broken tarmac.

Her cheek rolled against it, and it was icy cold.

She should scream now, she realised, but somehow it was all too much effort – she couldn't think straight, she couldn't speak, and it hurt, and now, with a preternatural strength that even in her bewildered stupefaction she realised was powered by a vicious, bottomless need, he was dragging her towards the van, his iron hands under her armpits, and her knees were grazing bloodily, the tights ripping against the road.

She had to do something.

Lashing out, like a paralytic drunk, one arm flailed in his direction, connected uselessly against his hard shin. It was little more than a pat.

With a casual backhand he slapped her head so hard her teeth rattled, the darkness deepening, and she was being thrown forward into the gaping void at the back of his van, and with a slam, the doors were sealed behind her, trapping her in darkness.

23

I was awake long before Adam's tedious alarm (the theme to *Grange Hill*, of all things) burst into electronic life down the hallway.

I sat upright against the headboard in the thin pre-dawn light, a novel I couldn't concentrate on lying open on my phone. The cat sprawled over my thighs, sighing deeply, as though I exasperated her.

Within minutes of the alarm, I could hear them stirring, one of them moving into the bathroom – Adam, I suspected, while Sid padded downstairs. She felt close enough to touch, and yet already on the other side of the world. Soon the kettle was boiling.

In my lap, Tallulah twitched her feather duster tail into my face, making hungry meowing noises.

'Patience,' I murmured, as the toilet flushed. 'Wait.'

Downstairs, there was no sound, except an occasional murmur of voices.

Perhaps they're being quiet so as not to wake you. You know Sid is avoiding you. And, let's be honest, you are avoiding Sid. At least for now.

Then there was the sound of tyres crushing the gravel outside. This must be the taxi. For the first time that morning I heard Adam's voice – a swift barked 'Come on' – and the pair of them moving through the hall to the door – I was glad I had resisted the temptation to sneak out on to the landing.

I peered out through the window, keeping low. Adam was crunching out on to the drive below me, and I could see the coin-sized bald spot at the top of his head. He looked much older from this angle, so much so I wondered for an instant if I was looking at the right man. He leaned in to talk to the taxi driver, a pale, middle-aged woman I didn't know with tired eyes, who was climbing out of the cab, popping the boot open.

Behind him, Sid appeared, dressed in dowdy, saggy jeans and a faded red top, slowly dragging a large wheeled case. Her pale hair shone like a living flame in the pre-dawn gloom, and I felt a spark of grief, as though she was leaving me forever. She looked dazed as the driver took the case from her, while Adam hopped into the back seat.

'Come on,' he snapped from inside. 'We'll miss the plane.'

I wanted to vault through the window at him, I realised. I saw myself landing on the gravel below like some kind of nightshirt-clad ninja, just before I ran up and smacked him right in his spoiled, petulant mouth with a curled fist.

My hand tingled, as though the ghosts of his loosened teeth had scratched it.

Just then, as I was distracted, daydreaming, Sid's head turned, and she stared up at me from the drive.

I blinked, and then, before I knew what I was doing, I had dropped to the floor, my head dipped beneath the sill.

She couldn't have seen me, I said to myself, not in the semi-darkness and with just the top of my head and my eyes showing. She couldn't have.

I waited, for a long moment, and it was only as I heard the car driving away that I realised what I'd been waiting for — it was for her to come up here, to pet Tallulah's head, to give me a hug and say goodbye.

And I would have wished her a safe trip, and for her to have fun, even though I didn't believe for a minute that she would.

Still.

They were gone now.

I climbed to my feet. It was time to act.

24

The door to our main home office was locked.

I'd been meaning to look carefully through the bills and payroll, perhaps find the password for the banking. But I had never known this door to be locked. The key had stuck out, unturned, from the keyhole ever since I could remember, from when this room had been my mum's domain.

But someone had used it now and taken it with them, as the knob resolutely refused to budge more than a few degrees. I peered through the keyhole into the office beyond. The old computer sat on the desk, quiescent and blameless. Behind it, the windows were firmly closed, probably locked. Papers were stacked in high, untidy piles; some had been there so long that they had started to fade and discolour in the sunlight.

I leaned back on my heels.

'Shit,' I said softly to myself.

I stood up and stomped off to the bedroom, looking for my phone.

Tallulah glanced up from her nap as I quickly texted Jimmy, who I had taken into my confidence –

He's locked the office door.

I wasn't expecting a response – it was still only quarter to six in the morning. But to my surprise he responded instantly:

I sighed.

I know.

The phone rang.

'How can it be locked?' He sounded belligerent, as though this was a personal affront. 'I didn't know there was a lock in it.'

'No. It's always had a lock, and a key in it, we just never used it.'

'You should ring him and ask where he's put the key. Do it now. Make some excuse. Tell him . . .'

'No, Jimmy, I won't. I don't want to give him any advance warning that I think something's up. What if he comes back?'

'But, Cass, he must already know you think something's up if he's locked the . . .'

'Not necessarily. I don't think he would have gone at all if he had any idea what I had in mind.' I brushed my hair behind my ears, walking back into the hall to the offending door. 'He's probably been locking it for a while now, and I've just never noticed it before. He's a controlling guy, it probably comes naturally to him.'

Silence. Then, 'So what are you going to do?'

I bit my lip, considering it. 'I'm going to look for a key.'

It was a big house surrounded by at least five outbuildings, not counting the tiny garden shed, so of course I searched for at least an hour, and found a bumper crop of orphaned keys, rattling around the bottom of drawers, lying abandoned in dusty repose in old vases, hanging from hooks in our garage like tiny silver bones. Of the dozen or so I found, only three would have stood a chance of fitting the mortice lock, and of course none did, not even remotely. I was hot and bothered by the time I threw the last one down on to the pile and sat back on my haunches, scowling at the wood.

The key was doubtless in Adam's pocket. I was wasting time.

Maybe I should admit defeat and head down to the shop for a council of war with Jimmy . . .

The shop.

'All right,' I muttered, getting to my feet, while Tallulah, having slept through the morning and now hungry, came purring and rubbing her smoky self against my calves. I reached down and tickled her behind her arms. I hadn't thought of checking the shop. 'One last try.'

As I came in, Erik glanced up from the computer, again with the aura of someone who has been interrupted in the middle of an argument.

'Hi,' I said, curious. 'You're in early. What are you up to?'

He raised a dark eyebrow at me. 'Logging dives. I could not do this yesterday.'

'You couldn't? Were we busy yesterday?'

He shook his head, with something like pity. 'No, Cassandra. I did not have the paperwork then. We were not busy.'

'Oh.'

He considered my crestfallen face for a long moment. 'I sold a wetsuit. And some kid tried to steal a dive mask from the display.'

'Really?' I asked. I was astonished at their boldness. I'm

not sure I would try stealing anything with Erik behind the counter, myself.

I sighed, my mood already sinking, and headed into the little office at the back.

Once more I turned everything upside down, but there was no sign of any keys.

I also riffled through the big metal filing cabinet. Normally we filed client and admin paperwork here, and things that required some measure of confidentiality, like payroll and bills – in short, the things I was interested in – up at the house.

I could see that nothing much within appeared to have been touched or added to since last year.

That included the folder marked *Insurance*.

My fingers stilled, as I plucked it out of the steel drawer.

I looked through the documents, twice. No sign of any new ones since March 2020.

My heart was pounding.

This was potentially very serious. The insurance covered us for all the usual things – fire, theft, flood – but crucially, it provided liability in case one of the customers had an accident and sued us.

We specialised in what insurers would call a *high-risk activity*. Rich, frequently older people undertook to breathe pressurised air in fraught, dangerous underwater environments like shipwrecks with us. Even under the very best management my dad could provide, there were constant minor scrapes and near misses.

If Russell Bowermann sued us, we could potentially lose everything we owned. Perhaps even go to prison . . .

I sat down at the desk, trying to think, or perhaps more accurately trying not to cry.

Come on, Cass, pull yourself together. Sid at least wouldn't be that stupid, surely. Surely. They might have done it online. It could be at the office, in those piles of paper.

I tried ringing Jimmy, listened to his phone go straight to voicemail, then remembered that he was taking the *Mustang Sally* in for a repair this morning, and might be out of phone range.

I needed to get into that office at the house. *Now.*

And it seemed then that my fears, that I'd been trying to keep at arm's length, were collapsing in on me. Adam was running our business into the ground and Sid could not be depended upon to help me.

And now I suspected that they hadn't paid our liability insurance.

'Hey.'

I looked up, startled. Erik stood in the doorway and was waggling a mug at me. 'Coffee?'

'Um, yes, please,' I mumbled.

He vanished, then reappeared a second later, his dark blue eyes sharp. 'Are you all right?'

I opened my mouth, about to insist that yes, of course I was all right, but then the words simply wouldn't come.

I sat there, like a baby bird, aware of myself as ridiculous, as illogical, and burst into tears.

He started, as though I had done something visibly threatening, and vanished into the hall, like a fish disturbed in a coral forest, flickering to some hidden hole.

I buried my head in my arms on the table, and now, in the absence of witnesses, my unhappiness and terror burst forth, soaking my hair where it lay across my face. What if we were uninsured and taking people on high-risk scuba courses? What if Adam had embezzled our money, left our taxes unpaid? What if we . . .

A shadow fell over me.

Erik was staring down at me, holding a small water glass filled with clear liquid.

'Drink this.' He set it down next to me on the table with an unforeseen delicacy. A faintly alcoholic aroma arose from it.

I was so surprised that I stopped crying, instantly, like children do.

'It's *akvavit*. It will be good for you.' He folded his arms.

'Um, thank you,' I said, taking it into my hands.

He fell into tense, silent waiting, so I felt somehow obliged to take a sip. It blazed all the way down, burned into the centre of my chest. I burst into a round of staccato coughing.

He watched me with an appraising expression tinged with approval, as though I was reacting in the correct way.

'Uh, thanks,' I squeaked out again. I swallowed against my excoriated throat, breathing in an astringent, earthy aftertaste of caraway and citrus. I swiped at my wet eyes. 'Sorry. I'm making a fool of myself, I know . . .'

'You are not making a fool of yourself. It is none of my business, true, but it's difficult for you. I can see this.'

I glanced up sharply at him. He was a man who, as far as I could tell, only ever noticed me in the periphery of his vision. I wondered what he thought he knew about me.

I sipped again, to avoid further conversation.

'You are looking for something here, yes? Perhaps I can help you find it.'

'I'm looking for a key to the office up at the house. Did you see Adam or Sid leave a key here . . .'

'Cressida leaves nothing here.' His eyes narrowed into dark blue slits. 'She never comes here. Only him.'

I blinked, lost in thought. He'd told me this before about her.

Sid never came here . . .

A moment of clarity, then.

I had been inclined to think Sid's absence from the business was about my dad and the accident, based on what she'd told me. It may even have been that, in the beginning.

But now it occurred to me that it probably didn't suit Adam to have Sid about, dealing with bills and banks, asking too many questions, seeing how little work he actually did.

Oh, I'm not leaving. I'm not going back to Australia, even if I could set off there tomorrow.

I'm not going anywhere until I get to the bottom of this.

'What is it?' Erik cocked his head at me. 'Are you all right?'

'Yes,' I said, possibly with too much emphasis. 'I'm fine.'

He made a tiny grunting noise, as though doubting me.

'You said the office is locked?' he asked.

'Yes.'

'You have no key?'

'No.'

'And you don't want that man to know you have been there?'

I paused. This was a boundary, I realised. If I answered this, I would be drawing Erik into my confidence. I'd better be sure I trusted him first.

Yet it took me a mere moment to decide to cross it. I don't know why I did. I knew nothing about him.

Only that his contempt for Adam was so ingrained that he hardly ever referred to him by name.

At that moment, this seemed an excellent qualification.

'That's right,' I said.

'Have you tried picking the lock?'

'What? I . . . I don't know how to do that.' I craned up at him, curious. 'And you do?'

'It is like most things.' He offered me a wide, thin expression that was not quite a smile. 'Easy when you know how.'

Erik certainly made lock-picking look easy. He tersely requested two hairpins, which he bent and twisted with his strong, thick fingers as though they were putty. Within moments of applying them to the lock he threw them down, muttering that he needed something stronger.

'Like what?' I had not yet found the courage to ask him where he had learned this occult skill.

He scratched his head, thinking.

'Maybe I can double up the hairpins. Maybe. Get me two more.' A pause. 'Please.'

When I returned, I was surprised to see Tallulah sitting on her haunches a mere two feet away from him, watching him thoughtfully as he peered through the keyhole.

Normally, Tallulah fled whenever strangers entered the house, like a gun-metal ghost flickering for a moment on the edge of your vision then instantly vanishing.

For some reason, he intrigued her.

'You have them? Good. Excellent.'

Again the arcane, effortless twisting of pins together,

bending them into gnomic angles, while I watched, as fascinated as Tallulah, and before I knew it, he had pressed them into the keyhole and there was a couple of tiny clicks, then a single loud one.

He reached up, pulled on the handle, and the door swung open.

He grinned then, his teeth as sudden, white and visible as a shark's before it attacks.

I was almost shocked. I had never seen him really smile before, I realised.

'See? Easy.'

The office smelled close, a little musty, but somehow, underneath it all, was the very faintest ghost of the incense my mum had once burned when she worked in here, a shimmer of jasmine scent. My dad would not permit her to burn it anywhere else in the house – or more properly, moaned endlessly about the 'hippy stink' if she tried to. But this place had always been her preserve and her will had been law here, and catching the whiff of it now I felt her presence around me, buoying me up.

'All good?' he asked from the door, lingering on the threshold like an uninvited vampire.

'Yes, fine . . . wait – how do I lock it again?'

'I will do that. When you're finished.'

I nodded.

Maybe I didn't want to lock it again.

Sunlight streamed in through the windows – the room was small, true, but cosy and full of light, despite the untidy sheafs of paper and lack of proper airing.

I slid into the old office chair with its overstuffed red cushion, feeling it creak beneath my weight as I faced the computer screen. And as I did, I felt, despite my unhappiness, my dread, an undeniable sense of rightness, of belonging. Whatever I discovered here, I was realising that it would be my responsibility, not Sid's, to rescue us.

Erik folded his arms, studying me. It was as though whatever I felt, he could see it in me somehow.

He had been an absolute boon to me today, I realised.

'Sorry, Erik, do you want a cup of tea before I get stuck in here?'

'It's all right.' He was turning on his heel. 'Perhaps I'll make *you* a drink, Boss Lady.'

25

This tiny moment of newfound self-confidence lasted for roughly five minutes – not even until Erik set the mug at my elbow with an unsmiling wink that seemed to suggest that this was a special treat and I should not get too comfortable with it.

First of all, I'd finally been able to log into the business bank account. Despite the fact that everything – the papers, the computer screen, the desk – was covered in a fine coating of undisturbed dust, there was a single brand-new Post-it note attached to the PC itself, listing our business bank account number and also a string of numbers and letters that proved to be the banking password.

It must have been changed recently, I thought, looking at the note, perhaps in the last couple of days. How odd.

When I left in September 2019 there had been nearly £47,000 in the current account.

We were now down to our last £5,000. I had no idea how we were even going to pay Jimmy or Erik next week, never mind insure the business.

Blue Horizons was in phenomenal trouble.

From what I could see, no bills had been paid out of it for months, and that included anything that looked like an insurance premium.

But the thing that really made the little hairs on the backs of my arms stand up was that Jimmy, Erik and Grace O'Donoghue had only been paid sporadically, and almost never on time. Both Adam Fulmore and Cressida Brownrigg had been paid, both to the same bank account, from money that appeared to have come from the HMRC – I guessed that this was the furlough money the government had paid during the lockdown.

By the time I had skimmed through the statements I was shaking. Large sums of money, about two or three thousand pounds at a time, had been transferred out of the account under the reference DIRECTORS WAGES.

'Are you all right?' Erik asked.

I was shaking, I realised. I didn't even have my dad's little bit of inheritance any more. I had blown most of it on the ticket from Australia, which had been nearly eight thousand pounds.

'No . . . not really. We're almost broke.' I couldn't bring myself to tell him he might not get paid. Instead I said, 'We're not insured . . .'

To my surprise, he merely considered this for a long moment, then shrugged.

'It's not the end of the world. If the shop has been mostly closed, then why spend thousands of pounds insuring against accidents when there are no customers?'

'B . . . but there are customers now.'

'Yes, yes. But we can insure it now. There are no dives or classes until Wednesday.'

'But what about Russell Bowermann? What if he sues us?' Tears were pricking at my eyes.

'What about him?' asked Erik, with a trace of a snarl. 'He disobeyed instructions and left the line.'

'But if he sued us I don't think there's . . . I don't know how we'll afford it. Even afford a lawyer. Afford any of it . . .'

Afford to pay you, even.

My mobile rang. It was Jimmy. I glanced up at him.

'I better take this.'

He nodded.

Ten minutes later Jimmy was parked outside the house in the people carrier.

I was wondering how much we could sell it for.

Blubbering like a little girl, I wept out what I had discovered, while he wrapped me in his arms.

'Right, Cass,' he said, 'very first thing, like, right now, you need to get a business loan out to cover the wages and insurance, all right?'

I nodded, swiping at my wet face.

'We need to ring up every supplier we have and talk to them, find out what's up, make terms with them, all right? They won't be surprised to hear from you. Every dive shop in the world is in the same boat right now. Okay?'

I nodded again. Already I felt calmer, less helpless.

'Now,' he said, holding my shoulders tightly, 'the other thing you have to do is kick that bastard out of the business accounts.'

I was about to nod – stopped.

He was on a luxury holiday with my sister, who desperately needed the break. I could strand him abroad in a heartbeat and feel pleasure doing it – but I couldn't do that to her. I began, spluttering, to explain this . . .

'Cass,' he said, calmly raising a hand to stop this flood of speech, 'you *cannot* leave him with his hands in the till any more. Do you understand? You have to kick him off the business account and bar his access. Right now. Anyway, won't he have his own money?' Jimmy scowled up at the screen, and the list of withdrawals. 'Looks like he's been doing all right to me.'

I sat there in an agony of speechless indecision.

I tried to imagine what would happen if Adam and my sister were about to sit down for a romantic dinner, to go for a drink, all those good things that Sid deserved and should have.

'But if his card is declined while they . . .'

'What are you talking about? You're scaring me, Cass. He shouldn't be using the business credit cards for holidays – isn't that embezzlement? And Sid already knows this, even if he doesn't.' He snorted. 'If he is, he deserves all that's coming to him.'

But that wasn't how I saw it. I only knew that if I cut Adam off he would be humiliated – and then what might he be driven to?

And after all, surely, they both ought to have the chance to explain themselves. Wasn't that fair? Perhaps I didn't have all the information.

It was a wan, forlorn hope, true, but surely Sid would never have been foolish enough to be a party to all this deliberately?

Imagine how hurt she would be if I got this wrong . . . The thought made me literally nauseous.

'Jimmy . . . I . . .'

'Come on, Cass – you're only cutting him off from the business!' Jimmy's frustration with me was growing palpable, his voice rising. His hands were on my shoulders. 'You know, it doesn't end here either. Eventually you are going to have to get the police involved. You might as well do it all in one fell swoop. I can do it for you, in fact. Right now.'

'You are not calling the police!' I gasped in panic. 'Not until I'm sure . . .'

'Is everything all right here?'

Erik was back at the door, peering in at me.

'Erik, no offence, but you need to mind your own business. This is family . . .'

I stood up, shrugging Jimmy off. 'I need to think hard about this,' I said to them both. 'If he's innocent, he has to be allowed to explain himself. If he's not, then I can't abandon my sister abroad somewhere with some . . . some abusive crook who might take his rage out on her.' I ran my hands through my hair. 'I don't even know where she is in the world – but if he doesn't even allow her to have her phone, she'll have no money. He's probably controlling it all.'

'I have a suggestion,' said Erik mildly. 'Don't kick him out. Just freeze his cards. If there is a problem, he will call you – just tell them that the bank thinks someone might have got the card number and there have been fraudulent transactions. You could even persuade him it could be because he has gone abroad, and not told the bank.'

'But what's the point?' asked Jimmy passionately. 'He'll *still* know something's up. He can still transfer money out. You might as well make a clean break.'

Erik shrugged at him.

'Not necessarily. One way he just hands over the card, the other he has to log in and see how little there is. And Cassandra is correct. She doesn't know if he has done anything wrong. He could be entitled to that money or have withdrawn it for some legitimate purpose. Anyway, Cressida would also need to be consulted . . .'

'Ugh,' said Jimmy throwing his hands up in the air. '*Sid*. She let things get in this mess in the first place!'

Erik's eyes narrowed. 'Yes. It is, as you say, *family business*.'

Jimmy coloured. 'Well, forgive *me*. I've only worked here for twenty years, and known these kids since they were little girls . . .'

'Jimmy,' I said. 'Stop. It's fine.' I went to put my arm around his shoulders, and he seemed to subside.

'Sorry, love,' he said, patting my hand before clasping it. 'You're right. We all need to be calm. But we can't do nothing.'

'Indeed we can't,' I said. 'Erik's got the right idea. I'll freeze the cards to the business account now.' I wiped at my dewy forehead. 'And I'll go through all this stuff,' I gestured helplessly around the office at the stacked piles of unopened envelopes. 'We've no clients until Wednesday, right?'

'No,' said Erik.

'Hmm,' I said, sitting back down again, feeling utterly hollow, filled with dread. Oh, Sid. What have you got us all into?

A lightning lance of sheer rage went through me then. However furious I was at Adam, ultimately I blamed Sid. She had let this snake into our home, had shown him all our gold . . .

'Want me to start sorting these?' Jimmy asked, nudging one of the stacks of unopened post.

I sighed. 'Yes, please.' I tried to pull myself together, staring about the piles of paper. 'We should open all of this, stack the relevant things in date order, and then see what we've got.'

Jimmy nodded. 'Well, that's my weekend spoken for,' he said, leaning across the desk as he grabbed some letters. His expression was still slightly strained – I was disappointing him on some level, I knew.

It was too bad. I would do nothing until I knew more. I owed Sid that much at least.

Erik turned on his heel and left.

I would have called out after him – to say what, I don't know. *Thank you. Stay.* But Jimmy was already pulling up in the other chair and had started ripping the envelopes open.

'Hang on,' I said. 'I've got a letter opener somewhere . . .'

I was sure we did. My mother had had one, in the shape of a small jewelled dagger, that she'd brought back with her from a Spanish diving trip. I remember Sid and I sword-fighting with it in the garden once and she'd come running out, shouting. Sid had been so startled she'd dropped it point down on her bare foot. After the ensuing pandemonium, my mum always kept it in the top desk drawer.

I pulled the drawer open, ruffling through the contents, but there was no sign of it. Adam had probably moved it. I sighed, opening each of the drawers in turn, but nothing.

When I reached the final drawer on the right and dragged it open, having almost given up, I paused.

Lying on top of the sheets of blank printer paper and rolls of old Sellotape was a richly patterned blue scarf I had never seen before.

It was made of some silky material and obviously belonged to a woman.

I reached down and picked it up, wondering. It was fringed in scarlet thread and looked expensive.

What it didn't look like was anything Sid would have ever owned.

'Jimmy?'

'Yeah?' He had seized a brown envelope and was about to tear it open.

'Do you recognise this?'

He peered at it. 'No,' he said dismissively. 'But I'm a man.' He offered me an apologetic smile. 'I'm no good at noticing women's clothes.'

'Hmm,' I said.

On an impulse, I raised it to my face and sniffed tentatively. Nothing, but no – a little aroma of grassy perfume – Gucci Bloom, I suspected – and traces of moisturiser and the animal scent of somebody's hair.

But not my sister's. Whoever this belonged to, it was not Sid.

26

At around eight, Jimmy suggested fresh fish and chips from the shop in Fore Street for dinner, and I succumbed. He drove down to the village, so the food wouldn't be cold by the time he got back.

As helpful as he was, and as glad as I had been of him, I relished the peace once he was gone.

The day had utterly drained me. It was impossible to concentrate on anything but the ringing between my ears.

This man has almost bankrupted us in the space of twenty months. And he's out in the world somewhere with my sister, and I've no idea if she's safe.

And always, in the back of my mind, was that alien scarf in the desk drawer.

What was that? Why was there some strange woman's clothing in our office?

After all, I brooded coldly, if he was unscrupulous enough to rob us, then he would certainly have no qualms about cheating on my doting sister.

I went downstairs and snapped the kettle on in the empty house.

We'd not accomplished much beyond confirming that all we had suspected was true, which I supposed was a success, albeit a demoralising one.

I supposed I should be dwelling on how bewildered and distressed I was, but I didn't feel that way. My primary emotion, strange to say, was a kind of resigned relief. I knew the worst now. I had a sense of what I was up against.

I couldn't decide. Was Jimmy right? Sid or Adam might have an explanation for this, but it looked unlikely. We needed to get the police involved at some point. But when?

Maybe now *was* the right time. Adam would have no warning and no notice.

Events could sweep him up and away, for a change, instead of me.

I paused at the kitchen window, looking out to sea. Beyond, the sun boiled away into the horizon. The street-lights had flickered into life, and out in the Channel the endless row of ships twinkled with lamps.

And from far away, borne by an easterly wind, came the faint, plangent notes of the Manacle Buoy.

I wanted to speak to Sid. I wanted to warn her, tell her what we had found out, even though I knew that whatever I sent, Adam would see it first. Before I knew what I was doing I had mounted the stairs, looking for my phone.

It lay on the desk. I stared at it for a long moment, my heart aching with worry and grief, before snatching it up.

Hey Sid – how you doing? Where did you go in the end? Hope you're having a fab time! Send us a picture when you get a chance! Cxxx

Even as I hit Send I knew it was a mealy-mouthed, disingenuous message.

After a moment I added, just on the off chance she might get to see it:

I'm sorry we fought. I want you to have a lovely time. You deserve this holiday.

Another pause.

I love you. xxxx

I waited, holding the phone, but there was no response, and that was how Jimmy found me when he walked into the kitchen with paper bags of cod and chips and a six pack of beer.

And now I was alone in the house, and all was quiet.

I was at my kitchen table, while the old dishwasher swished and rumbled behind me, and the windows were dewed with steam.

'I'll be back tomorrow morning,' Jimmy told me, shrugging himself into his jacket. 'Around eight.'

'You don't have to . . .'

'It's no trouble.' He waved this off. 'Are you opening the shop in the morning?'

'No,' I said. 'I swapped my shift with Erik.'

'Hmph,' he snorted.

There was a significant pause here. I had the sense that I was supposed to ask what it meant and to pry, to ask him what he thought about Erik, but I didn't have the energy to do so.

We had reached the door and I opened it, letting him out into the warm twilight.

'Will you be all right here on your own?' he asked.

'Jimmy, I'll be perfectly fine.'

He peered at me, as though he would have liked to contradict me.

'You won't be headed out again tonight?'

'No, I don't think so.'

He cocked his head, as though he didn't quite believe me.

'I know you don't want to hear this,' he said, his dark brows bristling. 'But there are some dangerous people about.'

'I know,' I said with feeling. 'Believe me, I do.'

He regarded me for a long moment, then nodded, leaning in for a kiss on my cheek. 'All right. See you tomorrow, Cass love.'

Now I was finally alone in the kitchen, sat at the table with a cup of hot tea. In front of me, on my laptop, I was collating every tiny bit of information I had on Adam.

Something flashed in my notifications, a news story, and I clicked on it.

FEARS GROW FOR ANOTHER MISSING WOMAN

After the disappearance of Olivia Simpson and the discovery of an unidentified young woman in a Cornish shipwreck, police are concerned that another woman has vanished in suspicious circumstances.

Last night Shannon McDaid, 22, from London was reported missing when her broken down car was discovered on the verge of a country road near Gwinear Downs, ten miles from St Ives. Devon and Cornwall Police have indicated that evidence at the scene suggested Ms McDaid might have 'come to harm'.

Gwinear Downs . . .

A mere twenty miles from Anvil Point.

I pulled open the article on my phone, a faint chill moving over me.

This new disappearance is the latest in a series of suspected crimes, after Olivia Simpson, 19, went missing from Anvil Point on 18 June. In addition, the body of an unknown woman was found on 5 July within the wreck of the MV *Undine*, two miles offshore from Porthoustock in Cornwall. Her cause of death is currently unknown.

That was three people now. All within half an hour's drive of our village. What the hell was going on?

DCI Tom Trevelyan of the Devon and Cornwall Police described Shannon as 'an ambitious, successful but fun-loving daughter, friend and girlfriend. We are appealing to any members of the public that happened to be in the area of Gwinear Downs on the evening of the 6th of July, particularly if they were travelling along Merivel Lane between the hours of 10:30 p.m. and midnight, to contact us immediately if they saw anything out of the ordinary – it doesn't matter how small or insignificant.'

Police have refused to confirm whether the abductions are linked but are not ruling anything out at this stage.

I read the story through twice, lingering on the photo of Shannon, a slender, neat young woman in an impeccable charcoal suit, her brown hair meticulously upswept on to the top of her head, her only make-up a slash of red lipstick. But she had wide green eyes and the light danced in them, and I thought that she looked like someone who loved to laugh.

Another tourist, just like Livvy Simpson had been. This woman in the *Undine*, had she also been a stranger here? Somebody just travelling, here to have fun?

I glanced out of the window, into the setting darkness, the lights of Anvil Point twinkling below.

Was there a serial killer out there somewhere?

I'd always thought that I understood about predators. They were, after all, my life's work, what I study. But sharks are different. Sharks take only what they need.

What was happening now was something from a different world, one I didn't understand at all.

I sighed, turned away from the window.

However dire things were, I had my own troubles to reckon with right now.

I turned back to my search on Adam.

I had gathered very little.

Google had been absolutely silent on the subject of Adam Fulmore. No Facebook, no Twitter, no Instagram, nothing. Or rather, there were accounts with that name, but it was clear that none of them were him.

I buried my head in my hands, thinking.

Redruth.

That's where he'd told me his sister was based.

I leaned back in my chair.

Maybe, when we'd first hired him, he'd emailed us a CV. I went through the shop's email account with a fine-tooth comb, but there was no sign of a CV – though I did find an email from Dad about his start date from 5 July 2019, and his reply – **That's great! Really looking forward to it! Thanks so much for the opportunity!**

No sign there of what was to come unless you counted the excess of exclamation marks.

I stood up, my tiredness vanishing. It didn't matter if I couldn't find the email, there would be an application form. His references and his dive log would have been checked. The employee files were all kept at the shop, in the filing cabinet in the office.

Within seconds I was shrugging myself into my thin green cardigan, snatching up my keys and heading out the door.

27

It took me a little while to find what I was looking for.

Adam's application form, neatly lettered in blue pen, wasn't in his file (there was nothing in his file, it was resolutely empty) – it had been sorted with *Pending Applications*, which is where we put promising people who applied on spec but for whom we didn't have a job open at the moment.

Part of me wondered whether, if it had been in his file, it would have gone missing along with everything else about him.

Why would you hide your CV?

I held it up beneath the desk lamp. Beyond the office door, the shop was dark and silent.

Ah-ha. Adam Fullmore – with two LLs now – interesting. On the bank accounts, there had been only one.

It could be a typo. But who misspells their own name? It listed his address as 7 Skye Close, Redruth, Cornwall.

I googled the address. I'd been expecting a block of flats, or some kind of bachelor-friendly conversion, but Street View showed a nice suburban cul-de-sac near a school, with a small but modern detached house, a garden and a Nissan Micra in the driveway.

Could this be the troubled sister's house? What had her name been? Ah yes, I remember – Jem.

I googled her too but got nowhere. I thought Jem might be short for Gemma or Jemima, but there was no

Jem, or Gem, or Gemma, or Jemima Fullmore or Fulmore that remotely fitted the bill, and Jem/Gemma/Jemima and the address likewise turned nothing up. Perhaps she was a half-sister, or more likely, lived under a married name.

He'd listed two previous dive shops as references – one was near Inverness, the last in Egypt, in Sharm El Sheikh.

I photocopied Adam's application form, watching the blue light seep out from under the machine's cover and vanish, flash out and vanish, and my mind strayed, lost in thought . . .

There was a sudden hammering on the big glass door of the shop.

I let out a little squeak of shock.

I was so startled that I dropped my phone, which bounced and then skittered away under the filing cabinet. I found I was retreating, silently moving backwards into the office, trying to still my breathing.

Then, horrifyingly, the jangle of keys, turning in the lock in the door.

Who could this be? The others would all be off for the night.

Oh no . . . Was it Adam? Did he somehow know we were on to him, was this him returning?

But how? demanded the last rational part of my brain, the part that wasn't paralysed with fear. How could he know? And how could he get here so fast?

Maybe, I thought grimly, he never left.

Remember, he lies.

I dropped to my knees, trying to get at the phone, but in my haste and panic my fingers seemed to be poking the phone even further under the filing cabinet.

'Shit,' I hissed.

The front door of the shop swung open, letting in a cool night breeze.

I froze, even my breath stilled.

The little signs and taped pieces of paper in the kitchenette opposite stirred faintly as the glass door was closed again. Heavy footsteps were making their way across the shop floor with a steady tread.

The shop's landline extension was in here, but I didn't think I would get time to use it. I glanced wildly around me for something, anything, I could use to defend myself with.

I clambered to my feet and shrank back behind the open office door, wrapped a shaking fist around the Anglepoise lamp on the desk. Whoever it was wasn't pausing – they were heading here, towards where I was – they must have seen the light on.

I was shaking so hard now I could feel it through the soles of my feet, as though I was caught in my own mini-earthquake.

'Hello?' came a voice.

'Erik?'

His head poked around the door, to where I cowered behind it. His gaze moved from my face down to my hand and the lamp clenched within it, and back up again.

His eyes narrowed.

'Are you . . . are you okay?'

I snorted in relief, barked out a false little laugh. 'Yes, I'm fine. Sorry. It's been a very strange day.' I shrugged, as though inviting him to find it funny too.

He didn't join me, instead tilting his head slightly to the left to study me.

After a moment of this silent consideration I felt compelled to speak, to fill the unspoken void with chatter.

'You don't have to worry, you know.' I gestured at the lamp with a flippant wave. 'I wasn't actually going to hit you . . .'

'You thought that man might have come back.' His gaze was flat.

I considered denying it, exhaled, and then replaced the lamp on the desk, shrugging again. 'Yeah. I . . . Yeah. That's what I thought.' I sighed. 'And you know – I've been reading about those missing girls. There's another one gone, up near Gwinear Downs . . . it's made me a bit . . .' I gestured helplessly at the lamp. 'You know.'

'Yes, I know.' He stepped into the office, looked around. He seemed to make the place shrink around him. He glanced down at me. 'I saw that another woman is missing. But what are you doing here now?'

'Oh.' I shut my mouth with a snap. 'Well, I just wanted to look through the HR files, you know, find . . .'

'That man's details, yes, yes,' he said, rubbing his chin. 'That makes sense.'

I was embarrassed. I shouldn't have to be explaining myself. This was my business, after all.

'Anyway, what are *you* doing here?' I asked, possibly a little rudely.

He didn't reply straight away, instead reaching over the desk and picking up an iPhone lying under a couple of sheets of paper. 'Getting this. I forgot it earlier.'

'Ah. Right.' Again I tittered out some inane fake laughter.

He regarded me with great attention, unsmiling, while I let the false chuckle drain away.

Then he said:

'I was going to use it to call you.'

'Me?'

'Yes. You are the licensee of the *Undine*.'

Of all the things he could have said, this I had not been expecting. 'Yes. Well . . . I'm one of them. Sid's the other . . .'

'You're the only one that counts at this moment.' He dropped into one of the chairs at the desk, which creaked to take his weight. 'You said you noticed something new about the wreck before you discovered that woman's body.'

'I didn't discover her, really, the client, Russell did, and . . .'

'Don't talk to me about that idiot,' said Erik with cold distaste. 'If I ever see him again, I may kill him.'

I stared at him. 'What? Why?'

'He posted his video on YouTube. He is saying he got lost in a dangerous part of the ship because of our poor guidance.'

I let this sink in.

'What?' I asked after a long moment. 'He swam off on me! What am I supposed to do, put him in handcuffs?'

Erik waved this away. 'He came to promote his own agenda,' he said. 'He is that sort of creature.'

'I . . .' Was this my fault? 'Well, he can say what he likes, I suppose. This is the Worst Dive Shop in Cornwall, according to all the reviews.' I gave him a despairing shrug. 'I can prove it with spreadsheets and PowerPoint. And y'know, I don't even care.'

'That's a lie,' he said, watching me. 'You care enormously.' He crossed his legs at the ankles. 'It's breaking your heart.'

I opened my mouth, closed it again.

There is a moment that occurs in your life, sometimes,

when you realise that just for a single instant, you – the secret hidden you – have been wholly seen and understood by somebody else.

I stepped back from him, overwhelmed. I had so many feelings. A terrifying, unwanted sense of intimacy and recognition, a roiling confusion, and finally, at the bottom, a tiny, inexplicable flickering flame of pure joy.

I looked away, keen to change the subject, to master my feelings. 'Why are you asking me about the *Undine*?'

'Because I have been thinking about it this evening. You said when you came up that there was a current, a new current, in the lower corridor.'

'Yes. There was.' I wrapped my arms around myself, remembering its cold embrace.

'You keep the official maps of the wreck here, yes?' He stood up, towering over me once more.

'Yes.' I squinted up at him. 'Why?'

'Because Jimmy and I did a survey of it in the spring and I think this new current and the dead woman are connected.' He was opening the filing cabinet, looking for the hard-copy maps we kept of the *Undine*.

'How?'

'I want to check something out,' he said, as though I had not spoken, taking the maps out, laying them on the table.

His thick finger moved along the lower deck, pausing by the engine room.

'Hmm,' he said. 'Just as I thought.'

'What is it?' I asked, puzzled.

'I want to check the engine room. That's the logical place for the current to come from, as it faces out to sea. It was sealed on our last survey.'

I peered at the drawings. The engine room lay at the end of the corridor, cheek by jowl with the Forbidden Hold.

That was why Russell had attempted to swim that way.

Erik was standing back now, stroking his chin, then he gave me an appraising look. 'The police reopened the *Undine* to divers a couple of hours ago. I think it will be busy tomorrow. It's slack tide in an hour. We need to go now.'

'What,' I snorted, 'dive the *Undine*? Right now?'

'Yes. Dive the *Undine*, right now.' He paused. 'It is underwater. That is the only way to get there.'

'But it's *night* . . .'

'It's only twenty minutes past sunset, actually.' He swung his heavy kit bag off his shoulder. 'But yes, it will be a night dive.' His tone was perfectly reasonable, somehow making me sound hysterical in comparison.

'You're really going to dive it *now*?'

'Yes, we are.'

And this time I laughed, genuinely laughed. 'Um, no. I'm not. You wouldn't catch me in the *Undine* in daylight now, never mind at night.'

'Cassandra, you have to come. I think this new current is because there is a hole in the hull that's appeared since the last survey we did. Maybe the woman came in through it. It is safest to check it between tides, which is now. We have to go and look.'

'I . . . I'm sorry. There's no way. I can't go there in the night.' I was backing away. 'I can't . . .'

He caught my arm, held me still. 'You saw bad things. And now you can't stop seeing them.'

I could not reply, merely nodding.

'Cassandra, I have also seen many bad things in my time. Things I cannot even tell you about. I know it is hard, but you need to come to the ship with me. This woman,' he gestured out to sea. 'She cannot hurt you. But if people dive the *Undine* tomorrow because of the publicity, and there is a collapse, *they* can be hurt. We must look. And the tide is right to look *now*.'

I was frightened, suddenly and terribly frightened, and not just at the thought of sailing and swimming in total darkness, past the same room where we had found the woman. My heart had started to beat faster again. 'I don't think that . . .'

'Come on. You work with sharks. I know courage is not a problem for you.'

I looked up, startled. I had not considered what I did in that light.

'You will be perfectly safe,' he continued. 'I dive the *Undine* solo at least once a week. And you, you dive inside wrecks all the time, and it is dark in there, yeah?'

I swallowed. 'Well, yes . . .'

'So come. A dive would do you good. The sea is a different world at night.' He met my gaze. 'Come.'

And incredibly enough, I found myself saying, 'All right.' I offered him a final tiny shrug, as though this was no big thing, and smiled wanly. 'I mean, why not?'

There was a tiny flash of triumph in his eyes then, quickly banked.

'Indeed. Why not?'

28

'Nearly ready,' I called out to him, checking my air. 'Do you really solo this dive a lot?'

He nodded. 'I prefer to dive alone.' That almost smile again. 'Most of the time, anyway.'

We had loaded our kit into the *Mustang Sally*, and Erik had already clipped mobile lights to the boarding ladder on the side with a practised ease that led me to believe he'd done this on his own many times before.

It was a very strange thing to think of him out here, alone in the deep in the dark of night, a shark shimmering through the void. It was so antithetical to the way that I dived at the Institute – rigorously safety conscious, always buddied up – that there was something shocking, almost miraculously audacious about it.

He reminded me of my father.

'Are you ready? We won't be long.' He was pulling his hood on. 'I have a theory on how the woman ended up in the cabin.'

I nodded my head, the wind tousling my hair. 'Okay.'

'You're shaking,' he said, and I realised it was true. A little tremor was running through me.

'Well, lots happened here . . . you know . . .' I looked away. 'The woman . . . and I know it was nearly two years ago, but . . .'

Silence, with only the roar of the boat engine, the slap of the waves.

'Of course,' he rumbled. 'I'm sorry.' A long pause. 'That was insensitive of me.' He seemed to be thinking. 'If you must, you can stay on the boat . . .'

I was about to say yes, that would be better, but somehow this impulse, as soon as it was born, died within me.

I was sick of hiding from things, I realised. I was sick of hiding from my worries about Sid, my suspicions of Adam – I wanted to strike out.

I wanted to face things.

The *Undine* was my responsibility too, almost my second home beneath the waves. I was its guardian. We had lived in its flickering marine shadows all my life. I had tackled my fears at home. I would not be defeated by the wreck.

'No,' I said. 'It's fine.' I shrugged, chilly despite my drysuit.

Erik didn't reply, as though he knew I hadn't quite mastered my emotions.

'And it would be cool, you know, to see it at night. You're right. I don't think I ever have.'

'All right then, Boss Lady. Let's go.'

We synched the dive computers on our wrists – I knew the values for an *Undine* dive the way I knew my own phone number, and read them out to him as he steered the boat with one hand, its lamps igniting the sea around us, leaving us a tiny island of light in the darkness.

My heart was already starting to pound long before we reached the Manacle Buoy, heard its sad toll over the waves, a tiny counterpoint to the slowing of our boat engine.

All around us was darkness, the silky ocean a mirror for the shining moon, slapping the sides of the boat almost playfully, each blow a brine-scented kiss. The tide was low, about to turn, as he weighed anchor – waving away my help – while mere hundreds of yards away the bitter, razor-sharp teeth of the Manacles twisted upwards through the waters as though some dread creature below was trying to bite through a gleaming veil at the stars.

A dangerous place, I reminded myself. A place where people died.

We helped each other into our kit, and even though I had done this a thousand times or more with other divers, somehow it felt unbearably intimate as I checked his fastenings, tugged at his weights, at his air tank, and then he did the same for me. His movements were strong, sure, as he tested the buckles, lifted up my air tank effortlessly as my arms found their way through the straps.

He handed me my diving light and my spares. The last thing we wanted was for our lights to fail down there in the utter darkness.

'Ready?'

I took the regulator mouthpiece between my lips, sucked in air to check it.

'Yeah, ready.'

He nodded, and suddenly his face vanished behind his mask, his own breathing apparatus.

'Let's do it.'

29

Below II

The water is shockingly cold, but no worse than during the day. We are descending, and Erik is keeping the light focused on a place beneath our feet, a tunnel of illumination when all around us is in milky darkness shot with moonlight.

I am afraid, yes, but I am also, I realise, unbearably excited as we fall together towards the *Undine*, my heart pounding. Above me, the waxing moon is as pale and gauzy as a mirage, growing smaller and smaller. I might as well be in outer space.

Looking back down, I momentarily catch Erik's dark eyes through his mask.

He raises a hand, a little gesture of *Are you okay?*

I answer him with the same gesture.

Beneath, his flashlight is beginning to pick up the steely outlines of the *Undine* far below.

I breathe out a stream of bubbles, conscious of my rising nervousness, the effect it will have on my air supply. Around us, all is darkening, an underwater night that is utterly opaque except where our flashlights shine. Anything could come barrelling out of that darkness, any combination of scales and sharp teeth.

The light of my torch slides off the wreck, on to the nearest of the rocky pinnacles holding it in place.

I feel like a trespasser here, an absurd sentiment, but one I cannot escape, as though I am breaking into the house of a close friend while they are asleep.

We near the bottom, and with surprising grace for such a large man, Erik has zoomed off with unerring speed towards the dark void in the *Undine*'s hull and vanished within. His trim is excellent, better than mine. I have to swim hard to keep up, to keep the light steady.

Within the *Undine*, lurking in the crevices and in the lee of rusting walls, fish sleep alongside the jewel anemones and branching coral, barely stirring even as the lights flash over them. A yellow eel drifts across my path like a ribbon, with the slightly dazed expression of someone looking for a bathroom in the middle of the night in a strange house.

Beyond the beam of our lights, all else is utter darkness. The moon no longer intrudes now we are inside, and through the portholes there is nothing but a shadowy blue-greyness, that while paler than the rest gives off no illumination. For a flickering second I imagine what it would be like in here if our flashlights were to go out, then drive this thought firmly from my head.

How can Erik bear this alone?

Very easily, it seems, because he doesn't linger, moving deeper into the ship, as though the three rooms we show the public hold no appeal. He is a careful diver with impressive balance, stirring very little debris in his wake, and it is a refreshing change from the students.

We move through the shattered crew mess, on to the lounge, where I think he might pause for a second amongst the slow-moving ghost crabs picking their way carefully over the ruined decking, but no – he turns right, towards the empty stairwell that Russell had vanished down, and I gesture to him, to tell him to slow down – but he does not even turn to look at me.

I have to hurry to catch him and keep the light on him as he swims downwards, into the bowels of the *Undine*, the thin trail of bubbles from his regulator the only sign of his passing.

He swims so *fast*.

I follow him along the remains of the steel passageway, the *Undine*'s main internal artery leading past the old crew quarters.

It is how I had left it, tilted to an unsettling 30 degrees to the left, wallpapered in rust and tiny waving fronds of anemones, metal doors thrown wide and rusted into position to display destroyed furniture festooned with creeping sea stars.

The new current that so worries us is weak but still present – it is slack tide, so it won't get up again for a little while.

I try to calm my breathing, not race through my air, as we pass the cabin the woman had been in, very carefully not looking within.

What if there are more dead people? I try, desperately and unsuccessfully, to close off this avenue of thinking, to dismiss it from my mind.

And then I hear the noise.

Impossible to describe what it is with the sound-twisting effect of the water, with the glug of my respirator and its accompanying bubbles.

I stop, tempted to hold my breath to listen, realising this is impossible. It's fatal to hold your breath while scuba diving.

It is like . . . it is like *singing*. Like someone singing through an old-fashioned radio, high and full of static, the signal sighing in and then out.

Then, as quickly as it had started, it stops.

Erik stops moving, looks back at me, his expression quizzical.

What the hell can it be?

Certainly, Erik seems oblivious to any danger. He doesn't stop to even shine his light into the abandoned cabins.

The darkness and silence, broken only by the rasp of my respirator, oppresses me. I hurry after him, careful not to stir up the silt and blind myself.

He is heading for the engine room.

The *Undine*'s engine room is in its back, or stern end, and for years it has become increasingly apparent that this part of the ship is not safe – whatever that means in the context of a crumbling shipwreck that could theoretically collapse in on us at any moment.

And here is the safety notice we had commissioned, nailed to the bulkhead with a skull and crossbones at the bottom:

PROCEED AT YOUR OWN RISK PAST THIS POINT – THIS IS AN UNSAFE STRUCTURE.

For more information please contact
Ms Cressida Brownrigg
Blue Horizons Diving School
Anvil Point
Tel: 01326 473030

The idea that this expected catastrophe might happen right now, here, while I am trapped deep in the interior, in the dead of night, fills me with a dread so profound that I want nothing more than to turn around and swim back up to the *Mustang Sally*.

But even as I glance over my shoulder, I realise that I am too frightened to do this. It is too scary and too dangerous to swim back through the *Undine* alone, and Erik's fins and trail of bubbles are now well ahead, and I can see the reckless bastard is about to turn down into the rotted freshwater tank and disappear from view.

I swim hard after him, stirring up a cloud of silt in my haste, a stupid and dangerous error, and glance at my dive computer. We'd said three quarters of an hour, including a decompression stop halfway to the surface, and with the descent it has already been nearly fifteen minutes. We need to turn around soon.

Erik pauses at the torn mouth of the tank. The hatch that once led below decks is buried under tons of rubble, so now, in the rare moments we visit it, we get down through the old freshwater storage tank and access the engine room that way.

He turns, and grins through his mask as I raise my own light to him. He makes the hand gesture, *follow*.

Erik disappears now, slipping through a rent in the tank wall crusted with barnacles, and taking us both into the only surviving bottom deck section of the *Undine* – the engine room and the boiler room, most of the latter now crushed by the decomposing steel superstructure of the wreck above into spaces too narrow and dangerous to dive in.

Just great. My least favourite place in the ship.

The wrecked boilers are lined up like silent dark giants in the light of his flashlight, standing watch in disapproval.

Carefully I sidle in, join him amongst the massy rusted columns of the boilers. The current is stronger in here, and the delicate twigs of plant life and sea creatures that manage to subsist here in the perpetual twilit gloom flutter out and then relax, flutter and relax, as though something gigantic is breathing nearby.

We float there for a moment, getting our bearings.

The hull walls have crumpled and perished below us, the keel now buried deep in the seabed, so beneath us all looks like sand, dotted with shells and darting fish stirred awake by the currents of our fins.

I'd be lying if I said it isn't impressive, that I don't feel that surge of wonder, of adrenaline, every time I come here.

But we've come far enough. I haven't seen any massive changes from the last time I was this far into the wreck.

I make the signal *go back*, hold up my dive computer.

He ignores this, instead focusing his light on a gap between two of the boilers.

I see nothing but sheets of rusting debris, am about to pull back, but then he physically grabs me. *Look*, he mouths, taking out his regulator for a moment.

Dutifully I swim forward.

He is pulling away the decaying pieces of rotten iron piled up between the boilers, letting them fall on to the floor of the wreck behind him in drifting slow motion.

I am puzzled, unsure.

Then I see it.

Hidden behind a rusting piece of steel plate is a

massive, jagged tear in the iron wall, and peering at it, I can see the edges are fresh.

This has not perished from rust, but has been torn open, buckled, by some massive force – very likely the weight of the ship above us.

Erik has already pulled out his camera, is snapping images of it.

It is as tall as I am, but not very wide – to enter, you'd have to take all your scuba gear off, squeeze through the crack, and then put your gear back on.

All the while hoping that you didn't get stuck in it, or that the ship didn't fall down any further, trapping you inside.

Beyond it is the bottom deck, a place that has been effectively completely sealed off since the ship sank. The Forbidden Hold. We've been surveying the wreck for years and never found a way to access this space before.

I am stunned, swimming forward to peer through it. The tears in the steel are warped in such a way that you would have to physically go through the gap to see what was on the other side, but I glimpse things in my dive light nevertheless – a rusting bulkhead, painted numbers, the bent girders holding up the deck above.

I glance at my dive computer. We've reached the end of the dive.

I tap his shoulder, make the signal.

He nods and signals acceptance, but in a distracted way, as though he is humouring me. He looks above, raising his flashlight through a hole in the overhead, peering into the circle of light at the metal deck skeleton above.

Intrigued, I glance upwards. I notice nothing out of the ordinary at first, but then . . .

Something up there is moving slowly, back and forth, a tiny pale shadow, and I realise it is the moon, appearing and vanishing, appearing and vanishing.

Somehow, up there, is an exit to the surface. But what is that thing that is waving back and forth . . . ?

In an instant I understand.

It is the ship. Or more properly, it is the quarterdeck ceiling, moving slowly backwards and forwards, and as it does so, the noise begins again.

The problem of course is that the quarterdeck should not be moving at all.

It is meant to be stable – yes, bits fall off, and it is a dangerous place, but it does not move. It is meant to be wedged in tight between the pinnacles, held in place like the rest of the hull of the *Undine*.

Soon it will come free.

It weighs hundreds of tons and if it was to collapse on top of us . . .

And now the noise again, only louder.

Underwater, sounds behave peculiarly because the little bones in your ear cease to work – you have to feel them instead of hearing them, vibrating through the water and against your skull.

The *Undine* is singing again, a strange tetchy staticky noise, and now I can tell where it is coming from – above us.

I've dived enough to know that if I heard this noise on land, whatever it is, it would be very loud indeed.

This is a conversation I cannot have with hand gestures, so I whip out the slate tied to my BCD and write DO YOU SEE THAT?

He gently pinches the stylus out of my hand, writes YES under the circle of my shaking flashlight. He seems

to think for a moment, then adds, I THINK ITS GET-
TING WORSE.

All of the blood drains away from me then. I am numb
with horror.

I immediately make the signal for *abandon dive*.

He looks at me, shrugs. I think he'll argue, but with a
single strong push, he swims back through the tank, up to
the passageway, and I follow him, trying not to panic, to
control my shivering, to not burn my way through my air
in my alarm.

Now I am listening for it, it is as clear as day – a rhyth-
mic squeal of metal, distorted by the sea, audible over the
glug of my bubbles and the sighing of my respirator.

And then it stops again.

I let out a long trail of bubbles, a sigh of relief, as I follow Erik back down the passageway, past the frozen
cabins, as my light trembles over him in the darkness.

This has been a close call – but already my mind is
whirring. We have to think about how to handle . . .

There is a bump of pressure above me, as though
something huge has swum past me in the corridor, buf-
feted me with its current.

And then, impossibly, the ceiling is dipping towards
me, the steel tearing in places like paper, the corridor
shrinking, and then even this vanishes as everything is
suddenly clouded by swirling silt, thicker than any fog,
and I am rolling in it, tumbling against the steel walls, my
balance lost, and my light can make no headway against it.

I hear that most terrible of sounds, an underwater
scream, and I realise I am making it. My regulator has
been torn out of my mouth and mud and steel is against
my lips. I cannot see an inch before my face. I cannot tell

if I am facing up or down. My mask is filled with water and silt.

I struggle wildly to find the regulator, craning over my shoulder for the tube coming out of my air tank, when suddenly a hand is on my arm, dragging me, and Erik is at my side, and he swims me forward, into the opaque darkness. My mouthpiece is being forced between my teeth and he is pulling me.

He didn't need to pull. I am *leaving*.

We swim for our lives, shooting out into the stairwell and into the dining room, where I quickly clear my mask and finally we can see again by the light of Erik's flashlight. All is pandemonium amongst the residents, and woken fish stream out through the broken portholes in flashes of silver, darting deeper into the sea.

Out of the mess we pass, and finally out of the hole in the *Undine*'s breast, and we are swimming up now, to the comparative safety of open water. Above us the moon shivers as though she is cold.

Erik gestures at me. *Okay?*

Okay, I gesture back, though I am trembling, a bone-deep adrenaline trembling.

Below our fins, in the circle of my flashlight, coils of silt rise around the *Undine*'s skirts, and fish swim upwards and out and away, as though she is an explosion happening in slow motion, blowing silver shrapnel in all directions.

But still, she looks the same, her superstructure intact. What is it that has collapsed in there?

Above us the lights around the *Mustang Sally* twinkle in welcome. I need to get on board, to get a hot shower, to wrap up warm with a mug of hot chocolate, to think . . .

I glance sideways at Erik.

He has persuaded me to do this dangerous, foolish thing – is this somehow his fault? The *Undine* has been stable for years – has he, in these nocturnal wanderings, broken or moved something?

You know, I think, you don't know this guy at all.

But threaded through all this is a little tug of realisation.

He's saved my life.

30

'Hi, Doug. It's me again, C-Cass Brownrigg. You told me to call you back on this channel.'

I was shivering as I stood on the deck of the *Mustang Sally*, whether with cold or adrenaline I couldn't tell, and my unfastened drysuit was still dripping around me. Erik was setting out the emergency buoys and then stopped briefly, to gaze across the black sea, to where the faraway but ever-present queue of ships in the Channel twinkled faintly, and then back at me.

'Hi, Cass, thanks for calling back. How you holding up?'

Our family has known Coastguard Doug, or Maritime Operations Officer Calvery, for years, since he transferred over to Falmouth from Brixham.

'Um, been better,' I tried on a little self-deprecating laugh, which choked in my throat, stillborn.

'You want to tell me what happened?'

I drew breath, martialled my thoughts. 'Yeah. So. On the dive where we found . . . when the body . . .'

Once again, I was there, in the bowels of the *Undine*, with only the woman for company, grinning at me in the cold floating darkness . . .

I clamped my jaw shut, swallowed against a dry throat.

'Yeah. Sorry. I got talking to Erik tonight in the shop about this new current and we – we decided to go out and have a look.' I licked my lips, tasted salt. 'We had a bad feeling.'

'You went out to the wreck? In the middle of the night?'

Erik stalked up to me, gently grabbed my hand, steering the radio to his mouth. 'It was a *very* bad feeling,' he said distinctly, before releasing me and walking back to the stern of the boat.

'Right,' said Doug, while I eyed Erik's turned back.

'Anyway,' I said. 'We found a gap leading to the lower deck that wasn't there before, that had been hidden by debris. We were checking it out when the upper gangway nearly collapsed on top of us. We were lucky to get out. The whole wreck needs sealing off.'

I heard the sound of a long, exhaled breath. 'I see.'

'Look, I'm freezing so I'm going to get off.'

'Sure. We'll flag the wreck and let all the right people know. You'll need to come in and give a statement, probably, but anytime tomorrow is fine.' A pause. 'Good night.'

He was gone.

'Are you all right?' Erik asked me from the wheelhouse after a long while. He stood in front of the wheel in his drysuit, his big fingers deftly operating the controls.

'I . . . I don't know.' I looked at him. 'How are you?'

'I'm all right, Boss Lady,' he rumbled mildly, the wind tousling his short dark hair, as though the question was ridiculous, and discovering the entrance to Forbidden Holds and escaping from being crushed to death in the bowels of collapsing shipwrecks was something he did every day of the week.

I sighed.

As mad as it sounded, there was a great deal for me to be grateful for here, I told myself. We'd both survived and we weren't even injured. And we'd found the source of the new current.

But the *Undine*, our prized dive, the draw that kept us afloat with Dad gone, was now far too unstable and dangerous to dive. However it had happened – the police search, our own carelessness, the unstoppable entropy that envelops all things that fall beneath the surface of the sea – there was no way we could take students there on penetration dives, ever again. At least not until it fell into rusting spars. It would need to be sealed off, forbidden to recreational divers. It had to be declared hazardous.

But without the *Undine*, our star attraction, what would happen to our embattled business? What would happen to me, to Sid, to Jimmy, to everything our parents had worked for?

Was this the final blow that would finish us off?

It was too, too much. At least until we got back to dry land.

I dropped my cold hands into my lap, shivering a little. 'What do you think happened?'

He shrugged. 'The sea. The ship is breaking up.' He glanced at me, back at the horizon, to the lights of Anvil Point. 'The bridge is falling into the main hull. But slowly. A little at a time, but there is no telling when it will happen again. Only that it *will* happen again.'

'It was so weird. I thought I was going to be crushed to . . .' I swallowed, looked away to sea. 'Thanks.'

'For what?'

'For saving my life.'

'You don't have to thank me.'

'I think I do. That was a dangerous, dangerous place. Nobody would have blamed you if you'd turned around and just swum out.'

'I would have blamed me. And anyway, you would have done the same.'

I very deliberately didn't look at him. I wasn't at all sure that I would have gone back into such peril.

I was still aware that he was merely smiling at me.

'You don't believe it,' he said. 'But I think you would have. You are a rescuer. That's who you are.' He chuckled. 'After all, you are Rob Brownrigg's daughter.'

31

'You should shower,' said Erik, as he set a cup of coffee in front of me. It gave off a little wisp of steam. 'You are cold.'

I was back at the shop, sitting at the table in the briefing room.

Everywhere I looked, there were images and references and posters showing the *Undine*, papering the walls, surrounding the big map of it unfurled across the briefing room. Come see the *Undine*, the only penetration wreck in Cornwall still accessible to divers! Learn wreck diving on the *Undine*! Take a tour of the *Undine* with Blue Horizons, established in 1991 by legendary divemaster Rob Brownrigg!

I had been seeing these words and images all my life, to the point where they no longer even consciously registered with me.

Until tonight.

I pushed my wet hair out of my face, blinked. It was becoming hard to see the words, and I realised that this was because my eyes were filling up.

Erik pushed the mug towards me. 'Drink.'

I glanced down at the coffee, bit my lip.

No, I would not sit here crying.

My dad would not have sat here crying, I can promise you that.

'Okay,' I said, swallowing a sip down against my closing throat.

Erik took the seat opposite me, and to my surprise leaned forward on the table and looked expectantly at me, almost as if he was about to interview me for a job.

'So,' he said. His camera was at his elbow. 'I'm no expert on these things, but I am starting to have some ideas now.'

'Yeah?'

'So,' he said again, holding up a finger, as though summoning quiet, trying to hear the slow gears of his own thoughts. 'Suppose . . . let's suppose that I am a murderer. I need a place to hide bodies . . . what do I do?'

'I have no idea. Not something I ever had to think about before.'

'If I bury these bodies,' he continued, as though I had not spoken, 'they can be found. If I dump them at sea, they may float back to land, end up in a fishing net, or lying on a beach.'

'Yeah, it's a problem, I'm sure,' I raised my cup with a cynical tilt. 'The answer seems to be to not kill people . . .'

'But I am a psychopath and I hate women and killing them makes me happy, so what am I to do?' He said this absolutely expressionlessly, his gaze on mine. A shiver moved through me, a reminder of the real cost of what we were discussing. 'If I had a safe place under the sea to store these bodies, the ocean would do all the hard work for me.'

I raised an eyebrow at him.

He picked up the camera, showing me the digital viewfinder, the image there. It was of the slit in the boiler room wall, leading down into the Forbidden Hold.

He passed me the camera.

In the little screen I could see the picture he'd taken of the rent in the wall. Its edges shone, but it was still difficult to see because of the debris stacked against it.

'I see the tear in the bulwark,' I peered into it. 'That's how the current is getting through, I'll bet you. But I don't see an opening big enough for a person to get through.'

'No. You wouldn't. Somebody has deliberately piled things against it, to hide it.'

I stared at him, then at the picture. It looked completely natural to me, a haphazard collection of rusting steel and plastic.

But then, when you enlarged the picture, focusing on the detail, it could seem that a couple of the big pieces of steel had been placed there, and the rest thrown against them to look like the work of the currents, of the wreck itself.

'You see it?' he asked.

'I . . . I don't know,' I said. I was too tired to deal with this, to think straight. 'Why would you hide a body behind there, though?'

He shrugged. 'Lots of reasons. It is actually very smart. In an evil way, yes, but smart.'

'It's not that smart . . .' I snorted. 'First off, it straight away tells me you're a scuba diver, which is a pretty specific thing to know about a person.'

'Yes, yes, but this particular body was *found*.' Erik was peering into the camera again. 'She was never meant to be found. If you had access to a place in the wreck where nobody else could go, it is a great place to hide a body.'

I leaned back in my chair, following this horrible logic.

'It will decay very quickly,' he said. 'The fish, the crabs, the sea lice – they'll do your work for you. Devour all your evidence. Also, you forget,' he took the camera out of my hands to peer into it himself. 'The *Undine* is not just an attraction. It is also a grave. Everybody on board her died when she sank, and they never recovered all the bodies. If you were diving and found human bones there, Cassandra, what would you think?'

'I'd think . . .' Oh God, I was seeing his point. 'I'd think they were the crew. Somebody missed in the original recovery.'

He did not answer me, merely shrugged, as if to say, *voilà*.

I shook my head at him, with a short laugh. 'But it would still be crazy. The *Undine* is a super popular wreck site. It's full of dive tourists snapping underwater pictures, all the time, especially in summer. Anyone could see you . . .'

'It's busy, true, but not all the time. Not late at night . . .'

'But . . .'

'It wasn't busy just now, was it?'

I was about to reply, then stilled. No. We'd been the only people there tonight. Thankfully.

'I often dive at night and there is nobody there. Remember, it's only accessible by boat,' he rumbled. 'I can tell from the shore if anybody is already diving out there with just a pair of binoculars.'

I sat back in the chair, thinking, trying to encompass the audacity of it, the focused madness. The pictures of the *Undine* all over the walls seemed to flutter in my tired vision. It was a fantastical idea, yes, but if you had a secret way in to the Forbidden Hold, then . . .

'I think,' Erik said, 'whoever it was that put the woman in this sealed hold was disturbed, perhaps . . .' his dark gaze flickered then sharpened, as though he had had an idea. 'No, no, what am I thinking? It is so much simpler than that. They had already hidden the woman, they weren't even *there*. The *Undine* is collapsing, right? Having these little . . . these little convulsions all the time. One of these has knocked over the covering of the hole in the engine room, and it has been lying open.'

I could barely breathe, thinking about it. Of course. Like a restive volcano, the *Undine* was probably in constant motion in her accelerating death throes, an unquiet sleeper tossing in her darkened underwater dreams.

'And her corpse escapes, driven by this current from the deep sea,' I murmured. 'Her body is pushed through the hole that is now uncovered. She comes up out of the engine room, is hurried along the central corridor. But at some point, she floats into one of the cabins . . .'

It was blossoming in my head, this scenario, and almost without noticing, I realised I could think about her without being filled with sick fear and disgust.

'And in the cabin she's protected from the current. She's trapped in there . . .' I continued. I could just see it, see *her*, cut and battered from being forced through the rent in the bulwark, drifting up the corridor, twirling in some eddy, suddenly in the dark cabin, slowing, coming to a stop.

'Floating in the cabin,' I whispered. 'Waiting to be discovered.'

Still horrifying, yes, still pitiable, but yet somehow also active in her own cause, active in her desire for justice, even in death. Somehow admirable.

'Yes.' Erik leaned back in his chair. 'Waiting to be discovered.'

For a long moment we sat there in silence, each in our own thoughts.

I felt cold, both inside and out. The thought that

someone might use the *Undine* for something so wicked, so depraved – it was unthinkable.

Previously I had been filled with remembered fear, my horror and disgust at my discovery, but for the first time it no longer felt like something I wanted to blot out, to forget.

Whoever had done this, I wanted to find them. To stop them.

But . . .

'There's only one problem,' I said.

'Yes?' He leaned his large head on his arms now, obviously as exhausted as I was. Only his dark crown was visible.

He seemed so vulnerable that for a moment I wanted to reach across and touch him.

Needless to say, I didn't.

Instead, I said:

'That hole can't have been uncovered, though, or at least not enough to let a body out.'

He looked up at me. 'Why not?'

'When the police divers came through a couple of hours after we found the body they would have seen it, surely? We told them the lowest deck was closed off and they never came back to us. I know they went down to the engine room.' I rubbed my tired eyes, tried to repress a yawn. 'If they thought there was a big accessible space in there, then the *Undine* would have been closed off for a lot longer than forty-eight hours. And I'm the licensee. They would have asked me questions about it.'

'That could be true.' He raised himself up from his arms, regarded me carefully. 'Alternatively, whoever did this had some warning the ship was to be searched and was able to cover up this hole again before the police arrived.'

'That's crazy — how could they?' I protested. 'Only a handful of people knew about the body until the police showed up.'

'Only a few did?' He looked hard at me. 'How many?'

'Well — the other students knew about it, and I called the coastguard once we reached the surface.' I strained to remember. 'And I texted Sid from A&E . . .'

My breath caught then in my throat, stilled.

Oh God.

'What?' Erik cocked his head. 'What is it?'

'I . . .'

'What?'

'Sid didn't have her phone with her,' I said, the pieces falling into place. '*Adam* had it. And Adam didn't respond, not all day. He seemed surprised when I told him about the body, but . . . I dunno. Of course you'd pretend to be surprised!

'And something else,' I said, turning urgently to him. 'He had . . . okay, I know it sounds crazy, but when we broke into the office, there was this woman's scarf in one of the drawers. I remember thinking it was something that Sid or my mum would never have worn. It was like something I would wear.' I was shaking. 'Oh God, I dunno what I thought at the time, like, maybe he was having an affair . . .'

Erik was silent for a long moment. Then:

'Where was he? That day you found the body?'

'I thought he was teaching a class — but it turned out he was visiting his sister!' I pushed my wet hair out of my face impatiently. 'But this is the thing, Erik. That man lies like a rug – lies all the time, about *everything* . . . What if he came back here, after seeing my texts to Sid? To tidy up after himself, before the police arrived?'

It was all too much to process.

Somebody had hidden a drowned woman in the bottom of our shipwreck. This seemed incontrovertibly true, based on all we had learned, and all the police had hinted to us.

And it had been done by somebody who knew the *Undine* very well. Someone who had found the Forbidden Hold.

And while nobody knew who this dead person was yet, she was one of a growing number of missing women, in a swirling whirlpool of circumstance that was leading us back again and again to Anvil Point, and the *Undine*.

And to Blue Horizons.

And to Adam, who was robbing our business blind and controlling my sister to do it.

Who had somehow got rid of almost all information about himself from our records – I had only found his application form by accident, because it had been filed in the wrong place.

Who spelled his own name differently as it suited him.

What was he hiding?

'Oh God,' I said, only now realising, my insides turning to icewater. 'He's somewhere out in the world with my sister. Right *now*.'

32

I did not sleep that night, though my tiredness was bone-crushing, as if I was wading through tar.

Once the night changed from darkness to a weak, watery morning, I called Jimmy and told him about the collapse.

He was shocked into an entirely uncharacteristic silence. Once he recovered, he offered to come round immediately. I refused. I was too exhausted to deal with him, with anyone.

'We need to contact everyone signed up for penetration wreck dives and let them know we can't take them in the *Undine* for the foreseeable future,' I said, my hands clasping my hot coffee cup. The bone-deep chill of the wreck seemed to have soaked into my very soul. 'We don't have to tell them it's forever because we don't know it's forever. I mean,' I said, hearing the hitch in my voice, 'we just suspect that. Suspect that a lot, admittedly.'

Jimmy took a long moment to answer. 'They're going to realise. Sooner rather than later, too . . .'

'Eventually, yes, they'll know.'

'Bloody hell,' he breathed. 'The end of the *Undine*, eh?'

I remembered that I was not the only one with an attachment to her. 'Yeah. It's one thing after another.'

'I'll get on to that then . . .' he said. 'I was heading into the shop later today anyway.'

'Jimmy?' I asked, tentative. 'About Sid . . .'

'What about Sid?'

'You don't . . . she didn't happen to mention where Adam was taking her, did she?'

'No. To be honest, Cass love, I don't think she knew. And he certainly didn't say anything.'

'Okay, thanks, Jimmy.'

A pause. 'Look after yourself, girl.'

I switched the call off and looked away, over to that Lalique vase on the mantelpiece, the one my dad had been given for recovering a body.

My heart was breaking.

Dad had only been dead for not quite two years and already everything was falling apart. The dive shop. The *Undine*. Me and Sid.

The little ship of our lives was wrecked, was lost at sea, in a storm out of a clear blue sky.

All I wanted to do right now was sit here and drink tea and eat toast and watch shitty TV. I found I was understanding my sister much better than usual.

Unfortunately, however, I had an appointment.

I pushed myself to my feet, stretched, padded up the stairs to the shower in my en suite.

As I passed my dresser, the scarf from the office drawer was lying next to my jewellery box in untidy folds.

It sent a shiver of dread down me.

I picked it up to fold it again. It was a pretty thing.

I ran my fingers over the slippery fabric of the scarf and noticed something then, an irregularity in the dense pattern.

In one corner, near its deep red fringe, were three coin-sized maroon stains.

I held it up again, peering at them, as my mouth went dry. Yes. My first instinct had been right.

It was definitely blood.

33

'So, hi again,' I said to DCI Trevelyan.

'Call me Tom,' he said, though his cordial expression still had something guarded in it. He was wearing a hooded sweatshirt with the Devon and Cornwall Police logo on the breast, and chinos.

Behind his rimless glasses though, his grey eyes were flinty. I could not imagine calling him Tom, not really, under any circumstances, so I offered him a wan smile instead.

We were in a small interview room in the Helston police station. Erik and I had been offered coffee and I had accepted water, which I held carefully in a dented plastic cup.

'Right. So how can I help you?'

Once more unto the breach, I supposed.

I took a deep breath.

'We're here about . . . well, first, we're here about the wreck of the *Undine*.' I sipped the water, which was lukewarm and tasted stale. I put the plastic cup on the table before me, folded my hands in my lap.

'Right.' It sounded more like a question than a statement.

'So,' I said, gathering my thoughts, 'first of all, we were diving the wreck last night and there was a major collapse in the lower corridor while we were in there. So, the wreck is now barred to all divers. I forget what the limit is . . .'

'A five-hundred-foot radius,' supplied Erik, crossing his

legs at the ankles, appearing to dwarf the plastic chair he was seated in.

Those flinty eyes settled on us. 'Diving it last night, eh? You were both keen to get out there again, I see.'

Something in me recoiled, as though I was being accused of something.

'I . . .' I stammered. 'Ah, well, that is *we*, thought it would be a good idea to inspect it, informally . . .' My throat was dry.

'The news about the new current moving through the ship was a cause for concern,' Erik intervened. 'It called for immediate inspection during the next available tide.' He crossed his arms. 'So yes, we were very *keen*.'

Call-Me-Tom's mouth turned up slightly at the corner.

'And it sounds like the ship nearly fell on you, so you were probably right to inspect it, yes?'

'Um, yes.' I blushed, with a small laugh of nervous relief. 'Anyway, something else came up before the collapse. During the dive we discovered a new way to access the lower hold – we call it the Forbidden Hold.'

'I don't . . .'

I got my phone out, pulled open the map.

'This is the *Undine*. So the purple outlined bit, the lower hold, has been sealed off for years and years.'

'Okay . . .' He peered into my phone at the map, a trio of tight lines drawing down across his forehead.

'But last night, Erik spotted a tear in the bulkhead near the engine room. This would let you swim into the lower hold.'

'We think that someone may have been attempting to hide this hole. From other divers,' said Erik. 'It was covered up with debris.'

'Right. Why would someone do that?' asked DCI Call-me-Tom, those grave eyes running over us, assessing us.

'Erik and I thought that the way the current works, there was no way this woman drifted into the ship from the open sea . . .'

'We think somebody had hidden her body in the lower hold.' Erik was pulling up his photos. 'And she was pushed out by the new current.' He found the right ones, pulled wide to show their detail. 'We thought we should share these with you.'

I took the opportunity to peer at them again, the images Erik had taken both before and after he'd uncovered the rip in the steel. Even though he'd already shown them to me, it still took me a second or two to recognise that the camouflaging debris was actually artful design instead of an accident of the sea.

How observant he was. It was kind of scary, truth be told.

'Hmm . . . can you email these things to me?'

'Yes.' Erik was putting his phone back in his pocket.

'Great, thank you.' I sensed DCI Trevelyan thought we had reached the end, was getting ready to usher us out. He'd risen out of his chair.

'There's one more thing,' I said. I could hear the anxious tremor in my voice, and it was hard to master it. 'It's all a bit . . . it's sensitive. Actually, it's very sensitive, and I can't – I'd really rather that nobody found out it was me that talked to you about this.'

He lowered himself down again, and I watched him school his face into a neutral expression. I was to be offered no promises of anonymity, it seemed. 'Yes?'

I swallowed hard. 'We were trying to think who could

have covered up this hole between me finding the body and the police searching the wreck. Seeing as how the hole *must* have been covered up in that time, or the police divers would have noticed it.' I picked the cup up again. 'Only a handful of people knew about the body being found. It was a couple of hours before the police divers could get there.'

'Right,' he said, but there was a slight change in his posture. I no longer had the sense he was keen to go.

It was making me nervous. I was about to say something that could have devastating consequences for Sid, for me, for the business. I bit my lip.

Beside me, Erik shifted in his chair, his chin dipping down to his chest.

'Anyway, we've been having some . . . *I've* been having some problems with my sister's boyfriend. He's out of the country right now. With my sister.'

'Riiight.' DCI Trevelyan looked hard at me.

'He's a very experienced scuba diver with good knowledge of the *Undine*, and he was one of the first people to know about the body.' I was shaking a little with the realisation of my own treachery. What if he found out about me saying all this? What if Sid did? The thought made me nauseous. 'He says he was visiting his sister that day, who I think lives out in Redruth. I don't know, though.' I shrugged. 'He lies. A lot.'

He was silent, creating a silence for me to fill.

'Secondly, there's this scarf.' I picked up my tote bag, pulled out a plastic bag within it. 'I found it in the bottom drawer of the desk in our home office. It doesn't belong to me or my sister, I don't think.'

I handed the Sainsbury's bag to him. 'I don't know

much about evidence, I hope this is okay. I mean, it's possibly not even evidence. I hope it's not evidence. It's just with these missing women, and . . .'

'This is a scarf,' he said, 'from your office.' He didn't look very impressed.

'Yes,' I said. 'It's got blood on it.'

That got his attention.

'And where is . . . sorry, what's his name?'

'Adam. Adam Fulmore. We don't know if it's one L or two, he writes it differently in different contexts, which I also find a little bit peculiar. Anyway, he's taken my sister away on a surprise trip. He didn't tell us where. He didn't tell *her* where. It might be Egypt, or Malta. I haven't heard from her at all, so I don't know.'

'When was this?'

'Yesterday. They're due back on Tuesday. She thought it might be Tuesday, anyway. But I just don't know. I – I don't want to raise a big fuss over nothing,' I said, and my voice cracked, just a little. 'But just in case, just in case there is something in this, I don't like the thought of her being alone in the world with him somewhere.'

'I see,' he said. He picked up the bag. 'Visiting his sister, you say, on that day?' He peered at me over those rimless glasses. 'You wouldn't have an address for her, would you?'

34

'You sure you don't want me there?' Jimmy asked.

I glanced over at the antique grandfather clock – quarter to three.

They could return at any moment.

I shook my head. 'No. I'll be all right, Jimmy.'

What I didn't say was that I was actually desperate for him, for anyone, to stay, to ride out this miserable, humiliating meeting with me.

But the fact remained that this would have been an unconscionable way to treat Sid, to expose her failure in discernment to anyone outside the family.

It might be a lost cause trying to salvage anything from this, but I felt it regardless.

'Are you sure?' he asked, getting to his feet and looking down at me, 'Because you don't look it.'

'Quite sure.' I felt sick.

He let out a whistling sigh, 'All right. I'll head off. But you know you can call me, don't you? Anytime.'

'Will do.'

I sat there for a few moments, listening to his retreating footsteps, the slam of the front door.

We'd spent the weekend calling resorts, looking for them both, with no success, an endeavour that had ended abruptly with a single text to Jimmy from Adam:

Back tues flight gets in at 9am

They'd probably land in London, I thought, so it would take at least six hours to get back here – it was what it had taken me only nine days ago. I was torn between the twin poles of anxiety and rage – why hadn't Sid texted me? Was it that she was angry at me? Or was she being prevented?

Despite this, I'd been quite efficient. I'd prepared a spreadsheet of the missing money, and the unpaid bills from suppliers. Jimmy had given me good counsel – I'd rung every one of them up over the last few days, explained the trouble we were in, come to terms with them.

How we were going to meet those terms was another matter, a problem for a different day.

I picked up my phone, pretending to myself I was going to play a game rather than obsessively check it for a text from Sid. Back in the old days, of course, before Adam, she would have been texting me throughout the day – all about the journey to the airport, the check-in process for getting home, complaining about the fuss, the rush, whoever she was sat next to on the plane, her ETA – an endgame for all the texts and pictures she would have sent me during the holiday, scattered throughout with emojis, kisses and exclamation marks.

This time she had been resolutely silent throughout. My initial texts on Thursday had not garnered a single reply.

I glanced at the spreadsheet on-screen again. I had a sudden sense of how preposterous I would appear if Sid and Adam arrived now, in my big chair with my computer open on a spreadsheet describing their sins, like some stereotypical CEO.

Maybe I needed to be conciliatory, sympathetic. They

could discover me downstairs, perhaps, in the midst of loading the dishwasher. I could offer false and lukewarm questions on their trip before cutting to the chase about the criminal fraud.

Perhaps I needed to come to Sid alone, while Adam was distracted, maybe lure her upstairs on some pretext, appeal to Sid's logic, her reason . . .

Yeah, I thought bitterly. Why not. That worked before.

I stood up, restless and desperately unhappy, striding over to the window, and that's when I saw the taxi purring up our mountainously steep driveway. The flash of a tanned arm, capped by an orange sleeve, was at the passenger window, and in a flash I recognised Sid, her eyes hidden by shades, sporting an enormous straw hat.

I let out a long, slow breath of relief. Until that moment, I hadn't realised how terrified I had been that she wouldn't come back at all. That it would just be Adam, alone, telling me some fantastical tale about her being abducted by bandits or drowning off the shore of Sharm El Sheikh.

I drew back from the window.

I don't have to be intimidated here, I reminded myself. This is my home.

I realised that if I was going to do this, I needed to do it straight away, like ripping a bandage off. I started to walk down the stairs, Tallulah mewing at my heels. Car doors were opening and slamming, and there was the muted sound of voices carrying across the gravel. I looked down at my hands and was pleased to see that they trembled only a little.

Remember, he's a thief, possibly even worse. He's stolen from you – from us. You don't have to be nice to him. You owe him nothing.

Sid is the one you need to care about.

The key was rattling in the lock, and I felt suddenly breathless as I sat down at the kitchen table, waiting for the front door to swing open with its familiar creak.

When the door pushed open, it was Adam alone.

His expression was unreadable, but despite everything, there was something flickering behind his mouth, some kind of suppressed triumph. Considering the situation, it struck a note of deep unease in me, but it also filled me with enough hot fury to carry on.

'Hello, Cass,' he said. He widened his smile, letting his hands rest on the kitchen table as he leaned towards me.

'Hi, Adam,' I said, looking up at him, which took all my courage because I was finding his proximity, his obvious self-satisfaction, very intimidating. 'Did you have a nice trip?'

'Oh, *wonderful*.' He cocked his head jauntily at me. 'How were things here?'

'Could have been better. The *Undine* collapsed and is closed to visitors indefinitely. On the plus side, I unlocked the office door.'

I searched his tanned face carefully, looking for some inkling of surprise about the office, or even the *Undine*, but saw none – it meant nothing, of course, because he was obviously a practised liar, but still, I was disappointed.

There was no sign of Sid. Was she hiding from me?

'I don't know what you mean about the office being locked.' He offered me an apologetic smile, and my sense of alarm was deepening. 'But clearly something is bothering you.'

At this point, Sid appeared. Presumably she'd been paying the taxi driver.

'Hello,' I said to her. 'How was Malta? Or wherever it was?'

Her face set like concrete, only her eyes gleaming with some unknown emotion. As unfriendly as she was being, it squeezed something in my heart.

She's in trouble.

'We didn't go to Malta,' said Adam.

'Have you told her yet?' Sid asked him.

'Told me what?' I asked, my alarm returning.

'We went to Las Vegas instead,' he said, and his triumph shone out as he caught hold of Sid's sunburned hand, and there, on her wedding finger, was a band of gold. 'We got *married*!'

Quickly Sid snatched her hand out of his.

'You were planning this?' I asked, looking at them both, hardly able to believe it.

'Um, no, no.' Sid had the grace at least to look shifty, her cheeks glowing red. 'Adam surprised me.'

I could only stare at her, stupefied. Was she mad? Why would she do such a thing?

And then, in the middle of all this, there was a loud knocking on the door.

'Aren't you going to congratulate us?' Adam was asking me, with a big smile that showed all his teeth.

I opened my mouth to say something, but I felt sick, and all I wanted in that second was to be away from them both. I stood up, feeling as though a bomb had gone off between my ears. She'd married him.

She'd married him.

Oh, how stupid she was. How were we going to get out of this?

And in a way, I realised, I might have triggered this

reaction in him. I had been difficult, ultimately hostile. Any fool could have seen that I was going to upset the balance of power around here.

Why hadn't I been more cunning, more circumspect?

Now he wasn't just an employee any more. Now he owned half of Sid's half of the business.

I yanked open the door, planning on getting rid of whoever it was as fast as I could.

Standing on the step were two uniformed police officers, a man and a woman. 'We're looking for Adam Fulmore?'

Oh, I thought.

It seemed one of my arrows had hit its target. Had they found something out about the scarf? About his whereabouts on the day I found the woman in the *Undine*?

Things suddenly appeared to be spiralling upwards, into a weird unreality.

They were staring at me, expectant, almost suspicious.

'Um, yeah, yeah,' I murmured, stunned. 'Come in, he's just here.'

At that moment he emerged into the hall, still gloriously smug, and I had a tiny fraction of satisfaction in watching his face pale, his grin drop. In that instant, he looked as guilty as any man alive.

'Hello. Adam Fulmore?' asked the woman.

He nodded, his eyes round.

'I'm PC Cobham and this is PC Kelly.' The other officer, a man with short grey hair and heavy jowls, offered us a curt nod. 'We're with Devon and Cornwall Police.'

'Whah . . . what is this about?' Adam asked. He offered her a weak smile.

She did not return it. 'There has been an allegation of theft made against you concerning your place of business,' she said. 'I'm not privy to all the details, but they can discuss it in more detail with you at Helston. We're just here to take you in to answer some questions.'

'What?' He seemed genuinely amazed. '*Theft?*' He stepped back. 'That's ridiculous. I'm not going.'

I stood there, blinking at them. I could not have been any more shocked than he was.

I had mentioned nothing about the money to the police. What were they doing here?

Sid appeared behind him.

'Adam,' she began, her voice high and anxious, while the two officers exchanged a look.

'It really is in your best interests to . . .' began the man.

'This is a mistake,' Adam barked at them. 'I haven't stolen anything.'

'Now now,' said the male officer. 'Calm down. We only want to ask you a few questions at the station. You're not under arrest.'

'Adam?' said Sid, her face ghastly. 'Adam love, you must stop arguing with them . . .'

I backed away as he caught sight of me, his eyes wide.

'Did you do this?'

'No!' I said. I was, in truth, as astonished as everyone else. Well, maybe not that astonished, but still. Those things I'd said to Call-Me-Tom – had he really arranged for Adam's arrest? But if so, why about the money? They didn't know about the money. Only a handful of people knew . . .

I thought Adam would hit me for an instant, but he paused, frozen, considering.

'All right. This is all ridiculous,' he said. 'But I'll go.'

Without another word he stalked out of the house, the

officers in tow, while Sid followed behind, listening to him bellow instructions to her on who to call on his behalf while she wrung her hands.

I watched from the doorway as they let him into a police car, gently unpeeling Sid as she laid her hands flat on the windows, shouting 'I love you!' to him through the glass.

When they drove off, she watched them go from the drive, waving helplessly after him as though he was off to war.

When she turned back to me, her face was scarlet and tear-stained.

'*You did this!*'

'What? No! I didn't know this was going to happen . . .' Which was true, as far as it went, but I had an inkling who might have been responsible. I might not have called the police specifically about the money, but ultimately Jimmy would have had no such compunction.

I felt my face, my chest grow hot.

Jimmy.

I needed to have a word with him.

'You're so jealous,' she hissed, her mouth a square of flashing teeth. 'You think you're just fucking *it*, don't you? Swanning off to Australia, being a "scientist". You can't bear to see anyone else be happy!'

I recoiled. 'Everything you said is ridiculous. Completely ridiculous. And for the record, he is a thief!'

'You're lying!' Her face was red, water streaming out of her nose and eyes, her voice hoarse with grief. 'He would never steal from us. Never!'

I couldn't let this stand, and like a fool I shouted: 'Yeah? It looks like he's stolen thirty-seven grand from us!'

She did a double take, her eyes huge and pink. 'You just told me you knew nothing about it, you lying cow!'

I hated to fight with her like this and I wanted to stop, I really did, but also – I was so, so angry at her. Dangerously so.

'What the hell, Sid? He's stolen all that money, and now he's married you just so he can steal more!'

I knew it was a terrible thing to say even as her palm connected with my cheek in a ringing blow, which I think was the only thing stopping me from lunging at her, catfighting with her as we had when we were little girls.

We glared at one another, breathing as hard as if we'd been running a marathon, until I turned on my heel and stalked back into the house.

35

Jimmy.

Oh my days. Jimmy.

This could only be him.

I'd decided to walk to the cottage on Hellys Street. However helpful he had been, it was time for me and Jimmy to have a serious talk.

It was something I would not have thought twice about a year ago, but as I strode down the footpath along the headland that would take me into the village, I felt anxious, as though I was being watched.

Anyone could come for me here and nobody would see or hear, I realised, passing down the winding dirt path, dark trees overhanging me with their branches, and not even reaching the relative light and busyness of Fore Street could wholly soothe me.

Jimmy must have been expecting me, because I didn't even have time to rap on the blue paint of the door before it swung open, and he stood back to let me in.

I didn't enter.

'Jimmy,' I said. 'What have you done?'

He let out a weary sigh.

'Is this about Adam?' he asked.

'Yeah. It's about Adam. Of course it's about Adam! The police have just driven him away. I specifically said to leave it until we knew more, until I could talk to Sid. I said it more than once, too.' I crossed my arms in front of me. 'I know you heard me.'

'Girl,' he said, coming forward to stand on the step, since it was clear I was not coming in. 'I only did what you would never have had the courage to do.'

'What?' I blanched. I felt the truth of this accusation, but still . . .

'You would have let Sid talk you round,' he said mildly. 'I . . .'

'You would have, you know it and I know it. You would have wrung your hands and angsted about it all but would have done nothing about it. He's a thief. I spared you some trouble.' He shrugged. 'It's true, isn't it?'

I smarted a little against these words. After all, hadn't I wanted Adam to be investigated?

I had. Just not for this. Not right now. Not when there were bigger fish to fry.

'Jimmy, we don't know he stole that money,' I said. 'Tonight was devastating for Sid. True or not, you cannot be making those kinds of decisions for us.'

'I just . . .'

'*We are not children any more.*' I stared at him, even though part of me was dying inside. 'Do you get it?'

The silence was absolute, thick as concrete between us. Somewhere gulls were calling over the harbour. Sprightly footsteps were coming down Hellys Street on the other side of the road.

'Jimmy, I am grateful for your help. I am. That said, you are not in charge of our affairs. Do I make myself clear?'

'Cass . . .' He looked heartbroken.

I couldn't stay a moment longer. I realised that if I did, he would talk me round, just as he'd claimed Sid would.

Don't get me wrong – I had no love for Adam, God knows. I'd told the police I thought he might be a killer. I'd handed over that scarf. I suspected he might have covered up that entrance to the Forbidden Hold and I'd told the police why I thought that.

But Jimmy was now making executive decisions about our lives, just as he had when he and Mandy had looked after us as kids.

I just couldn't let him. I couldn't let him interfere with the real business in hand and muddy the waters.

If Adam was a killer, I needed the police to concentrate on that – to prove it. More than anything, I needed them to get him away from Sid.

So as much as it hurt, I turned on my heel and stalked off down the hill, leaving Jimmy standing there.

36

'Hey, Georgia – how's it going?'

'Caaassss! I was just talking about you last night. I was telling this guy we met about your shark research.' She winked. 'He was very impressed. And so cute. He's taking me out for drinks on Saturday . . .'

Despite myself, I laughed out loud. 'I'm so glad I could help.'

'That's what I love about you, babe, you always help a girl out.'

'Maybe you can help me out, then. Can I tell you something?'

'Of course you can, pretty lady.' Georgia sank back into the squashy grey sofa. I remembered that sofa, how often I'd laughed with her on it, how I'd fallen off it, how I'd woken up hung-over on it on more than one occasion.

The sight of it filled me with an ache that was exactly like homesickness.

'Shoot,' she said.

'I . . .' I shut my mouth, thought for a moment, while she watched with expectant and slightly ironic patience. 'Don't think I'm crazy, all right?'

'That ship has already sailed, Cassandra.' She grinned at me. 'Just spit it out.'

I smiled despite myself. 'Okay. So here's the thing. And it's . . . it's quite serious.'

'Yeah?'

'I think my brother-in-law might be a murderer.'

'Adam?' She was about to laugh, prepped for the punch-line, but my silence must have made an impression on her. A pause, while her smile died. 'What?'

'Yeah, exactly that.' I thought about what to add, decided that I'd just about got the subject covered.

She didn't reply, her brows furrowing.

'I get that it's a lot,' I said, after a long moment.

'I mean,' she rolled her eyes upwards in thought, 'I know that you don't *like* him . . .'

'Well, yeah, yeah. I don't like him, true. But that's not . . . it's incidental.'

She blinked. I could tell instantly that she didn't believe me but was prepared to give me a fair hearing anyway. It was one of the things that I loved about her.

'Do you want to tell me your reasons, then?'

Yes, I did. I told her everything.

By the time I had explained about the rift in the *Undine*'s bulkhead she was pale and silent, her eyes huge, her hand clenched in her long black hair.

'Cass, I mean, I know it's suggestive, but still . . .' Her fun, girlish affect was gone. 'You know, this is all circumstantial. You can't let your dislike of this guy, however well deserved, get you into trouble . . .'

I shrugged helplessly. 'There's nothing more I can do anyway. I already told the police everything I know. It's up to them now.'

We stared at each other for a few moments down the phone, before Georgia, dropping her hand, turned and looked away, deep in thought.

I sighed. 'Y'know, I don't even have anywhere to stay tonight. I can't go home to the house with Sid like she is.'

'You can't go home anyway,' said Georgia quickly. 'He might not be a killer, but you can't be anywhere where he is.'

'He's not there now. He's at the police station.'

'But they're only questioning him.' She looked at me. 'Remember, if it's just about the money, all Sid has to say is that he took the money out with her permission, and they'll let him go.'

I sighed, stirred uncomfortably. I wanted to sob. 'How can I leave her alone with him? I mean, if only one tenth of the things I think about him are true . . .'

'Cass, I know it's hard, but try not to worry,' she urged. 'If the cops are paying attention to him for this, he'd be very stupid to try anything with her, and he doesn't sound stupid.' She leaned into the phone. 'She's his supporter, his cheerleader, his meal ticket. You, however – *you*, he's angry at.' She put her chin on her hand. 'You really have no place to stay?'

I shook my head. 'Nope.'

'Not Jimmy's . . . ?'

'Nope.' A pause. 'I'm furious with him.' I rubbed my face. 'What if this theft thing distracts the cops from looking into Adam properly? What if they start thinking this is just some petty grudge I have with him over money?' I let out a long sigh, wanting nothing more than to curl up into a little ball. 'I can't . . . oh, it's just too much.'

'Okay, what about Ben?'

Yeah, what about Ben? I thought bitterly.

I had heard nothing since my last text. He must have been aware of what I had been going through.

Why hadn't he . . .

'Don't panic,' said Georgia with brisk authority. She

had accurately gauged my expression. 'There must be *somebody* you can trust to put you up?'

'Hello.'

'Hello, Boss Lady,' Erik replied, eyeing me suspiciously from around the door. I wondered for an instant whether there was somebody else in there, and was surprised at the visceral pang I had at the idea. 'How did you know where I live?'

'It's in your file in the office.' I shrugged. 'I am overstepping a thousand boundaries, I know.'

'It's okay.' He narrowed his eyes at me. 'The times are very strange.'

'Can I come in?'

I thought for a ghastly moment he would refuse, but instead he held the door wide for me, standing back as though I was a bomb that might go off.

Erik lived in a tiny flat above the Old Fish Market, which had moved out of the village years ago further up the coast, many years before I was born. The lower level was composed entirely of a coffee house and gift shop; the upper was a couple of flats that didn't appear to have been renovated since the eighties.

I knew these flats quite well. People who came in the summer to work at the shop often lived in one or the other. As a teenager I remembered impromptu parties, barbecues in the tiny yard behind the gift shop, beer cans lined up on the low wall, men in surfing shorts and mirrored sunglasses, women in bikini tops and cut-off denims, the scent of burning weed, voices and accents from all over the globe, gathered together in one place.

It seemed a vision from a lost world now.

One thing had not changed – the view from the windows, though I remembered that in bad weather they shook in their frames and the wind whistled and howled through them. Beyond lay the sea, deep blue and quiescent, glittering in the dusk.

'What are you doing here, Cassandra?'

What an excellent question. Why was I here, and not at Ben's?

I didn't know the answer – I only knew that I had been walking and thinking, and somehow, without knowing I had decided, I had ended up here.

'Adam took my sister to Las Vegas, not Malta. She says it was a surprise.' I waggled my head noncommittally, trying not to cry. 'I think I believe her.'

'Not much diving in Las Vegas,' he remarked, offering me an old brown fake leather recliner after quickly moving a stack of dive magazines from the seat. 'Isn't the Devil's Hole near there?'

'I don't think they got much diving in. He married her.'

'Married her?'

'Yes.'

'Oh.' I realised it was the first time I had seen him surprised. 'That's not good.' He looked down at me. 'I take it you wished the happy couple all the best?'

'I didn't have time. The police arrived and took him away for questioning.'

His dark brows went up and he considered me for a long moment. 'That was fast. They must have heard us when we spoke to them.'

I shook my head at him. 'It wasn't that. Jimmy went behind my back. He told them about the theft.'

He narrowed his eyes at me. 'Jimmy. That is also not good.'

Erik sank into another armchair opposite me, seemingly deep in thought. He was clad in a light grey fleece and loose blue jeans, his large, strong feet bare. Coiling scars covered the left one, leaving weaving white marks against the tanned flesh. An old jellyfish sting, and a nasty one too.

He saw me looking. 'Ah, that was me being stupid. Ignore it.'

'I find it hard to imagine you doing stupid things.'

He grunted out a laugh. 'Thank you, but you don't know me that well.'

Touché.

I told him all that had happened since we last talked, and he soothed me by not having a loud, dramatic reaction to it, instead listening quietly until I reached the end. I was emotionally exhausted and so managing other people's feelings demanded more energy than I felt I could spend.

I was taking away that Erik didn't do expressive, visceral reactions to things as a general principle.

After I finished talking, silence fell, letting the murmur of the tourists out on Fore Street in through the leaky windows, the quiet underlying rush of the sea.

'So he is under arrest?' asked Erik, regarding me thoughtfully.

'No. At least not yet. They're just questioning him about the money.' I sat back in the chair, let out a long breath. 'But I can't help thinking they've brought him in for the wrong thing ... What if they decide this is just some stupid domestic and stop looking at the evidence we gave them?'

He waved this away with a single gesture. 'It doesn't

matter what they question him for now. It is out of our hands. They have him and will learn what kind of man he is.' Erik folded his arms, regarded me. 'They have the bloody scarf. They have our evidence about the *Undine*. Either he is guilty or he is not. If he is guilty, then this marriage to your sister will go away very quickly, I think.'

I bit my lip. Before, I had been convinced of his guilt. But now the police had taken him in for questioning, I was in an agony of doubt and second guessing.

What if we were wrong?

I was destroying Sid's happiness. I had to believe it was in a good cause.

'What do you think?' I asked him.

'What do I think?' He raised his eyebrows at me.

'Yes. Do you think Adam did it? Killed that woman in the *Undine*, maybe even the other missing women too?'

Erik shrugged. 'Somebody killed that woman and hid her body in the Forbidden Hold. They took the trouble to hide her. Did they kill the others that have gone missing? I don't know that, but it seems possible. Somebody also knew that the police would come and covered the hole in the boiler room up again. Was it him?' Erik closed his eyes. 'That I do not know either, but he was one of the few people that could have known the divers were coming to recover the body.' He opened them again, fixing me in that dark blue gaze.

I looked away first. 'It's almost too much to imagine,' I whispered.

'There is no point thinking about it now.'

I had no reply. He was right. But it didn't do anything for my bubbling anxiety.

I gazed out of the window, to the sunset.

'It's a nice view in this flat,' I said. 'But freezing in the winter, if I remember rightly.'

He stirred, surprised.

'Freezing? Your winters are never freezing. Back home it is freezing.' He nodded towards the sea. 'The world is too hot and noisy anyway.'

'Where is home?' I asked.

'Mortensrud. It is a suburb of Oslo. In Norway.'

I narrowed my eyes at him. 'Here was me thinking that Oslo was in France. Or perhaps Paraguay.'

That almost smile was back. 'I apologise.' I was awarded an ironic little bow as he got to his feet. He raised a warning finger. 'Not everyone I meet in this country knows where Oslo is.'

'Do you miss it?'

'What?' He looked discomfited, as though he had been caught out.

I blushed. I had been too nosy, perhaps. 'Sorry, I . . .'

Again that decisive hand wave. 'No. I don't miss it. I haven't lived there in years. I don't even have family there any more. I went into the Navy, ended up in the Marinejeegerkommandeon – special forces, you would say. I travelled. There's nothing left for me in Mortensrud. My parents are both dead now.'

'I'm sorry to hear that.'

'Yes, we are both orphans.' He appeared to have no interest in discussing the matter further, instead tilted his head at me. 'Do you want a drink?'

'A drink drink?' I asked hopefully.

'Oh yes, a drink drink. The situation calls for it, no?'

'A drink drink sounds perfect,' I said. 'The only thing that will work.'

While his back was turned, I gazed around the flat. It was fastidiously neat. He had a bookshelf full of well-thumbed paperbacks, mostly histories and biographies, dive magazines, and a television attached to a single beat-up laptop and a pair of speakers. Very little else, apart from a framed movie poster for *The Cabinet of Dr Caligari*.

He was somebody that travelled light, I saw.

I accepted the bottle of beer he returned with, gently clinked it against the one in his own hand. 'Cheers.'

'*Skål.*'

'You know,' I said, 'there was a girl that used to live in these flats, called Mona, and she claimed this place was haunted. She was so scared she moved out.'

He was pulling out his keychain, which had a bottle opener on it in the shape of a dolphin. 'Interesting. Grace used to say that too.'

'Grace?' I asked.

'Yes, she was my neighbour,' he gestured at his front door, towards the landing leading to the other flat. 'All the time, she would say it. It didn't bother her. She said it was a "friendly presence".'

I stared at him, wide-eyed and fascinated. I had been haunted lately too, I felt, by the woman on the *Undine*. She seemed to shadow me constantly. 'Did she ever see anything, hear anything?'

'No, just felt a presence. But then, she was not likely to see or hear anything since ghosts aren't real.' He shrugged.

'Not a believer, then?'

'No.'

'What was she like? Grace?'

He regarded me for a long moment. 'Irish, pretty, punky. Why do you ask about her?'

'I don't know,' I said. I had the feeling I had touched another nerve. 'When I was looking through the online reviews, I saw a lot of positive stuff about her. She was nice, helpful.' I sighed. 'It's a shame she's gone. I would have liked to say thank you.'

He seemed to ruminate on this, then:

'I liked Grace. She was adventurous.' A pause. 'She saw the good in people.'

I had the strangest feeling he was talking about himself, that the good she'd seen had been in him.

A tendril of jealousy wove about my innards, sharp as a jellyfish sting.

'She was in love with the *Undine*,' he continued. 'We dived it together, all the time – I would film her for her channel. She made YouTube videos, she was very good at it. The *Undine* was the reason she stayed so long, despite the fact that she was unhappy. We were all unhappy. You have already guessed this, but that guy is a terrible boss – charming to your face, but lazy and disorganised.' He popped the cap on to the table, placing it carefully. 'Anyway, she had a big fight with them about her money, just before you arrived.' He handed me my own bottle. 'I just heard about it afterwards. I was disappointed.' He looked wistful. 'She did not say goodbye.'

'That's a shame,' I sighed, little envious knives digging into my heart, and I wondered at how much they hurt. 'It's too bad they couldn't do right by her. Sid always hated handling that stuff. I kind of saddled her with it.'

'Hmm,' he said.

'What?' I asked, feeling a brush of disapproval.

'You talk constantly about how you left your sister alone here.'

I shifted uncomfortably.

'But she had her boyfriend. All her friends were here.' He regarded me levelly. 'You were the one that went into exile, not her.'

I snorted, wiped at my face. 'It was the Gold Coast, hardly Siberia . . .'

'This thing,' he said, pointing at me with one thick finger, 'that is happening at Blue Horizons, this is not your fault.' He waved his hand at me. 'It is very sad that her father died. Especially while she was diving with him and supposed to be looking out for him. But he was an experienced diver and knew the risks. Cressida is not a little girl. She is a grown woman and this was her responsibility.'

Silence then.

I felt again the crushing weight of failure and blame she had been shouldering all along. Pity wracked me. I wanted to call her, wanted to talk to her.

'She must feel terrible,' I said eventually.

Erik gave me a cynical glance. I was stung into resentment by his surety, his judgement.

'Look,' I said. 'She was only what . . . twenty-eight, and had just lost her dad, and . . .'

'Excuses, excuses.' He flapped his hand, dismissing this. 'You know what I was doing when I was that age, Cassandra? I was being shot at by the Taliban in Afghanistan.'

I was astounded, tried to imagine this, found I could, very easily.

We sat in silence at this impasse, finishing our bottles, while I thought furiously. Out of the window, the sun was setting, boiling scarlet into the sea.

'Did you and Grace – were you a thing?' I asked.

'What? What kind of question is that?' He didn't seem offended though, more amused.

'I was just curious . . .' I was actually mortified. Where had that come from? My cheeks were burning.

'No. I was not her *type*.' Again that faint smile.

'No? It just seemed like . . .'

'Grace liked girls.'

'Oh.' I fell silent, crucified by embarrassment. What was I doing? How strong was this beer, anyway?

He merely stared at me, as though he had every right to do so.

I stood up. 'I'll just put this in the kitchen,' I said, needing a moment to gather my thoughts out of his gaze. 'Do you want another . . . ?'

He had stood up too, and slowly he stepped over to me.

I was shaking, I realised. 'Um . . .'

He lifted the bottle carefully out of my hand, set it on the table. 'In a minute.' His broad hands were on my hips, pulling me closer, where the heat radiated out of him, his eyes not leaving mine, and when his lips descended to my own I pulled him closer, closer still, my arms winding around his back, his shoulders, and catching him in the tresses of my long hair.

37

It was quiet in the shop.

My mood was sombre. Nevertheless, I'd relished the early morning peace as I'd parted from Erik at the sea wall with a squeeze of his hand and walked alongside the harbour. It was a strangely thin and misty morning. The gulls were invisible behind the veils of fog, only their cries giving their presence away. Both sea and sky had blended together into a single opaque, creamy whole.

It gave me a shivery feeling, as though I was trapped on an island adrift in a pale and moving golden light, attached to neither heaven nor earth.

We'd picked up a couple of croissants and some filter coffee from the shop below the flats, and Erik and I were going to enjoy this together once he got back from the *Mustang Sally*. He'd left something undone on board, he told me.

He hadn't said what it was.

Inside the shop, as I pondered what news today might bring, the phone rang.

'Hello, Blue Horizons, can I help you?'

'Where the hell are you?' It was a man's voice, with a strong Welsh accent.

I blinked at the receiver.

'I'm sorry, who is this?'

'Alan Howard. I have a private lesson booked. With Adam Fulmore.'

'Uh . . .'

'He told me he'd pick me up. I've been waiting at the train station with my gear for the last hour. Is someone coming to get me?'

A private lesson? I'd seen nothing about it in our calendar.

'I . . . I'm sorry, I'll just . . .' I was firing up the achingly slow computer, the flush of embarrassment creeping up to my hairline, the beginnings of panic hammering in my chest. Not this. Not now. 'Let me check that . . .'

'. . . I've been calling his mobile all morning, and he's not answered. I've come all the way from Cardiff, love, and I've got to say, I'm not amused . . .'

'I'm so, so sorry,' I said, thinking on my feet. 'Adam's indisposed. But of course I'll be coming to get you. I'm on my way right now . . . you're at Falmouth?'

'Yes, I'm at Falmouth. I've been at bloody Falmouth since half six this morning . . .'

'I'll be there as soon as I can.'

'Make sure you are.'

He hung up.

My heart pounded in my throat. All I knew was that I had to pick this man up now before any more reputational damage could be done to Blue Horizons.

Frankly, we needed all the help we could get. We'd had to borrow thirty thousand pounds just to keep the business afloat, to afford insurance, to pay the wages.

We would have to pay all of that back. Somehow.

The door swung open. Erik stood there, and despite all that was happening, I felt a burst of unreasoning happiness at the sight of him, even while I held up the phone.

He did not speak, merely raising his eyebrows.

'Erik, sorry, I have to go. Adam's gone and booked some private dive and not put it in the calendar. The guy is supposed to be picked up from Falmouth . . .'

'It's all right,' he rumbled. 'I can go get him . . .'

'No.' I shook my head. 'I need to go get him myself. He's going absolutely mad.' I shrugged at him. 'It will need a full-on charm offensive.'

He narrowed his eyes at me. 'Are you trying to imply that I am not completely charming?'

I laughed, kissed him, and he tasted of fresh coffee. 'Of course not. See you in a bit.'

When I arrived at the top of our long, winding drive I was covered in a light sweat which was not wholly down to exertion.

After how I had left the house yesterday, the idea of returning filled me with dread.

But what I needed was the people carrier. The van had not been cleaned since yesterday since we'd not anticipated using it, and I wanted to make a good first impression. Or at least, second impression.

The people carrier was parked near the house, its blue logo of leaping dolphins the only splash of colour visible in the mist. I glanced hopefully in the driver's side window – perhaps the keys had been left in it.

No such luck.

Damn it. I was not looking forward to the next part.

With a sigh, I unlocked the front door of the house and pushed it open, then froze in surprise.

My sister stood in the hall, her hands on her hips, dressed in a grey suit and pale pink blouse I had never seen before. Beneath her make-up, her eyes were small and red.

That hateful gold band glittered on her hand.

On so many levels she seemed like a stranger to me at that moment. She was even dressed like one.

'What are *you* doing here?' she snapped.

I blinked at her.

I glanced around the hallway, half fearful that her new husband might leap into view behind her.

Be nice, Cass. Try to be nice.

'I'm here to pick up the car. We've got a private lesson booked today.'

I nearly added, *Remember? Private lessons? From that business we run?*

I'd told myself, as I scrambled up the hill from the village, that I had to be gentle with Sid if I ran into her, no matter how angry I was. That really, she was a victim in all this. I needed to be compassionate, and understanding, and in short, to be the bigger person.

However, all this had been easier to sell to myself when I expected her to be grieving and volatile and crying hysterically. But now there was something cold and hard in her face, something spiteful.

And I shouldn't have been surprised, not really, because if you'd asked me, at any other time, how my sister would handle all this, I would have told you that even for pre-Adam Sid, the best form of defence was always attack.

In the animal world, they call it 'threat display'. It is a cover for vulnerability.

She scowled at me. '*I* need the car today.' She tugged at her little grey jacket, a self-conscious movement. 'I need to be at the solicitors in Truro for nine-thirty.' Her tone was accusatory.

She was going to the solicitors? Alone? 'Use the van.'

Then, before I could stop myself, 'Like your arsehole boy-friend should have done.'

Her eyes narrowed as her chin came up. 'He's my hus-band, actually.'

'Your arsehole husband,' I snarled back. '*Sorry.*'

She glared at me.

'Sorry,' I repeated, swallowing down my unreasoning rage. 'Look. Just because we don't agree about Adam is no reason for us to fight.' I met her chilly stare. 'We're in big trouble now, Sid. We need to pull together.'

She didn't even flicker, and I could feel it building in me again, that irrational, unthinking fury. Like when she had borrowed clothes I'd wanted to wear when we were teen-agers or told on me to our parents.

But then she lowered her eyes, sighed.

'Where's Adam?' I asked.

She froze, just for an instant.

Oh my God, I thought. 'Did they charge him? What with?'

'Oh, assaulting a . . .' She paled, then bristled. 'Don't sound so surprised. It was what you wanted . . .'

'For God's sake,' I snapped. 'It was not what I wanted. I did not tell the police that Adam was stealing from us.' I sighed in the face of her unwavering glare, aware of how disingenuous I sounded. How disingenuous I was actually being with her, if I was to be honest.

But how could I possibly tell her what I'd really sus-pected him of?

'Yes,' I admitted. 'I knew he'd been taking out a lot of money from the business account. Yes, I knew we were broke . . .'

'Then how did the police know?'

However angry I was at Jimmy right now, I found myself unaccountably reluctant to drop his name to her. After all, I had set this course in motion, not he. But still, we'd all been lying to each other quite enough recently.

'I don't . . . Jimmy helped me go through the bills. I think he might have said something.'

'Oh, it's Jimmy's fault now, is it?' she hissed in disgust. 'Adam's right, you're such a piece of work. Just so deceitful. So manipulative.'

I went very still for a long moment. So still, in fact, that she took a tiny step back from me.

'Here's what I want to know, Cressida,' I said coldly. 'I want to know how you can stand here, shrieking at me about how deceitful and manipulative I apparently am, when, let's not forget, for nearly two years you've been telling me that you're too busy to chat, and the business is doing so well, when all of that is clearly absolute bollocks.' I threw my hands wide. 'Was I even speaking to you most of the time in those texts? I don't know! I have no idea, and I don't trust you to tell me the truth. And you think I'm the deceitful one?'

'I don't expect you to understand,' she said, but there was a tremor in her voice now, as though she had almost comprehended me. 'Adam loves me. He's only trying to protect me . . .'

My jaw dropped in amazement. 'Protect you? From what? From *me*? From *reality*? You know what, Sid? You sound like somebody in a cult. You're stood there, blithely explaining to me why it's okay that your boyfriend controls every aspect of your life because "he loves you". Like this Las Vegas thing – I'm curious – was that your idea of a dream wedding?'

'Of course I knew we were going to get married eventually . . .' Her cheeks were taut, her lips trembling.

'Eventually?' I snorted. 'I mean, did he even propose to you at any point, or did he just pitch up at the Little Chapel of Love straight from the airport and expect you to get your "I do" on?' If she had been nearer to me I would have grabbed her, shaken her. 'Can you not see how this is Not Normal? How this is dangerous? How *he* is dangerous?'

'He helps me,' she shouted, but her voice was cracked, her expression twisted, conflicted. 'It may not work for you, but it works for us!'

'Sid,' I said, my anger gone, because I realised that, for the first time since I had come home from Australia, we two were on the brink of having a genuine conversation about Adam. 'Whatever it is you think he's achieving, it's not helping you.'

She looked panicked, lost, and for a second I thought there would be a breakthrough, or at the very least a glimmer of nascent self-awareness in her.

But the moment passed, and she sighed, briskly dabbing at her eyes with a well-used scrap of tissue she pulled out of the pocket of the little jacket she was wearing, her chin jutting forward at me. 'I can't do this with you now, Cass. I have to get to the solicitors.' She sniffed. 'He's got a bail hearing at the magistrates' court this morning and I can't be late.'

Something struck me as odd about this. I was no expert in these matters, but . . .

'Why didn't they bail him straight from the police station?'

'There was . . .' A hard light came into her eyes. 'Well, it wasn't for theft, so you can get that look off your face!'

'I don't have a look on my face,' I snapped impatiently. 'Just tell me. If they didn't charge him for theft, why does he need to be bailed?'

'It was . . . it wasn't his fault!' She looked shifty yet imploring. 'He . . . there was some trouble at the police station. They wanted to ask his sister some questions for some reason so they wanted her address, and he . . . he lost it with them. He might have pushed one of them. I don't know the details, he didn't want to worry me.' She threw me a challenging glance. 'He thought they would frighten her.' She raised her chin defensively. 'He's very protective of her.'

'Right.' I already had very strong views on Adam's version of being 'protective' towards the women in his life, but these were surplus to requirements now. I was aware of Alan Howard waiting for me in Falmouth.

But still. Why did the police want to question his sister if they were only interested in the theft? And more interestingly, why would Adam be so desperate to prevent this questioning that he'd assault a police officer?

I wondered what he was afraid she might tell them.

Sid waited in unforgiving silence.

'We can go to the shop,' I said. 'The van's parked there. But I need the people carrier for this customer.'

A pause, then a hint of assent in the tilt of her golden head, though her blue eyes remained flinty. She swept up the car keys. 'All right. Let's go.'

She stalked past me to the door, leaving a slight whiff of Coco Mademoiselle in her wake.

I glanced towards the living room. Sid's crisp, on-point appearance was at total odds with the state of the house. Clothes were strewn on the couch, and it looked as if she'd been sleeping on it. The house already smelled sad and musty – the sickly fake tomato scent of oven-ready pizza and last night's empty wine bottles lingered in the air. A dirty wine glass sat on the coffee table, glinting at me as I pulled the door shut.

She climbed into the driver's seat, and the car throbbed into sudden life. I swung in next to her, pulling the heavy door shut.

'Where are you going to take this person, this diver?' asked Sid suddenly.

'I don't know,' I mumbled. 'I don't know where Adam meant to take him when he booked it – probably the *Undine*. The *Mohegan*, maybe . . .'

'No way is the *Mohegan* going to satisfy him if he's come for the *Undine* . . .'

'Well, we can't go to the *Undine*,' I muttered. 'So that's that.'

'You can't just take him even to see it from the outside?' She moved the car into gear, frowned at the wheel, the pedals.

I thought about this for a second. It was so tempting. It was . . .

'No,' I said, because the answer hadn't changed. 'Not till the survey's done.'

'When will that be?'

'I dunno.'

'But you could just show him the damage and not take him in. He'd probably be into that. First to see it after the collapse and all . . .'

'Sid,' I said, 'I watched the ceiling split above me. I nearly died. The coastguard will arrest us if I try to lead a dive within five hundred feet of it.'

Shocked silence as the car rumbled towards the steep driveway that twisted down to the road.

'What are you talking about?' She stared at me. 'You were there? When it happened?'

'Well, yeah.'

'With clients?' She scowled through the windshield at the downwards-winding track.

'No. Just Erik.'

Her blonde eyebrows shot up. 'It collapsed while you were in it? You and Erik?' Her mouth was open, speechless, as she swung round the first bend in the drive, far too fast. Below us the railings lining the sea wall glinted in the veils of fog. 'What the fuck did you do, Cass?' Her hands tightened on the wheel. 'Did you *cause* this?'

'No!' I grabbed the door handle because the people carrier was picking up too much speed now. 'Don't be stupid! What, you're going to blame us for doing the things you and Adam should have been doing? And slow down, will you? Are you trying to kill us?'

She didn't answer, and I looked at her.

Her face was frozen, her eyes round, and in that instant, I realised exactly the same thing that she did, which was that though she was pumping the brake with those new black leather high-heels for all she was worth, nothing was happening.

Her sideways glance at me was filled with terror, and I understood.

The brakes were useless, and we were tearing down the hill, leaving the driveway, gaining speed with every second, and we were going to shoot out from the drive into Fore Street below, crash into the sea railings, and if that didn't kill us, we would be carried through them on to the tideless beach some twelve feet below.

Time stood still.

Ahead, the iron sea rails raced to meet us, and a slew of ideas flashed through my mind and were instantly dismissed. Open the door and jump out – no, never, it was too fast now.

And no way was I leaving Sid here.

Pull the handbrake.

I had hold of it and was yanking it up, and there was a screech, and a crunch, and instead of rolling we were jumping, like a jack-knifing antelope, over the bends of the looping drive, both of us existing now in some place beyond words, staring our own mortality in the face.

We landed in a crunching punch, my clacking teeth sinking into my tongue, flooding my mouth with blood.

Then Sid started turning the wheel, with huge sweeps of her arms, like a captain heeling a ship in the midst of a turbulent gale, and we were broadside to the road, the sea in my passenger window, but we were still moving at vicious speed . . .

We tore over the rocks lining the opening to the drive, the view suddenly at a tilting 45-degree angle, when there was a shattering bang from somewhere below as one of the boulders tore out the bottom of the car and we lurched forward in our seat belts as the airbags exploded into our faces.

I cried out against the smothering plastic, my voice lost.

Utter silence now, except for the murmur of the sea through the vanished windscreen.

'Are you all right?'

I turned. Sid was staring at me, her head weaving ever so slightly, her trembling hands coming to rest on the wheel, which had somehow moved a good six inches closer to her breast. Her coral lipstick was smeared on her deflating airbag like a kiss.

'Yeah.' I blinked. Behind the sinking airbag the windscreen had been replaced by dark green broken fingers of yew hedge that reached into the car to brush my face, as if concerned. 'Are you?'

She nodded, as though unsure this was the right answer. Her eyes fell downwards, to her left arm.

Then I understood what it was that had smashed the windshield.

Lying between us was the steel signpost for Blue Horizons, the sign itself sheared off, the pole now thrust headfirst into the leather of the back seat, tearing it open.

A foot or so either way it would have pierced either one of us through the chest. As it was, it had scored along Sid's arm, leaving a deep, thin tear in her pale skin through which bright blood beaded.

'Oh shit, you're . . .'

'It's nothing.' She stirred restlessly, as though she was asleep, though her eyes were open. Her other hand, the knuckles bloody, pushed at the door handle, and it swung wide. 'Need . . . need to get out.' Her voice was breathy. 'Got to . . .'

She slid out, vanished as she fell to the dirt.

My own hand scrabbled at the door handle, pulled. Nothing. I remembered someone telling me once that in modern cars nothing attached to anything else – there were only handles and levers that connected to sensors. As the handle flapped uselessly, I realised this was true.

On my other side, the broken signpost was a barrier, penning me in. I could crawl neither over nor under it.

'Sid? I'm stuck . . .'

Suddenly hands were there – flat palms spread, slapping against the glass on my window, an urgent freckled face peering in with wide eyes, a stranger with hair in a dark ponytail . . .

'Are you all right?' She sounded far away, speaking to me from another world.

'My sister . . .' My voice sounded thin, slurring to myself. A great tide seemed to be surging between my ears. 'I think my sister is . . .'

'Oh my God!' she shrieked, vanishing around the back of the car. She was standing on Sid's side, dipping down and turning now to some man, blond with a baseball cap on, who was running to join her.

'Don't worry,' cried the man to me through the open door. 'I just phoned the ambulance. They're coming now.'

'Is my sister okay?' I asked.

'We should help them out of . . .'

'No, no, don't move them, it's dangerous,' said the man. 'Let the ambulance people handle it.'

'Is she okay?' I repeated. I attempted to unclip the seat belt. Somehow my strength seemed to have deserted me.

I sighed, defeated, let my head fall back on the headrest with a little zinging pain. Outside, Sid was trying to persuade our earnest Good Samaritans that she needed to go up the hill to the house. They were having none of it.

Oh shit. Who's going to pick up the client now? thought a tiny nonsensical part of my brain. Is there any chance

I will be allowed to dive today? Maybe if I lie to the doctors about . . .

Erik. I needed to call Erik.

My phone was in my jeans pocket, hairline cracks spreading over the surface. Unsteadily I poked his number.

'Yes?'

'Erik, I can't pick the client up. You need to do it.'

'Good morning to you too,' he replied mildly.

'I've been in a car accident.' I swallowed. 'We wrecked the Audi.'

'What? Are you all right?'

I licked my lips, tasting blood again. 'The brakes wouldn't work . . .'

'The brakes did not work?' He was incredulous. 'How is that possible? Are you hurt?'

'No. Well, I did bite my tongue. That's it. But I can't get my seat belt off . . .'

A disbelieving pause.

'You are still in the *car*?' he asked. '*Now?*'

'Yeah, yeah, I'm at the bottom of our drive, where it joins the main road. I can't get . . .' I tried tugging the clasp free again. 'I can't get out.'

'Do not move,' he said with stern authority.

Then he was gone.

38

A&E was busy again. The curtained cubicles on either side of me were occupied, one by a man repeatedly crying out in pain. It was setting my teeth on edge, but it reminded me that there were people out there with bigger problems than me.

But you know, the more I thought about it, the more I wasn't sure how true that was.

Erik told me that the car had been towed to one of the garages in Gweek – he had been forced to wait outside for us in the waiting room.

Ten minutes ago Maz, one of the mechanics there, had rung me. I'd known Maz most of my life; we'd gone to school together in Anvil Point and spent our teenage years drinking together in the Wreckers.

'Hey, Cass mate – how are you doing?'

'I'm all right, considering.' My tongue was swollen, my voice felt like wet cement. My chin was being held up at an odd angle by a puffy neck brace that I'd been told I couldn't take off until I'd had my X-ray. 'They're just doing tests on me. But Sid's torn something in her wrist and needs an operation. She's already whingeing about the scar it will leave.'

'You did a real number on that Audi.'

'It was Sid driving, I'll let her know you said so.'

He let out a nervous laugh, and for the first time I had the sense that there was something serious about this call.

His voice lowered, 'Look, Cass, this is a bit awkward,

like, but it's just that, well, the brake failure on the car . . . it's looking suspicious.'

'Suspicious?'

It had already occurred to me that something was very wrong. The car was practically new. But somehow paranoid little me thinking it, and actual professional mechanics thinking it, was an entirely different experience.

'Well,' his voice dipped, the surrounding crash and rattle of a busy garage smothered, and I realised he was covering his phone. 'Craig just got off the phone to the police,' he was almost whispering. 'He's had to report it. I thought you ought to know.'

I blinked. 'I . . . I don't . . .' What a day this was turning into. 'What exactly is he reporting? What happened?'

'So we just had a look underneath, and somebody who knew what they were doing has just slightly nicked through the brake cables for both the front and back. Not enough to empty the reservoir of brake fluid and spark the warning sensor, not straight away, but once you start the car and pump the brake you put pressure on the fluid and it will empty through the cuts pretty quickly.

'And you live right on top of the Point, don't you? On that big steep cliff with the long windy drive? So you're probably hitting the brakes pretty hard right away once you take the handbrake off.'

I swallowed. My mouth was dry. 'Yes,' I said. 'Yes, that's right.'

'So I don't want to frighten you, Cass. I'm not supposed to be talking to you, Craig says. But . . . you know. You need to keep your eyes open.'

'Yeah,' I said, my voice barely audible. 'Thanks, Maz.'

'It's nothing.' A pause. 'Look after yourself, all right?'

My nerveless fingers were numb around my phone.

Adam. It could only be Adam. He wants to kill you, Cass. You and Sid.

Sid was awake when they let me in to see her, and though her blue eyes were still faintly cloudy with chemical sleep, she was sitting upright, her injured wrist in its splint lying across her belly, the ends of her shorn hair stuck to her dewy cheeks.

She managed a faint but genuine smile for me, as though she had forgotten we were fighting, or perhaps had chosen to forget.

'Hey,' I said. I had a little box of chocolate truffles with me, that I put on the cabinet next to her head. 'How's you?'

'I'm all right.' Her gaze fell to her lap, to her bound wrist in its foam cradle. 'It doesn't hurt. Yet.'

'What have they told you about it?' I asked, moving to the seat next to the bed, quietly shocked at the swollen shape of her arm beneath the clean white bandages. It was normal after surgery, probably, but still. It filled me with a fierce protectiveness.

She gave a tiny shrug, favouring her injured arm. 'It's going to be fine.' She glanced down at it, with a puzzled but almost affectionate glance, as if she was talking about a favoured pet.

'That's good.'

'What about you?'

'There's nothing wrong with me,' I sat down on the plastic chair. 'I am free to go.'

'That's something,' she said. 'Does anybody know what happened with the car?'

I licked my dry lips, couldn't look at her. I tried, as a

kind of thought experiment, to imagine saying *Yes, your husband tried to murder us.*

It was unbearable to me how frightened she'd be, especially in this unlikely peace we found ourselves in. I just wanted it to go on a second or two longer.

The only thing I didn't understand was how he had managed it.

He'd been taken away almost the minute he'd arrived home. And he'd been in custody until this morning. Hadn't he?

Perhaps he had accomplices. Perhaps the sister in Redruth . . .

'Sid? Sid darling!'

As though I had conjured him, Adam burst through the doorway to the little room, his arms wide, a gigantic bunch of roses clutched in one hand. I had a few moments to gather up a series of lightning impressions – his eyes were shadowed and bloodshot, and he had a nick on one cheek that was beaded with a couple of drops of dried blood, and as his arms were raised his pale T-shirt lifted up to show a flash of white belly and a few stray dark hairs peeking out above his waistband.

I was too stunned to speak. His posture, his voice, everything about him – it was a performance, and had he broken out into a Shakespearean monologue I would not have been surprised. I could almost have laughed if I hadn't been so horrified to see him.

And in a flash, so quick that I thought I might have imagined it, it seemed some very similar emotion fluttered over Sid's face, then vanished as though it had never been, as though she would never have dared to entertain such a thought.

He rushed forward, gathering her clumsily in his arms, and from my miserable plastic chair her yelp of pain set my teeth on edge.

'Sid, Sid darling . . .'

I didn't know what to do. At all.

I sat there, confounded, frozen into place. I didn't want to be in this room with the man who had robbed me and bullied and tricked my sister into marrying him, and who I quietly suspected might have been up to far worse.

On the other hand, I very desperately didn't want to leave Sid alone with the man I was sure had tried to kill us both.

39

I leapt to my feet.

'*You*,' I said, and then, before I could stop myself, 'what are you doing here?'

'What?' He looked the picture of shocked affrontedness, the mass of roses still in his hand. 'I can't visit my wife in hospital?'

'You've got an absolute nerve . . .' I was shaking, I realised.

This man had tried to kill me.

And God help me, I don't think I was the first.

'Cass, I don't know what's going on with you, but you need to calm down and stop this. All of those false charges were dropped,' he said, his face composed into compassionate gravity. He tried but didn't succeed to suppress his slight smile, so gazed down at Sid to hide it. 'I'm sorry, Cass. Perhaps this is all our fault,' he said. 'Sid should have been more honest with you about things at the shop after you left for Australia.' There was the slightest emphasis on the word *left*, as though I had abandoned the place. 'But she didn't want to worry you and I . . .'

'Oh, don't even try it,' I snarled. 'I know you're the reason Sid and I are in here in the first place.'

'What are you talking about?'

'You sabotaged the car. You cut the brakes.'

'Cass!' Sid looked aghast. 'That's a horrible thing to say!'

He blinked at me, expressionless, either with surprise that I knew or because he didn't trust himself to react.

'That's completely absurd.'

I was aware of myself as looking unhinged, of heads turning further down the ward, coming to peer through the ward door.

'I don't know how you did it, but . . .' I was stammering, 'I know you had something to do with it . . .'

'Cass,' he said firmly, 'I know you've been through a lot, but you're not being rational right now.' His expression tightened, and I had the sense that I'd alarmed him.

'Could you both not do this?' Sid was asking us both in a tiny voice. 'Just for two minutes, could you not? I've literally just got out of surgery . . .'

'It's been stressful for us all, Sid,' he said, but he was looking at me. 'This has literally been one of the most terrifying nights of my life.' His lips were thin as he took her hand. 'And now you've crashed the car.'

Sid's eyes widened in alarm, almost fear. 'Adam, the brakes wouldn't work, I don't know what . . .'

'It's all right, darling, it's all right.' He petted her hand until she fell silent. 'It's understandable, I suppose. You've been under so much *pressure* lately . . .'

'Don't you dare try to blame it on her!' I snapped, filled with crimson rage on Sid's behalf. 'It was nothing to do with her! Somebody tampered with those brakes and nearly killed us, and by God, I'm going to make sure they find out who!'

He threw his hands up in the air. 'You know what, Cass? You may not realise this, but you are absolutely incapable of reason right now. I need to get back to the shop before everything goes completely to pieces.' He shot me a glare. 'One of us at least has to try to stay in control of themselves.'

Without another word, he left the room.

I drew a deep breath, sighing in relief.

'You can't even try to get on with him, can you?' Sid's eyes were scrunched up with anger. 'What the hell was all that about?'

My mouth snapped shut.

If she couldn't see how bullying, how manipulative he was after that display, after physically sitting through it, how could mere words convince her further?

Silently, I gathered the flowers up, while she ignored me, fuming.

Now he was gone, I felt absolutely terrible. It had been stupid to go after him like that. I should have kept my mouth shut until I spoke to the police and found out exactly what was going on.

Speaking of which, it was time to make a phone call.

'I wasn't going to come back home tonight,' I said. 'Do you need . . .'

'Adam can take care of me,' said Sid, her voice cold, her head turned away from me.

'Fine,' I said. Our little moment of rapport was over, I saw. 'I'll see you later.'

It took a couple of tries to get hold of DI Small – Call-Me-Tom wasn't in and she was busy the first two times I attempted to reach her.

'I spoke to DCI Trevelyan last week,' I told her. 'About my sister's boyfriend, Adam Fulmore, and some things we found on the *Undine*.'

I'd be damned if I called him her husband.

'Ah yes, I know.'

She sounded compassionate but firm, which I couldn't help but interpret as a bad sign.

'You questioned him about this unrelated fraud, then released him.'

'He was bailed on an unrelated matter, yes.'

'Can I at least ask why you didn't take the evidence Erik and I brought any further?'

I noticed I was trying not to raise my voice and only partially succeeding.

'I can assure you, we took your concerns about the body in the shipwreck very seriously, Cass,' she said. Her voice wavered in and out, as though she was doing something else wherever she was, which was engaging her attention more than speaking to me. 'While Adam was at the station about the other possible offence, we did take the opportunity to ask him some searching questions about his whereabouts and movements.' She paused. 'And we also spoke to more of his family and friends . . . despite some reluctance on his part to give up their contact details.'

There was a chilly hesitation here, and I had the sense she would have liked to have said more, but she didn't.

'And?'

'The fact is, we have no evidence he had anything to do with the body in the *Undine*.'

'But . . .' I could hear the rising hitch in my voice. 'Are you sure? I mean, how do you *know* that . . .'

Erik, who had come to collect me from the hospital, was leaning forward over the wheel of the van. He glanced sideways at me then, and there was something in his dark gaze that said: *keep calm*.

I breathed in, tried to rein in my racing emotions.

'Cass, right now, there's no evidence linking him with that woman, which I know was going to be your next question. And despite the evidence you submitted, there's still only circumstantial proof that *anybody* deliberately placed that woman's body in the *Undine*.' She sighed. 'Obviously we're still looking into that.'

I swallowed against my dry mouth. 'But what about the scarf we found?'

'The scarf doesn't seem to be connected to any missing person, Cass. We tested it. And there was only a small amount of blood . . .'

'But what's it doing there? In our house?' I ran my hand compulsively through my hair, trying to control my trembling. 'And the car! And what about the way he lies about where he's . . .'

'We took all you said very seriously, Cass,' she repeated. 'But the fact is, all of the charges for theft were dropped – he absolutely had permission from your sister to withdraw those funds. And in regard to your other queries, he had an alibi for the day the body in the *Undine* was discovered. So . . .'

An alibi.

In a lightning flash, I understood. 'The sister,' I said. 'You've been talking to his sister in Redruth, haven't you?'

'I'm sorry, but this is part of an ongoing investigation, and I simply can't tell you everything that . . .'

'I mean, of course she's going to give him an alibi!' I snapped. 'That's what he does, get women like her to cover up for him!'

'Cass, I know that you have a difficult relationship with him, according to your own sister . . .'

I was so angry now I could hardly breathe. Sid. Of course *Sid* had had something to say. A seething sense of betrayal filled me. 'A *difficult relationship*? I'm just a spiteful, jealous cow, making this all up, is that what she told you?'

'Cass . . .' Her even tone enraged me. I felt I was being managed, like a drunk or a crazy person.

'Arggh! This is . . .' I fought to find the words. 'He's such a shady bastard! I mean, he stole all that money . . . you know it and I know it!'

'Cass, I know this is disappointing to hear, but we're satisfied that the money is a civil matter. He's being charged with assault, and that is all I've got to say on this subject.'

I couldn't believe it. The implications were becoming clear.

'You know, somebody sabotaged our car today and my sister and I were nearly killed. If I leave Sid in the house alone with him once she's been discharged from hospital and he's this . . .'

'Cass, we know about the allegations surrounding the accident. And naturally if more evidence comes to light . . .'

I was speechless. I was done. I was too upset to continue, and realised it was too dangerous to try. They already thought I was a bitter, resentful maniac.

'You know what, *fine*. It's fine. But this isn't the end. I know what he's like, even if you don't.'

'Cass, please try . . .'

'This isn't the end,' I repeated, and shut the call off.

Erik was regarding me with slow, grave attention. 'Do you feel better now?'

I sighed. A summer squall of light rain misted the windscreen of the van. Outside, a woman with a limp and a

296

stick glanced up, obviously having heard me shouting, and then continued hobbling towards the hospital, pretending to ignore us. 'Did I sound like a paranoid lunatic?'

'You may have sounded moderately paranoid.' He made a tiny gesture, holding finger and thumb close to one another. 'About this much.' He shrugged, gazed out of the window of the van. 'You have had a serious shock. One of a number of serious shocks. And you do have many things to be paranoid about.'

I shook my head.

He reached over and kissed me, and for a tiny moment, with the heat of his lips brushing against my cheek, I forgot my troubles.

Just for a moment, though.

'They're not after him for any of it, you know,' I said, letting the reality of it sink in. 'Just for getting punchy when asked for his sister's address. They're not even interested in the money.' I raked my fingers through my fringe, crushing my hand into the top of my head. I looked at him. 'How is that even possible? I mean, the money is still gone, right?'

Erik shrugged. 'I know nothing about that. If your sister told them he is allowed to remove money from the bank account . . .' His large hands rested on the steering wheel of the van, gently tapped it. 'It's illegal to steal, not illegal to be incompetent,' he growled. 'The police were involved too early. Jimmy was hasty. But at least they know who he is now.'

'I need to get back to the shop,' I said. 'You know Adam's going to . . .'

'No,' said Erik, starting the engine. 'It is not my business, but that is a bad idea. Everybody needs some time to cool off now. It has been a very long day already.'

'But he's in the *shop* . . .'

'Good.' Erik turned the key, and the van roared awake.

I was too surprised to speak for a second. 'What? Are you crazy?'

'It's good, Cassandra. Believe me. It's the best thing that could happen now. Let that guy be where Jimmy and I can keep an eye on him. Maybe he will do or say something that will trip him up. And he is away from Sid.' He ran his hand over mine. 'And you.'

'But . . .'

'No,' he said, pulling out of the hospital car park. 'There's nothing more to do. We have had all the drama we need today.'

40

I resisted all of Erik's plans for me to rest until I got back to his flat. Once I was there, I felt a bone-deep tiredness descend upon me. He was right – so much had happened lately, and almost the instant he was heading out of the door and back to the shop, I drowsed into unconsciousness in the armchair like a toddler, my tea cooling next to me in a chipped mug advertising fishing boat hire.

At some point I woke and bestirred myself to the bedroom, reduced myself to tank top and knickers and was out like a light in his rumpled bed, not moving until I heard someone opening the door to the flats below.

'Erik?' I called out sleepily.

No reply. He must not have heard me.

There was no window in this room but through the bedroom door the light was low and glancing. How long had I slept for?

I could hear him coming up the stairs, them creaking under his heavy tread. I waited for the sound of his key in the flat's front door, but instead the footsteps went on, and then a different door was rattling, being pushed open.

Grace's old room. Not Erik, then. There must be a new tenant there, I guess.

I rolled on to my back, stretched languorously.

Ah well. I couldn't lie here all day. I had things to do and my mind had started to race again. As exhausted as I was, we had to keep everything going at Blue Horizons. People were depending on us for their livelihoods.

Whoever it was in the other flat was opening drawers – they seemed to be in a hurry. It was as clear as if they had been in the room with me. Then the sound of moving furniture. The walls were paper-thin in here. It must drive Erik mad.

I rolled to my feet. I was hungry now – I'd not eaten all day, I realised. Perhaps Erik and I could get something when he got back – he couldn't be too much longer now. I should text him.

The sounds next door had risen in volume. Furniture was being moved, in haste and carelessly – cupboard doors banging open, wooden surfaces striking the walls, and under all was this heavy breathing.

On an impulse I cupped my ear to the wall, trying to listen, to stay still. My hair tickled my face.

Should I call someone? Interrupt by knocking on the door?

I stole into the living room, phoned Erik.

He picked up on the second ring.

'There's someone in the flat next door,' I whispered. 'They sound like they're ransacking the place.'

It took him only a second to get it.

'Do nothing,' he commanded. 'I'm nearly there.'

'Okay,' I said. 'See you soon . . .'

He'd already hung up.

I curled up in the chair to wait, and as I did, it creaked loudly, thumping against the wall.

Suddenly there was silence from next door.

Shit. Oh shit . . .

Did Erik lock that door behind him when he went out?

He might not have.

As quietly as I could, I rose to my feet, crept over to it. There was a simple Yale lock with a snib and below it, a sliding security chain which hung loose.

With trembling fingers, I leaned forward, lifted the end of the chain, preparing to slide it into the slot . . .

Under my feet, the floor creaked.

Startled, I dropped the chain, and it rattled heavily against the wood.

Silence – a pregnant silence, of someone thinking, and then a rush of footfalls on the stairwell.

They were running.

I ran to the windows, peering down, trying to see who it was as they emerged, but though I heard the outer door swing open and slam shut, it wasn't possible to see whoever it was as they fled – the corner of the coffee shop's red brick bin shelter hid them.

I leapt up, determined to follow them before they got away. Fore Street was not the same as a deserted flat, after all, and I had much less to fear there. I ran for the door, cramming my feet into flat tennis shoes and realising I had no shorts on, wasted precious moments finding them, ran for the stairs.

Standing in my way was Erik, looking mildly surprised.

'Cassandra . . . ?'

'They just left!' I shouted. 'Did you see them? They would have gone straight past you!'

He turned and raced out into the road, with me hard on his heels.

'Did you see which way they went?' He was shading his eyes against the slanting sunlight, turning his head this way and that. Towards the harbour there was nothing but boatmen and children fishing for crabs off the quay, and Fore Street was a mass of swarming tourists still.

I shrugged helplessly at him. 'I don't know,' I admitted. 'I never saw them.'

'Are you all right?' His large hand was on my shoulder, guiding me towards his chest where I was gently crushed for a moment before being released.

'Yes, I'm fine.' I wouldn't have minded being hugged for a moment longer – he smelled really good. Despite my alarming afternoon, I was not above noticing these things.

'Tell me exactly what happened,' he said, steering us both back inside, up towards Grace's flat.

As we approached the other flat, I explained how I'd fallen asleep, been awakened, the creaking floorboard. The door was lying open, letting us both into the rifled space beyond.

This flat was smaller than Erik's, little more than a studio, with a tiny shower and kitchenette.

It was completely vacant. The wardrobe doors opened on a handful of empty hangers. The drawers were empty, the bed stripped.

All around everything was lying open, rifled, as though it had been turned over by the police.

I looked at Erik, who gazed about himself in amazement.

'This is so strange,' he said. 'The flat is empty. It's been this way since the day she moved out. She took everything with her. There's nothing to steal here.'

'That's so weird,' I breathed. 'Why would somebody break in here?'

'Who knows?' He shrugged down at me. 'Could just be a thief or a druggie deciding to take a chance . . .'

I shook my head. 'No, no, Erik. This wasn't random. Think about it.'

'Cassandra . . .'

'Whoever it was, didn't expect anyone to be here. They weren't taking any care to be quiet, they were in a hurry. Somehow they knew you were out, and also that you would be back soon.' I wrapped my hands around my arms. 'And they freaked out when they heard me in here.' I sucked in my breath, remembering my terror. 'They expected to be alone.'

He looked at me for a long moment, and then away, behind us.

'This is all very strange,' he said, pulling me close.

I gave a hollow laugh, and he glanced at me, surprised.

'Well, at least it isn't something I can blame Adam for,' I said. 'He was at the shop today, right?'

Erik did not smile back. 'No. He never showed.'

'What?'

'Your sister phoned, looking for him. Jimmy had to drive out to fetch her from the hospital, since he never came back to pick her up.' He reached up, scratched his head.

I remembered his departing back as he'd stormed out, the roses he'd brought on the bed.

Guilt washed through me. 'Sid's on her own? At the house?'

Collecting her was my job if Adam wasn't around. Why hadn't she called me?

'Erik, I think I'd better . . .'

'She does not want to see you.' His embarrassment was plain. 'Jimmy happened to be in the shop when she called. He suggested very strongly to her that you should come get her, stay with her, and she refused.'

'Oh,' I said. A slice of sadness went through me, like a knife through butter.

'Don't worry. She will get over it.' He took my hand, squeezed it. 'We need to call the police. I think you should stay here, for now.' He looked around Grace's sullen, disordered flat, rubbing his chin thoughtfully. 'But not alone. Never alone.'

That night, after the police left, Erik took me out on his Triumph motorcycle to a quiet patch of beach in Porthleven. I pretended to be completely cool with being on the back of a two-wheeled death machine clinging to a man, in fairness, that I barely knew, and he had pretended to believe I was completely cool with it too.

We sat on the beach on a perfectly ironic tartan picnic blanket he kept in the bike's top case, gazing out to sea, eating fresh Newlyn crab rolls and drinking cans of Orangina we bought from a café on the way. I pretended not to keep glancing at my phone, not to worry about Sid, and he pretended to believe I was fine.

But I had the sense that had I chosen not to pretend, that would have been fine too.

When we returned home, we peeked into Grace's flat – nothing had changed as far as we could see. Erik had plucked one of the dark hairs from my head and laid it over the doorknob to his flat, and it was still there when we returned.

We went in, and our pretending was over, at least for the night.

41

Erik and I had woken late, snuggled in together. I'd offered to make us coffee, only to discover that we had no milk, which we both agreed was nothing short of high tragedy. I'd chosen to walk up to the Co-op on Fore Street to source a bottle while Erik showered, having left him a note in the condensation on the bathroom mirror.

The morning was fading away now and there was a kind of mugginess in the air, which made me think a storm was coming. The sky was a thick blue and full of scudding clouds.

I felt good, calm.

I should have known it wouldn't last.

My phone vibrated.

It was Sid:

Have you seen Adam?

I blinked at it. No kiss, no greeting, but at least she was speaking to me, if only virtually.

No

A few seconds went by. Then:

He didn't come home last night.

I paused on the pavement — around me, the tourist crowds were nearly bumping into me, a man muttering rudely as he passed.

This is stupid, I thought to myself. We should be talking. This is too serious for us to be playing these games.

I called her.

'You have been diverted to the voicemail service of . . .'

Dammit, Sid.

If it was even Sid at all, I thought with a little chill, putting the phone back in my pocket. How would I know?

There was also a message from Jimmy, from a few minutes ago. It simply read:

Cass

Nothing else.

I tried calling him but he didn't answer; it just went straight to voicemail.

When I walked up to the Co-op and into the cool space within I was distracted, anxious, so it took me a moment to realise that Ben was standing by the chocolate section, his back to me.

I had a split second to prepare myself before he turned around and saw me.

'Cass,' he said. His eyes travelled up and down me. He smiled, his slow, seductive smile. 'How are you doing? Not seen you in the Wreckers lately.'

I raised an eyebrow at him. 'Ah well. You know, I've had a lot on. How are you?'

'I'm good, good.' He licked his lips, a quick, tiny gesture. 'I hear it's been tough lately. Been missing seeing you around, though. You should come down tonight.'

I blinked at him while he grinned widely at me.

Despite all that had happened to me – the discovery of the body, the collapse of the *Undine*, Adam's arrest – all things the local grapevine would have carried unerringly to the Wreckers – he'd not contacted me once to ask how I was.

I turn up at the Co-op in short shorts though, bed-headed and sexed up, and suddenly he's full of sympathy.

Oh my God, I thought to myself. For nearly two years of my life I've been letting this guy waste my time.

'Sorry,' I said, with a slight smile. 'I've got plans tonight.'

I brushed past him, paid for the milk and paper at the counter, and let myself out of the shop, into the sunshine, and out of his life.

42

Well, I thought, heading back down Fore Street to Erik's, Jimmy would be pleased I was done with Ben. He'd never liked him . . .

And as I thought of Jimmy, a spark of uneasiness went through me. However angry I was with him right now about reporting Adam's fraud to the police without my permission, I still relied on him.

That text had been distinctly odd. And it was not like Jimmy not to answer his phone, especially if it was me calling.

I glanced over my shoulder, up the street.

It would take mere minutes to call by, to see what was up.

By the time I crossed his neat garden on the paved path all was quiet – there was the noise of bees in the overgrown hedges, the faraway cries of gulls, the tourist voices from the town reduced to a distant murmur.

I knocked on the door, stepped back.

Where was he? I knew he wasn't on the rota for the shop today. I put down my milk and newspaper and sat down next to them on the cracked step, which felt chill despite the heat of the sun, and tried ringing him again. No answer.

That's when I first heard it – a kind of low groan, like a wounded beast.

I froze, listening.

It was coming from inside the house.

I stared at the cracked blue door, the phone in my hand forgotten. I felt a powerful sense of horror – it was long and low, with a slight hitch at the end, a sound of deep distress, of someone crying out for help.

I reached forward and very lightly pushed the painted wood.

The door, unlatched, swung inwards easily.

I was already over the lintel, standing on the polished wooden floor. Orange wallpaper lined the hall, a narrow corridor leading down towards the kitchen.

The boards creaked beneath my feet as I moved, the space stifling with trapped heat.

'Jimmy?'

The kitchen door was ajar, flecked with what I realised was blood.

A thrill of horror went through me. 'Jimmy?' I shouted. 'Jimmy, are you okay?'

The groan again, only this time longer, more urgent, as though my voice, recognised, was having a galvanising effect on him.

I rushed through to the kitchen.

He was lying on his face on the lino, for all the world as if he had fallen asleep there, half-curled into a foetal position, his eyes closed until just a glimmer of cracked wet grey was visible through them.

Bending down, I could see the patch of blood in his dark curls.

'Jimmy, what happened?'

No reply. His final cry must have drunk up the last of his energy. He was absolutely still, only the rising and falling of the blue shirt he wore indicating that he was even alive.

But one thing was clear, I realised, as I punched in 999. He was on his front and yet these injuries of his were all on the back of his head.

Someone had done this to him.

But who?

43

I'd come up with all these stratagems as to what to do if Sid didn't answer, but in the end I needed none of them. She picked up on the second ring.

'Sid?' I was too surprised to speak for a moment.

'Yes?' I detected tetchiness, as in *Who else could it be?*

I resolved to ignore it.

'I'm here at Jimmy's. He's been hurt. Someone broke in here and attacked him.'

'What?' She sounded frightened. 'Is he all right?'

'I think so . . . they're going to check him out.'

'What do you mean, attacked him? Do they know who it was?'

'No. He didn't see them.' I looked over to where he sat between two paramedics, one of whom was peering at Jimmy's scalp. 'Crept up on him and hit him on the back of the head. It isn't as bad as it looks, they say, but he'll need scans. He should be home tonight.'

She was silent again. I could practically hear the cogs in her mind turning down the phone.

'Anyway, thought you should know. We're shutting the dive shop today. We all need . . . we need to stop and figure things out.'

More silence, but it had a strained quality, as though she would have liked to say more.

'Have you heard from Adam?' I asked, because that was the question that most needed answering.

'No,' she said, and her voice broke on it towards the end, finishing on a choking sob.

For all we had fought, her naked misery wrung my heart.

'I'm coming over,' I said. 'Let me sort Jimmy out, and I'll see you soon.'

'You off, girl?' Jimmy was sitting on the floor, bracketed by ambulancemen.

There was something so matter-of-fact about him, despite all that had happened and him being covered in blood, that I laughed out loud.

'No, not yet. We've got to get you to the hospital . . .'

'There's no need for that,' he said. 'I'm absolutely fine.'

'You are *not* fine,' said the man on his right, tying a bulky bandage to the back of Jimmy's head.

For my part, I was distracted by the sound of a heavy tread in the hallway. I looked out to see Erik approaching, seeming to fill the house.

'Cass?' He wrapped his arms around me, squeezed, and for a second I let myself melt into it. He looked bewildered, as well he might. 'What is happening here?'

So much for the gentle morning together we had planned.

'It's fine, I'm fine,' I murmured. 'But Jimmy's hurt. And Sid called – Adam didn't come home last night.'

'He didn't?' asked Erik.

We exchanged a glance.

'I'm not hurt, it's just a scratch,' Jimmy grumbled, but there was a sharpness in his face, a suspicious awareness, and I realised that he hadn't known about me and Erik until now. 'The girls are in trouble.' He offered Erik a fixed stare. 'We need to . . .'

I frowned at him. 'Jimmy, go with these guys now, and I promise I'll go to Sid's. You can come over the minute they let you out.'

'I will take her over there now,' said Erik.

Jimmy considered this for a long moment, seeming to turn it over in his mind.

'All right. You've got a deal. I'll see you both up at the house later.'

I nodded. 'Okay. Take care of yourself, Jimmy.' I waved at the ambulancemen. 'Look after him.'

Sid answered the door in a pretty blue sundress, her hair brushed and with a slick of coloured lip moisturiser, her little anchor necklace glinting at her throat. Above it her eyes were pink and tired, her skin pasty.

I realised this was all for Adam's benefit and my skin prickled, as though I was in the opening haze of lightning strike. The very air crackled around me.

These missing women, the car crashing, Jimmy being attacked – something terrible was happening around us, and every moment it was becoming clearer and clearer that it was intimately connected to Blue Horizons, and to the slumbering mass of the dying *Undine*.

As far as I was concerned, and despite everything the police thought, Adam was a very dangerous man.

Somehow I was able to suppress all the bitter things I wanted to say to Sid, that desire to shake her until she saw reason. Instead, I just hugged her, fiercely.

'Are you okay?' I asked.

She looked about to say *yes*, then shook her head, and burst into hysterical sobbing.

'Sid! Sid . . . it's going to be fine. It's going to work out.'

It was the opposite of what I was really thinking.

So I just led her into the kitchen, where Tallulah rose up off the kitchen table, arching her back and fluffing out her heavy tail, as though we were disturbing her.

I poured Sid a cup of coffee as she sat down, swiping at her face with a tea towel.

'That cat's not supposed to be on there –' Sid hiccupped through her tears, reaching out towards Tallulah on the table. 'Adam hates it when she does that –'

Adam, Adam, Adam. It had been the litany since I got home from Australia.

Never mind. Both Tallulah and I were going to have to hold our tongues in the interests of familial peace. I swiped up her lithe little body, cradling her despite her stiff annoyance, and set her tenderly on the floor.

'Oh God, do you think something has happened to Adam?'

Her fear was heart-breaking.

I sighed. 'Tell me what happened after I left.'

'Apparently he texted Jimmy and Erik to let them know he was going to work – he was going to get a taxi to the harbour, he wanted to check out the *Undine* himself, inspect the damage, but they say he never showed.' Her voice was full of ratcheting hysteria. 'He's not answering his phone, nobody's seen him, the boats are all there so he can't be at the wreck . . .'

'How would he be getting about?' I asked. 'We've got the van. The people carrier is totalled.'

Sid shrugged. 'Maybe his sister picked him up?'

The sister, of course.

'Have you contacted her?'

'Um . . . I don't have her number.'

'That doesn't matter,' I said, forcing down my surprise. 'We can track her down. Her name's Jem, isn't it? What's her last name?'

Sid's face went slack with confusion. 'I don't know.'

It was getting harder for me to control my impatience, but I tried. Please believe me. I tried.

'You've never met her?' I tried to smother my incredulity but she saw it, and that little pilot light of defensiveness glowed out of her gaze.

'She has a lot of problems, all right? She gets jealous. And he protects me from a lot, you know? You've not been here, but it's been tough for me.'

I looked down at my hands. They were shaking with rage.

I love her and I wanted us to forgive each other, but I was getting tired of this narrative where everything was my fault, and her only option was to get together with some guy who was trying to kill us both.

But now was not the time to get into this.

'I wonder if this Jem might live at the address on his application form down at the shop,' I said, forcing my voice to be calm. 'I'll try it.'

Sid merely stared out of the window, nodding, her jaw set. She was clearly miles away.

'Okay,' I said. 'Sid, I need you to be careful, okay? Don't go out. And the minute Adam comes back, I need you to tell me, okay? I think we need to tell the police he's gone missing.'

'You do?' And there was something so painful, so pathetic, about how at cross-purposes we were. This suggestion pleased her, animated her, because she thought that, on some level, I was worried about him too.

Well, I *was* worried about him.

So much was certainly true.

44

I sat in Maz's courtesy car from the garage, the engine idling, and looked at the house.

It was late afternoon now, as it had taken Erik and I some time to source the car, for me to drive out here, to press on Sid the importance of keeping the house secure and staying in touch in case of trouble.

I had lied to Erik about where I was going. I had the unmistakeable sense he would not have approved.

I'm not even sure I did.

The address itself had also been difficult to find, being located in some brand-new estate – a medley of snaking circular roads with similar names themed around Scottish islands, lined with immature trees and identical houses.

Number 7 on Skye Close had been the address on Adam's application form, though I'd no way of knowing if it was where Jemima lived now. It was on a T-junction, which made clandestine parking difficult. I settled on a space between a plumber's truck and a little red Hyundai, over the top of which I could see the front door. I was conscious of curtains twitching in the house to my left.

Here I was, being spied on by a stranger while spying on a stranger.

What had my life come to?

An abandoned child's bike lay on the grass, and a

couple of errant weeds poked their way up between the paving stones on the path to the door.

The driveway was empty, and ringing the doorbell had elicited a deep chime but no answer.

Now what, Cass?

I sighed, crossing my arms over the steering wheel, resting my head on them for a second.

There was nothing to do but wait.

On an impulse, I picked up my phone.

Erik had told me that Russell Bowermann had made a video about his adventures on the *Undine*, and how his injury was the fault of my poor leadership skills.

I should probably watch it, I told myself, though in all honesty I would rather have thrust needles under my fingernails. Just thinking about him filled me with dull anxiety, though the way things were going of late, it would have taken very little to terrify me.

I tapped in *russell bowermann undine*.

A list of suggestions came up – I didn't see any results for Russell on the first page, but one in particular caught my eye. It appeared quite high up – clearly lots of people had searched for it before – *Grace O'Donoghue dives the* Undine.

I remembered Erik telling me about Grace and her videos, so I tapped the link.

There was a burst of upbeat but generic music, accompanying a few jump cuts showing the ruined inside of the *Undine*'s engine room. It was a place far too dangerous to take any divers – even I preferred to avoid it when possible.

It clearly wasn't putting Grace off any.

'Hi, everyone, welcome back to my channel Wrecking Crew!' It was bright daylight, and a smiling woman in a drysuit with a gap between her teeth waved into the camera. She seemed oddly familiar – I wondered if we'd met before. Diving can be a small world.

She stood against what I recognised as the stern of the *Mustang Sally*. The sea breeze blew her hair into wild shapes as the Manacles tossed in the background over her shoulder. 'As you can see, it's a lovely soft day here off Porthoustock, perfect conditions for diving the *Undine*.' She had a charming accent: a sweet Irish brogue, and a gentle, low voice. I could see now how she must have been popular with the clients. 'I've been promising for a while that we're going to take a look at what little is still accessible of the lower deck, and the weather today's just right. So, let's crack on!'

Footage then of her under the water, wavering schools of fish, folky fiddle reels playing in the background as the *Undine* appeared out of the darkness. I'd assumed she was alone, but it soon became clear another person was filming her, following her as she moved through the stairwells and passages of the *Undine* without raising a trace of silt, slid after her as she entered the lower corridor, the very one I had chased Russell down.

She swam to the rotting old freshwater tank at the bottom of the corridor, the only way into the engine room. The shots and footage were beautifully presented and edited – they put my own efforts in this department to shame.

She spun around in the boiler room itself, smiling through her mask at whoever was filming her, giving them a pair of happy thumbs-up.

Behind her, the pile of decaying metal and debris that covered the hole to the Forbidden Hold appeared in one or two glancing frames – I paused the video, peering at it. It was chaotically lit by the dive light of whoever was holding the camera, and very hard to make out, but it looked very similar to the pictures Erik and I had taken when we had gone out there.

The next thing, she was back on land, sitting at what I immediately recognised as one of the picnic tables behind the Old Fish Market, clad in a yellow bikini top and a batik print skirt, her curly hair with its henna red streaks now flowing down her shoulders. On the table were two open bottles of craft beer and a smartphone, the case decorated with the striking image of a beautiful lilac and blue jellyfish, its trailing tendrils wrapping around the edges of the phone.

She waved at the camera, smiling hugely. 'Thanks so much for watching! I hope you enjoyed that, and if you did, please like and subscribe as that helps us enormously! Huge thanks also to my colleague, Erik Magnusson at Blue Horizons, who did the filming but is too shy to appear on camera himself . . .' In the background I heard Erik's rumbling chuckle. 'And I hope to see you all again soon! Happy Diving!' She raised her bottle, toasting the camera, grinning.

I sat silently for a moment, thinking. The hole to the Forbidden Hold had been right there. Lying there in plain sight.

So strange that it would be there all this time – why had Erik only noticed it now?

Perhaps I should ask him about it.

Some more searching turned up an Instagram account, so I sent Grace a DM, telling her who I was, that I liked her video, and her jellyfish phone case, and that I really wanted to get in touch with her.

In all this time, there had been no movement at Number 7 Skye Close.

I sighed, feeling self-conscious, a little lost.

What exactly was I doing here? What was I expecting this woman to tell me, once I confronted her?

When did you last see your brother? Where is our thirty-seven grand? Did he kill those missing women? Is he hiding in your guest room even as we speak?

I'd had some half-formed notion that I was going to sit here and watch the place until he appeared, but now I was here, I saw how hopelessly impractical this plan was. I could be sat here for days and achieve nothing, and in the meantime, life would continue falling apart at Blue Horizons.

Also, Adam might see me first. If I was right, he'd already tried to kill me once.

Start your car, turn around and sod off, you ludicrous mare.

I glanced into the sky. Twilight was already falling.

I sighed, defeated, about to turn the engine on again, when a car breezed right past me and pulled into the drive of Number 7.

I had glimpsed the face of the female driver only briefly as she went by – straight dark blonde hair in a ponytail, an oval face. No discernible family resemblance.

I froze.

She drove a Nissan Micra that looked like it had just gone through a carwash, and she jumped out to release a small boy from the back seat, who clutched a red ball to his chest.

She was dressed in a playsuit in some silky material, patterned in big yellow flowers. In one hand she carried a large summer bag full of what looked like towels and swimwear.

I watched, mesmerised, as they walked up the path and she let them both into the house, saying something to the boy that I couldn't hear but which made him smile and rush in before her.

She, however, stood on the step for a long moment, looking up and down the drive, as though searching for someone, her large eyes passing over me, slowing, before moving on. She turned on her heel and went in, letting the front door close behind her.

Before I could change my mind, I was out of the car and walking up to her front door.

Time to get this over with.

I raised my hand to that gleaming knocker, when it suddenly opened.

I went perfectly still, staring at her round-eyed.

'Can I help you?' She was pretty, in a sharp-nosed, fine-featured kind of way, her skin dewed faintly with sweat, her shoulders gently dusted in freckles.

'Oh!' I said. 'Sorry, you startled me. But . . . well. Yes. Maybe.'

'Is this a charity thing? I'm in a bit of a rush, I'm afraid. Liam needs his tea.'

I wanted for all the world to say sorry, perhaps I could call another time, as though I really was collecting for a charity, and to flee.

Don't be a coward, I told myself sternly.

I met her gaze for gaze – something about my expression was making that polite, business-like smile wilt around the edges.

'Um, no.' I breathed in. 'I'm here about Adam.'

Her mouth opened. She blinked, too quickly. Immediately I saw that she was pretending to be surprised. On some level, she'd been expecting me, perhaps even when she'd been looking up and down the street on the doorstep.

'Adam?'

'Um, yeah.' I folded my arms. 'Adam Fulmore. He's gone missing. We wondered if he came here?'

'I'm sorry, I don't . . .' Her cheeks had blushed a furious red, and this colour was flooding down her throat and into her bosom above the low neckline of her playsuit. Her expression hardened. 'Who are you, exactly?'

'I'm your new sister-in-law, Cass Brownrigg.'

And it seemed everything changed.

Her mouth opened. 'I'm sorry . . . *what?*'

In a lightning flash of insight, I realised that now she was genuinely surprised.

'My name's Cass Brownrigg. Adam's just married my sister, Sid.'

Her mouth snapped shut.

'I . . .' She took a deep breath, and again that quick look up and down the street, her darting eyes full of panic. I wondered suddenly if she was expecting him, or perhaps just frightened of what the neighbours would think.

She drew herself upright. 'That's impossible. I don't know what your sister told you, but Ads isn't remotely interested in her. She needs to stop harassing him.'

Now it was my turn to be surprised, and it was tinged with a growing anger. 'Harassing him? Harassing *him?*' I could hear that ratcheting volume in my voice, fought in vain to control it. 'He's run off on my sister with nearly forty grand of my family's money! And you think *Sid* is harassing *him?*'

Jem was scarlet. 'Look . . . I know it's d-difficult, having all the issues she does, but she can't just . . .'

I looked at her, astounded at her nerve. She was talking about *Sid's* issues?

But her eyes were huge and she appeared on the brink of tears.

Something was way off here. There was, yet again, something I wasn't seeing.

I took a deep breath. 'I know you're his sister and expected to stick up for him, but Adam is in a lot of trouble. And if you care about him, you need to tell him that the sooner he . . .'

She was speaking, saying something, but it was so low I could barely hear it.

'I'm not his sister.'

'What?'

'I'm not his sister.' She looked about to faint, grey and crumpling. 'I'm his partner.'

All of the hair stood up on the back of my neck. '*What?*'

'I'm his partner.' She blinked at me. 'We've been together for seven years.'

The inside of the house was untidy but clean, strewn with Liam's toys, and messages and reminders on gaily coloured Post-it notes were stuck to the fridge. Liam himself sat on the couch, tucking into a cheese sandwich, glued to *Ben 10*. I could see him from my seat at the kitchen table, a cup of weak tea in my hands, which shook around it.

I was astounded, almost speechless. I had expected every bad thing from Adam. But he had still managed to surprise me.

'I knew something was up.' Her eyes were pink and wet. 'He told me he'd got this job on an oil rig, doing commercial diving. We didn't see him for months at a time, but he was sending a little money home, so we didn't . . .' She sighed, a breath like a sob.

So much for his weekly visits to his 'sister', I thought bitterly. I'd seen Adam's CV. There was no way he was rated for deep-sea commercial diving. How had she not known this? I thought, looking at the crown of her dark blonde head as she bent over, trying valiantly not to cry.

Somehow, though, it made sense that Adam would be with a woman who didn't ask too many questions.

I felt like a monster. Though I had no hand in its creation, I had brought this trouble into her house.

'I mean,' she said, 'I don't know what your sister told you about being married to him . . .'

'It wasn't my sister who told me she was married,' I said, having decided that the best policy was to give her the plain, unvarnished truth. 'He did. He came through the door with her. They've just come back from Las Vegas. It was nearly the first thing out of his mouth.' I looked down at the grey cup of tea in my hands. 'I'm sorry. I'm not any happier about it than you are.'

'But . . . but I . . .' Her mouth screwed up ferociously, as though a wasp had stung her. 'How would he . . . why . . .'

I gave her a quick look. 'We think he married her for control over our business.'

Her face was ghastly, suddenly, as though, despite her distress earlier, she was only just getting it now. 'But he's with *me*!'

The silence following this seemed to go on for a very long time. Long enough for me to drain my horrible tea to the bottom of the cup, at any rate.

'Is this what the police want with him?' she asked eventually, in a voice barely above a whisper. 'They were asking about his whereabouts a couple of days ago. He was in touch to say it was all a misunderstanding about some money, that the charges were dropped.'

'Partly a misunderstanding.' I couldn't look at her. In the living room, her son – Adam's son, with his same oblong face and fair hair – put the plate down on the couch next to him, still enraptured by the television, quickly licking a few crumbs off his top lip.

'I'm sorry,' I said again, because I was. I nearly went on to say that both she and Sid were in the same boat, and then realised this was a bad idea. Sid had been swept off her feet in under two years. Jemima had . . . Jemima had been with him for the best part of a decade. They had a child together.

'Have you seen him?' I asked. 'I mean in the last twenty-four hours?'

She shook her head, not speaking, and somehow I believed her. 'No.' Her lips became thin, bitter. 'Not since a week last Monday. Something about the oil rig job ending early because of the boss getting Covid, or something.'

I examined my fingernails, nodding thoughtfully.

God, I thought with a pang of pity. He could tell her anything.

How like Sid she was.

But something was niggling at me. A week last Monday . . .

Oh God.

'So he did really come here then?' I asked, incredulous.

Jemima glanced at me, surprised at my urgency. 'Yes. For the morning at least.' She nodded. 'He was going to take Liam and I out.' She shrugged helplessly. 'He told me they'd found someone to cover for him so he could have the day off. I didn't want to go. I couldn't take the time off work. And . . .' she moved shiftily, brushing her hair back from her forehead, 'I didn't want to go far. He told me that your sister was stalking him. She was an ex from years ago that had reappeared and wouldn't take no for an answer . . .' She looked away. There was embarrassment in her manner, but also a needle-thin sliver of malice. *He slandered her too, you know. Not just me.* 'I was frightened she might do something to the house.'

I tried to tamp down my own ember of fury. Of course. He had to say something in case Sid ever pitched up here, and I knew by now that there was nothing he wouldn't say or do to get his own way.

But still. How dare he.

Oh God, I thought – what am I going to tell Sid?

'Sid?' I said into the phone, as I pulled the door of the courtesy car shut after me. No messages from Erik, I saw. That stung.

'Cass, where the hell are you?' Her voice sounded scratchy, as though she'd been crying. 'You've been gone hours . . .'

'No, stop, listen. I've got to talk to you. I . . .' My mouth clamped shut. Maybe we needed to be doing our next conversation in person.

'What is it?' A beat of silence. 'Cass, I know something's wrong, you might as well just . . .'

I stared at the phone, in an agony of indecision. 'It's about Adam. He's . . . he's not been entirely honest with you.'

'What?' She sounded tiny, lost.

'Look, we can talk about it when I get home.'

'I'm not waiting till you get home,' she said. Little spikes of anger were appearing in her voice, and I did not want to fall out with her again. 'Tell me now.'

All right. I breathed in.

'Sid, listen. Jemima's not his sister.' It burst out of me, like a scalding wind. 'She isn't his sister, and she's not mentally ill. She's . . . there's no easy way to say this, but she's *with* him. She has a kid with him. She thought he was doing commercial diving, on an oil rig, and that's why she hardly ever saw him.'

The silence on the line was so profound that for a moment I thought we'd been cut off.

Then:

'What did you say?' Sid's voice was breathy, wounded.

I felt like an absolute heel.

'Listen, don't worry about it. I'm on my way home now.' I started the car. 'We'll talk then, okay?'

45

It was getting late by the time I chugged up the hill to the house – the sun was low, the shadows long.

For the first time, as I climbed out of the car and trudged towards the porch, I felt a tiny chill within the breeze, the kiss of autumn in summer's embrace.

My first inkling that something was wrong was when I realised that the front door was open. Just a crack, but it was enough.

'Sid?' I called.

Nothing.

I ran up to the door, shoved it.

Within, all was dark, but everything had been swiped from the side table as you came in, sent to the floor – there was a shattered bowl my mother had loved lying there in pieces, a spread of trampled potpourri lying on the stone tiles.

'Sid?' I called again, my heart in my mouth.

No answer.

The smart thing to do was probably wait outside and get the police here, but while I was on the phone to them straight away, no power on Earth could have kept me out.

Every room was full of chaos – evidence of some terrible fight. In the living room, the Lalique vase given to my dad had been hurled against the fireplace and lay in a thousand shards, the television was on its side, in the kitchen everything on the counters was lying on the floor, and my shoes crunched through muesli and scattered pasta.

'Sid!' I shouted, my voice cracking in panic. 'Sid!'

'Police, what's your emergency?'

I glanced down at the phone.

'Oh, hello? I've just this second come home and someone's smashed up our house. And my sister's missing.'

'What's the address?'

'It's, it's Blue Horizons, Anvil Point, Cornwall. The house, not the dive shop. We're at the top of the Point.'

'All right, is anyone in the property now?'

The bedrooms were ordered, quiet and empty – the wave of destruction had not ascended the stairs. I dropped to my knees, looking under the beds. Under mine, two yellow eyes gleamed back at me.

It was Tallulah. Apart from her twitching tail she was absolutely still.

She looked terrified.

'No, no one's here,' I said, reaching out to stroke Tallulah's head. She was not mollified. 'I . . .'

Oh God. The training pool.

I was running over the crunching gravel to the indoor pool house. The interior lights were on.

'Sid?'

The door was open wide, a sure sign something was wrong. I sucked in the hot, humid air.

Within, the fight had continued, or perhaps it's where it had started. The pool cleaning machine whirred away, unattended. Spilled kit lay on the pool verge, knocked out of the shelving where it was stored.

There was no sign of her there now.

*

'I'm sorry, Cass, I can't allow it. It's just too dangerous.'
Call-Me-Tom shook his head. 'They say in the morning, if
they can, they'll send a submersible drone of some sort to
look around the wreck.'

We had been arguing it out for what seemed like forever, standing outside the pool house, while precious time
was being wasted.

I had been thinking, and the more I thought, the more
bleakly frightened I had become.

And the more frightened I became, the more I faced up
to the terrible answer.

She could be in the *Undine*. What Erik had said was
playing endlessly in my mind.

*But I am a psychopath and I hate women and killing them
makes me happy, so what am I to do?*

Erik. Erik who was not answering my calls or texts.

'I know you don't believe me, but this is Adam, I know
it.' I was almost shouting, unable to control myself. 'He's
doing all this! He's sabotaged the car! He's attacked
Jimmy!'

'You don't know that.'

'I *do* know that!'

*If I had a safe place under the sea to store these bodies, the ocean
would do all the hard work for me . . .*

My chest was heaving. 'Who the hell else could have
done all this? It's the only thing that makes sense! I'd just
told Sid about his girlfriend! He called her or came back
here and she confronted him and . . .'

'I'm not arguing with you, Cass.' God, he was so reasonable, it made me want to kill him. 'And we are looking
everywhere for both of them.'

'I know you think I'm this paranoid lunatic,' I said,

trying to control my emotions, to make him see reason. 'But it's him. It's always been him. He's the one that hid that woman in the *Undine*, I know it! Sid could be down there right now!'

There was the ghost of compassion in his eyes. If Sid was down there, she could wait for a drone to look for her. Could wait indefinitely, in fact.

The *Undine* would not wait indefinitely, though. The *Undine* was dying, collapsing back into her grave, and would take all of her evidence with her.

I would have stalked back to the house but looking at the damage was more than I could bear. It reminded me that I had not been here, had not been guarding her. Instead, I got back into Maz's scruffy car, shut the door after me, and rested my forehead on the wheel.

But a storm was brewing in my breast. This monster had taken my sister, had taken others, and if they didn't believe me and didn't dare to look – well, what could I do?

What could I do?

Then it came to me.

Excuse me, aren't you Rob Brownrigg's daughter? Haven't you been diving that wreck since you were out of nappies?

You go. You must go. You always were the strong diver, had the best trim, you can just slip in and out of there and the *Undine* won't even notice you've been.

Look into that Forbidden Hold.

Make sure your sister isn't there, along with who knows what else.

And if she's not, then get on your knees and thank God. Return here meekly and wait for news, like they want you to.

In the meantime, however, I needed that answer. I could not live without it, could not bear the idea that she was down there, floating, becoming like the woman that I had already met down there . . .

I glanced into the rear-view mirror at the place where the police stood, talking.

I could not let them see me now.

They would try to stop me. In fact, everyone would try to stop me, I realised – Erik, Jimmy, even Sid herself were she here to have a voice.

Everyone who loved me.

It didn't matter.

Instead, I texted Jimmy. Unlike Erik, I had not taken him into my confidence about my suspicions about Adam and the *Undine*. He didn't know about the discovery of the Forbidden Hold, would not be able to guess my plans, to thwart or dissuade me:

Adam's come back and attacked Sid. I don't know where she is but have a feeling and it's not good. Look after yourself. He might come after you again. Love, Cx

I slipped out of the car and away from the pool house, looking as if I was heading back indoors, before dipping sideways and down our rutted headland footpath towards the sea.

I was gone before I even realised I had made up my mind.

I am insane, I thought, as I anchored the *Mustang Sally* near the hazard buoy, stared back at the coast, now drowned in shadow.

All was silent. Red warning buoys winked around the

perimeter of the *Undine*, but there was, thankfully, no sign of other ships.

If the coastguard caught me here I was done. If a night fisherman or diving boat came out here and reported me, I was done.

But it was the strangest feeling. It was as though another Cassandra was blubbering and whining about all this, a frightened girl who never dived alone, who looked outwards for approval every day of her life.

All that mattered to me now was finding out whether Sid was down there or not, alive or dead. And if she was down there, she was almost certainly dead.

I stood for a long moment, thinking, the deck bobbing beneath me. The logical next step was to switch the boat's waterline lights on, to make it more visible to passing shipping.

Do you really want to do that? I asked myself.

It was illegal not to, like driving a car without lights after dark. If the coastguard happened by, if someone from one of the big container ships in the Channel saw . . .

Nobody was going to come out to a collapsing wreck in the dead of night, I told myself firmly. Or at least, I thought with a flicker of fear, anyone with any good purpose.

If you're that worried, just leave the mast light on.

And so it was in darkness that I pulled on my kit, checked it under the dim illumination of my dive torch. I had enough gas for one hour, which was forty minutes at the *Undine*'s depth, so I would have to be quick.

The tide would be coming in soon.

I had tried calling Sid, but the line just rang and rang. I wanted to call Erik once more, tell him what I planned, but realised I could not. The things I wanted to say were too huge, and besides, if he realised what I was up to, he might come out here.

I could risk my life. I could not risk his.

Just go in, I said to myself. Just go in, look – and then get out.

And stop fretting like this. You'll burn through your oxygen.

I stilled for a moment, tried to calm myself. I could feel my drysuit, tight across my chest, the weight of my tank on my back, the salty air stirring through my hair.

I had never done anything like this before – diving alone in the darkness, in a forbidden wreck.

Don't think about it.

Just do it.

And with the next intake of breath, I rolled off the transom of the *Mustang Sally* and into the dark water.

46

Below III

The damage to the *Undine* is much worse than I remember.

As my torchlight picks her out in the misted darkness, I can see the *Undine*'s superstructure, all the way up to the bridge. It is twitching now, moving with the tide, and I have never seen it so mobile. It fills me with a thudding horror, just beneath my breastbone.

The water is cold, so very cold.

Calm down. At least it's not completely collapsed.

It might be better if it was.

You are imagining all of this, I tell myself firmly.

But just in case. Just in case . . .

I let my hand fall on my dive knife at my thigh.

If you so much as see a whisper of anything that justifies your suspicions, you will get out.

She is singing again, that terrible song of hers, only now it seems to have been joined by more voices, like a swelling chorus.

I try not to listen. I would plug up my ears if I could.

Many more opportunities to reconsider my actions come up as I drift through the *Undine*, past the mess, past the lounge, down this fateful stairwell with the rising current pushing me back, like a living thing. I'm terrified of meeting another dead woman, perhaps even Sid, as my light flickers over the openings into the abandoned cabins, but in my heart I know I would do better to fear the living.

The hole in the freshwater tank beckons at the end of the crushed corridor, and down I go, into the engine room.

Something has changed.

The steel-lined gap is covered up again now, and a big piece of rusting metal has been laid up against it, to hide it better. It takes some effort to move it away, send it crashing down to the remains of the deck.

And am I imagining it, or does the gap itself look bigger than it did a couple of days ago?

I glance at the dive computer on my wrist. I have about twenty minutes, all told, before I have to start making my way out again.

Time to see if that will be enough.

Putting my head through the hole, I shine my dive light in.

It opens up into a shadowy room below me – I can't see all of it, but it is large, at least half as large as the hold above, and the collapsed floor is about twenty feet below where I float. It's at a strange angle though, sloping off and downwards towards the stern of the ship, where the ceiling crumples into it, the wall between them utterly crushed.

This corner of the Forbidden Hold, or at least all I can glimpse from this angle, this hidden space that has so agitated the dreams of divers all over the world, seems to be full of nothing but ragged plastic debris, broken cargo containers, of the kind that you hitch up to the back of a lorry, and the silty residue of the sea bottom. Rotting and rusting pipes and ducts scar the far wall, which the remains of white safety paint identify as CAR O SECT. B1.

I feel a flicker of disappointment – often, as a child, I imagined the Forbidden Hold as being full of treasure, or a palace inhabited by mermaids, or some other glorious hidden thing adults did not want me to see or know about, but looking at it now it seems little more than a rusting junkyard full of places for unpleasant things to hide in wait.

A death trap, in short.

The water visibility is good, not perfect but okay, like it would be through a fine mist on a November evening.

That said, this part of the ship has been sealed up for the best part of fifteen years. It will be full of silt. If you so much as brush the bottom, you will be blinded until it settles.

My pulse is racing at the thought – which is in itself a very dangerous thing, and wasteful too.

I turn, look back down the corridor, the way I have come. Nothing stirs there.

C'mon, Cass, nothing is following you.

Somehow I am unconvinced, some atavistic instinct at work in me.

I switch off my dive light, look again.

The blackness is complete, beginning at my mask. There's no one following me, unless they are diving in total darkness.

Flashing the dive light on again, I point it at the ceiling of the Forbidden Hold, but it shows nothing but welded squares of rusting steel, dotted with wandering sea stars. As damaged as it is, there's no sign of another safe exit, or even an unsafe one. It seems that this slit is the only way in or out.

I peer through desperately, but there is no sign of Sid

or indeed anything out of the ordinary in the slivers of view this angle affords me.

I duck my head back out, swallow against the dryness of my tanked air, consider my next move.

First of all, that depth change down to the deck floor will burn through my air that much faster, particularly if I get into strenuous physical activity.

Which leads to the second thing – I can get in there through this gap in the wall, but not with my dive gear on.

This is the madness. I will have to strip off my tank and BCD, crawl through the hole without getting stuck, then drag my kit after me and then fasten everything on again. This would almost certainly constitute strenuous physical activity.

It is all so dangerous.

Are you going to do it or not? I ask myself.

Every instinct I have screams *Hell, no*.

It will take you five minutes to just swim round, check out the rest of the room that you can't see from here, and leave. Which is good, since five minutes is probably all the air you will have to spare.

Nothing ventured, nothing gained.

There is nobody down there. No boats nearby. The only thing that can hurt you here is your own imagination.

I wish, though, oh how I wish, that Erik was with me. Or even Jimmy.

Or Sid.

I tie a new line to the one I've already laid and try not to notice that my hands tremble inside my gloves. If anyone comes behind me, they will see this new, bright yellow line, heading down into the void. It announces my presence for both good and evil.

But there's nothing I can do about that now.

I unbuckle my BCD, slide it off, trapping it against the wall with my knee, the tank still attached to it. I tie this to the line, my regulator still in my mouth.

I feel utterly vulnerable without it, but there is no help for it.

Right. One deep breath and let's go. Into Bluebeard's Castle.

Now the tricky part.

With the new line in my hand, I turn around, pointing my fins at the gap, and start to slide through.

It's tight – tighter than I expected. It squeezes me at my hips, my breasts, which require a little wiggling, makes me panic a little.

How has Adam got through this? He's bigger than I am. I don't think he could have. I just can't see it.

And the thought hits me like a slap – maybe there really is another way in or out of here after all.

But I am committed now. As I slide through, I pick up my gear and guide it after me, and before twenty seconds are up I am strapping my tank back on to my back, sucking in sweet air, already panting slightly.

Done.

Now hurry. You don't have a lot of time.

I let myself fall gently towards the floor of the Forbidden Hold, my light travelling over the abandoned containers, the walls. I see nothing out of the ordinary.

The temperature change is sudden, startling, as though I have stepped into an icy bath.

I stop six inches above the silt and sea creatures that stir faintly in the light current, circuit the room. That's all the time I have, I realise, glancing at my dive computer again while I ply my dive light over the decaying detritus, swimming towards the bow end.

I am passing the black opening of a cargo container, lying on its side, its walls lined with broken plastic boxes, when something glints in the ray of my torch, right at the very back.

I stop, peer inside.

Whatever it is, the light from it leaps out of the grey and rusty morass – it gleams metallically, as if new. It rests on top of an old yellow fish crate, placed upside down against the back wall of the container. The fish crate itself is perched on top of some bulky rectangular base.

I swim within, my heart hammering.

Whatever this incongruously neat arrangement is – the yellow crate, the base, which I now see is a suitcase – it is man-made. A space has been created for it in amongst the racked plastic boxes, spilling rusting tools on to the metal floor.

Resting on top of the yellow crate, like offerings at an altar, are a collection of objects – a pair of Bottega Veneta high-heeled mules with pebbles inside them to weigh them down, neatly placed as though their owner had every intention of coming back for them, an amber pendant tied with a black cord that floats vaguely, stirring as I approach, as though trying to escape the stone that holds it, a tiny silver ring held to the bottom of the fish crate with a piece of threaded wire, and the shining thing that had reflected my dive light and lured me in here.

It is a Samsung Galaxy.

This is all so strange, down here in this watery world where nothing from the surface survives, I stop breathing for a moment.

It looks absolutely pristine, as though it was placed here very recently.

I pick up the phone, turn it over in my gloved hand.

The case design on the back is of a blue and lilac jelly-fish, its tentacles wrapping around the edges of the phone.

I have seen this recently, this striking design, but it still takes me a moment to remember where from.

Oh.

Oh.

I hold it out in front of me, as though it is cursed, while above, the singing grows momentarily louder, fades away, grows louder again. Because of course now I know who it is that I met in the cabin days ago, floating in the darkness.

The one woman who had not been reported missing, because everyone thought she had left of her own accord.

She had been here all along, and looking at this collection of hoarded trophies, I suspect that she had not been alone.

I kick out in panic, knocking the crate and its treasures off the top of that tartan suitcase. It looks so familiar, with its faded patterning, hidden under silt and patches of algae. I have seen it somewhere before as well, back in the mists of time . . .

Nothing on earth could induce me to open that suitcase. Absolutely nothing.

Shaking, I thrust the phone into my net dive bag and turn to get the hell out of there.

That's when I realise there is somebody inside the container with me.

My racing mind puts it together – the shape of a shoulder, the gleam of a tank, hidden against the shadows, the dangling silhouettes of fins brushing the container's silty floor.

Hanging there, in the freezing darkness, is a dark-clad figure in a drysuit.

I scream in a burst of bubbles, flail backwards. I snatch at my leg for my dive knife, but even as my hand closes around the handle I realise that something is wrong.

Whoever it is – was – gives off not the slightest hint of bubbles himself.

He simply hangs there, against the container wall, like a human suit.

Despite every instinct screaming at me to flee, I turn the light on his face, gasp.

It is Adam.

47

His skin is as chalk white as a fish's belly, his open eyes cloudy and dead.

For a moment I can do nothing but stare in unblinking horror.

Has he done this to himself?

It could make sense. He knew he was about to be caught, go to prison . . . Has he come down here with the evidence of his crimes and . . . what? Opened his tanks?

As much as I have hated him, and wished him ill for hurting my sister, and possibly more, I cannot resist a flicker of pity. What a horrible way to die.

I look at him more closely, trying to calm my heaving heart, my racing nerves, to *think*.

His white skin, his sightless eyes – he's been dead for a lot longer than an hour or two. I'm no expert, but based on what I've learned since finding the woman, he has probably been here since he went missing, which was over twenty-four hours ago.

What could it mean?

It means, I realise, that there's no way he could have been the one to attack Sid at the house tonight.

And in that case, who did?

What have I missed, while I have been so laser-focused on Adam?

I move the dive light down his body, and there, over his heart, are three deep, savage cuts, going all the way through his drysuit. Whoever had done it must have possessed enormous strength.

I force myself to remember to breathe.

My dive computer beeps, twice.

I am out of time. I have reached my safety limit and must turn around. This mystery will have to wait for the surface.

Terrible suspicions roil within me now, as I rip my gaze away, moving out. No sign of Sid here. Please God, she has never been here at all. I recognised nothing of hers in that gruesome collection of objects.

It doesn't matter. I'm going to run out of air before I surface unless I leave *now*.

I swim up to the rent in the wall, my dive light fixing on it, finding it hard work to breathe at this depth.

If not Adam, I'm thinking, if not Adam, then who was behind this? I'd been so sure. Everything pointed to him.

Perhaps it was meant to.

No time for this now. I must concentrate on getting out in one piece. I've nearly reached the tear in the bulwark, where my yellow line leads back to the engine room like a golden thread, and I'm unfastening my BCD, my tank, to get out again, while in the background, the *Undine* sings her unearthly song.

And as I do, there's a sound, not the singing this time, more of a *thud*.

With this thud there is a flashing shimmer of decayed metal and silt, falling like a fine waterfall from the rent in the wall above, catching like dust motes in my dive light.

Somebody is blocking the hole up again.

Oh God. Oh no . . .

I fly up while more thuds follow – whoever it is, they're

stacking debris against it, quickly, urgently, and as I reach it, I push helplessly at the slab of rusted steel within.

It won't budge. Because, of course, there's nothing for me to grab, nothing to push against – I am floating unsupported in the deep.

I try grabbing the torn wall edge with one hand, pushing through with a finned foot, but it's hopeless, for I can gain no purchase at this awkward angle, and whoever is on the other side is continuing to pile debris against the steel.

I hammer on it, kick, aware that I am blowing through my rapidly dwindling Nitrox, but nothing.

For a moment, time stands still while I process this, fighting it every step of the way.

I have been sealed up in here to die.

Despair overwhelms me, like a net tightening on me with every breath.

There is no way out.

No, Cass.

Think.

Adam is in here, and with his tanks too.

Tanks.

Adam might have more air.

I swim back, forcing myself to be still, to be calm. Panic drowns you down here.

At this depth, I have another ten minutes of air, total. Then nothing. Nothing for the ascent, even if I could make it out of here.

Even in death Adam is determined to be awkward – it's hard to manoeuvre him in the confined space of the container, and when I drag him to its opening, feeling every

346

bump of his head as it scrapes across the roof, my breath hoarse and rattling in the regulator, he wants to float away out of my grip, like a grim balloon.

This gives me a bad feeling, beyond the very obvious bad feeling I already have – if his tanks were full he would be less buoyant, and I would be finding him easier to manage.

I think he has dire news for me.

I grab his air gauge, shine my light on it, while he bobs next to me and I try not to think of him as a person, a murdered person, left here to rot alone in the darkness. He'd been a terrible boyfriend for my sister, but he hadn't deserved this.

The air gauge on his aluminium tanks displays empty.

Oh no. *No.*

I try to slow my laboured breathing, to think.

And as I float in the darkness, Adam rising away from me now, to the surface of the Forbidden Hold, it comes to me.

Someone had got Adam in here in full scuba gear, despite the fact that I – much smaller – had had to remove my kit to get through the gap. Someone who'd also got that large suitcase in here.

There must be another hidden way in and out, one I had not discovered but the killer had. There *must* be.

You just need to find it.

Look for it. Look for it *now*.

I swim, turning the dive light this way, that way. Nothing on the roof, the walls, except for an access door that has rusted into place. Nothing on the . . .

The deck.

Everything is covered in its veil of fine silt, but near the

347

far wall, almost hidden by another rusting container, there's a shadow my dive light can't illuminate.

It's an irregularly shaped hole, about four feet deep, that seems to just end in more silt. In the middle of it is a huge broken boulder.

The *Undine* had come down, wedged in the rocks and settled on this, and it had torn this thumbtack hole in her hull bottom.

I'm about to swim on, to look further, when I glimpse, hidden in the lee of the boulder, a gap running under the deck.

Surely not.

The dive light shows a straight, narrow passage – in the briefings we give we sometimes tell people that the *Undine* had a double bottom hull – a gap between the inner and outer wall of the ship that had held ballast – and I realise I am looking down a surviving section of this, that has somehow not been crushed into the seabed.

It's just wide enough to fit me, without me being able to turn around. And it will silt up, uncontrollably – there'll be no way round this.

I have no idea where it will lead me. It could, conceivably, lead me out to sea. Or it could be a dead end.

I have mere minutes to choose, and if I choose wrong, I will die.

But if I don't choose, I will definitely die.

I choose, clipping a line to it, so at least, if anyone comes looking, they will find my body.

In I go.

48

I swim through the narrow tunnel, trying to stay calm, though it's getting harder – the depth, all of this activity – I'm growing short of breath, and breath is the one thing I can't spare, and my visibility is gone – the dive light can't penetrate the underwater dust storm I'm raising in the tiny space so I have to feel my way along all four walls.

I can't escape the feeling that these walls are drawing in, the tunnel getting smaller and smaller . . .

Above me the inner hull of the *Undine* appears in flashes, festooned in barnacles, then vanishing in the silt my bubbles raise.

Just keep going, I tell myself grimly.

The price of imagination is fear.

Do not imagine things.

There's a sullen rumble then, that shakes the walls, the water, the silt, and me. Another one of the *Undine*'s tremors, and I swim, finning my way through the tunnel, expecting any minute for it to collapse on top of me.

Suddenly the ceiling is gone.

My hand reaches up, encounters nothing. I have no idea where in the ship I am but I rise, out of the silt, into an unknown space lined in rusty metal.

I have never seen it before. I have no idea where I am.

But suddenly the *Undine*'s singing is back, that aching, creaky, unearthly noise of the radio tower waving in the current, and it's loud, as though the *Undine* is a violin and the tower a bow – a symphony in grinding, rocking steel. The very sea seems to bend with it, the walls to vibrate. It fills the world.

Head towards it. If you can reach the bridge, you can get out.

I swim, upwards, and fast, and immediately the pressure on my chest begins to lift. Swim so fast, in fact, that I nearly miss the square gap in the wall in front of me, where an old plate has decayed into fragments.

I knife through it, my fins catching on the rusting torn pieces, and with a start, realise where I am.

This is the Upper Hold – the one we show to divers. I was here last week with the class.

Only this time I'm on the wrong side of the deadly thicket of decaying farm machinery, which surrounds me on all sides like the bars of a cage. A not very stable cage, as once again there's a tremor, and it all shakes, gently, as if it's cold.

I stare about myself – how can I get through it all before my air runs out?

Then I see the line.

A dark red nylon wreck line someone has laid, running through the barrier, vanishing in the mass of metal, and without hesitation I follow it, squirming past rusting tractors and the blades of steel ploughs, and there is no doubt they are moving, starting to roll, infinitesimally slowly, towards the other side of the hold, with a series of loud squeaks and groans, like a reluctant crowd.

It's beyond unstable in here – I must go. I scrabble out from under an upturned machine with a large rusted bucket and kick upwards, heading for the entrance and the open sea.

Someone grabs one of my fins.

I'm so stunned I stop breathing.

I turn around, already furiously kicking them away, my teeth meeting so hard on my mouthpiece that I nearly bite it in half.

So panic-stricken am I that it takes me a good few seconds to see that it is *Jimmy* – Jimmy, of all people.

I am so overwhelmed I could weep. It is Jimmy.

He can share his air with me.

I smile at him, sighing out in relief.

Is Erik with him? I can't see anybody else, but I've never known Jimmy to dive alone. He is gesturing frantically at me to stop.

He's beckoning at me to come closer, smiling around his regulator, as relieved to see me as I am to see him.

I am about to swim back towards him, but then, almost without realising it, and in spite of my panic, my grave danger, I stop.

There is something urgent, yes, but also something . . . something hard, something predatory in his eyes. They shine out through his mask.

And I am beginning to think now my panic is lessening, starting to wonder.

What's he doing here?

How did he know to look for me here? Was it that text I sent?

I never mentioned the *Undine* in it. We've never discussed our theory on the Forbidden Hold with him.

He surges towards me, his teeth gritted.

I turn tail and swim. Swim for my life.

He snatches again at my fin, and there is no more pretence. I was right to suspect him, I was right – I feel the vicious rage in him through the rubber itself. I kick out, lunging for the door out of the hold, but like a crocodile he has hold of me suddenly, and pulls himself up my body, his hands swarming towards my air tank.

If he switches it off, I will never be able to reach behind myself to switch it back on. He is going to drown me.

I twist on to my back, trying to shake him free, kicking at him furiously with my fins, but it is no use. He's as strong and vicious as a barracuda, and he's on top of me, and we're both sinking down to the deck, as I try to writhe out of his grip, the dive light on my arm flicking on and off his crazed, furious face.

Oh God, I realise. I'm going to die. Die just like the others. Like Livvy Simpson and Shannon McDaid . . .

And Grace.

And then suddenly he's gone and I'm free, whirling in the water, lost and disoriented.

I turn over, and there is Erik.

It takes me a second to recognise him, hidden behind his mask, but his sheer bulk and strength is unmistakable, even here, in the flickering of my dive light.

He has hold of Jimmy by the throat.

Erik pushes him hard against the bucket of a nearby machine, making a shower of particles leap up from it, hard enough to jar it against the deck.

I'm up, tugging at him, signalling *low on air* frantically at him.

The *Undine* rumbles around us, gently at first, and then she begins to sing to us again. The machinery is in motion, tumbling now off the deck, falling towards us all.

The silt is rising.

He releases Jimmy, turns to me.

We have to go. I have to . . .

Something buffets me then, something vast, knocking me over, sending me free-falling into sporadically lit darkness, while the *Undine*'s song reaches an ultimate, rising pitch.

I am whirling in pitch blackness now, expecting any moment to be crushed by the oncoming machinery. I fight to still myself, to find my light, to right myself in the cold water, and when I do, it reveals Jimmy – squirming and furious – pinned beneath one of the rusted scythe-like blades of some giant harvesting machine. The ragged point has thrust through his drysuit and rammed itself into the steel wall of the *Undine*'s hold. A little cloud of blood floats within his mask, veiling and unveiling his wide eyes.

Erik swims up, draws to a standstill above him, regarding him. Jimmy starts to thrash harder, like a speared fish, almost as though he's prepared to let the blade slice right through himself in order to escape.

It's impossible to describe the pain, the rage, and ultimately the pity of that moment. Even if we wanted to, there's no way to save him in time, before all of us drown, and yet he fights, desperate and filled with a terrible unstoppable determination, an animal courage that thinks of nothing but itself.

Erik turns to me. His dark eyes are unreadable, fathomless.

I desperately signal *low air* at him again.

He gestures into his chest, encouraging me to take a deep breath from his spare regulator.

And then, with a tug, he pulls the regulator out of my mouth.

I grab helplessly after it – what is he doing? Are they in it together?

He holds up a commanding finger before my face. *Wait here.*

In his hand, gleaming, is his massive titanium dive knife, drawn from its holster on his leg, and I realise with a thud of horror what is about to happen next.

Erik wants Jimmy's air.

And Jimmy wants to fight him, his hands coming up, his pale wrists visible, the tendons cording as his gloves claw at Erik's face, trying to rip the mask from his eyes, the regulator from his mouth.

But he's slowing. He's dying and nothing can save him. His hands are falling away from Erik, to his sides, and his eyes are rolling backwards.

With a flash of the blade Erik tears through the nylon loop holding the tank on to Jimmy's drysuit at the top, the frayed edges waving about Jimmy's chest, which pumps dark purplish liquid into the sea in slowing heartbeat time, stilling as his eyes cloud over, then stopping.

Meanwhile, my last single gasp of air is almost gone, my lungs contracting within me . . .

I am desperate too, I realise.

I swim in, seize the buckle holding Jimmy's tank on at the back, snap it up and loose. The tank falls, clanging dimly against the floor of the *Undine*'s hold, vanishing in the rising haze of silt.

I snatch up Jimmy's free-floating regulator, which has been torn out of his mouth, and suck in that glorious air, feel the sweetness and relief of it, as Erik grabs my arm, none too gently, and steers me to look ahead.

There can be no doubt.

The rusted farm machinery silted into place on the *Undine* is still moving, sliding towards us, slowly, slowly now but with gathering speed.

It's raising gouts of silt like revenant spirits, so our lights can't penetrate them, as though they are solid, like a marching army.

Suddenly, the singing stops.

There is a perfect moment of silence.

Then a scream of metal, a hard boom, vibrating at us through the dark water.

The radio mast has fallen over – that must be it – landing on the top deck, and its weight on the superstructure is more than the *Undine* can bear.

The deck above us is collapsing, and now this deck is too.

We must get out.

We must get out *now*.

There are flashes of steel moving closer, picking up speed, gliding over the barnacled deck, and I seize Jimmy's tank from beneath his limp, twitching body, and my last image is of him impaled there, dead, his mouth hanging half-open as though mid-gasp.

I hug the tank in my arms as Erik propels us both upwards, out of the way, I hope, but there is no way to know as the silt is engulfing us now, and the terrible noise of tearing, screaming metal surrounds us.

We can't see anything. Any idea of finding the main line again is a fantasy. We will have to feel our way out, if we are allowed, if the *Undine* does not fall down around us.

But we swim, every so often Erik's steely leg or arm brushing me, and his animal strength gives me inspiration, gives me hope. I too am not helpless, and I tap him, steering him in our blindness, leading us both upwards, towards the ceiling of the hold, out of the way of the careening cargo, and I can feel it, that slight current that grows stronger as we near the old cargo doors. I feel my way, in this ship I have been diving for nearly all my life.

When my free hand reaches out and closes on the lintel of the hold doors in the silty sightlessness, I almost weep.

I want to scream to him, but we can't risk the air. I don't know how much Jimmy had left, but I know that it can't be much after our games of hide and seek below.

Instead I just grab Erik, pull, as the tank strains the muscles of my other arm, and as he too feels the lintel we are both through it, and in the growing current a tiny sliver of visibility is returning, just a few inches from the ceiling above, and ahead I can see through the wreck, all the way to the mess, which somehow looks different, smaller and more cramped.

We need no further encouragement. Beyond the mess lies open water.

I can no longer carry the tank one-handed, my arm aching, the strain like torture. I embrace the tank instead, my muscles trembling against the aluminium.

Keep swimming, Cass.

You have to get out of here.

You have to tell them all . . .

But the *Undine* is twisting, contorting around us, sliding downwards on her port side, and the world is revolving into a 45-degree angle, sending plumes of silt after us, raising terrible grinding sounds, and debris is falling on us now, rocks and coral and rusting fittings, like meteors out of a watery sky.

This is it, I realise. *This is the hour.*

She is dying.

We need to get out, or she is going to take us with her.

Suddenly one falling piece of decking tumbles down, hitting Erik hard, taking him with it into the moving fog of silt below us.

I know what I should do. Keep going. What can I possibly do down there as the deck collapses, amongst sliding objects moving around, as big and heavy as cars?

My arms are full of Jimmy's tank still. I can't even feel for Erik properly.

I kick downwards anyway, searching for anything that feels like Erik against my body, against my fins, and suddenly with a bump that makes my teeth clack together around my regulator he has risen against me, one hand knotting in my BCD, and we're rising, and my arms are so tired, my legs, and things are falling on us, hitting us, small at first but at any moment it could be girders, giant rocks, pinning us within, and . . .

Then we're out.

It's as sudden as leaving a cloud in an airplane. Our lights pick up the sea again, the surface, the swarms of glittering fish abandoning ship and heading out into open water, just like us.

I draw breath, so relieved, so . . .

And then, silently and suddenly, the air in Jimmy's tank runs out.

I should be expecting it, but my horror, my dread, is absolute, like a stone in my throat.

I signal desperately at Erik, the slicing gesture across my throat. *Out of air.*

He holds up his own air gauge.

It's in the red.

We must be at least seventy feet from the surface still.

He knocks the empty tank out of my hands, pulls me close, and we're heading up, him pushing his spare regulator into my mouth.

We're kicking up, fast and hard, and he's inflating his BCD with the dregs of his tank.

Oh shit. Shit.

After all that has happened, are we even going to have enough air to get to the surface alive? And if we do, will the bends just kill us anyway?

Up we go, trying to control our ascent, but we aren't kidding ourselves, there's no way we'd be making a safety stop.

Above us, so very far above us, in the velvet darkness, is the watery, wavery white circle of the moon.

We'll never reach it in time.

I'm going to die exactly the same way that my dad had.

And then, beneath us, an echoing roar, pulsing through the water, as the *Undine* at last crumbles into metal and dust, collapsing in on herself, sending out a shockwave that we can feel beneath the soles of our fins.

It's not much, but enough, enough to nudge us on our way, and as we rise, the gases in our body expand, making us both more buoyant, and we're rising faster and faster, swimming hard, not daring to think of the danger this explosively growing pressure is putting our very lives in, because there is absolutely no alternative.

And my head breaks the surface, and all is moonlight.

I think I scream, suck in a lungful of the sweet night air, fall briefly again below the surface before kicking myself to the top again.

Next to me, Erik rises above the sea, then sinks back into it once more.

I grab him, pull him up, because he is floppy, drowsy almost, blinking around himself as though in a dream, wanting to slide beneath the waves.

Both of Blue Horizon's inflatables are here, presumably the one Jimmy took and the one Erik followed him in. But the *Mustang Sally* is nearest, so I haul him towards her.

Once there, bobbing against her hull, I realise the dive ladder is almost too much to face. It feels as though the deck of the boat might as well be on the other side of the world.

But I have to get us both up there. We both need the 100 per cent oxygen stored in our emergency locker, and we need it *now*.

'C'mon,' I mutter. 'Climb.'

He doesn't answer – he's dazed, his eyes unfocused. He has had enough.

'Erik,' I snarl, gathering every remaining inch of my strength. 'Get in that fucking boat.'

I should swear at him more often, because he seems to notice the dive ladder for the first time, and slowly, very slowly, climbs up it, and he does not stop until he reaches the top.

When he does, he collapses over the side and falls on to the deck.

I follow, terrified at the thought he might be dead.

I realise that I cannot bear to lose him.

I tear off his dive mask, find our emergency supply of O_2, apply it to his face, watching him breathe it in.

I feel sick, I realise, freezing cold even in the mild night, and no matter how low down I sit in the boat, I am dizzy and nauseous, as though I am about to fall over.

It's the bends, all right.

'Grace,' I whisper, afraid I may die before I tell any-body.

He doesn't speak, but his eyes narrow, forming a question behind the oxygen mask.

'Grace. The woman was Grace.'

'Whuh . . .'

'The body in the *Undine*.' I have exhausted nearly all of my words, but I manage: 'I found her phone. I recognised the case, with the jellyfish. In the Forbidden Hold.'

I am sagging now, my head too heavy to hold upright.

He watches me.

Then, very gently, he pulls me down, my head on to his chest, and the mask with the oxygen is now against my face, then his, then mine, then his.

And this is how the coastguard finds us.

Epilogue

Sid

'All right, everybody, time for some final checks. Make sure your buddy is ready to dive!'

Cass stands there, in her grey drysuit, her dark hair tied behind her head, and the other divers have all turned towards her, like sunflowers following the sunlight. She's grinning, easy, as she moves amongst them, checking them all before the dive, and Sid is struck once again by how good she is at this.

Good like I used to be.

No. No, she is not going to do this intense negativity any more. She promised herself.

Good like you'll be again.

She'll miss Cass desperately when she goes back to Australia at the end of this month.

There's a happy, excited chuckle amongst their clients as they all realise this is *it*. At the bow, Erik stares out to sea in his Blue Horizons hoodie, one massive hand shading his eyes as he gazes at the Manacles.

He grunts, then turns to Sid, where she stands grasping the wheel of the *Mustang Sally*, making tiny adjustments to compensate for the lively current.

'Are you ready?' he asks.

Sid nods.

'Good. I'll see you both when you get back.' He nods

back at her, brisk and curt, before taking over the wheel.

Sid is not offended. They have been working together – properly working together – for over a year now, and she has grown used to him.

She'll miss him too, if she's honest.

She reaches down to the bench, picks up her scuba tank, straps it on.

Today the *Undine* has finally reopened after fourteen months – well, no, Sid reflects. Not reopened – her days as a penetration wreck are well and truly over. There is nothing left to penetrate, at least for anything larger than a mackerel. But she has been judged sufficiently dead that it is safe to take divers down to ooh and aah at her collapsed bones.

The *Undine* is shattered into a hundred thousand pieces, and already the currents are blowing her over an ever-widening arc amongst the rocks.

For the past year, Sid has known how that feels, as the scale of Jimmy's crimes has become more and more apparent, more huge, more terrifying.

Sid never had Cass's relationship with Jimmy – she has known all along who was the favourite between the two of them – and she had always found him a little overbearing, someone who had never really regarded her as an adult. But she never once dreamed he could be capable of such terrible acts.

Now some time has gone by, she finds herself reviewing the past, and while she could not – obviously could not – foresee that he was so wicked, so depraved (so much had come out about his early life up North – had her parents known, there was no way he would have been allowed into their lives), there are things that make her think, in retrospect.

The first is the dive weekends he used to take away with Mandy, Mandy who was afraid of the sea. The police have started to track them, using Jimmy's dive logs, and in more than one instance they coincide with attacked and missing women. It might have been down to Jimmy. It might not. But when she thinks about it, about those days she and Cass spent in his company, while he was going away to who-knew-where and up to who-knew-what, it fills her with a slippery nausea.

For an instant, she is shocked to realise that she is almost glad her parents are dead, so they never had to learn who they had left their children with.

The other is the disappearance of dour Mandy, Jimmy's wife. Like Cass, Sid remembers that ugly tartan suitcase. It is buried now, beneath the *Undine*, so its contents will remain forever unknown, but the police have since discovered that once Mandy left Anvil Point in June 2005, she never again used her national insurance number, paid any tax, or accessed her bank account.

She might be living it up abroad somewhere, but considering where her suitcase was discovered, and recalling the harassed, hunched little woman from her memory, Sid thinks it unlikely, and Cass even more so.

'It was like a shrine down there,' Cass murmured, as they sat in a cocktail bar in Truro after the horrifying, debilitating inquest into Adam's death. The coroner had ultimately decided that Jimmy probably lured Adam out on the boat, perhaps to inspect the *Undine*'s damage, and killed him shortly before or after he entered the water.

It was as good an answer as any, considering answers were thin on the ground.

Jemima hadn't made it all the way to the end of the inquest, excusing herself after giving evidence on the final day.

'A shrine to his own murders,' continued Cass, her voice little more than a sigh. 'That tartan suitcase was the base. And on this crate were these things . . . things these women had owned.' She had stirred her straw through her gin and tonic, her face lost in ghastly memory. 'And I recognised that suitcase. I just didn't know where from straight away.'

Sid had stayed silent, as did Erik.

There'd been nothing to add, really.

Instead she'd looked at Cass, for a long moment, thinking.

After listening to the whole inquest, it was humbling to realise that while she'd desperately resented, indeed hated, her sister for those fraught couple of weeks, she'd actually been within a hair's breadth of losing her multiple times. If Jimmy had caught her alone in the *Undine*. If she'd burst in on him while he ransacked Grace's flat, where he'd gone to check that he had left nothing incriminating behind and his prints were wiped . . .

Sid realised that she had been caring about all the wrong things.

'How many people do you think he killed in the end? Do you think there are more that we don't know about?' asked Cass in a hoarse whisper, looking around herself, as though voicing such an idea was enough to make it come true.

Erik had shrugged, shook his head, wrapped his hand around Cass's. 'More than we know.'

*

Sid has heard many theories on this since, from pundits and journalists and police, and some of them have had the terrible ring of truth.

She believes with all her heart that Jimmy killed Adam by luring him out on the boat to check out the *Undine*. With his hidden body undiscovered, it would be easy to make out that Adam had fled after the murder of Grace and the others.

Jimmy had been so cunning, so creative. Once Grace's body had floated free and was discovered (by Cass, of all people!) he must have known the danger he would be in.

After all, they would have identified Grace eventually, and sooner rather than later. She was popular, after all, and almost famous. Sid had learned in the inquest that her family in Ireland had started asking questions about the abrupt way she'd left Blue Horizons, questions that Jimmy had taken it upon himself to answer without telling anybody else. It would not have been long before the right phone call was received by the right person, and she was identified.

Jimmy had turned everything around with lightning speed. Knowing that Adam was reckless and spendthrift, he set Cass upon him, planting Grace's scarf in the office before locking the door and pocketing the key to pique her suspicions, even helpfully leaving her a clean new Post-it note on the dusty monitor with a password so she could access the business's bank accounts.

His insidious guile had been relentless. The very morning after he'd killed Adam, he'd staged an attack on himself in his own home that had been meant to point to Adam as the killer.

Sid has no doubts that she was meant to be next. With

her out of the way, either in the car crash, or failing that, when Jimmy had burst into the training pool with death in his eyes, she and her entanglements would be out of the way, leaving Blue Horizons with his Cass, the girl he was obsessed with.

If Sid hadn't been able to push him into the pool and run out into the woods, it would have ended very badly for her. Her torn arm was aching, her body weak with shock and lack of exercise. When she'd finally crept out of her hiding place and back to the house, lured by the blue and red lights of the police cars, Cass had already vanished.

Why had he murdered Grace? Cass thinks that Grace discovered his route into the Forbidden Hold, perhaps found his suitcase, his trophies.

But who really knew why he'd killed any of these women?

Sid didn't know.

She suspected Erik was right. She would never know.

She only knew that that night in the house, she'd nearly been one of them.

Sid's loneliness suddenly covers her like a neoprene wetsuit – tight, cloying, cutting off her ability to feel. Like a reflex she cannot suppress, she finds herself missing Adam.

Strange as it is, somehow it would be perversely easier to bear Adam being gone if he were here to comfort her through it.

Yes, she understands that he was controlling, deceitful, and no prince. She wouldn't have looked twice at him if she hadn't lost her dad. Despite all evidence to the contrary, she thinks ruefully, she's not a fool. But she also remembers the relief that someone, anyone, was taking over responsibility for the split timbers and howling gales of her burning-down life.

This past year, with its electrifying revelations and their attendant humiliations, has been a baptism of fire for Sid. She has been forced to confront her own deceptions and abandonments. She could, at any time, have questioned Adam's spending, his decisions, his whereabouts – it seems as amazing to her now as it did to Cass that she had never met Adam's 'sister'. Her sense of shame is like a channel being dug with a chisel through the very centre of her chest, right into her gut.

Rage ... regret ... rage ... regret ... she is lobbed between these twin poles constantly.

She stands, stock-still, and despite the brightness of the day, the happy clients, she is suddenly overcome with emotion, can hardly move another step.

She sees Cass looking at her, concerned.

'Are you all right?' her sister asks.

Sid screws up her bottom lip.

She's going to do this, she realises. She's going to make this right. She is going to be the true mistress of Blue Horizons now, and for the first time in forever, she is starting to feel that she is ready for the challenge.

'Yeah.' She shades her eyes, glances back at Cass. 'Yeah, I'm all right.'

Her gaze falls back towards the sea, beneath which the wreck of the *Undine* sleeps.

The missing dead have never been found, and after several failed attempts, they are no longer expected to be. This year their families came, jointly, and threw white wreaths on the sea where the *Undine* lies.

But in the quietude of three, four in the morning, while Cass and Erik sleep and there is no one else awake except for the tender paddings of Tallulah about the house, set upon her own business, Sid wonders about these dead.

What happened to her dad, down there in the *Undine*, doing his intense and finicky inspection of the shipwreck? Had he found the Forbidden Hold, perhaps excitedly pointed out the entrance of it to Jimmy, thus sealing his own fate?

She shakes her head, and feels a sudden, unbidden calm come in, like the tide, surprising her.

It's impossible to know what was in Jimmy's head, as she has been repeatedly told. He is past all human justice. He lies entwined with the rusting spars of the *Undine*, pierced through with her knives, and by now he will be nothing but bones bundled inside a torn drysuit.

He exists trapped beneath the *Undine*'s iron heel, and so he'll remain – until he disintegrates, or she does.

'Are you going to be all right going back down there?' Sid had asked Cass earlier that morning.

She'd discovered her sister in a quiet moment, sitting at the kitchen table, gazing into the middle distance. Sid unerringly knew when Cass was thinking about those times – there is a certain drawn tightness around her sister's eyes that smites Sid's heart.

Cass shrugged, and rested her chin on her hand on the table. 'I don't know. I think so.'

Sid drew up a chair next to her.

'Cass, you don't have to be a hero. We can get Ryan or Sammy to take the tour down. They'd be mad for it. It's just going to be swimming over the wreck anyway. You don't have to . . .'

'No,' Cass waves this away. 'They'll both get their chance when I go back to Australia. But I *want* to do this first tour. It'll be good for us. It's going to look so different now, anyway.' She sits back, faces her sister. 'And we are still the *Undine*'s guardians.'

Sid sighed. 'Yes, I know.' She paused, thinking. 'Aren't you a little bit frightened, though?'

'Frightened of what? It's all gone. It's just a pile of rusting girders now. There's nothing there any more.'

'Well, no. But it's still a grave.'

Cass looked surprised. 'But the *Undine* was always a grave,' she said. 'I used to tell you this, and you accused me of being "gothically morbid".'

'Oh yeah,' Sid raised the ghost of a smile. Those days seemed a million years ago. 'I did, didn't I?'

Sid and Cass have been astonished by the uptake for this tour. Cass joked that when they started offering it and the first places sold out within a day, they could probably just do this for a living now.

They have worried about ghouls and dark tourists, but ultimately they have been protected by their refusal to do any interviews or press, which was hard, as they were offered handsome money and they had absolutely none. *Do not let your tragedy be bought*, Erik had said, *or it will define you*, and he'd been proved absolutely right.

And at a hundred feet, the *Undine* had proved too inaccessible really for the casual murder tourist. The kind of people able to visit her are those who are curious about her for all of her other charms as well – the artificial reef she has become, her history, the anti-intuitive beauty of entropy that she wears now like a gown. All things must die, after all, even shipwrecks.

But still, thinks Sid, there is a life in the *Undine* yet – a new life, a different life, but a life nonetheless.

The first couple of divers splash into the water, while Cass leans over the transom, checking they're okay, and Sid moves to join her.

Together they urge their party into the water, and then, finally, both roll off the back of the *Mustang Sally*, and into sea.

Acknowledgements

It's a very funny thing to be writing a novel about ship-wreck diving and Cornwall when you're actively forbidden to leave your small flat in Cambridge with nothing to help but YouTube and JustEat, but I've got the pandemic to thank for the joke. All my usual means of hands-on research were proscribed to me, and so much of the time I felt I was stumbling around, blindly, as though lost in my own dark wreck. But it's not all bad news. Part of me hopes that some part of this feeling comes out in the book.

Nevertheless, I'm wholly indebted to Craig Mainprize and the rest of the crew at the sadly now defunct Hydro-active Dive Centre, who did all they could to teach me to scuba dive before the dive schools closed. Everything I got right in the book I owe to them, whereas any errors (of which I am sure there are more than a few) are entirely my own fault.

I am hugely grateful to my editors at Michael Joseph; Joel Richardson, Clare Bowron, and Grace Long, for all their fabulous suggestions and painstaking work – I could not be more proud of the final book. I'm grateful also to Sarah Bance, Riana Dixon and all the team at Penguin Random House.

As always, none of this would be happening without my wonderful agent, the unflappable Judith Murray, for her unfailing support and advice.

I'd like also to thank Jenny Kane and Alison Knight for hosting their Imagine writing retreats at Northmoor in Dorset – every time I go, I find myself falling in love with this whole writing project all over again. Thanks again for everything.

It was hard to write a novel during these last few years, with their fear and bleak loneliness – but one of the things that made it easier was having good friends. Many thanks to Kathy and Raymond Dickey, Lucia Graves, Dave Gullen, Sumit Paul-Choudhury, Gaie Sebold, and as always, Julie Revell.

Finally, all my love to Mum and Dad, and to John, Joseph, Darla, Aiden, Arcadia, Finn, Rain, Oliver, Remy, Jacqueline, Lance, and Ralf. We don't get to choose our family, but I could have done a lot worse.

Read on for an extract from
NIGHT FALLS, STILL MISSING

'A gripping, atmospheric and dark thriller'
Sun

Caithness, Scotland, January 2020

It was only three o'clock but the sun was already slung danger-ously low on the horizon, a bright, burning orange. Small lakes reflected its failing light, and looked filled with molten gold.

Fiona Grey leaned in with the petrol nozzle, careful not to let her new red coat brush against the thick caking of mud and road salt smeared all over her little car. She already suspected that her boots were a write-off.

She was heading north.

Her breath steamed before her, a fragile plume, as the old-fashioned pump grumbled and pulsed and the stink of petrol was everywhere. Apart from this everything was silent, hushed by the snow – only the occasional splashing of a passing car through the slush on the nearby road intruding. The lively wind was fresh against her face, as though it was slapping her awake, and she was grateful.

She would be more grateful for a hot coffee, however.

She had set out from Inverness after breakfast and stopped to shop for some suitable cold weather gear – there had been no time to do this in Cambridge as Madison's summons had been too urgent, too peremptory – and this, she thought, eyeing the sinking sun, had been a tactical error. It would be long dark before she reached the ferry port at Scrabster, and the drive, which had followed a perilously winding cliffside road through towns with evocative names like Golspie, Dornoch and Dun-beath, had been beautiful but hair-raising in equal measure.

The car filled, she went inside to pay a large, pleasant blonde woman, who looked in danger of being crushed to death at any moment by the enormous number of boxes, cardboard stands and groaning baskets full of car fresheners, almost-out-of-date chocolate bars and window scrapers festooning the shop.

'That'll be thirty-nine pounds six, hen,' she said. 'Is that all you're after?'

Fiona took her card out of her pocket. 'Actually, I wondered if I could get a coffee . . .'

The woman shook her head, sighing at the panoply of goods surrounding her, as if mourning the lost opportunity Fiona presented to be rid of some. 'Ah, sorry. The machine is broken. Are you heading out for the ferry?'

Fiona admitted she was.

'Sailing for Orkney tonight?'

'Yes,' Fiona said, her mouth growing a little dry.

'Where are you from?'

'Cambridge.'

The woman nodded. 'You on your holidays, then?' she asked, putting the sale through before offering Fiona the card terminal.

'Um . . . well, I've been asked to go up and visit a friend who's working there. She . . .' Fiona stilled, having caught herself just in time. 'She says she needs my help with something.'

The woman raised an eyebrow while Fiona keyed in her PIN. 'That's a long way to come to help someone.'

Fiona had only shrugged.

Before getting back into her car, she took out her phone and captured a quick photo of the magnificent melting sunset.

She texted the photo to Madison, with a quick message – *Getting closer! Fx*

She was not expecting a response at this time of day – about now the dig was probably still in full swing.

Hi hows it going? Mx

Fiona, surprised, tapped in her reply, smiling.

Hello stranger – all good here! Not long now . . . Already bought some fizz! x

She buckled herself into the car while she waited for the reply.

Sounds good! Missed u sooo much! Be great to see u! Mx

Relief flooded Fiona. Madison had been cagey throughout this journey northwards, and they hadn't spoken since Fiona had left Cambridge.

You too! How are you? Are you okay?! x

There was a long pause before the reply came.

Yeah, why wouldn't I be? Sry gotta run. See you when the ferry gets in! Mx

Fiona frowned at the screen, her cheeks heating as though she'd been slapped.

If everything was fine, what was she doing here?

Before she knew it, Fiona had hit the number and was calling her friend.

Almost immediately, it was answered.

'Oh, hi Mads, I just wanted . . .'

'The person you are calling is not available,' interrupted the answerphone message. 'Please hang up and try again later.'

Madison had disabled her voicemail months and months ago, on the advice of the police after the court case, and then never reinstated it.

Fiona sighed, dissatisfied, then shrugged, throwing her phone on to the empty passenger seat next to her.

Doubtless all would be revealed, she thought, attempting to put it from her mind, despite the coiling disquiet in her belly.

* * *

'What do you need me on Orkney for?' Fiona had asked. She'd been in the bath, her phone resting on the tiled border next to her beeswax-scented candles.

Her heart had leapt when Madison had called – she'd missed her, she realised, missed having someone to share the minutiae of her life with, missed her spiky sense of humour, missed that communion with someone who really knew her.

They had been friends since they were little girls, growing up in the same village together, fascinated by the same things, but actually living worlds apart. Fiona had been raised by her alcoholic father, after her mother had abandoned them both. There had been an Aunty Lisette, busybody and virtual stranger, who'd occasionally visit and cluck over Fiona's ragged clothes and her dad's collection of empty lager cans that rolled about under his bed, but after she'd died the extended family had promptly dropped the pair of them. Perhaps they'd had troubles enough of their own.

Madison, in contrast, had lived in the biggest house in the village, a sprawling seventies concoction on the very top of the hill, bookended by ugly extensions. It was presided over by Madison's American father, Gulf War veteran and self-made man, a distant and dark creature who somehow managed to make the whole family fall into nervous silence the minute he entered the room, and Judy, Madison's fragile, impeccably turned out English rose mother who, without ever saying as much, had always made it perfectly clear that Fiona was not welcome.

It had made no difference. From the day they'd started at Blackdown Hill Preparatory, they had become inseparable – Madison the bold, ballsy agent of chaos who feared nothing, and Fiona her studious, long-suffering antithesis, picking up the pieces.

And it had seemed to Fiona that she could foresee no time that this would ever change.

How little Fiona had been able to foresee, in the end.

'What? I can't ask my bestie to come visit me?' Mads had been mulish, almost sulky, and Fiona felt her heart sinking.

'You can . . .' she said, dipping her toes back under the cooling bathwater. 'But you know it's difficult for me in term time . . .'

'It's not term time.'

'It *is* term time,' said Fiona, trying to be conciliatory but firm. 'Term starts on January the fourteenth . . .'

'Oh, so at most you'll miss a day or two. And you can pass it off as research. You know,' said Mads, warming to her theme, her voice becoming silky and persuasive, 'it's this big exciting dig, in this beautiful part of the world with a celebrity archaeologist, potentially going to make everyone's careers, with lots of fab metalwork . . .'

'Yeah,' said Fiona, before she could stop herself. 'An uninhabitable Scottish island in the middle of darkest winter. I'm sure the digging is *fabulous*.'

'There's no need to be sarky,' snapped Madison, her charm offensive abandoned.

Silence.

Then, a tiny, contrite voice. 'Are you still there?'

Fiona let out a stiff little sigh. 'Yes.'

'I'm sorry,' said Madison, and for the first time in the phone call she sounded like her genuine self. 'I'm just . . . I can't tell you what I think is going on. But I don't feel safe here. Not at all.'

'Hang on.' Fiona eased upright in alarm, the water swirling around her. 'What do you mean, you don't feel safe? Has someone threatened you?'

'I . . . no. Well, maybe. I dunno.'

'What does that mean?' Fiona's thoughts leapt forward. 'Is Dom back?'

Silence again, then, 'I told you, I don't know.'

'What?' Fiona was stunned. 'Who else could it be? What's that twat doing now?'

'Oh, the usual. Someone's tweeting bollocks at me. Whoever they are, they're on Orkney.'

379

'He's up there on *Orkney*? How do you know?'

'It says so. On one of the tweets.'

'Have you spoken to the police yet? What did they say?'

'No, I haven't spoken to . . . I don't know it's him. You know. Dominic.'

'What?' Fiona's jaw dropped open. 'Who else could it be?'

'I don't know!' snapped Madison. 'You know, this isn't my fault!'

Fiona took a deep breath, tried to calm herself. 'I know. I'm sorry, I'm just worried about you.'

'I know you are,' said Madison, with a sigh. 'And it's not like I don't love you for it. But you need to relax.'

Fiona stared at the phone. Madison's attitude didn't make any sense. 'Why do you think it's not him? Why aren't you worried he's on the island with you?'

There was a pause, Madison's breath hissing softly as she thought.

'I can't explain it. But it's just different this time.'

'You need to go to the police again,' said Fiona urgently, trying to rein in the desire to reach through the phone and shake Madison. 'Isn't that why you want me to come up, because it's bothering you?'

Now it was Madison's turn to be quiet.

'I don't understand,' said Fiona, frowning at the phone. 'You're out there in that cottage on your own and he might be . . .'

The silence expanded.

'Madison?'

'Yeah?'

'What's going on?' asked Fiona. 'I mean, *really* going on?'

'I . . . Look, I just need you here. I need to show you something. The only way you will get a chance to see it, to see what I mean, is to come up here.'

'Mads, it's not that simple.' She tried not to sigh again, caught between the competing impulses of frustration and alarm. 'Whatever it is, you must be able to talk about it . . .'

'Fee, I . . . no. I can't. Not right now. I don't even know what I think is going on. But I need you here now. I'm freaking out.'

'Mads, it's not that . . .'

'You never fucking believe me.' Madison sounded angry, and close to tears again. 'You think I'm crazy, I know!'

'Calm down. Yes, I do think you're crazy. It doesn't mean I don't believe you.'

'Then *come*,' she said, and Fiona heard her blatant, exposed need. 'Please come. I have never been so fucking miserable. I'm losing my mind . . . Please do me this one favour. Please come. *Please.*'

* * *

'Oh hi there, Nanook of the North,' Adi said, his voice pleased. He'd answered almost immediately. 'I was just thinking about you. How's it going?'

All was darkness, except for the sodium orange light of the harbour. Through the windscreen of her little car she could see the ferry approaching the terminal, and against the black sea and black sky it seemed to be a tiny floating island of light, trapped between heaven and earth.

'I'm okay.' She'd smiled, feeling herself relax against the driver's seat, letting the warm chocolate of his voice melt over her. 'Got to the ferry port in one piece. Just waiting to drive on.'

'How are things?'

'Things are freezing.'

He snorted. 'It's Scotland in January. What did you expect?'

'I dunno,' she said. 'That they would be freezing.'

He laughed. In the background music was playing – Amy Winehouse's 'Tears Dry on Their Own'. 'When's your ferry?'

'It leaves here in forty-five minutes.'

'I bet the views will be gorgeous.'

'They may be, but it's too dark to see anything, and anyway, they'd be wasted on me,' she said. 'You know I get terrible sea-sickness and I'm frightened of boats.'

'But you've put the patch on, haven't you?' he breezed.

Her hand drifted up to the little plaster behind her ear. 'Well, yeah, but it just takes the edge off . . .'

'You'll be fine. Most of motion sickness is just psychological anyway.'

'I dunno, Adi.' She shifted in the car seat. She'd managed to put off thinking about the boat for most of the day, but this discussion was stirring unwelcome feelings. 'It doesn't seem "just psychological" when it's happening . . .'

'Hmm,' he said, but there was something distant in it, as though she was being deliberately obstructive. 'Never mind. What are you up to right now?'

'I've been sat in the car brushing up on my Early Norse metalwork, since there is a very real danger celebrity archae-ologists might attempt to have intelligent conversations with me about it.'

'Ah yes,' he said, then loudly performed the trumpet-driven theme music from *Discovering the Past* in the form of raspberries, eliciting shocked laughter from Fiona. '"And now, the glamor-ous Professor Iris Barclay fills us in about an exciting discovery from Britain's mysterious prehistory . . ."'

'Philistine,' she hissed in mock contempt.

'Yeah, yeah, yeah,' he said. 'Anyway, I hope your meeting with the great woman goes well. Make sure you put some lippy on. And laugh at her jokes.'

'What do you mean?' asked Fiona, confused.

'I mean,' said Adi with barely concealed surprise, 'Iris Bar-clay would be a great contact for you. Obviously.'

'I suppose. She's really highly thought of in feminist archae-
ology at the moment – her paper on gendered grave goods in
the Tpaletske Roman-period cemetery was astonishing . . .'

'What? No, I don't even know what any of that *means*, you
ludicrous creature. I mean a *media* contact. You know, for getting on TV.'

'What? Me?' Fiona rolled her eyes. 'That's an adorable idea,
but . . .'

'No . . . well, yeah, it is adorable, true, but that would be a
brilliant move for you right now.'

'You say the sweetest things.' She laughed again, but she was
blushing with pleasure. 'No point making much of that, anyway. I'm here for Mads, and I'm pretty sure she isn't going to
want me hanging around her boss much.'

'Hmm.' Adi sighed, a tight little exhalation of breath.

'What is it? What's wrong?' she asked.

'Fiona, you should *make* Madison show you the dig. You
should *make* her introduce you to Iris Barclay . . .'

'Well, she *will*, of course she will . . .'

'She will on her terms.' Adi's voice was tinged with strain,
frustration, and ultimately, pity. 'She should introduce you
properly, put you together. It's the very least she could do.'

'What do you mean? Why should she?'

'Because you've dropped everything and come all that way
for her? Because it could be good for you, professionally?' He
snorted. 'If Madison was a real friend, she'd make a point of
helping your career.' His voice was cold. 'She never lets you in
on anything if there's any danger of her having to share any
glory.'

She felt herself flush. 'That's horrid. Why would you say that?'

'Because it's true.'

Fiona tried not to sigh. Adi did not like Madison, and he
wasn't being fair.

Madison wanted something of her own. Fiona's career had taken off in ways that Madison's never had and Fiona knew she felt it. Iris's patronage was the best thing that could have happened and, rationally or not, Mads was nervous and insecure about losing it.

Fiona understood Madison, even if Adi could not.

'If it makes you feel any better,' she said, 'I'd rather be going to Zurich with you tomorrow.'

He made the *hmm* noise again, as though she had not really answered him.

'To be fair, it could all be worse, you know,' he said, relenting. 'Beautiful Scottish islands and dead Vikings and *buried treasure*,' and at this last his voice grew low, mimicking a pirate's. 'Arrr! It sounds awesome.'

'I wish you were here instead of me, then,' she said. 'My feet are blocks of ice right now.'

'You miserable cow. You don't know you're born. Do you want to know what I did in work today?'

She grinned despite herself. 'What did you do?'

'I gave a presentation on international insurance legislation as it relates to investment banking,' he said, full of mock annoyance. 'And it was every bit as exciting as it sounds.'

She giggled, shifting her phone to her other hand. 'How thrilling.'

'Nail-biting. Absolutely nail-biting.' He yawned.

'You know, I just wanted to . . .' She was reluctant to begin again on this subject. 'Well, about Mads . . .'

'What about her?' His tone was suddenly short, brisk. 'Has she told you what she needs you for yet, or is she still being mysterious?'

'No,' Fiona admitted. 'But it will be about that ex of hers – Dominic Tate. I know it.'

'But something's bothering you, isn't it?'

384

Fiona sighed, looking out at the sea and the distant lights of the ferry.

'No. Well, maybe yes.' She scratched her temple.

'Which is?'

She bit her lip. 'It's probably nothing, but it just stuck with me. She said something in a text. I asked her if she was okay and she said, "Why shouldn't I be?" It just – I dunno, I thought it was strange, since she'd asked me to come up at such short notice. Like she'd no idea what I was talking about.'

'Yeah?' Now there was cool anger mixed in with the pity. 'A tenner says you get all the way up there, and all this ex-stalker drama she needed you for is over and your trip's been for nothing. It's just that she didn't want to tell you.'

* * *

The ferry was called the *Hamnavoe*. With its blue cloth seats and polite safety announcements delivered in a soft brogue that was almost Scottish, almost Scandinavian, it was deceptively comfortable at first.

Fiona sat in one of the lounge chairs, the rain pattering gently against the darkened windows. Her fingers drummed on the armrest next to her. She was too anxious to read, to look at her phone – to do anything.

In the beginning she thought she would be all right as they pushed through the flat sea, but once they pulled out of Gill's Bay and joined the tidal race of the Pentland Firth she could feel it, that sickening tug and rock, as though giant hands were pulling and pushing the boat up and down. She sat blinking and swallowing her excess saliva, fighting the dragging current of her nausea while her coffee cooled in front of her, untouched.

Through the window the vanishing harbour lights appeared and disappeared with the rolling of the ship. Somewhere below in its bowels, a car alarm started to wail, like a squalling child.

You have the patch on. And Adi is probably right. It's just psychological . . .

Madison hadn't responded to any of Fiona's more recent texts. This was normal, she reminded herself, as there was no signal out on the islet the dig was on. But as seven became eight, then eight-thirty, Fiona had found herself growing uneasy, and not just with seasickness.

On an impulse, she jabbed Mads' picture, lifted the phone to her ear. This time it went straight to her recorded message.

Hi Mads, where are you? Just tried to call. Are you meeting me at the terminal still? Fx she texted instead.

A pause before the phone chimed once.

Sorry – not ignoring u! Things r MAD here! BIG BIG FIND on site here at Helly Holm!!! Can't talk now but SO MUCH catching up 2 do! See u in 30 mins! MXXX

Wherever Mads was, there must be signal of some sort.

Sounds exciting! What did you find?

Another pause, then the chime.

Take 2 long 2 text. Tell u when I see u!

Fiona sighed.

All right – keep me in suspense! See you soon. Fx

* * *

As Fiona rumbled out along the steel plates of the ferry on to solid earth, she was greeted by the sight of a picturesque stone town built into the side of a hill, the restless dark sea lapping at its edges. This must be Stromness, she realised, and the street-lights illuminated intriguing sandstone buildings threaded with narrow flagged streets, and a harbour full of boats, their masts a thicket streaked in moonlight. The stars above were hard, sharp and impossibly numerous, like sugar grains spilled across the sky.

Despite her journey, her doubts, she felt a little flicker of excitement, now that she was back on dry land. Fresh sweet air swept in through the open crack in her car window, tasting of salt.

Madison must love it here, she thought.

A great longing rose in her then to see Madison, and in that moment she realised how much she'd missed her these past two months. The reasons for their quarrel, which had made her so furious, evaporated in her mind as though they'd never existed.

They would have a few drinks and talk, and Madison would tell her why she had summoned her all the way to the very northernmost tip of the country, and together they would solve everything – whatever it was.

First, she had to find the terminal office, where Mads was going to meet her. She pulled slowly in front of the ticket office near the car park, gulls wheeling above it by the lights of the harbour.

And waited.

* * *

'Are you all right there?'

Someone was tapping on the driver-side window.

Miserable and furious, Fiona was still sitting in her car, in the dark.

She pressed the button, lowering the window, letting the cold in. An earnest man with a heavy, jowly face was now leaning over her, his hooded jacket zipped up to his chin and striped with hi-vis markings. The battering wind seemed to have no effect upon him.

'I . . .' Fiona wanted to cry, was aware of this as a building pressure. 'I'm waiting for my friend – she's meant to meet me here, but she's not answering her phone . . .'

The other cars had rumbled away, one after the other. A small knot of foot passengers in weatherproofs – men, women and children – had waited patiently at the flat terminal building, new cars arriving to drive them away in twos and threes.

Soon all were gone, even the gulls, except for three men locking up the offices, who must be making their way home for the night.

And Fiona.

By then she'd been there for over an hour, with no word from Madison, and no answer to her numerous frantic phone calls.

'Meet you here, aye?' The man had kind eyes and a low, lilting accent – an Orcadian. Around him, through the gap in the window, the cold sea air blew in, stirring her unruly hair and the forgotten shopping bag with its celebratory bottles of fizz.

'Yeah,' said Fiona, already feeling calmed by the man's measured manner. 'She's called Madison Kowalczyk. She's an archaeologist, over at Helly Holm . . .'

'Oh aye, they're doing some work out there, aren't they? Do you know where she's staying?'

You know, thought Fiona, *I do*. 'Yeah, it's . . .' She thumbed through her phone. 'Langmire. The village is Grangeholm . . .'

'Aye, I know it. It's on the other side of the island. If your friend doesnae show, you can head out that way yerself. You'll probably meet her coming,' he said, scratching his head under his bright orange hood.

'Oh, thank you. I don't know what I thought. I just haven't heard from her since before I got on the ferry.'

He nodded. 'They do work some late hours out on Helly Holm sometimes. Are you one of them, then? An archaeologist?'

Fiona demurred. 'Yeah. But I'm not here to dig . . .'

'No? I hope you packed warm anyway. Ye've picked the time of year for it,' he said placidly.

* * *

After he'd delivered his directions and gone, she rolled up the window, letting the car's heating once again flood the interior. She was overreacting, she realised, and making a fool of herself – if the others had found something at the site, no wonder Mads was delayed.

You're just tired, she told herself. *You've been travelling for two days, after all, and you're missing Adi. A couple of glasses of Prosecco and a good laugh and a good night's sleep in a warm bed will set you as right as rain.*

Fiona picked up her phone again, tried to push down her annoyance. However busy Madison was, she should have let her know she'd be late. Fiona knew she was being treated in a cavalier – in a (let's be honest) *Madison-like* way.

Say something, murmured a voice in her ear. It sounded like Adi's. *You're here at her request.*

But what would the point be? And why start fighting with Madison again, before she had even arrived at the house? Why spoil everything now and possibly ruin the whole week?

Fiona sighed, staring out across the blackness of the sea lapping at the harbour.

Check her social media.

Of course. If there was something going on at the dig, the team might tweet it.

Almost without realising it, she had gravitated to @HellyHolmDig, the Twitter feed for the dig Madison was working on.

Madison did not appear publicly on Twitter, Facebook or Instagram, and had not done so for some time. Fiona knew that this had been hard for Mads, who treated all forms of social media with the narcissistic enthusiasm pundits on the television were endlessly warning the world against.

There were only two pictures today, all taken at least four hours ago in full daylight. Fiona tried to batten down her disappointment.

One showed the excavated end of some tapering shadow in

the earth. This must be the Viking boat they'd found – the wood had wholly rotted away, leaving only its dark ghost in the soil.

Above it stood a man in a grey woollen hat, perhaps in his late thirties, adjusting some surveying equipment – squinting through the sights, unconscious of the camera. His eye, focused on the device, was a very pale blue. This was Dr Jack Bergmann – site supervisor and Iris Barclay's right-hand man.

The second image was of a tray of rubbly pieces of decayed iron, little more than black nuggets of rust, being held up by a woman, her head uncovered despite her hair being tugged at by the wind, her smile wide and gleaming.

This was Iris Barclay, Madison's famous boss.

@HellyHolmDig: A lovely surprise! @ProfIrisBarclay shows off rivets from rescue of 10th-century Viking boat burial! Rare survivals. #HellyHolm #Archaeology

Fiona thumbed through both pictures again while the wind shook the windows in her little car. She frowned into her phone, trying to make sense of things. The recovered rivets were nice – interesting, true, especially to an expert on ancient metals like herself, but hardly show-stopping. Even a professional like Madison would not have described them as a *BIG BIG FIND!*

Madison must be referring to something else.

Idly she tapped Madison's Twitter handle in the search box: @MadsKow.

She knew there would be nothing from Madison herself, but there was a new tweet from a stranger, someone that had tagged her.

It was from @BH9JTqwwx – a fake account, Fiona realised, doubtless attached to some fake email address. The profile icon was a drawing of a sinister smiling man, his eyes whirling.

Fiona's breath stopped in her chest. She felt cold and sick.

It was happening again.

@MadsKow *YOU CAN GRUB IN THE DIRT TILL THE ENDS OF THE EARTH BUT I WILL FIND YOU AND CUT YOUR FUCKING TITS OFF CHEATING WHORE. #golddigger #youllgetyours*

What if your parents had been lying to you since the day you were born?

'An enthralling and compelling page-turner'
Claire Douglas

Would you risk your life to save a stranger?

'Riveting' 'Accomplished' 'Thrilling'

Helen Callaghan

Dear Amy

Please find me

THE SUNDAY TIMES BESTSELLER

'Haunting . . . this story will stay with you'
Jane Corry

NURTURING WRITERS SINCE 1935